TOURIST TRAP

MORGAN ELIZABETH

To the Jersey girls, because everyone knows we have the most fun.

PLAYLIST

The Middle - Jimmy Eat World
Wildest Dreams - Taylor Swift
A little Less 16 Candles - Fall Out Boy
Florida!!! - Taylor Swift
Rose-colored Boy - Paramore
Girls do What they Want - the Maine
Treacherous - Taylor Swift
Back to You - Selena Gomez
Thinking of You - Katy Perry
Under the Boardwalk - The Drifters
Sweet Nothing - Taylor Swift
Belong Together - Mark Amber
Quarter Life Crisis - Taylor Bickett
Ocean Avenue - Yellowcard
Dumb and Poetic - Sabrina Carpenter
You Are in Love - Taylor Swift

A NOTE FROM MORGAN

Dear Reader,

I grew up in central New Jersey (it's a real place), and when I was in middle school, my mom moved to Monmouth County, giving me a much-desired street cred of being someone who lived *down the shore*. After high school, I went to Monmouth University, which is a college a few blocks from the beach in Long Branch, NJ. I spent all of my summers at the Jersey shore, and when I started college in the fall of 2009, also known as the same year the TV show *Jersey Shore* came out.

It was an *experience*.

Fast-forward three years, and my now-husband took me to Point Pleasant on a random September night and proposed to me on the beach right in front of Kohr's, the ice cream place his parents took him to as a kid and where we now bring our own kids multiple times a year. (For the record, I was and still am a Strollo's girl, though when I was pregnant, Hoffman's was my go-to.)

That being said, a lot of this book comes from my heart, both from my love of the show and my affection for the New Jersey beach towns where I grew up.

Claire is a piece of my soul, with her desire to bop around from job to job, living life and trying to figure out what she's good at and what she wants to do. I feel like I spent my entire twenties figuring out what I wanted to do. (That, and having babies, but that's a whole other conversation and, honestly, the pregnancy trope is not for me) It's hard to explain to people, especially the older generation, that you don't want to waste your life away doing something you hate when to outsiders, it looks like you're wasting your life trying to find what you love.

If you're in a position like Claire, I urge you to keep looking. Try new things, go new places, make new friends. Eventually, you'll stumble into something that you love, something that, when you try it, it feels as natural as breathing, something that consistently makes you happy.

The whole "if you love your job you'll never work a day in your life" is bullshit, because every job has a part you don't like, but that doesn't mean you can't get really fucking close.

Finally, Tourist Trap features adult situations, a lot of the word *fuck* (I am from Jersey, after all), and features a narcissistic ex/family member. Oh, and theft of half a dozen hermit crabs. Always remember that reading is supposed to be our happy place!

I love you all to the moon and to Saturn.

-Morgan

ONE

CLAIRE

Fuck someone on a lifeguard chair.

The laugh that leaves me is almost worrisome as my best friend from college slides the paper back over to me. This has been going on for almost an hour now as we write things onto my summer bucket list, trying to plan for the most iconic season possible.

Something I desperately need.

"That sounds illegal," I say with a cough as I catch my breath, wiping tears out of my eyes.

"Probably is," she says with a shrug. "But it would be fun."

I skim over the list filled with fun, random, classic, beach bum things we want to do while down the shore for the summer.

"Are you ready for that?" June asks after a moment of hesitation.

"Fucking someone on a lifeguard chair? I mean, I don't know if anyone is really ever ready for *that*, you know?" When I look at her, her face is more serious than I expected.

"I meant hooking up with someone," she says. "You know, after Paul?"

I think about her question, then shrug. "I don't see why not. It's not like he was *good* at it."

She continues to stare at me in the way best friends always seem to be able to do: reading past whatever bullshit you're saying and finding the truth you don't want to admit.

That's because six months ago, I broke up with my boyfriend of a year and a half, one I met two summers ago while visiting her. After a summer of what I now see as love bombing and then a year of things being...okay, I finally came to my senses, but not before I moved across the country to be with him.

Since the breakup, I've been slowly trying to get my shit together and, admittedly, failing miserably.

But tonight is not for worrying about that.

Tonight, we're celebrating the fact that I am officially moving down to Seaside Point, June's hometown, for the summer. Yesterday, Helen, the director of the recreation department, called to offer me the position as head lifeguard, and I accepted instantly, excited for the change of pace I so desperately needed.

Then I packed up my things and drove here from Evergreen Park this morning. I'm staying in June's tiny apartment for the night since Helen found me a place to rent for the season, and I'll be headed there to meet my new landlord tomorrow.

"Me next. Get drunk at a tiki bar," I say, changing the subject and putting a hand out for the pen so I can add it to our list. She continues her assessing look for a moment longer before deciding to let it go.

"Oh, god, no," she says with a laugh, shaking her head and moving the pen out of my reach.

"What? Why not?"

"Because locals wouldn't be caught dead at a tourist trap like that. And you're a local now, babe."

I roll my eyes at her. "Come on. That's the fun of it! We can pretend we aren't locals." She rolls her eyes and shakes her head like she can't see the perk of doing so.

"Just imagine it! We go to the most touristy bar, get hammered and flirt with guys we'll never see again." I sit up, already mentally committing to the idea and smiling as June looks over at me, a look of understanding in her eyes. Understanding that she would have to go through a mountain of effort to convince me off my path, no matter the fact that I just thought about it.

"Tonight!" I stand to grab my phone. "I'll call Lainey, tell her our plans have changed, and we're going out," I say. Lainey is June's childhood best friend who is supposed to come here for movies and takeout, but she's always down for some chaos.

June looks at me skeptically. "Please? We have nothing else to do. Let's celebrate my moving down here for the summer. It'll be fun! The first official girls' night of the summer."

After a long beat, she lets out a deep sigh, then smiles. "Okay. But what do we wear?"

TWO

MILES

"That was Helen," I say, walking back out into the garage where my best friend for as long as I can remember sits.

I opened Miller Automotive four years ago and since it opened, Grant has given me shit for working so much, telling me the only way he ever sees me is if he comes by the garage I own and hangs out while I finish a job. Unfortunately, he's not exactly wrong, which is why we're here tonight.

"She said she found someone who is looking for a place to rent for the summer. They'll be at my place around noon tomorrow to see if it's a good fit."

I don't exactly want to rent out a room in my childhood home to a total stranger, but with my brother breathing down my neck to buy him out of his stake in the house we inherited, I need all the extra cash I can get. Plus, it's just for the summer, and Helen says the new head lifeguard is incredibly responsible and comes with stellar recommendations.

"Maybe it'll be a hot chick," Grant says, leaning back on the chair he's sitting in. I give him a dark glare before lifting the ratchet I abandoned to take the call, and he lets out a laugh. "I'm just saying.

You're so busy all the time; there's no chance you've gotten laid in a while."

As much as I hate to admit it, he's not wrong. With my overtime work at the garage and picking up whatever odd jobs around town I can to make extra cash without causing alarm from my mother, my personal life has fallen far on my priorities list.

"Don't think hooking up with a renter I'm charging to live here is really the answer. That feels...illegal."

He shrugs and takes a sip of his beer as if he doesn't see a problem with it.

"So, do you really think he's going to take you to court?"

I set the tool down again and lean against the bumper with a bone-deep sigh, crossing my arms on my chest. "With Paul? Who the fuck knows."

After my grandmother passed almost six years ago, she left the house in equal part to my brother and me. Paul had no interest in the property, and I couldn't afford to buy him out, but I desperately wanted to keep the house my grandfather built.

The agreement was simple: I'd cover the back taxes and much-needed repairs that had stacked up, and he could have or sell anything of value in her home. After that, I would pay him rent for the next ten years to settle the rest of his stake before it would be mine, free and clear.

I'm sure my wannabe rock star brother thought by now his career would take off, but now that it's becoming startlingly clear that's not going to work out for him the way he hoped, he's back to being a fucking bloodsucker on our family.

"Does your mom know?" he asks, and I shake my head before shooting him with a serious look.

"No, and if she finds out, I'm kicking your ass first and asking questions never."

Paul and I were raised by our single mom after our father died when I was eight and Paul was five. She always wants to see the best in my younger brother, blaming his selfish and often lazy behavior on the fact that he only had our mom and grandmother, refusing to admit that Paul is just...Paul. It would absolutely gut her to know that he's trying to force me to sell my grandmother's house.

"All right, all right," he says, lifting his hands as if to fend me off. "So what's your plan?"

I shrug and let out a sigh that feels like it takes the last vestiges of my energy with it. Thinking about the shitstorm that is my relationship with Paul always leaves me feeling this way: exhausted and hopeless.

"My lawyer says if he's hurting for money, which common sense says he must be, he's not going to be able to afford a lawyer to force me to sell, but the place is pretty valuable real estate. He could, in theory, sell his stake to an investor who would have the time and money to fight me for it." My jaw goes tight at the reminder of how I'm backed between a rock and a hard place by my own flesh and blood. "So I'm saving up to try and get the money to pay him in full while offering to double his payments in the meantime. The goal is to keep him happy so he doesn't feel the need to look at alternate options."

"So you're basically at Paul's whim?"

I cringe at the way he says it, though he's not wrong. "I'm going to try and buy him out by the end of the summer. I've got a good amount saved, but I'm not quite there yet."

"Is there any way you can get a loan?"

I think about how my brother fucked my credit by pulling out credit cards in my name and maxing them out years ago. On top of that, being self-employed and owning my own automotive shop makes loans a distant possibility.

I shake my head. "No, not feasibly, at least. For now, I'm going to offer up my monthly payments to him and hope Paul is just in a bind and needs money."

He looks at me with a pitying look. His face goes contemplative, and before he even speaks, I know what he's going to say. Grant is more of a brother to me than my actual brother, meaning we both would do just about anything for each other.

"You know, I don't think I have all of what you'd need, but I could—"

"No," I say quickly, nipping that offer in the bud before it gets any further. "No." I've prided myself on paying for everything myself for as long as I can remember, saving every penny I can, and I don't plan to change that anytime soon.

"Look, man, I know you hate taking help, but—"

I shake my head and cut him off again. "I've got it. Seriously," I lie. "I'm taking on more surfing lessons this summer and upped my fees for tourists."

He smiles at that. "You know they're good for it."

I return the grin because this is more sure footing, complaining about the tourists who flood our town from May to September. While they help keep our small town running, the tourists that visit during the summer season are a pain in the ass and something the locals love to complain about, myself included.

"Exactly. So I'll make it work." Silence fills the garage, and I turn to go back to the job I was working on before, but as is his way, Grant breaks it.

"But back to the important stuff, you should consider getting laid soon. You're too young to let your dick shrivel up and fall off from misuse." I cringe at the visual and open my mouth to argue with him, but his phone rings. He lifts his cell and looks at the screen before moving to answer it. "It's June," he says, referencing his baby sister.

June is six years younger than him, and considering both of their parents are shit, he basically raised her. Because of that, if June calls, he's answering.

"Hey, June bug, how's it—" Grant pauses his greeting, his brow furrowing in confusion before he sighs. "She's drunk?" Another pause before he adds, "Lainey's there too? Fuck. Yeah, okay. I'll be there in a few. I'm over at Miles's garage."

He puts his phone down, then looks to the concrete shop ceiling, sending up a prayer of patience, I've seen more times than I can count, before looking at me.

"June's over at Surf," he says, mentioning the tourist trap of a bar next to my house on the boardwalk. I grimace. During the day, it's a luxury beach club where sunbathers can have an all-inclusive day at the shore, and when the sun goes down, it turns into a nightclub I avoid at all costs.

"Surf? Why are they there?"

"No idea. Who knows why they do half the shit they do. Deck called me on June's phone. Apparently, they decided to be tourists and get drunk. Lainey's with her, and they're causing a scene."

Decker Elliot is two years younger than Grant and me and is good friends with June. They weren't friends in high school, but since he's the gym teacher at the elementary school where June teaches, they inevitably became friends.

"A scene?"

Grant shrugs but stands to leave. "He didn't really give me many details about what that meant, partially because he was laughing the entire time he was on the phone, and there was hollering in the background. But June making a scene is never a good thing." This is definitely true and has been since she was a kid. "I have to go pick them up."

He steps toward his car, and I grab a rag to clean off my hands before moving to follow. I could use an entertaining distraction in the form of Grant having to deal with his baby sister begrudgingly. Again.

"Oh, I'm coming," I say when he looks at me with confusion. "I'd rather focus on your shitstorm than mine."

He rolls his eyes but doesn't argue as we slide into his car then drive across town toward Surf. When we park behind my house, we make our way to the hideous building next door. It was built nearly four years ago now, after Baker Inc. purchased five lots on the boardwalk, tore down each one, and built this monstrosity in its place.

It's the bane of my existence: the noise, the eyesore, the litter, the damn principle of the matter. It doesn't help that the owner's son, Brad, has been bugging me for years to sell my property to them, despite my continuously and adamantly saying no every single time.

But I can't think of that when we walk to the entrance, nodding at Mike, an old friend from high school, before walking into the chaos. The lights are dim, though strobe lights flash on and off, lighting up different sections of the nightclub as music I faintly recognize bumps through the speakers at a near-deafening level. The song changes, and there's a loud, excited shout before the crowd at the center of the room shifts.

"You've gotta be fucking kidding me," I distantly hear Grant rumble, irritation evident in the words as he walks with a mission toward the bar in the center of the room, dodging tables and people dancing.

As we move, the crowd grows thicker, mostly men cheering, hooting, and hollering at two forms on top of the bar. One I recognize to be June, with the dark hair her brother also has, pulled into a ponytail and a glass in her hand.

But that's not what has me hesitating as Grant moves closer, calling his sister's name as he does.

It's the woman up there with her, long blonde curls tumbling down her back, a wide smile on her lips as her head tips to the ceiling as she scream-sings the words of the song out loud, and my heart stutters just a bit before ramping up once again.

Claire Donovan, my brother's girlfriend, is standing on top of the bar, dancing. Claire, who I have diligently avoided anytime she was in Seaside Point for the past two years because just seeing her reminds me of how fucked my relationship with my brother is.

I don't need to look around the room to know everyone is watching her. There's something so fascinating about her, the way she grabs the attention of everyone in the room, drawing them in instantly and forcing everyone in the vicinity's eyes to her, and I'm not immune to her magic.

I never have been. While I'm watching her, I spot Brad Baker, the heir to Baker Inc. and the bane of my existence, standing at the bar at her feet. You'd think the owner's son would be trying to get the drunk girl off the bar top, but instead, he's smiling, trying to talk to her and get her attention. I'm only one person away when his hand reaches up, brushing against her bare calf, seemingly trying to get her attention. It works. Her head snaps down, a small frown forming on her lips as she shifts her leg away. The sudden movement throws off her center of gravity, and her body shifts, making her lose her balance. As she teeters, I push someone aside and lunge toward the bar as she falls.

Right into my arms.

Without a lick of the panic pounding in my chest, she looks up at me with those wide blue eyes I've been trying to hate and smiles. The woman *smiles*, and looking back, I realize that was the moment where I became completely and truly fucked, because that smile stops my irritation in its tracks, intrigue and an unnamed warmth taking its place.

"Hey, Miles. Long time no see."

THREE

MILES

We settle the girls' tab quickly, after Grant convinces his sister to climb off the bar rather than fall like her friend, before ushering them out of the bar. June and Lainey, stumble along though Claire seems pretty steady on her feet despite falling off a bar top minutes earlier.

"What were you thinking?" I ask as we step into the night air. It's a warmer night than usual for early May, but the breeze off the ocean is still cool. Without my conscious permission, my mind wonders if she's cold in the tiny tank top and shorts she's wearing.

Claire gives me a confused look, her cheeks still flushed from dancing in the warm bar. "What?"

"Dancing on top of a bar? You could've broken your neck." The thoughts of her getting hurt makes my hand clench and my gut twist, and I have to remind myself the only reason I'm worried about her safety is because she's Paul's, and I've spent my entire life protecting Paul.

She's just an extension of that.

"I wouldn't have *broken my neck*. God. You're so dramatic."

"The only reason you didn't is because I *caught* you," I argue.

She rolls her eyes at that, crossing her arms on her chest and facing me. "I only fell because you *startled* me."

She crosses her arms on her full chest and I try to focus on the irritation brewing in my bones and not the low cut of her top or my unsettling urge to move the hair that the ocean breeze is blowing around from her face so I could see her better.

It's always been this way with Claire, ever since I first met her when she was far, far too young for me when she came to visit June that first summer. She was nineteen to my twenty-five and just as wild as she is now.

"You were in a busy nightclub. You were bound to be startled at some point."

She shrugs and smiles. "Well, then, I guess I'm lucky you were there to catch me, right?"

I glare, and she smiles sweetly back before I shake my head, deciding it's not worth the effort. "Where's Paul?" I ask. From the corner of my eye, June's shoulders shake as she lets out a snort, then whispers to Grant, but I can't focus on them *and* Claire before me.

"Paul?" she asks, looking confused.

"Paul. My brother. Your boyfriend? Where is he?" She tips her head to the side and gives me a strange, quizzical look I don't understand. Am I in a fucking twilight zone?

"Well, I'm assuming back in California, but who knows, maybe he already ran out of money and had to move somewhere else."

My brows furrow, and then I watch as slowly a smile spreads across her lips, understanding hitting her.

"Oh, you don't know, do you?" She tips her head a bit, hair tumbling to the side as she puts her hands on her full hips, looking at me in what seems to be a new light.

"Don't know what?"

"We broke up. Six months ago or so?" She looks to June who nods, confirming the timeline.

"You broke up?" I ask, fervently ignoring the unsettling way my body and mind are reacting to this new information. "What happened?"

I shouldn't ask because I shouldn't care, but here I am.

Asking.

Caring.

"Let's see, I gave him an ultimatum to treat me halfway decent or I would leave and, well, you know Paul. He seemed to think that was the most outlandish request, so I left."

This is news to me, but suddenly, his new need for money makes sense.

Fuck.

This new reality tumbles over me.

Claire Donovan is single.

And in my hometown.

I need to get her home and myself away from her as soon as possible.

"Come on. Where are you staying? With June? Let's get you home," I say, looking to Grant, who is clearly saying the same to his sister and Lainey.

"I don't want to go home yet," Claire says defiantly.

I shake my head and put a hand to her elbow, feeling the jolt of electricity that shoots through me when I'm near her. "Too bad. You made enough of a scene for one night, and it's getting late. Let's go."

She tips her head, looking at me curiously. "You're not my dad, and you're not my boyfriend. I don't have to do what you say. You realize that, right?"

I close my eyes and sigh with exasperation.

"I don't want to be doing this all night, Claire."

She shrugs out of reach and takes a step backward, a twinkle in her eye I very much do not like before she speaks. "Then don't." Then she's turning on her heel and walking down the boardwalk, away from me.

"Claire," I call out as I watch her move toward the set of stairs leading to the beach. She turns and begins walking backward with her eyes on me, a playful smirk on her lips. "Claire, what are you doing?"

She has some plans I know I am not going to like.

"I want to go swimming," Claire says suddenly, then looks at her friend.

"Claire, it's going to be freezing," June says with a drunken laugh. "It's May."

Everyone here knows the ocean doesn't really warm up until late July at the earliest, but Claire shrugs as if hypothermia only impacts the weak before slipping her shoes off on the boards.

"So?"

"It's dark." I add to the list of reasons this is a terrible idea, crossing my arms on my chest and watching her take the first stair. "You could get hurt." Clearly, that was the wrong fucking thing to say because she turns back to me with a wide smile, her face gleaming in one of the overhead lights that flicker on at dusk, and steps into the sand.

"Claire," I say in a warning. What exactly I'm warning her of, I have no idea, and she knows it when she glances at me over her shoulder, thoroughly entertained.

"Who's coming with me?!" she yells, then starts moving toward the shoreline.

"Literally no one," I shout, as I jump over the railing. I don't move toward the water yet, but I start slipping off my sneakers, somehow already knowing I'll have to go in after her.

That's confirmed when she gets within five feet of the waves and tosses her wallet into the sand. "Claire!" She looks over her shoulder at me once again, the dim moonlight glinting off her wide smile as she shrugs off her shorts, revealing a tiny thong and her perfectly shaped ass.

Fuck me.

I force my gaze to move to the sand and my feet to start moving in her direction. While I keep my eyes averted, I hear the splash of

Claire running into the water, and my eyes shift back to her figure, finding her already waist-deep in the ocean.

"Claire, get out of there," I say, moving toward the water as she dives under. She takes off her top and throws it onto the shore, the wet fabric landing next to me with a loud thwack. I'm not sure if she has a bra on underneath, but I hope to all that is good in the world she does. I'm not sure I could handle a topless Claire right now.

"Make me!" she shouts, and Grant lets out a loud laugh from the boardwalk behind me. I look over at my best friend, standing there with his arms crossed over his chest, a wide, entertained smile on his lips, and know I am completely fucked.

No one is going to help me.

"Claire, get out of the ocean before you drown." If June and Lainey are anything to go by, Claire is hammered, and everyone knows drunk people and large bodies of water are a terrible combination.

"Come get me!"

"What?"

"Come and get me," she repeats, then goes under the water, coming up with her blonde hair slicked back. "You know you want to."

Something about her invitation hits somewhere it very much should not. I can't feasibly deny that Claire Donovan is fucking gorgeous. Everyone who encounters her knows it, and worst of all, so does she.

But she's also Paul's. Or at least she used to be.

There was a small moment in time when I thought maybe she could be mine, but as always, my brother gets what he wants, or, more accurately, what he knew *I* wanted, and Claire was no different.

Except now she's apparently single and drunk and she's swimming in the ocean, begging me to come in with her. A siren, promising to ruin me.

"Isn't it freezing?" I ask as I step closer to the water, already coming to terms with the fact that I'm going into the water to get her and drag her to dry land. I reach behind me, grabbing my T-shirt and tugging it off before throwing it on the sand, my wallet, phone, and keys following.

"It's not warm," she says with a smile, leaning back and flipping her legs up into the air as if she has not a care in the world.

"So why are you in there?" I take a step closer, and the tide comes up, lapping at my feet, making me shiver. The water is fucking *freezing*.

"You ever do anything just...to feel alive?"

I shake my head and watch her swimming as if she's in a heated pool.

"No."

"No?" she asks with a laugh.

I feel idiotic, yelling back and forth over the ocean like this.

"No, I just live, and then I feel alive. Like a normal person."

"You're a bucket of fun, aren't you?"

"At least I'm warm. You're going to freeze to death out there."

"Warm and boring," she taunts.

I let out a deep sigh and cross my arms on my chest. My toes have started to get used to the cold, though I very much do not want to test it on my entire body.

"Come on, Claire, Get out of the water."

She shakes her head. "You're going to have to come in and get me if you want me to come out."

"Claire, get out of there so I don't have to tell your family you drowned on my watch."

"I'm not going to drown, Miles. I'm a strong swimmer."

I groan aloud, looking to the night sky. "That's what everyone says in the movies right before they drown."

"Then come save me, oh, knight in shining armor," she says with a tease in her voice, then dips under the water again.

Once she's out of sight completely, I wait.

And I wait.

And I wait for what feels like an eternity, though it's probably just a few moments before panic starts to sink in. Without even looking at our friends on the boardwalk, I move on a mission, making my way into the water toward where Claire disappeared. The water isn't too deep, but I know where she was standing. The sand drops off a bit, making it so she probably can't touch the sand. Freezing cold water sloshes around me as I move to where I think she could be, panic blocking out the cold as I frantically search for her, a dozen worst-case scenarios running through my mind.

I'm into my ribs when blonde hair pops up, a bright smile greeting me.

"What the hell, Claire?" I ask, staring at the woman in front of me. Relief tinged with irritation rushes through me as my eyes move over her, assessing to make sure she's okay.

"Were you scared?" she asks, beaming at me as she drifts to her back, staring at the stars as she floats in the water.

The sea is relatively calm tonight, and we're past where the waves break, so she bobs up and down as gentle waves pass us. She has a bra on, thank fuck, because I already got a good look at her ass: I don't need to remember what her tits look like, too, every time I see her wandering around with June.

"I don't want to watch you die in front of me. You were underwater and drunk. That's a terrible combo."

She turns her head to me with a smile, her hair fanning out around her in the water before she shifts her body until she's upright again.

"I'm not drunk."

"Claire," I say, giving her a *don't bullshit me* look, and she lets out a small laugh in response.

"I had one drink and two shots over a two-hour span. June? June is hammered, Lainey is pretty sloshed, but I'm not drunk. Buzzed, yeah. But not drunk."

"You were dancing on a bar."

She shrugs. "It sounded like fun and our song came on." I bypass that explanation, moving to my next example.

"You ran into the ocean." This time, she splashes cold water at me with a giggle. I wipe it out of my eyes as I tread water.

"It also sounded like fun."

"You disappeared under the water, Claire," I say through gritted teeth, partially from the frigid water and part from irritation that she isn't taking her safety—or the concern of others—into consideration.

Just like Paul, she refuses to care about how her choices impact those around her.

I shift back toward the shore until my feet are on sand, done with this game of hers.

"I was on the swim team. I can hold my breath for a while." Her smile widens, and she elegantly swims over to me as if we're not in freezing cold water before putting an arm around my neck. Her body is warm against mine, a relief in the frigid cold of the water, but I force my mind not to focus on that. Not even when her hand is moving up to my cheek, her eyes zeroed in on my face as her thumb brushes a drop of water from my mustache. "Were you worried about me, Miles?"

She says it so softly and so sweetly, it takes me aback.

A beat passes before I answer. "I wouldn't want something to happen to you," I tell her honestly, but the words come out like a deep growl.

Suddenly, this moment feels so much more intimate than it should be. I don't know if it's in my head, but if we're being honest, sometimes that's the most dangerous type of intimacy.

"You're cute, you know," she says after a moment.

I sigh and shake my head, taking a step backward, closer to the shore, and taking her with me. "Claire, come on. Clearly you're starting to lose it. Let's get you out of this water before you freeze to death." I soften my words, trying to take the irritation out of them that's simmering in my veins.

"I'm serious, I always thought so. Ask June." She lets go of me as I attempt to take another step toward the shore, swimming a few feet away.

My pulse skips a beat at her words, but I shake my head again. I don't care what she says, I'm convinced Claire is drunk off her ass, or else she would not be acting like this.

"Well, I always thought you were a pain in my ass, so," I say, hoping I sound the least bit convincing, considering it is a huge fucking lie.

I reach for her again, fully prepared to drag her to shore if I have to, but she shifts out of reach once more before I can.

"Claire, you're going to put the man into cardiac arrest!" June says with a laugh. Her words and Grant's following laughter snap me out of whatever trance Claire had me in.

"Come on. We really have to get you out of this water," I say in earnest now. "I'm fucking freezing." I tip my head toward the sand where Grant, June, and Lainey are now standing.

She rolls her eyes, but finally her soft hand slides into mine, and she follows as I start to trudge toward the shore, the cool night air making me shiver as more skin breaches the water.

"You're insane, you know," June says to her friend, and Claire shrugs.

"Life's short."

"Shorter when you've got a death wish," I grumble, and she lets out a small laugh.

"You're a fun one, Claire," Grant says, and I glare at him for encouraging her. "What? She is!"

"She's gonna freeze," I say, looking at the woman as she bends in her fucking underwear, ass aimed at me, twisting her long blonde hair and wringing the water from it before she reaches for the shorts June is holding out for her. She grabs a clip from the belt loops I didn't see before, pinning the wet locks up with it.

"I'm not going to freeze," she says with another roll of her eyes, but shivers a bit despite herself. When she reaches for her top, she finds it soaking and covered in sand before she cringes at it.

"Your lips are blue," I say, looking at her, and a bolt of unwanted alarm rushes through me.

"I'll be fine," she says as she slides her dry jean shorts on. "Nice to know you're looking at my lips, though."

How does she do that? Turn everything into some kind of taunt or flirt, some proof that I'm looking at her, thinking about her.

I am, but I don't need *her* to know about it.

I sigh, grabbing my T-shirt and shaking the sand out of it before offering it to her. "Here."

She puts a hand to her chest, and I force my eyes not to follow it to her full breasts cupped in a soaking wet bra.

"For me? A true gentleman."

"You're cold, that's all."

I expect her to argue, but she just shrugs before sliding the shirt on. It's huge on her petite frame, the hem covering her shorts.

Thankfully, before my mind can settle on how much I like seeing *Miller Automotive* cross her chest, I'm distracted when she pulls her arms inside the shirt and starts fumbling under the worn fabric. Before I know it, her bra slides out the bottom.

I close my eyes and pray for patience, realizing she doesn't have anything under my shirt now.

Lainey drunkenly looks from me to Claire, a smile spreading along her lips before she speaks. "All right, well, that's enough fun for one night. Thanks for saving her, Miles!"

"He didn't save me!" Claire argues, but Lainey ignores her.

"Come on, June. We should get you guys home," Lainey says.

Claire sighs, putting an arm around her friend and moving her up the sand toward the boardwalk. June stumbles a few times in the stand, and her brother moves next to her, always wanting to help but knowing she's too stubborn to accept it.

But all I can do is watch Claire Donovan move up toward the dunes in my shirt.

And fuck, does it look good on her.

"See you around, Miles," she says over her shoulder.

For my sanity, I sure as fuck hope not.

FOUR

CLAIRE

The morning after Surf is rough.

Lainey was the worst of us all, probably because, unlike June, she didn't get sick last night and instead just felt like trash this morning. I woke with a bit of a headache and a crick in my neck because June's bed is not meant for three, but that was nothing a greasy breakfast at the local diner couldn't fix.

"So can we talk about it yet?" June asks after we drop Lainey off at her place after breakfast. I can feel her stare burning on me as I drive, but I refuse to look at her. She'd been planning this, I know that much, since she's aware I'm always much more willing to spill my guts to her if it's just her and me. Lainey is her childhood friend and has become one of my best friends as well since I started coming down to Seaside Point in college, but June knows spilling my thoughts and feelings isn't my *favorite* thing to do.

"Talk about what?" I lie because, of course, I know exactly what she wants to talk about. June Walker is the best friend a girl could have, but also a huge fucking pain in the ass if you ever want to process something internally or, say, forget it altogether.

June is a *talk-it-out* kind of person, and I know even as I drive, she's dissecting every thought that shifts across my face, taking note of every bit of my body language.

It's what makes her an *amazing* fifth-grade teacher.

"What was that at Surf?" she asks, just as her apartment building, where I'm dropping her off before I go to meet my new potential roommate, is in sight now.

Internally, I groan because that means I won't have the distraction of driving in a moment or two.

"We got drunk? We danced?" I ask.

"Don't play dumb, it's not cute on you, Claire," she says as I pull into a spot right up front, putting my car into park as I turn to her, eyes wide.

"Excuse me? I *always* look cute, especially when I play dumb, and you know it."

She glares at me before rolling her eyes. I smile, then pull my visor down and pretend to check my hair in the mirror.

"I meant more *Miles Miller catching you when you fell off the bar then going skinny dipping and forcing him to come in with you.*"

I turn to her with wide eyes, a finger lifted.

"I did *not* force him to come in with me, and you know that. I also was not skinny dipping." I tuck a strand of hair behind my ear and look back at the mirror. "I was in my underwear."

"Claire," she says, the same patient voice I'm sure she uses on the kids she works with, as I reach into my very full backseat for my purse.

"Nothing happened," I say, even if it feels like a bit of a lie.

But it's also the truth: *nothing happened.*

Nothing happened, and yet for some fucked reason, it's all I've been able to think about since Grant helped me get Lainey and June home safe. His hands on me when he caught me, the way, according to Lainey, he panic-ran into the ocean because he was worried about me, the way he didn't flinch when I held onto him in the water, the way I *felt* his eyes on my ass.

And it's fucked because he's my ex's older brother. The one Paul repeatedly and near-incessantly complained about. Though, long before I even *met* Paul, any time we were at the same place, it was always Miles I would end up chatting with. The few times he was around after Paul and I got together, Miles would hang back with me while his brother was off getting drunk and into some kind of trouble.

At the time, it felt like I was bonding with my boyfriend's brother, both of us knowing intimately what an idiot he could be. And before that, it felt like Miles spent time with us begrudgingly because he'd tag along with Grant.

With him also being the best friend to my best friend's brother, we've been around each other more times than I can count in the six years I've been coming down to Seaside Point, and even though he always acted like I was a nuisance of a girl, always getting into trouble, he always said it with a hint of adoration.

Of brotherly acceptance.

Except for last night.

That was not brotherly in the *least*.

And now old thoughts and feelings from before Paul love-bombed the fuck out of me are creeping out of the box I very carefully and meticulously shoved them in.

"Claire," June says, but I grab my lipstick from my bag and start a touch-up, continuing my need to distract myself.

"I'm serious," I start, snapping out of my memories. "Nothing happened. He was worried I was drunk and wanted to make sure I didn't go all Jack in *Titanic*."

The silence is deafening as I continue to fiddle with my lipstick, pretending to touch up the edges. Through it, June's patient glare burns on me, though I don't dare meet it.

And then, because June is my best friend and a bit of a loose cannon, she says, "You should fuck him."

I'm glad I already pulled the lipstick away from my face, or else it would be smeared across my face.

"What?" I ask, turning to her aghast.

Her grin is near solar with how wide and bright it is. "You should fuck Miles. It would be pretty iconic."

"June." I laugh, putting the lipstick back into my bag. "You're insane."

"Why? You always had a thing for him, and until Paul came sniffing around, you two were always flirting back and forth." She says Paul's name like he's some grand criminal instead of simply an idiot. "You guys used to be friends."

I shake my head. "Miles and I were never friends; he is simply friends with your brother, which meant he was always just *around* when we all hung out. He couldn't stand me even then, which is why I'd flirt with him in the first place. It's as easy as that."

I put the cap back on my lipstick and rub my lips together.

"Paul always gave you shit for being friends with his brother, and in the end, he was a dick. What better revenge would there be?"

I sigh and close my eyes because this is not the first time we've had *this* conversation. "I don't want revenge on Paul. I just want to move on with my life."

I met Paul Miller two summers ago, and he instantly swept me away with grand gestures and sweet words, always giving me his full attention. His sweetness started to fade over our first winter together, but when it returned with the warm weather, I chalked it up to some kind of seasonal depression.

He was an aspiring rockstar, so I agreed to follow him to California last December. But when he was the only one I knew out there, and I had zero distractions from how shitty our relationship was, I ended things and headed back home to Evergreen Park to lick my wounds.

Now I'm here, spending my summer in Seaside Point.

"I'm just saying...you'll be here all summer."

Finally, I turn to her with an eyebrow raised. "And as you always tell me, this town is teeny tiny. I'd probably have to see him all the time after. It would be awkward."

"You could have a summer fling!" When I tip my head with a

raised brow, she rolls her eyes. "Awkwardness gone because you'd be fucking him all summer long. Then in the fall, you leave. No bumping into him."

That is definitely *not* how that would work, but I know that argument would fall on deaf ears. "You know I don't do flings."

She rolls her eyes exasperatedly. "Maybe you should," she grumbles under her breath.

"June."

"I'm just saying. I always told you he had a thing for you, and you love flirting with him—" I sigh and throw my hands up.

"Because he's an easy target, and I like flirting! I flirt with everyone."

"No, you don't. You don't flirt with Grant," she says.

I raise an eyebrow, finally looking her in the eye. "Do you want me to start?" I ask with a smile.

Her face screws up with disgust. "Ew, no. That's my brother, Claire."

"Perfect. Now drop this. Miles Miller has never and *will* never be into me."

"What if he saw you with Paul and realized he was a big giant idiot not going for it all those summers, and now that you've gotten your head out of your ass and dumped his brother, he's ready to give it a shot? Would you be into him then?"

I roll my eyes.

"You're going to hurt yourself with how far you're stretching this. Either way, this summer is not about that. It's about me having fun and maybe, hopefully, figuring out what I want to do with my life. Now go. I have to go meet my new landlord."

She looks me over, then seems to realize I don't want to continue talking about Miles or Paul and smiles again.

"Maybe *he'll* be hot, and you'll have a sweltering summer fling with him instead."

"Jesus, June, maybe you're the one who needs to get laid."

She shakes her head with a sad look on her face. "There's no maybe about that. We both know my dry spell is just about past saving. You're my last hope for hot sex by osmosis."

"You're out of your fucking mind," I say low.

My best friend gives me a wide smile and then reaches over, tapping my cheek with a loving hand. "And you love it." Then she looks at me again. "Sorry, I'm a nudge. I just want you to have the most stellar summer possible."

I smile before leaning over the center console and hugging her.

"I know. I appreciate it. You're the mastermind behind this plan, and it's already shaping up to be amazing."

"It's only going to get better. Call me after you go to the house. Tell me whose it is, and I can give you all the tea on who they are and if we should trust them with your life. Remember, if it's Old Man Rafferty, run. He's a weirdo and will absolutely steal your panties."

I cringe at the visual and shake my head.

"I don't think Helen would do that to me," I say with a laugh. "You said Mr. Rafferty is on Bayside Drive?" She nods. "Yeah, this is on Ocean Ave."

"Ocean Ave?" she asks curiously, and now it's my turn to nod. "Hmm. Interesting. Well, call me when you know more!" She steps out of the car, and I think I see a strange look on her face, but I may have just imagined it.

"Later," I call out, pulling out of her parking lot.

Now that I'm alone, my nerves take over. I graduated from college almost two years ago, and I still don't know what I want to do with my life. After my plan to follow my then-boyfriend across the country totally crashed and burned, I gave myself one year to figure it out before I had to start thinking *realistically* instead of *idealistically*.

Except I'm nearly six months in, and...nothing. I still have no idea what I want to do for the rest of my life.

After the breakup, my life pretty much settled into the same rhythm it had before: I went back to living in the cottage behind my brother's house, working at his girlfriend's dance studio, and babysitting my niece when needed.

The only difference was the looks I was now getting from my family. Even *they* knew I was faking it through each day, slowly wasting away with anxiety as I tried to figure out what I wanted to do.

It's why I needed to get out of that town, if only for a few months, because as much as I love my family, and I'm so glad I had them to fall back on after everything fell apart, I was suffocating.

This entire chaotic plan started about two weeks ago during one of our incessant FaceTimes when I finally confessed to June how lost I've been feeling.

"Everyone..." I bit my lip, feeling silly saying it out loud. "Everyone around me knows what they want to do. And I...don't."

"You're young!" she said with a wave of her hand. "You have time!"

"I'm twenty-five, June. I feel like I was supposed to spend the last two years since graduation figuring it all out, and instead, I spent it babying Paul." She gave me a tight look because, from the time I met him at a party, she didn't like him for me. "And now I'm home again, back at square one. Except my entire family is secretly judging me for not having it all figured out."

A frustrated tear rolled down my cheek, and I cursed my inability to hide emotions. Normally, I think it just makes me me, but right then, these tears exposed me too much.

She gave me a contemplative look before she nodded like she knew exactly what the answer was. "You know what you need? A hot girl summer."

I let out a snort of a laugh and shook my head at her, wiping away the few tears that escaped and already feeling a bit better.

"I'm serious! Spend the summer having fun, being silly, and living it up, then, in the fall, you can figure out what you want to do. You can't make big decisions like that just by thinking about them non-stop." A pregnant pause filled the line before she spoke again. "Okay, it might sound crazy—"

"I love crazy," I said with a smile she returned.

"What about Seaside Point?"

"What?"

"Come down here for the summer! It's perfect, actually. Helen, the recreation manager? She's looking for some lifeguards for the season."

I rolled the idea through my mind, then stumbled on the first obstacle.

"Where would I live?" I asked, knowing her apartment is no bigger than a shoebox. "I love you, but—"

"But college was rough enough. I almost killed you. Doing that again might be the end of our friendship."

I rolled my eyes at her. "That's because you're a neat freak."

"No. It's because you're a tornado."

I smiled, accepting her dig because it was not completely wrong. I could only see the top of her head as she tapped away at the screen of her phone.

"We'll find you a place down here, I know a ton of people. We have to get you the job first." My phone pinged with a new message. "That's the website for the recreation department. Fill out the application for summer positions."

I moved to my laptop and opened the link, finding the application quickly and opening it. "Is this crazy?" I asked with a laugh, typing in my name.

"No crazier than any other things we've done."

I shrugged because she was not wrong, then focused for the next few minutes while she rambled on about plans and what kind of fun we could have if we lived in the same town for a few months.

"Okay, application sent." A sense of excitement and purpose rushed through me, feeling good to finally take control of this morose feeling that had been plaguing me.

Maybe a change of pace was all I'd need.

"Ah! So exciting! Tomorrow I'll talk to Helen and make sure she knows how perfect you are for the job. You'll get the job."

That was two weeks ago, and in that time, I got the job, packed everything up from the cottage I was living in behind my brother

Nate's house, and moved down here. I'll be living down the shore for the summer to give myself some space and a bit of fun to try and figure out my life. My plan is to have one last carefree summer and, along the way, hopefully, figure out what I like and what I want to do with my life.

Or, worst-case scenario, in the fall, get a big girl job, and then I'll have this fun, chaotic summer to look back on when I'm a depressed paper pusher.

Either way, this is *my summer*.

FIVE

MILES

After spending the night trying not to think about Claire Donovan and our dip into the ocean, I wake up before the sun and go for a run to attempt to clear my mind. Then, I spend the rest of the morning tidying the house for the arrival of my new renter, despite my barely even touching most of the rooms throughout the week.

Finally, at noon on the dot, the doorbell rings, and I make my way to the front with an overwhelming sense of dread.

The truth is, I don't *want* a roommate. I don't *want* to share my home with someone else, not when this is the one place I can hide away from the tourists that will flood this town in the next couple of weeks.

But I *do* want my brother off my ass and to finally have this shit behind me, and this is the easiest way to get that done without having to ask for help. So, with my hand on the doorknob, I take in a deep breath before opening the door.

"Hey—" I start, but stop when I see the last person I expected to see.

Claire Donovan.

Claire Donovan is standing on my front step, her face clear of makeup, her hair pulled into a ponytail, a loose Atlas Oaks T-shirt tucked into the front of a pair of jean shorts.

Her pristine, bright yellow car is parked in my driveway next to my truck that's seen better days, spots of rust spackling it all over. Between New Jersey winters and their salted roads and the ocean air, cars don't have much of a chance around here unless you're incredible about your maintenance, of which I am not.

It's almost funny, the way they look next to one another, the perfect example of how different she and I are. She's had that same car for years. I remember June calling me to help them on the side of the Parkway when Claire ran out of gas and seeing the yellow Bug a quarter mile away. After that, it's how I always knew she was here, seeing it parked around town.

But it's never been parked outside my house.

"Can I help you?" I ask, unable to mask my irritation.

Irritation because somehow, she's prettier than normal, and annoyingly so. Her eyes are bluer than they were last night in the dark, the color of the sky on a clear, sunny day. Now that she's smiling at me in broad daylight, I see her set of dimples for the first time in what might be a year. Then she lets out a laugh, that ringing, magical laugh she's always had.

"God, the world really does work in mysterious ways, doesn't it?" she says cryptically, putting her hands on her full hips. She's thoroughly entertained by something I don't quite understand and don't have the time for, since my renter should be here any minute.

"What are you doing here?" I ask, looking around to see if June is somewhere nearby.

Or maybe a camera crew for some idiotic prank show. It sounds like something Claire would sign up for.

"This is 14 Ocean Avenue, right?" My brow furrows as she reads out my address, and in the back of my mind, something starts to move, warning bells ringing out.

"Yes?" She lets out an entertained laugh once more, and my irritation grows. "All right, look, if this is some kind of joke, I—"

Her laughter dies down, and her smile turns sweet before she cuts me off.

"I'm not here for a joke—I was sent here by Helen. She told me you have a place I can stay at for the summer."

For a moment, I stare at her, trying to piece together the words she's saying, before finally, it clicks.

I'm such an idiot.

How didn't I see it the second she showed up at my door?

Claire is the renter Helen recommended. When Helen originally called, I didn't bother to ask for a name since it didn't really seem to matter, but now I'm seeing the catastrophic mistake that was.

"No," I say instantly with a shake of my head, stepping back and starting to close the door. "No way."

Her foot moves out, stopping me from shutting her out.

"Helen said you said I could stay here," she explains, her voice taking on a pleading note that does something I very much do not like to my chest.

"She didn't tell me it would be *you*." Something I realize was probably intentional since Helen knows every*thing* about every*one* in this town and definitely knew that Claire used to be Paul's girlfriend.

Claire must know that to be true as well, something that becomes clear when she says, "Probably because she knew if she told you it was me, you'd say no without even giving me a shot."

"Well, she was right. I'm saying no." I try to close the door, but she's stronger than she looks. I could force it closed, but I'd probably hurt her in the process, and while I might be an ass, I'm not *that* much of an ass. Regardless of how frustrating I find her, I don't want to hurt her.

"Please, Miles. You know me. I know you. This is kind of a best-case scenario because now you can rent to someone who isn't a total stranger, and I can move in knowing my new landlord isn't a serial killer."

I shake my head in the negative. No matter how she sells this, her living here would be a terrible fucking idea.

"No."

She sighs, and a look of resignation comes over her face, while a sense of relief washes through me. She's not going to fight me on this for once in her life. But then her face shifts, an alarming level of determination taking over, and that relief is gone.

I should have known it wouldn't have been that simple.

"Come on, if you don't let me stay here, my next option is staying with Old Man Rafferty, and June said that's a bad idea."

Instantly, I shake my head because everyone knows that Mr. Rafferty is weird. Over my dead body will Claire stay there.

"You can't stay there; he's a creep. He'll probably watch you sleep or something."

A smile plays on her lips, hope in her eyes, and I realize I fucked up.

"So you'll let me stay here?" she asks.

I run a hand through my hair and let out a bone-deep sigh. "I don't know..."

It's a terrible plan, and not just because she's my brother's ex. Not just because when they were dating, I was never able to look at them together and not feel a soul-crushing level of jealousy. It's why any time she was in Seaside Point last summer, I worked overtime, avoiding going anywhere but work and home.

The first summer they were together was torture enough. I couldn't put myself through it a second time.

"I can pay rent through September upfront. All four months."

I hesitate then because that kind of money upfront could shut Paul up, if only for a bit, while I get the rest of the money without him breathing down my neck.

But before I get ahead of myself, I remember Claire is flighty and irresponsible, just like Paul. Last night was proof enough of that. I doubt she has that kind of money just waiting around. "That's almost six grand, Claire."

Her eyes go wide, a clear hint of hope and excitement filling them.

"I'm good for it! We can go to the bank right now. I'll get a check for you. Or cash, whatever you want. Under the table, official, I don't care. Whatever you want. I just need a place to stay for the summer."

"How do you have six grand just sitting around?"

She tips her head to the side, reading me, then smiles.

"Stripping. How do you think?"

My head jerks back, eyes going wide with shock, not because there's anything wrong with being a stripper, but because I can't imagine *Claire* being a stripper.

That voice in my head that was having highly inappropriate dreams last night pipes up. *But she'd definitely do a damn good job.* I shake my head, dislodging that voice before she laughs, crossing her arms over her chest.

"God, you should see your face. I forgot how uptight you are."

"I am not uptight," I lie, glaring when she rolls her eyes.

"You've been uptight since the first time I met you."

"You were hammered, and you were nineteen. I was probably annoyed that Grant and I had to babysit you and June."

"So you're telling me you remember meeting me, huh?"

I remember every fucking minute I've been in Claire Donovan's presence, not that I'll be telling her that. "June puked on my shoes, and I had to throw them out. So yeah, I remember that night."

"And you glared at me, fighting the all-consuming urge to give me a talking to, I'm sure."

She's not wrong; although if I'm being honest, that wasn't the only all-consuming urge I felt that night. But that's just another reason I absolutely should not let her stay here for the summer.

An entire season stuck under the same roof as her would be a complete disaster.

"Come on. For old times' sake? I start work tomorrow, and I don't have time to be house hunting and making sure it's a safe place *and* unpacking and getting settled. I obviously can't stay with June because the place is basically a shoebox."

"You took a job here without somewhere to stay?"

She shrugs, her blonde hair bouncing as she does.

"I knew I'd figure something out eventually. And look!" She waves her hands in my direction, her smile going wide. "I did! A safe place with a friend!"

"I'm not your friend," I say, crossing my arms on my chest and leaning in the doorway. This all feels so surreal, like some kind of stupid prank Grant would pull on me.

"Oh, stop it, yes we are! Remember when you came to my birthday in the city?"

I remember the January before last, Paul calling me last minute and accepting the invite to the lavish restaurant only to be left with the bill, the last straw in my relationship with Paul and another reason why I ignored them both the following summer.

"Or I came down the summer before last to spend the Fourth with your mom?" she added.

I remember having to hound Paul for a *month* to convince him to come and him constantly telling me Claire wanted to party for the holiday. It took me threatening not to send his monthly rent payment digitally and instead hand him a check in person to convince him to come down to celebrate our mother's birthday.

I also remember Claire coming with the most extravagant gift for Mom and being confused as fuck, because the woman didn't *seem* disappointed not to be at some rave that night.

"What about all the times we went shell hunting together? You're my lucky charm," she says, and that one has me hesitating. "Come on, Miles. Please?"

I don't respond still, and her face changes again. I always found that so interesting about Claire, the way her face shifts and changes at the drop of a hat, always so fucking expressive. She can't keep a secret to save her life, but it's entertaining to watch her try.

"At the very least, your mom loves me."

"What does that have to do with anything?" I ask, confused.

Her cuteness fades, and she cocks out a hip, clearly sliding into another angle to get her way with such smoothness it almost startles me.

Trouble. So much damn trouble this woman is.

"How is she going to feel if I call and tell her I'm living on the streets when you have a nice, clean, open bed for me to *pay* to sleep in?"

I roll my eyes at her dramatics, but something tells me she would actually do it. And if she did, a few things would be for certain: Mom would be upset Paul fucked things up with Claire, absolutely over-joyed that Claire was here for the whole summer, and she would be beyond pissed I wasn't giving her a place to stay.

Still, the idea of an entire summer with her...

"Claire—" I start, but she must sense my resolve weakening and keeps pressing.

"I'm very quiet," she lies, and even though I know that's a lie, she continues speaking before I can argue. "You'll barely even notice I'm here! Plus, I'll be out by September tenth."

"What are you doing after?" I ask.

"After?"

"I want to make sure I won't be conned into letting you stay indefinitely after September. Do you have plans?"

Am I actually considering letting her live with me? I think to myself.

I think I am.

Because some petty part of me likes the idea of Paul's ex living in this town he hated, with the brother he can't stand, helping me buy back the house he wants to sell.

She shrugs and smiles, but beneath it, her normal, blissful confidence is gone. In its place is self-consciousness and doubt.

"I'll go back to Evergreen Park, where my family is." It's a logical answer, even if she seems miserable over it. Regardless, I feel my jaw tighten with the knowledge as I run out of reasons to tell this woman not to live here.

She knows it, too.

"So does this mean you have a new roomie?" Claire asks, and I don't miss how she makes it seem like *I'm* the one benefiting from this.

"You can really pay upfront?" She nods excitedly. "Can you follow the rules I put together?" She nods slightly less excitedly. "Can you promise not to make a huge fucking mess?"

"Pinky swear." She puts a hand out, her pinky pointed toward me, the nails painted a buttery yellow that matches her car.

A pinky promise.

This is what I'm getting myself into: a woman who wants to secure a summer rental with a fucking *pinky promise*.

Her smile continues to widen as I hook mine with hers and hold it there.

I look at her, then where her little yellow car is parked, then back to her. "I'm not helping you with your bags," I say begrudgingly.

"Oh, of course not. I would never expect you to be a gentleman." She smiles like she finds this wildly entertaining as she skips to her car, opening the trunk before hefting a duffel bag over her shoulder. She lifts out another suitcase before walking back up the stairs. "Do you mind at least holding the door for me?" she asks.

I glare at her, and she smiles wider as she makes her way in. I lock eyes on her trunk and see two more suitcases, one of the two almost as big as she is, before I groan and jog down the steps, grabbing both and making my way up the stairs again.

"Well, look at you. You *do* have manners."

It's then I know I'm in for the longest summer of my life.

SIX

CLAIRE

After Miles helps me bring my bags in and shows me to my room, I don't see him again. Not after I unpack, not after I call June to tell her the news, of which she laughed maniacally, and not after I run to the store for a few essentials.

When I wake up early for my first day of work, his car is already out of the driveway, and a pang of guilt hits me as I realize he's probably avoiding me.

Thankfully, my day is pretty busy, so I'm distracted enough that I can't overthink things.

I arrive at the main lifeguard station, a raised, enclosed building on the sand with windows all around where everyone clocks in and where Helen keeps her office. She shows me around the small building, assigns me a cubby for my things, and has me fill out about a million papers.

After that, I'm officially a recreation department employee, and we spend the next six hours talking to what feels like everyone in town: the mayor, the first-aid crew, the fire chief, and a bunch of the people who work at or own the businesses on the boardwalk. Around four p.m., this season's lifeguards come for orientation, and I'm introduced to each of them.

A group of teenage girls instantly latch on to me, chatting non-stop and asking me a million questions, though I don't mind, since being from a small town myself, I get the excitement of someone new coming in. But my favorite is Jonah, a twelve-year-old junior life-guard. There's something about him that is so sweet and shy, and I instantly decided to take him under my wing this summer.

I'm exhausted but also excited for the prospect of the upcoming season when I finally make it back home to Miles's house at almost six, only to find he's still not home.

It's why at seven p.m. that night, when he knocks on the door-frame of my room, I jump, not realizing he'd gotten back at all as I watched the ocean from the small deck attached to my room.

When I turn to look at him, he looks comfortable, leaning against the doorframe and making me wonder just how long he's been there.

"Crap, you scared me," I say, putting a hand to my chest.

"I was standing here for a while," he says as if that absolves him from startling me. It doesn't, instead, it confirms he's been watching me for some time.

But why?

"Sorry, I was just taking in the view. It's beautiful," I say, looking back over my shoulder at the ocean. "Do you ever see dolphins from here?" He gives me a blank look and I continue rambling on. "I love them, and I always wanted to see them in real life, living their little dolphin lives in the ocean."

He stares at me as if he's trying to understand what I'm saying before he shakes his head.

"You haven't seen any?"

He shakes his head again before finally speaking. "No, I have a few times. You can see them if the ocean is super warm and it's still pretty cold out there. As you know."

I can't help the small smile that comes to my lips. "Yeah, I guess."

He's silent as he steps further into what is now my room, stopping at the white dresser where I laid out all of my shells. I don't know exactly why I packed them up and brought them, but I like seeing them, and I suppose that's a good enough reason.

"What are these?" he asks, touching a dark blue scallop shell delicately, his fingers barely grazing over it.

"My shell collection," I say with a smile. "You should recognize most of them." He turns to me, a bit confused, and I smile wider. "Since you were there every time I found the good ones. You're basically my lucky charm."

Miles continues to stare at me for long moments before he seems to snap out of some kind of daze, averting his eyes back to the shells. "Hmm," he mumbles.

The urge to continue to pull conversation out of him the way I've always done tugs at me, and I move, sitting on the edge of my bed and chatting. "It's on my list, you know."

"Your list?" he asks, stepping away from the dresser.

I lift my phone where a photo of the list I made with June lives and wave it toward him. "My list of things I want to do this summer. I'm planning on getting the full beach bum experience." He gives me a look, and I'm surprised when he speaks instead of just moving past it to whatever he actually came in here to ask me about. "Anything I should add?" I ask, looking at him.

"Add?" he asks, confused as always.

"Anything you think I should add to my list?" He stares at me blankly, and I laugh. "What do you do for fun around here in the summer? I'm sure you have *something* I can add."

"I don't do things for fun," he says quickly, then instantly a mask comes over his face like even *he* knows that was the wrong answer.

I tip my head to the side curiously. "What do you mean you don't do things for fun? You're human."

"I don't..." He hesitates, then runs a hand over his hair, his tell that he's uncomfortable, and shrugs. "I don't know. I work a lot."

"So you don't do *anything* for yourself?"

He shakes his head to argue. "No, no, I do." I raise an eyebrow because suddenly, I don't believe him, not at all. "I surf," he says.

"Don't you teach surf lessons?"

"How do you know I teach surf lessons?" he asks, and I fight the blush that burns over my cheeks. I will not be admitting to Miles that I have spent the past six summers taking note of everything I can about him.

"I saw your ad in the rec center," I say, which isn't a complete lie. "But teaching lessons isn't fun. When was the last time you surfed for yourself?"

He stares at me for long moments, and I know the answer is obviously long enough that he can't easily remember, and something about that hurts my heart. Miles, who is constantly helping everyone and anyone who needs it, doesn't take time for himself. He shakes his head and stands up straight, clearly not interested in this conversation.

"It doesn't matter, enough about me. I came up here for a reason."

I smile at him. "It wasn't just to be a friendly roommate?"

He glares at me in response, pushing off the wall and standing up straight again. "I think we should go over the rules."

I quirk an eyebrow at him, lips tilting with a smile. "Rules?" He nods, crossing his arms on his chest as if he's ready to argue with me. "You should know now, I'm not great at rules. You can ask my dad. They always make me feel this unexplainable urge to do the opposite."

He shakes his head as if erasing some thought from it before he stands up straighter like he means business. "Rule number one, no parties."

"Bummer. I hope I can get my deposit back on the three kegs for next weekend."

He glares but continues with his rules. "No pets."

I look around the room as if I'm looking for one, then brush a hand over my forehead with fake relief. "Good thing I left my hedgehog at home."

He blinks at me a few times before responding curiously.

"You have a hedgehog?"

I shake my head and smile. "No, but if I did, it would be pretty lonely." I shift on the bed, curling my leg under myself and putting a fist to my chin like I'm a student paying attention to the teacher. "What other rules do you have?"

"No overnight guests. June or Lainey are fine. No...no guys."

My eyes go wide with fake shock because I wouldn't have even considered bringing home someone to Miles's house.

"What about daytime guests?" I tip my head to the side, my hair tumbling over my shoulder, and I use a finger to twirl a lock of it around. "Like, if they just come for a quickie. Is that allowed?"

"No," he says bluntly and quickly, and I fight a small laugh before giving him a salute.

"Got it. Take it to their place."

He rolls his eyes.

"Curfew is eleven."

"Curfew?" I ask with a laugh. "I haven't had a curfew since I was seventeen."

"Well, then we're going to pretend you're seventeen."

"That would make things very awkward between us," I say, wiggling my eyebrows, and as expected and hoped, a blush spreads across his cheeks.

His jaw tightens, and he points an accusing finger at me. "That. We're not doing that."

"Doing what?" I ask, innocently.

"That's my next rule. No flirting."

I cringe. "Ooh, that's gonna be a hard pass. Physically impossible for me."

He sighs and runs a hand over his face like he's questioning all of his life's choices, specifically agreeing to have me stay here. After a moment, he seems to have found whatever inner strength he was looking for and locks his eyes with mine, shoulder straightening.

"You can't flirt with me, Claire."

"Why not? I love flirting. It's basically one of my three personality traits. Hot, funny, a flirt." I tick them off on my fingers with a grin, and he opens and closes his mouth like he wants to argue before shaking his head.

"Because you're my renter, and I'm your landlord. And you're my brother's ex."

I roll my eyes at that.

"That means nothing to Paul, and I'm sure even you know that."

His head tips just a bit, and then his mouth opens like he's about to argue before he thinks better of it. "Regardless, no flirting. Pretend I'm your brother. Or your dad."

"That would make thinking about you very uncomfortable, Miles," I say in an exaggerated whisper. His eyes go comically wide before he stutters out an answer.

"*No*," he says. "None of that. End of discussion."

"But it's so cute when you blush and get all weird about me," I say with a smile.

He lets out a deep sigh, and god, it's like when I first came here when I was nineteen, when every time I was down the shore with June, I would purposely flirt with him, and he'd instantly get all red and nervous.

It's like a jolt of nostalgia hits me, aching because I truly did miss this.

"We're not doing that. No flirting."

I roll my eyes. "God, you really don't ever have fun, do you? Do you even *know* how to have fun?"

"Excuse me?" he asks.

"Do you ever have fun? These rules kind of make it so you can't have fun ever. No pets, no parties, no one-night stands, no flirting...no fun."

"I don't think anyone has fun like you do, Claire," he says, exasperation in the words.

I shrug.

"If they did, I bet people would live longer." He gives me a disbelieving look. "Because they wouldn't be so stressed and depressed, obviously."

"I don't know if that's how that works."

"You need some fun in your life," I say. "Or you're going to die young and not because you were enjoying yourself too much. From a boredom-induced heart attack or something equally tragic."

"I very much do not need more fun."

"You do. Even Paul used to tell me." He gives me a deadpan look.

"Well, Paul isn't the most responsible person, so I don't put much weight in that," he says, a fair point.

"June said it, too. And Grant. And Helen."

His jaw goes tight once again, clearly unhappy that so many people have such an opinion on him and his life. "Yeah, well, that's their opinion," he says, then turns away to leave the room.

"I think," I say, and he pauses, looking over his shoulder. "I'm going to make it my mission for you to loosen up this summer." He leaves without another word, and I smile as he walks down the hall, my new mission clear.

SEVEN

CLAIRE

When June suggested I move down here for one last summer of fun before I force myself to get serious about figuring out what I want to do with my life, we made our list of fun things to do this summer.

Most of them were silly, like watching a sunrise or getting a killer tan, but I'm glad Miles didn't ask to actually see my list because we also added insane things, like hooking up with a local and fucking someone on a lifeguard chair.

Both of which I would be more than willing to do with my new landlord, even if he clearly has no interest in that.

I thought for the slightest moment in the ocean with him that there might be...something, but I think that was me reading into the crush I've had since I was nineteen, not reality.

Happens to the best of us.

But when Miles told me he doesn't have fun, I thought maybe we could kill two birds with one stone. I knock out my summer bucket list and force Miles to have some fun this summer as well.

Definitely *not* an excuse to convince him to spend more time with me.

I was up with the sun the following day since I left the curtains wide open, not that I could really complain too much despite *not* being a morning person, since I'm now waking up on the ocean. Miles's house is huge, and the only thing between us and the actual sand of the beach is the twelve-foot boardwalk. There are multiple decks on the property overlooking the water, including one right off my room.

Could I be any more lucky?

Digging through my things, I find what I'm looking for, a small stack of colorful papers I brought because you never know when you'll need it, as well as the zipper pouch full of colorful pens. I'm grateful that I always pack like a wild animal, forgetting about one-third of what I might *actually* need and bringing a ton of shit I probably won't need.

It's for times like these when I suddenly need paper and markers to make a colorful list more than I need that comfortable pair of walking shoes I left at my sisters' place.

After I get dressed in a bathing suit, an oversized *Seaside Point Lifeguard* sweatshirt, and a pair of shorts, I grab my things. Moving down the stairs quietly, I quickly make myself a premade coffee, one of the few groceries I bought yesterday, and then sit out on the deck while I start my summer project.

Two hours later, my list is done and decorated. I'm still out on the deck, face down on one of the foldable chairs and tanning when the side door slams unexpectedly. I bolt up to sitting quickly, putting a hand to my chest as the flimsy fabric of my top almost falls down.

I'd been lying on my stomach and flipping through a tabloid magazine to see if I could find anything funny about Jules's friends, Ava or Harper, who always end up in these magazines to tease them about later, and kept the ties off my back to avoid tan lines. I already know that summer as a lifeguard is going to result in the wildest ones possible.

"Jesus, sorry," Miles says as I watch him step onto the deck and then stumble back, putting a hand to his eyes.

I don't think he saw anything, though I wouldn't care if he did. I always thought it was strange how men are allowed to go for a run with their nipples out for everyone and their mom to see, but a nip slip on a woman is worthy of front-page news.

"Nothing to be sorry about," I say, turning a bit to face him, still holding my top in place.

"Are you decent?" he asks, panicked.

I fight a smile as I answer. "I'm covered if that's what you're asking."

He carefully peeks around his fingers in a way that is almost, dare I say, cute, before he drops his hand completely when he sees I'm holding my top up and covering myself, my back to him.

"Are you okay?" I ask with a smile, looking over my shoulder at him.

His eyes are wide and stuck on my back that's bare. I know I'm not supposed to tan, UV rays, skin cancer, and all of that, but a few minutes out in the sun, tanning is almost a vice at this point.

"What are you doing?"

"Trying to get a base before the summer. Those lifeguard tan lines are going to be brutal," I say, draping the top ties over my shoulders and hooking the back clasp with ease.

"Without a top?" he asks, and when I look back at him again, his eyes are still locked on me, though he looks to his feet as soon as he notices I'm watching him.

"I have a top on," I say, draping the ties over my shoulders. I then grab my hair in one hand and lift it, turning my back to a still-silent Miles. "Do you mind tying this?"

"What?"

I look over my shoulder with a smile I can't fight.

"My top. Can you tie it? I don't have a hair tie, and if I do it on myself, my hair will get tied up in it, and it hurts." He stares at me for long moments, blinking a few times before he clears his throat. "Please?"

"I thought we made rules about you flirting with me."

"I'm not flirting, I'm just living my life." He glares at me, and I let out a small laugh because he looks so fucking flustered. "Sorry, sorry, fine. I'm flirting with you. I can't help it. But if I tie it myself, I'm probably going to show you or whoever is on the boardwalk my entire boob, so—"

He moves across the deck toward me so quickly, I have to choke back a laugh before his hands grab the ties. I grab my hair, holding it up high so it doesn't get caught in the ties. His fingers hold the ties loosely, and I look over my shoulder at him.

"Would getting a glimpse really be *that bad*?" I ask with a smile. He rolls his eyes before moving to tie my bathing suit top, and I look ahead as his fingers brush gently against the back of my neck sending goose bumps over my skin.

"Sorry, I don't mix with privileged tourists," he declares as he tightens the loops and steps back.

Ahh, so this is the take we're still going with. Got it.

"You're kind of an ass, you know that?" I ask with a laugh, not actually offended.

He smiles back because for as long as I've known him, this has been our thing: I flirt, he gets annoyed, and he bites back.

"I'll be sure to write that one in my diary. Really hurt my feelings, you know?"

"God, what I'd give to read your diary. *Dear Diary, today my brother's super hot ex-girlfriend came to live with me, but I'm secretly super into her, and it makes me so mad*," I say in a fake gruff voice.

His face goes red, and I wonder if I hit the nail directly on the head and if it would be worth his wrath to look through his room from some little black book with all of his darkest secrets. Once a nosy little sister, always a nosy little sister.

"You're a pain in my ass."

I smile as I gather up my things and make my way inside the house to get ready for the day.

"It's a nice ass, though," I say over my shoulder as he follows close behind, and it's not a lie: Miles Miller has a *nice* ass, though when I smile at him, I don't miss how he's looking at *my* ass.

"Where are you going?" he asks as we move into the kitchen.

"I have thirty minutes before I have to head to work, and I need to eat breakfast."

He glares at me as I reach into a cabinet and grab a colorful box of cereal and then a bowl before moving to the fridge for milk. I know he wants to make some kind of comment about the cereal not being a *real* breakfast, but he gets distracted.

"What is this?" he asks as I situate myself at the island, pouring my cereal.

"What's what?" I ask, spooning cereal into my mouth and not bothering to look up. I know he's holding the colorful piece of paper I pinned to the fridge this morning with the lone magnet on it and taking it in. When he doesn't answer, I give in, looking up at him and seeing his brow furrowed as he stares at the list.

He really is kind of hot when he's not being an uptight bore.

"Miles's and Claire's list of things to have fun?" he reads aloud.

"Oh, that's Miles's and Claire's list of things to have fun."

He looks up from inspecting the bright yellow piece of paper and glares at me. I smile in return.

"I can read. What *is* it?"

"It's a list on paper written in colorful markers," I say as if I'm writing the assisted data for a picture on the internet. He closes his eyes and lets out a deep breath, something I've noticed he does around me a lot.

"Yes. Got that. What is this list *for*? Why did you make it?"

I tip my head at him and give him a pitying look like he's too dumb to comprehend things. "I told you I was making it my mission for you to have more fun. That starts now."

"Claire, this is," he starts, shaking his head, but I cut him off.

"Humor me, Miller."

He glares at me, and I glare back, and then, to my surprise, he softens, sighs, and starts reading the list aloud.

"Spend a day at the beach. Watch the sunrise. Go fishing." He lifts his head and looks at me through squinted eyes. "I love fishing."

"Great, I've never been. We can do it together."

His eyes go a bit wide with that.

"We're doing these together?"

I roll my eyes at him. "My name's on it. I'm not going to just take your word for it, Miles. You're kind of an unreliable narrator."

He opens and closes his mouth a few times, and I take a bite out of my cereal in the meantime because soggy cereal is a crime against humanity.

"Do you *know* how to fish?" he asks.

I shake my head. "No, but it sounds easy enough."

His jaw goes tight, and I just *know* that irritates the fuck out of him.

Mission accomplished.

It really is too easy.

"Get ice cream?"

"A summer necessity."

"Pet a hermit crab?" he asks, putting the paper on the counter and glaring at me, exasperation clear on his face.

I shrug. "Yup. They're basically the mascot of the boardwalk."

He hesitates before asking as if he isn't sure he wants to know. "How does one pet a hermit crab?"

I look over to him and smile.

"With your finger, ideally. I hear earning their trust is very important." I take another bite and watch him struggle with how to answer that. I added this one and a few others that I knew would send him into a tizzy because watching the blood creep up his neck is funny, and it does *not* disappoint.

"How does one earn a hermit crab's trust?" he asks hesitantly, an eyebrow raised.

"I would imagine it's different for every crab, just like people?"

He sighs like I'm testing his patience even though I know he's secretly wildly entertained by me before he looks at me again, putting the list down and crossing his arms on his chest.

"What is this?" he says, tipping his chin toward the paper.

"God, I just told you. Is your garage well-ventilated? Because it's a bit alarming how quickly you forget things." I chew another bite of cereal, fighting a smile as he glares at me, unspeaking. "It's a list of ways for you to have fun."

He leans into his hands on the counter, and the muscles along his arms tense and ripple.

Despite it all, Miles Miller is *hot*.

I, unlike him, am not in complete and utter denial of the palpable tension between us, but fuck, watching his arms move like that? It makes that extraordinarily clear.

Paul hated when we came to see his family because according to him, his mom and brother *don't get him* and *always give him shit*, (i.e: request he do the bare minimum and treat his family with respect). Anytime we were down here, we'd get into an argument about my flirting with his older brother. I never would have crossed any boundary, of course, but sometimes I felt guilty about it.

But now that there is no boyfriend to speak of, keeping me on the straight and narrow?

My mind has a bit of a life of its own, making up scenarios of summer flings and hot, sweaty nights.

I blame June, really. She's the one that put the idea in my head.

"You know what I mean. What is it for?"

I snap myself out of my lust-filled haze to answer, beaming at him.

"To help you have fun," I say slowly like he's an idiot. He blinks at me, and I smile wider now. "All you do is work."

"That's not true. Last night I was home and chatted with you."

"And you gave me a list of *rules*," I laugh.

"I have to make sure we're on the same page so we can have a drama-free summer."

I roll my eyes at that. "You said I couldn't flirt."

"That's because you're trouble and Paul's ex-girlfriend."

My heart skips a beat because the way my brain interprets that is he might be amenable to some kind of flirting if I *weren't* his brother's ex.

That I can work with. I can *so* work with that.

"What does that have to do with anything?"

"You know exactly what it has to do with."

God, he *so* feels it, too.

"I don't think I do," I say instead of agreeing, crossing my arms on my chest and leaning back on the chair.

"It means I have to keep my distance from you no matter how much you test my patience."

"Are you?" I put a hand to my chest and gasp. "Are you admitting there's some killer sexual tension between us?"

"I have no idea how you got that out of that sentence."

"Body language," I say, then smile. "That and the beet red blush on your face as soon as I said it."

"I'm not blushing," he lies, the blush only going deeper.

"Ahh, yes, it must be a killer sunburn you got in the past, what, eight hours you were sleeping?"

He shakes his head and puts the list back on the fridge.

"Look, I gotta get to work. Just...don't get into trouble, okay?"

"I'll do my best. Can't make any promises, of course. I love wreaking havoc at eight a.m. on a Monday."

A small smile spreads on his lips.

"A smile? Did I just make Miles Miller smile?" His blush deepens, and even though he fights it, the smile spreads. I throw my hands into the air dramatically. "Call the press! Call the president! Miles Miller knows how to smile! He's not a robot!"

"I know how to smile, Claire," he says as he hefts a bag over his shoulder and makes his way out the door.

"Now that I'm in your life, of course you do. Have you met me?"

"For better or worse, Claire, I have."

Honestly?

I'm going to call that interaction a success. Mission *Make Miles Have Fun* has commenced.

EIGHT

MILES

"So wait, hold up, your brother's ex is living with you for the summer?" Grant asks with a loud laugh. "The hot one?"

I grit my teeth, regretting that I confided in him when I was drunk three years ago that I thought his sister's best friend from out of town was hot, even if she was way too young for me. More so now, that, for some unknown reason, agreed to have her live with me for the summer.

She moved in less than a week ago, and I already almost saw her tits and argued with her on the deck, gave her a list of rules she has adamantly ignored (okay, so she's just ignored the one rule, but it was arguably the most important one), had her make some *summer fun list* she's insisting I cross off with her, and had two sex dreams about her.

I'm not sure how the fuck I'm supposed to survive this summer in one piece.

"Shouldn't we be calling her your little sister's best friend?" I much prefer that descriptor since the reminder that she used to be with Paul makes my jaw tight every time.

In contrast, Grant smiles wider, loving my misery.

"Not with the way you've always looked at her. When you do that, we call her your little brother's ex that you've been into for years."

Have lifelong friends, they said.

It will be fun, they said.

I call bullshit. Complete and utter bullshit.

"She's a friend," I say, only half lying because, for a while, I did, in fact, consider Claire Donovan a friend. "And she paid four months up front." His eyes go wide with the same shock I felt when she offered that. "Six grand."

"Jesus, where did she get that kind of cash?"

I shrug.

"I'm not sure. She joked that it was from stripping, but then we got sidetracked, and it didn't seem right to circle back to that specifically." I run a hand over my hair, remembering the incredibly detailed daydream I had about that the day before yesterday.

"Do you actually think she's been stripping?" he asks, eyes wide, a mix of shock and intrigue in them. The mere idea of Grant being interested in Claire dancing for men makes my blood start to heat, but I brush the strange jolt of something I refuse to name aside quickly.

It's because in my head, despite my complicated feelings about my brother lately, I still care about him, and I've been trained to protect him my entire life.

That's all.

"No," I say with a shake of my head because I've considered all angles more times than I should. "If she had, she never would have dropped it: it would be her new favorite way to fuck with me."

Again, Grant smiles wider.

"She sure does like to fuck with you," he says, and I glare.

We're at Grant's place since I'm avoiding my own house like the plague, deciding the best way to survive this summer is to just not see her. Difficult when she seems to be *everywhere* in that house, from her shitty cereal in the cabinets to her array of flip-flops at the door to her seemingly million pairs of sunglasses left about the house.

"You know, things with your brother are a little dicey right now, and it would be pretty normal to want to get back at him a bit," Grant says while I'm lost in my thoughts, a playful smirk on his face as he tips a beer toward me.

I stare for a moment before I ask for clarification, though I don't think I need it.

"What are you implying?"

He shrugs but answers all the same. "A pretty girl living in your house for the summer, it might be the perfect time to finally crack that seal on your celibacy."

"I'm not celibate," I say exasperatedly, rolling my eyes.

"Might as well be," he chuckles, and as much as I don't want to admit it, it's not completely wrong. "When was the last time you went out on a date?"

I shake my head and tell him something he already knows.

"I don't date."

He gives me an annoyed groan. "That's because you don't make *time* for dating. Fuck, if I didn't force you to hang out with me, you wouldn't even make time for friends."

Guilt eats at me a bit at that, knowing the truth of it.

"I don't see a point in dating someone if I'm not in a place where I can offer them some kind of future," I justify. Grant gives me a look like I'm out of my mind. "You know how I feel about that shit."

My parents were young and stupid when they got married and had me soon after. My mom tells me regularly about how they were both working paycheck to paycheck when they had me, and when my dad passed before Paul was two, it left her with nothing. She moved in with my grandmother, who helped raise us, but it wasn't easy. It's why I refuse to start anything, even *casually,* until I feel like my life is settled, which it very much is not.

"All I'm saying is it seems like a perfect opportunity, having her right there. Convenient, even."

That word rubs me wrong, and I'm out of patience to hedge my words. "Claire isn't something convenient for me."

It reveals too much about how I feel about her and my reluctant protectiveness of her, and he knows it when he smiles wide.

"Is that right?"

I roll my eyes. "Stop reading into everything. I'm not going there. She's not my type."

We both know that's a lie. I thought Claire was beautiful from the first time I met her. Frustrating and annoying, yes, with the way she instantly made herself at home here, with the way she won over everyone in her stratosphere, but beautiful all the same.

But even if I were in the market for someone, it surely wouldn't be a party girl like Claire.

She's too young, too flighty, and too...Paul.

"You're a fucking liar," he says with a laugh.

"I'm not." I shrug, trying to convince myself of it the same way I need to convince Grant. "She's too young and too much of a party girl."

He takes me in for long moments, in a way only my annoying as fuck best friend can, before smiling. "She's my type. Maybe I should shoot my shot."

Instantly and without warning, anger flares through me. I open my mouth to...I don't know, but I'll probably regret it.

But I don't have to say a single thing, because Grant's head tips back, and a deep, full-bellied laugh fills the room.

"Oh, god, you should see your face!" He chuckles, wiping a tear from his eye as he catches his breath.

"Fuck off, man."

"You are so fucked, you know that right?"

I roll my eyes and ignore him until he changes the topic, but it doesn't change the fact that he's completely right.

I am, in fact, so fucked.

I'm at the shop the next day when an all-too-familiar car pulls up. When she turns off the bright yellow car, Claire opens the door and steps out, a brown paper bag in hand, before slamming it shut behind her.

She's in a tee that reads *Wilde Security* that she's cut the arms off of and made shorter so it barely covers her belly button and a pair of short jean shorts that should be illegal. The shirt rises to show off her tanned and toned stomach when she lifts her arm to put her sunglasses on top of her head, and I just barely see that she's wearing a bright pink bathing suit underneath.

"Car trouble?" I ask, stripping off my orange gloves as I make my way toward her, taking off my baseball hat and slipping it around to block the midday sun. She shakes her head and meets me halfway, stopping a foot or so away from me and putting the hand holding the bag out to me.

"Brought you an Italian from Joe's." Joe's is a deli a few blocks inland from the boardwalk that everyone goes to if you want a good sub for the beach.

"You brought me lunch?" I ask, confused.

She shrugs like it's no big deal.

"I'm off today. June is busy, and Lainey's doing inventory at work. I figured I'd grab a sandwich at Joe's, then lay out for the afternoon. But you know how big the sandwiches are, and I didn't want it to go to waste. I remembered you order the same thing as I do, and so I asked him to split it in two for me."

A light blush bleeds across her cheeks, and my gut goes warm at the sight.

"He threw in those gross cheddar sour cream chips you like and an iced tea. It's all in the bag." She shakes said bag, and slowly, I reach out to grab it, noting it's pretty heavy.

"They're not gross," I say without thinking.

"Barbecue is way better." It's an argument we've had many times before, and despite myself, I smile, shaking my head. "Anyway, I just wanted to drop that off. I'll get out of your hair," she says, stepping backward toward her car.

"You're not staying?" I ask, quickly pushing down the burst of disappointment that rockets through me.

She smiles wide and shakes her head. "No, I don't want to bother you too much. Just knew I'd never finish that sandwich myself and figured I'd share."

It's a lie. I know it is, just like how I know Joe, despite being a good guy, didn't just happen to throw in the drink and chips.

Claire did it to be nice.

I sigh and tip my head to the garage. "Come eat with me."

Her eyes go wide. "You're inviting me into your lair?" she asks in a stage whisper.

"It's not a lair; it's a dirty shop. But we can clear off a spot and eat." I hesitate, rethinking my offer. "Unless you're planning to eat on the beach and want to head out. Then—"

She shakes her head quickly, cutting me off. "No, I'd love to. Sand in sandwiches is the worst."

Then she turns back to her car to grab her bag, and I find a place to set us up.

Forty minutes later, I've dragged out eating a sandwich and chips as long as I can to keep her here, and Claire is finishing the last sips of her own iced tea lemonade before I look at the clock over her head and sigh.

It's been a good forty minutes, despite myself. We chatted and laughed, and I remembered why I always gravitated toward Claire when we were thrown together, why we always went for walks along the shoreline while she looked for her shells. When she's not flirting with me just to get a reaction and when I'm not being a dick who's making assumptions about her, we get along really well.

"I've got a client coming in ten minutes to pick their car up," I say, tipping my head toward the white car in the small lot.

Claire steps back, checking the time on her phone, and her eyes widen. "Jeez, I didn't realize how late it was getting. I'm going to miss all the good sun." She moves to clean up the deli paper before her, the makeshift picnic we created on the flat top of my rolling toolbox.

I shake my head. "Don't worry, I've got it."

She hesitates. "Are you sure?"

"Yeah, it's the least I can do. Come on, I'll walk you to your car."

She takes me in before nodding, grabbing her keys, and moving back toward her car. The sun beats hard on the blacktop, and Claire slides her sunglasses back onto her nose as she stops in front of her car, turning to face me.

"Thanks for having lunch with me," she says with a smile. "I had fun."

"Pretty sure I'm the one who is supposed to be saying thank you."

She shrugs like it's no big deal. "Whatever."

A gust of wind moves through the air, pushing her hair into her face. She giggles, and when the breeze stops, a piece of hair is stuck on her sunglasses. Without thinking, my hand lifts, grabbing the silky golden strand between my fingers and pushing it back behind her ear, my fingers lingering there, my thumb brushing over the soft skin of her jaw.

I could kiss her.

I could kiss her, and with the way her chin is tipped up to look at me, the way her lips are parted, I think she'd let me. My mind moves to the previous night, to Grant saying I should hook up with Claire, and for a split second, I consider it.

For a split second, I contemplate throwing common sense to the wind and just doing what *feels* right instead of what I *should* do.

And then the sound of tires crunches behind me, and I step back, the moment broken as my client pulls up.

"I'll, uh, let you get back to work," she says, her voice breathy as she steps away, a smile on her lips.

She opens the door to her car, and I hold it as she slides in and turns the key in the ignition before slamming it shut and tapping the hood of her car.

"Thanks for lunch, Claire. You didn't have to do that."

She smiles before putting her car in reverse, and I step away before watching her drive off.

Even though I get home long after she's shut away in her room because I have a side job across town, the warmth of her coming to see me carries me throughout the day.

NINE

MILES

My hands move over her smooth skin, reaching up to cup one of her full breasts, and a throaty moan falls from her lips as I pinch a rosy nipple, then lean to capture it between my lips, sucking hard.

Her back arches as I do, before she eagerly reaches between us, her hand wrapping around my cock and pumping once, then again before sliding the head along her wet slit. I groan at the heavenly feeling, and she lets out a light, tinkling laugh, always happy to enjoy my misery before she notches the head inside her.

She pauses, straddling me, barely an inch of my cock inside her. Eager to slide in, I lift my hips to slide inside her more, but she smiles wide, shaking her head. Then she moves to her knees, pushing her long blonde curls over her shoulder and smiling down at me.

"Why are you teasing me?" I groan, watching my cock sink another inch inside her.

She lets out a breathy laugh, her eyes fluttering with her own restraint.

"It's what I do," she says, and she's not wrong. She has always teased me, and this is no different. She lifts her hips up an inch, then sinks down, slowly fucking the tip. Her breathing grows shallow as she continues to fuck me but not nearly enough to satisfy me.

"Claire," I groan through gritted teeth.

She beams down at me, teasing, and I've had it. Both of my hands go to her waist, and I slam her hips down until she's filled before I roll us both so she's on her back.

"Miles," she whispers.

"Now we're doing this my way," I say and start to fuck her, hard and fast.

"Miles," she moans, her hips lifting to meet mine. "Fuck, it's so good."

"I know, baby," I say through gritted teeth. "I'm going to fill you."

"Yes, yes, yes," she moans. "Please." And who am I to not give her what she asks for so nicely?

BUZZZ!

My head shifts in the direction of my bedside table at the noise, but her hand moves up, gripping my chin and moving it to look at her once more. I dip my head, pressing my lips to hers, the pleasure building as I thrust into her. Her hair lies on the pillow like a halo around her, her lips swollen, and I feel my balls start to tighten again.

BUZZZ!

I jolt awake with my cock throbbing and my bed empty, the sun starting to peek in through the blinds. I slam my hand on my alarm before I lie in bed, staring at the ceiling for a few long beats before I realize what just happened.

I was having a wet dream about Claire fucking Donovan.

Unfortunately, it isn't the first time, though they seem to be getting more and more vivid, which is definitely a problem.

Grant is right: I need to get laid.

My dick throbs in agreement.

It's her incessant flirting, her need to get under my skin, that has me reacting like this, I tell myself. That and my long-standing dry spell. That's all.

My mind is still reeling when my phone beeps with a message, charging on the other side of the room. I mentally go through all the people it could be: Grant texting to continue to give me shit, someone canceling a surf lesson, or maybe someone needing a last-minute repair from the shop.

When I check my messages, I'm shocked to see a text from the lawyer I currently communicate with Paul through.

> I attempted to contact your brother's attorney about doubling the amount sent as a compromise but have not heard anything back as of this morning. I would suggest against sending the increased amount until we have it in writing that he agrees to increase payments to hold off on the full settlement.

I let out an irritated sigh, realizing tomorrow is the tenth, when we typically send out his payment. I'd already planned to send double the amount, but now I'll have to log into my bank account and change that before it processes.

With a groan, I move toward the closet, glad that the frustration at the very least deflated my hard-on, and reach for a pair of running shorts, hoping a run will put me in a better mood.

Unfortunately, even after I run four miles, I'm still wavering between being annoyed at my brother and being frustrated by my subconscious thoughts of my new tenant. I'm walking on the board-walk to cool down, my house in sight as I scroll through my emails and appointments for the day, when my day gets worse.

"Great day for a run," a voice says, and when I look up, I see the one person with the ability to irritate me more than Paul.

"Yeah," I grumble to Brad Baker, putting my head down as I do. I'm already in a shit mood this morning, and the last thing I need is this fucker making it worse.

"Oh, why so brusque? Can't you greet your neighbor?" He moves into my path, and I fight the urge to do something really fucking stupid.

Brad Baker is my neighbor only in the sense that he is currently managing Surf since his daddy owns the company that bought the properties the giant building now sits on, and let his spoiled son take over when it was built. Baker Inc. has been offering to buy my house since before my grandmother passed. On the day of my grandmother's *funeral*, Brad had the balls to come to my mother's house to ask about purchasing the home.

They bought up five consecutive properties above market value on the boardwalk directly next to my house, tearing down homes that had been there for decades to create the eyesore that is Surf. I know it really pisses off Brad they didn't get my property so he could expand it all the way since there's an empty lot on the opposite side of my house.

"Fuck off," I grumble.

"You still holding tight to this place?" Brad asks, hands in his pockets.

He looks like such a pompous asshole, and I wish I could punch him in the face. Unfortunately, I am also wildly aware that if I did, he would sue me until kingdom come.

"Not selling," I say simply, the way I have countless times before, trying to move past him, but he steps aside, blocking me again. I close my eyes and take in a deep breath because this morning is already enough to put my emotions on edge, and now I have this fucker in my way.

"Look, we're willing to up our offer," he says as if he's doing me a huge favor and I should be grateful.

"Not interested," I say, then step to the side to move around him. Unfortunately, he takes the same step, stopping me once again.

Punching him would be a horrible idea.

Reasonably, I know that. He has more money than God and the mentality of a privileged fuck who has always gotten his way: punching him would be certain bankruptcy, at best. So, instead, I take a deep breath to try and center myself before, once again, stepping to the side. He doesn't mimic me this time, and with relief, I walk past him.

"Is your brother on the same page as you?" he asks to my back.

My steps falter, then stop. Slowly, I turn, looking over my shoulder at him, a shit-eating grin I seriously want to knock off his lips.

"Excuse me?"

"You co-own the property with your brother, right? That's what the word around town is. He isn't on the title, but town gossip is usually more reliable anyway."

He's looking into the details of the house.

Fuck. Fuck, fuck, fuck.

"That's none of your business," I say as calmly as I can muster.

His head tips to the side with an arrogant smirk. "It could be," he says, and I start to walk again, realizing he's fucking with me and I'm giving him exactly what he wants. "I'm just saying, I wonder what your brother would think about my offer, you know?"

"Doesn't matter," I say as I continue to walk toward my house, my mind calculating the amount in my savings and anything else I could possibly sell. Even if I cleared it out, I'd be short, and if, God forbid, some incident happened, I'd be fucked.

I need to keep hustling, or there's a good shot I'm going to lose everything.

It's the reminder I need that I have no time, room, or energy for distractions, and this summer has to be nothing but working and trying to make the money I need to buy my brother out before I get fucked.

TEN

CLAIRE

Miles walks in the front door with no shirt and a pair of short running shorts that definitely shouldn't be as hot as they are, a thin sheen of sweat all over his body, and a grimace on his face.

Despite the grumpy look, for the millionth time since I've moved here, I'm blown away by how fucking hot he is. Okay, so I always knew Miles was hot, but living with him further cements the concrete proof that I absolutely dated the wrong Miller brother, and that alone seems like a giant shame.

He storms into the kitchen where I'm eating breakfast and avoids my gaze as he takes out a headphone and moves to the fridge for water. After he pours himself a glass, he stands and watches me eat cereal out of a salad bowl. The box of sugary cereal is before me as I read the back, my eyes winning the maze for the third time in an effort not to be a creep and trace the lines of his abs.

"Morning," I finally say with a smile before taking another big bite of the colorful stuff. He gives me a glare, and it's clear to me he's not having a great morning. I can't blame him, considering it's barely light out, and he just did physical exercise *on purpose*.

Could never be me.

"Don't you have work?" he asks, judgment in the words.

"Such manners," I say with a laugh he is obviously not entertained by. "No, I don't work until later today. Noon to five."

He rolls his eyes at me. God, he's *really* in a shit mood. I wonder what happened.

"Must be nice, only working for five hours." He means it as a barb, but I shrug it off. Miles thinks I'm some flighty little girl who flits around on a whim, and that's fine: he's not the first to see me that way, and he won't be the last.

At least, that's what I tell myself because, despite it all, I want Miles to like me.

I always have.

"My hours are shortened until the season starts after Memorial Day. Right now, I'm just learning the ropes before all the kids start next weekend," I explain, even though I don't feel like I owe it to him.

He continues to glare as he downs his water, and he must find my answer satisfactory since he shifts to a new subject.

"What are you eating?"

"Fruit Loops, obviously," I say, lifting the box. "Want some?"

"No," he says with a cringe, as if I'm eating rocks instead of food, and he's alarmed I'd push my agenda on him. "You're eating that for breakfast?"

I look at my non-existent watch, then nod. "Well, it's not dinner time."

"It's pure sugar," he says, and I shrug. "Maybe you should really try eating an adult breakfast."

"Maybe you should try having some fun occasionally."

The deadpan look he gives me could melt the paint off a car.

"What, like dancing on bars and nearly breaking your neck?"

I roll my eyes, though I do love the banter.

"If that's what it takes," I say with a shrug. "I'm just saying you need to loosen up. You're going to die of boredom before you hit forty."

He looks me up and down in a way that makes me shiver before responding.

"I think that's a chance I'm willing to take."

Taking the last bite of my breakfast, I chew, leaning back and crossing my arms on my chest. "You haven't even finished a single task on the list I made for you," I say, tipping my chin toward the fridge where the bright yellow paper is still pinned to the fridge door.

"Sorry to disappoint. We can't all just float from job to job, doing whatever we want, whenever we want. Some of us have responsibilities and bills," he says.

I roll my eyes, standing and closing up the box of cereal and putting it away on the shelf before I turn to him. But when I do, I temporarily halt at what I see there: seriousness and genuine irritation.

"You give me shit for being so serious and boring, but maybe it just seems that way because you don't know how to be an adult."

He doesn't mean it in an *eat less junk* way. He means it in a *you're childish, grow up* way. My stomach flips a bit at the refrain I've heard more times than I can count. His eyes track me as I stiffen, and my face tightens just a bit before I throw on my signature smile, brushing it off.

"Why would I grow up when I can be happy?" I move to my bowl to busy myself, dumping the leftover milk in the sink and rinsing it out.

"I don't know, so you can have a place of your own to stay, so you don't have to job hop? So you don't have to beg your ex's brother to give you a safe place to stay?"

It's a sore spot of mine that he hit dead on, the reminder that even at my big age, I don't know what I want to do with my life. June is a teacher; she knew she wanted to be that since I first met her. Nate is a contractor, and Jules owns a dance studio. Both of my sisters have big-girl jobs of their own.

And I'm...I'm just the girl having fun.

I don't regret the choices I've made in life. I'm happy with almost every choice I've made and the way each one has shaped me. But I do regret how the way I live makes others see me and how it makes them judge me against some societal norm. I'm supposed to be climbing the corporate ladder and finding a man to settle down with, not taking a seasonal job down the shore and hoping that somewhere along the line, I find some job I like and would be willing to work forever.

It's how everyone sees me, even if my friends and family love me enough not to hold it against me. I'm the girl with no direction, the one who doesn't know what she wants to do with her life, who can't hold down a job because she gets bored too quickly. The one who makes spur-of-the-moment decisions and who "followed her heart" to go live with her boyfriend across the country, only to come back barely a month later in tears.

I've been okay with it, but suddenly, with Miles looking at me like that, I wish I were different. I wish I were more responsible and knew what I wanted, or at least I could fake it believably.

With Miles looking at me like that, I feel momentarily ashamed before anger follows in on its heels because who is he to make me feel that way?

Still, suddenly, my sugary breakfast sits heavy in my stomach as I put the bowl and spoon into the dishwasher, adamantly avoiding Miles's glare as long as I can before I close the appliance and stand straight. In his defense, there's remorse on his face, but I don't care.

I thought Miles and I were getting somewhere after bringing him lunch yesterday, finding some even footing, but clearly, just like every other time in my life, I deluded myself until I believed in a reality that didn't exist.

"You know, everyone makes choices in life. I chose to make sure that whatever I do with my life, be it a job, a person, or a place, I'll be happy to be there forever. I haven't found something that makes me feel that way, and I'm okay with that. I'm okay with everyone thinking I'm just some mercurial girl who will never grow up because I won't settle down if it means that when I'm fifty, I won't look around and realize I'm fucking miserable. Can you say the same?"

He stares at me for a moment before I walk past him to leave the room.

When I'm out of the kitchen, I turn around again, needing to say more. That's when I finally look at him and see his face is stark with understanding, like I hit a sore spot. I don't feel any guilt, though.

"You hustle so hard to keep up with whatever status you've assigned yourself in your mind, and it's commendable, really. But what does it really matter if you aren't happy? I might not have it all figured out, but at the end of the day, I'm happy."

I stand there for a long beat waiting for him to say something, but he doesn't. Instead, I stand there long enough for my alarm to go off on my phone, reminding me to get out the door for work.

As I turn, he finally starts. "Claire—"

I shake my head, reaching down to grab the bag I packed this morning. "I gotta get going. To work, the place where I'm going to just be a giant child and save lives. Later, Miles."

And even though I think I hear him say my name again before he mumbles a curse under his breath, I don't look back. Instead, I slip out the door, desperate to get away from him and his suffocating judgment.

ELEVEN

MILES

"So Claire Donovan, huh?" my mom asks later that day when I stop at her coffee shop for a quick check-in disguised as a coffee break. I try to stop in a few times a week so I don't start to worry her, but this time, I regret it instantly, forgetting that the gossip mill runs rampant in this town and always makes a stop at Seaside Coffee. "Interesting that I had to hear about that from someone other than my own son, isn't it?"

I sigh, weighing my options. I could leave right now and avoid this interrogation, but that would just delay it. And honestly, it's better we talk about this than Paul or the house. If I direct this conversation correctly, I might be able to avoid her asking about *why* I took on a renter, something that would just give her undue stress.

"Sorry, I've been busy. She needed a place to stay, and Helen sent her my way," I say.

"Sure, sure. And I'm sure your willingness to house her has nothing to do with the way you always looked at her?"

My head moves back at that.

"Like she's a pain in my ass?" My mom doesn't argue but gives me a look that I've seen a million times over. One that says *you can lie to yourself, but you can't lie to your mother.* "She's a fucking headache," I grumble eventually, and my mom just shrugs.

"Sometimes a headache is exactly what you need to loosen up." It's a reminder of Claire's insistence I have more fun, and with it, a mental image of her happy, yellow list echoes in my mind.

So does the sad, hurt look she gave me this morning, twisting the knife in my gut.

"You know, Grant was in here," she starts, and my jaw tightens, realizing that's where the leak is from. I add punching him in the face to my never-ending to-do list. "And *he* thinks that there's some kind of chemistry between you two that you should act on. And you know what? I agree."

I blink at her a few times because I must have entered some other timeline, and I'm the only one who understands reality.

"She's Paul's ex," I say slowly, as if she's forgotten. Mom waves her hand in my direction as if that's a non-issue.

"She was always too good for him, and even Paul knew it." My eyes go wide, and she rolls hers as if I'm being dramatic for no reason. "Oh, come on, you knew it too."

I did, but I never would have said that out loud, much less to our *mother.*

But since we're on the topic, maybe I can get more information on how that all went down, or at least Paul's twisted side of it.

"Do you know what happened?" I ask, trying to play it off.

Mom shakes her head but answers with a heavy sigh all the same. "You know how your brother is. I have to read between the lines with that one. But from what I got, she left to follow him to LA, and then he, well, you know. Was Paul." I raise my eyebrows at that, definitely understanding how Paul can be. "He said she started nagging at him and"—her fingers move in air quotes as if she doesn't believe whatever it is she's going to repeat—"wouldn't stop bitching, so he dumped her."

I have to fight the instinct to tighten my jaw at the thought of Paul saying that to her because my mom will read into every reaction.

But the truth is, the idea of my brother saying that about Claire makes me see red.

"So she stuck up for herself, and he didn't like it," I say, knowing that's what Paul always says when someone asks for him to be semi-responsible or treat them with respect.

Mom shrugs. "That's what I think. But what do I know? Has she said anything to you about it?"

I sigh and shake my head. I don't tell my mom I haven't taken the time to ask, much less that I've spent the week she's been living with me, either judging her or ignoring her.

God, I'm a fucking asshole.

"I always liked that girl. A lot of fun, but super smart. I kind of always hoped she would help get Paul's head out of his ass, but I also knew he would fumble a good girl like her." I turn to her, surprised. "You know, she always looked at you with stars in her eyes..." She lifts an eyebrow as if I'm going to fill in with some new information or, better yet, a confession of love.

"Stop looking at me like that, Mom. That is never going to happen," I say, needing to nip my mom's hopeful expression before her mind goes any further.

"Why not? She's sweet," she says, aghast that I wouldn't even consider it.

See what I mean? Why has everyone lost every ounce of common sense?

"She's six years younger than me and insane and constantly getting into trouble." My mother stares at me for a moment, and I continue to explain. "She fell off a bar top at Surf the other day and then went into the freezing cold ocean. I had to go in after her."

My mom cringes, picturing the biting cold, but then shrugs.

"So she likes to have fun. Is it in a way where it hurts other people? Does it make it so she can't be relied on or trusted?"

I give that thought amount before I sigh and shake my head. "She used to nanny for her older brother's kid, and Helen gave her the head lifeguard position, so she has to be semi-responsible. But she's the youngest of four kids, so she's been babied her whole life."

"You know, I know because it was just you, me, and Paul that you had to grow up pretty fast. I always regretted not giving you the freedom to be a kid, to be a dumb teenager," she says, a hint of regret in the words.

I got my first job at twelve as a junior lifeguard because I wanted surfing lessons and a surfboard, and my mom couldn't afford it. I never stopped working when I realized it could help lessen the burden my mom held as a single parent, but I never saw that as a *bad* thing. It taught me to be hardworking, to save, and to be responsible.

In contrast, Paul got an allowance from Mom by the time he was in high school since the coffee shop was up and running, and he never had a job all through college. He never saved a dollar in his life, obviously, since he goes through cash like water.

Claire, on the other hand, clearly knows how to save, I remind myself, but I don't want to hear that right now.

"That has nothing to do with anything, Mom." She shrugs as if agreeing to disagree. "I think she needs to grow up."

"Why?" Mom asks, head tipping to the side with interest.

"What?"

"Why? Why does she need to grow up?"

"Because..." I pause because when she asks outright like that, I can't exactly think of a good reason. The same uncomfortable guilt I felt in the kitchen this morning moves over my skin, making it feel like I need to wash it off.

Why *does* Claire need to grow up?

Aside from eating junk as a large chunk of her diet, she's not living some grandly unhealthy life. She isn't hurting anyone, isn't causing trouble other than the harmless kind. She isn't racking up debt that I know of or taking advantage of people.

She's just...enjoying her life.

Is that so wrong?

The question tears at me a bit because if the answer is no, there's nothing wrong with her living her life the way she wants to. That also means I've been unfairly judging her, and I don't like the way that makes me feel, the way it makes *me* the bad guy in this situation.

Especially when I realize she has never once held my judging her against me. Instead, she jokes with me, flirts with me, and tries to help me find ways to loosen up.

Which is just another example of the sunshine and joy that is Claire Donovan.

"Looks like you might have some things to think about, kiddo," Mom says with a smile. "Like I always told you, just because someone is different doesn't make them wrong."

I grumble a response, and she laughs, but all the while, my mind is reeling, and guilt churns in my gut.

Someone walks into the shop, and Mom winks at me before standing from the table we're sitting at and walking behind the counter to help the customer. I stay for a bit longer before I say goodbye and head out to my car.

I sit there for a while, staring at my phone and trying to decide what to do next, all the while painfully aware of what an ass I've been. I took a shitty morning out on her, and she didn't deserve that.

> Sorry. I was a dick earlier.

Text bubbles arise almost instantly, then disappear, then appear again, my heart rising and falling with each change. It's like I'm a teenager waiting for some girl to call me back.

So fucked, Miller. You are so very fucked.

> Yeah, you were.

> There's nothing wrong with having fun. No one actually has anything figured out, and if they say they do, they're all lying. You're just honest about it.

> Plus, a world full of grumpy assholes trying to make ends meet would be a pretty miserable place.

She doesn't reply instantly, and I keep staring at my phone, more responses coming to mind. Most of them I manage to stop from saying, but one makes it through my raised guard.

> The world needs more Claires in it.

That one, she responds to too quickly.

> Even yours?

I don't answer for a long time, trying to figure out just what to say, how to respond, if I *should* respond. Then I realize I have to get back to the shop, so I type a response without thinking too hard and hit send.

> Especially mine.

On my way home from work, I make a stop at the grocery store. Claire isn't around when I get home, so I set my purchases on the counter before grabbing a pen and the yellow paper on the fridge.

When I leave to take a shower, I leave six different kinds of cereal in brightly-colored boxes on the counter, and the *Miles and Claire's list of things to have fun* on top.

At the bottom, I added an item.

Have a fun breakfast with Claire.

TWELVE

CLAIRE

It's dark when my name is whispered in a dream, half waking me.

"Claire," the voice repeats, but I snuggle deeper into my blanket, turning away.

"Claire," it says again, louder, and a part of me recognizes then that this is not a dream, especially when a hand touches my shoulder, shaking me gently.

"Go away," I grumble, turning away from the hand. "Sleepin'."

A deep chuckle fills the room, and with it, my body stills. Even in this hardly awake state, I recognize that laugh.

"Claire, come on," the voice says again, this time losing the quiet whisper, and suddenly, sleep is leaving my body. I look over my shoulder, one eye squinting to see Miles Miller hovering over my bed, his smile wide.

I must be dreaming.

There are so many reasons this has to be some kind of dream, but mostly because Miles is smiling at me.

"Miles?"

"Come on," he says one last time, stepping away from me and tipping his head to the door.

My eyes shift from him, dressed in a pair of loose shorts and a Miller Automotive T-shirt, then to the windows where I actually remembered to close the blinds last night. But there isn't sun leaking through the cracks, so I move back to him in confusion.

"It's dark out," I say, stating the obvious as I sit up in the center of my bed. He smiles so wide I wonder if there might be something wrong with him.

"Not for long."

"What?"

"Just come on, Claire," he urges, seeming to lose patience.

I look at him, at his genuinely pleading face, before I sigh, rolling and shifting until my feet touch the ground. That's when I see the time.

"Five a.m., Miles? Are you fucking with me?"

"You're already up, let's go." Then he leaves the room.

I watch him go, wondering if I should just go back to bed because it is fucking *early*, but my curiosity wins out as I stand, then follow him out into the hall.

"Miles?" I call out in a whisper as if there is someone else in the house soundly sleeping.

"Down here," he says from downstairs.

The sound of ceramic and metal hits my ears before I hear the sliding glass door opening. Once more, my curiosity prevails, and I move down the stairs. I probably should have put something more substantial on, since I'm wearing a tank without a bra and a pair of sleep shorts, but it's too late for that.

After making my way down the stairs, I see him, arms seemingly filled with items I can't quite make out, moving through the sliding glass door and out onto the deck, making a left toward the side that faces away from the ocean. Confusion continues to fill me, but I smell coffee and bacon and decide that I'll go wherever both of those are.

Stepping out onto the deck, I pause in utter bafflement for a beat as Miles bends to place a bowl onto the small table before he stands and looks at me, his shoulders straightening. He gives me a small, shy smile before he lifts a hand, rubbing the back of his neck. A sweet blush creeps up his skin, and suddenly, I feel inexplicably nervous.

Suddenly, *I'm* self-conscious and worried about my morning breath and my bedhead and the fact that there's a bit of a chill in the morning air, and I have two point five seconds before my nipples get hard. I cross my arms on my chest before that becomes a new thing to worry about as I take in the scene before me.

A couple of blankets are on the two chairs facing the boardwalk, and on the table before them are coffee, bacon, and three of the boxes of cereal he left out for me yesterday as well as my water bottle.

When I saw the cereal on the counter after work last night, warmth filled me. From his text, I knew he felt bad about hurting me that morning, but going the extra mile to get me more cereal and add it to the list that I made him tells me he genuinely regretted it.

"What is this?" I ask, looking around to try and figure out what's going on.

He bends again, picking up that familiar yellow piece of paper.

"Yesterday, I added 'have a fun breakfast with Claire.'" His hand reaches for a box of Lucky Charms and lifts it, shaking it. "And watching a sunrise is on the list, too."

My heart starts beating fast as I put the pieces together.

"Two birds, one stone," he says, a shy smile on his lips.

"You made me breakfast?"

"I mostly just made bacon, and I hate to say it, but it was a selfish act. I like bacon, and I think my body might stop working if I only eat sugar for breakfast."

"Everyone likes bacon," I say absentmindedly, barely paying attention as I take a step closer. "You set all this up?"

He shrugs nonchalantly.

"My grandmother used to do this a few times during the summer and made a big thing out of it. Wake up early, and eat a huge breakfast in our pajamas while watching the sunrise. It's one of the highlights of my summers as a kid."

"And now you're doing it with me?" I ask.

He smiles again, and that blush I like so much blooms across his cheeks. "I saw the weather was pretty clear today and thought it might be a good idea to..." He scrubs a hand over his face. "I don't know. Maybe it was stupid. If you want to go back to bed—"

"No," I say quickly. "No, this is...this is amazing. It's perfect." I look around. "I can't believe you did this."

He gestures for me to take a seat.

"I, uh..." he starts awkwardly, a hand moving to the back of his neck again, as I've noticed he does when he's uncomfortable. "I owe you an apology."

I sit back and cross my arms on my chest, tipping my head to the side and smiling a bit. "Go on..."

A blush depends on his cheeks.

"I was a dick to you yesterday. I was having a bad morning, and that had nothing to do with you, but I took it out on you all the same. That's not okay, and you deserve more kindness and respect than I gave you."

I roll my lips into my mouth as my eyes start to water. *Stupid fucking emotions.*

"Oh, fuck, I'm sorry," he says, leaning forward and grabbing my hand in his. It's warm, and he holds my hand tightly in a way that distracts me just enough to get a handle on myself again. "Don't cry. Or do. I don't want to tell you what to do. Fuck, I'm screwing this up."

I let out a laugh and shake my head, reaching for a napkin to dab at my eyes. He lets go of my hand, and instantly I feel the loss of them.

I shake my head and give him a watery smile. "No, no, I'm just a crybaby. I cry at everything. Cute baby videos, sappy commercials, those fucking ASPCA commercials with Sarah McLachlan."

I shake my head again and take a deep breath to center myself. "I'm good. And I appreciate it, really, but I understand. You're under a lot of pressure—"

"That's not an excuse. I'm serious, Claire. Don't make excuses for me. I was an ass. Let me apologize." I roll my lips into my mouth and lift my hands in surrender for him to answer. He lets out a small laugh and shakes his head. "I'm just saying, I'm sorry. I've been judging you for some time on a scale that was unfair to you, and I promise to do better."

I wait a beat to see if he's done, so I don't get yelled at again, and nod.

"I accept your apology." He looks like he wants to argue with even that, to tell me I shouldn't accept it before he lets it go. "You know, I'm just glad you've moved past your hatred stage," I say with a smile and a shrug. I say it to add some levity because I don't do well with serious conversations, but instead, he stares at me with soft eyes, a hint of sadness still there.

"I never hated you, Claire," he says gently after a long moment. "I think...I think I was envious of you."

"Envious?" I ask, fighting the disbelieving laugh bubbling in my chest.

"You do what you want. You don't let anyone else tell you it's wrong. You're giving yourself time to figure out what you want. I'm lucky. I like what I do. I like where I live, but you're right: I'm constantly hustling, trying to fulfill this sense of what I should do I created in my head. I don't make time for myself or for...fun."

I give him a small, sad smile, my chest tightening at the look on his face.

"You look tired, Miles," I say, letting out the concern I've been keeping in since I moved in. He does, and not because it's early as fuck. It's a bone-deep weariness that seems to hang around him.

"I am," he admits. I let that hang in the air between us, willing to let it be if he wants, but he surprises me when he continues. "I just..."

I sit there patiently, my heart pounding, to see if he'll finally open up before he looks at the ocean behind me and takes in a deep breath. "Paul wants me to sell this place."

"What?" I ask, alarmed, sitting up straighter.

"I don't know how much he told you." Knowing Paul, probably

not enough. "But we both inherited this place from my grandmother. I wanted to keep it. He wants to sell it. So, we came to an agreement about how things would go, with me paying him essentially a mortgage since I couldn't afford to buy him out outright."

My brows come together as I try to digest this new information.

"But...?"

"But for some reason, he wants more. He wants me to buy him out. He's threatening to try and force me to sell."

I sit there for long moments as I piece the story together, realizing that once a month, Paul would go on a bender of sorts, spending money I didn't think he had, partying, and buying shit he didn't need...

Now, with context, I can realize it was whatever money Miles was apparently sending him.

"Well, his cash cow is gone," I say without meaning to because, in those interim periods, I was the only one with money to pay for silly things like, say, groceries. I feel my eyes widen at the slip, and my cheeks burn. "I'm sorry, I shouldn't have—"

"Don't worry, I've already kind of come to that conclusion," he says with a laugh. "I think we both have a unique understanding of Paul and the way he manipulates people and the truth."

I nod with wide eyes, and then, for some reason, I continue spilling.

"He's jealous of you, you know,"

"What?"

"He wouldn't outright say it, but it was obvious. Always complaining about you, comparing himself to you." He shakes his head, but I continue. "We fought about you once."

"You fought about me? With Paul?" he asks, shocked, and I nod.

"Yeah. It was after my birthday party. Apparently, he didn't like that I was talking to you a bunch. He thought I was into you." I hesitate and bite my lip, guilt eating me at that. "We got into a huge fight that night."

"Why did you do that? Talk to me?" he asks.

"You didn't know anyone there, and Paul wasn't going to intro-duce you to anyone. And I..." I'm embarrassed at the reminder that he invited a dozen people I didn't know to what was allegedly a birthday party for me. Especially knowing that I stayed for another three months after that. "I didn't know a ton of people there either. They were mostly Paul's friends he wanted to impress."

He closes his eyes like the confession pains him.

"And I kept brushing you off," he says, then sighs, adding his own side of the disaster. "He invited me last minute and made it seem like he was being friendly, a brotherly gesture. It turned out he needed someone to foot the bill."

"No," I whisper, eyes wide as guilt rips through me. "Oh, Miles, I'm so sorry."

He shakes his head like it's no big deal, but to me it is: I should have *known* that was why Paul invited him, should have objected to such an extravagant night, but I was in such delusion then, that I didn't see the red flags waving.

"I should have seen it coming, it was typical Paul. He's always doing shit like that. But he told me you wanted this big thing and were giving him shit and..." His voice trails off, and a soul-deep sigh leaves his chest before he puts on a fake smile. "It doesn't matter. We're up at the ass crack of dawn for fun, goddammit. We're not going to let him bring this down, too."

I stare at him for a long moment before finally, I nod and smile.

"Lucky Charms or Fruit Loops?"

"That thing's a weapon," he says ten minutes later after I downed nearly half of my coffee, tipping his chin toward my pink water bottle, plastered with stickers.

I gasp. "Don't talk about Margo like that."

"Margo?"

"My water bottle."

"Full, that thing probably weighs like forty pounds." I roll my eyes. "I'm serious. If you threw that at someone, you'd probably kill them."

"God, you're so dramatic," I say with a laugh. "Leave my emotional support water bottle out of this."

"Your emotional support water bottle?"

"Yeah. I bring her everywhere. I feel naked without her."

With that, his eyes dip to my chest where my hard nipples are poking through the thin shirt. I bite my lip, and with his burning gaze, a chill runs through me, tightening them further.

Goddammit.

He clears his throat, then stands, moving to the edge of the deck. He looks over his shoulder and says, "This never gets old."

When I look behind him, I see the sky is a radiant orange, with a bright yellow center.

"Oh my god, it's beautiful," I whisper, moving to stand next to him and watching the colors fill the sky, the light reflecting off the ocean. It's the most gorgeous sunrise I've ever seen, with the way the water amplifies it.

It's absolutely breathtaking.

"Fucking gorgeous," he says low, his body close to mine and something wistful in his words, but I can't bear to look away from the magic before us.

A moment later, my alarm goes off upstairs. I turn to Miles to smile at him, but his gaze is already on me, a little dazed, like he's been staring for some time. My breath catches in my chest, and the sound of my alarm fades away. His hand lifts, tucking a piece of hair behind my ear, his fingers lingering against the skin there.

They're calloused and rough from what I assume are long hours in the shop, and for a slight, infinitesimal moment, I wonder what they would feel like on other parts of my body.

Without thinking, I lift my hand, placing it on his cheek and brushing my thumb along his mustache the way I did that night in the ocean. I'm shocked when his hand lifts, capturing mine against his face and holding it there before he finally speaks.

"Is that your alarm?"

I nod, then swallow as his hand drops.

"Yeah. Memorial Day weekend. Gotta..." I clear my throat, suddenly feeling tight. "I have to get there early." He nods but doesn't move, and neither do I. It feels like if I do, this moment might shatter, and I'll never get it back.

"I should get going for the day, too," he says. "I haven't taken my run, and I try to do that before the boardwalk is flooded with tourists."

Finally, he steps back and moves to the table to clean it off. A part of me fills with disappointment that this morning is over already, wishing I could call out of work, but also...this was good.

This was perfect.

I move over to the table to help clean up, but he looks at me and shakes his head.

"No, I've got this. Go get ready for your day."

"I can't do that," I say with a laugh.

"I insist. It'll make us even for my being a dick."

I want to argue, to tell him that we already agreed the slate was clean, but his face looks so sincere, I can't do anything but nod.

"Okay."

"Don't forget Margo," he says, tipping his chin toward my water bottle.

I let out a laugh and shake my head, grabbing her and making my way toward the door. I do feel guilty, but that alarm is still going off, and I barely gave myself enough time to get ready and be out the door when I set it.

Still, I pause at the door, watching him fold the blankets and stack plates.

"Hey, Miles?" I say quietly. His head turns my way curiously.

"Yeah?"

"Thank you. This was...amazing."

He shakes his head and blushes, busying himself with clearing things.

"Oh, yeah. It was...it was nothing. It was on the list, you know?"

I smile. "I don't think that's why you did it," I say, but don't push it more than that. I lean in the doorway before I ask, "Did you have fun this morning?"

With that, he stands up straight, arms crossed on his chest as he takes me in. Now it's my turn to be nervous and fidget with my water bottle.

"What?"

"Did you have fun this morning? That was the point, after all." It's silly, but my belly flutters with my question. More so when he stares at me for long moments before a small smile pops on his face as if he can't help it.

"I'm finding I seem to always have fun when you're around, Claire."

THIRTEEN

CLAIRE

Memorial Day weekend flies by in a chaotic haze of sunscreen and sand.

Because it's the first real weekend of the season, the beach was packed, and since it's my first full weekend working with the full crew, I made sure I was at the beach before anyone else and left only once Helen did.

But it doesn't even feel like work.

I laughed with the other lifeguards, and I argued with tourists a handful of times, but really, how much can it feel like work when my breaks are spent on the sand and I can have ice cream and boardwalk fries for breakfast, lunch, and dinner if I so choose?

That being said, I was excited for my day off today, and it was the perfect opportunity to make a little bit of chaos.

The front door slams shut at six p.m. on the dot, when I can typically expect Miles home, and I smile, waiting.

The last week has been...good.

Ever since Miles and I had our heart-to-heart and he apologized, things have been much less tense around the house. Most mornings, he sits with me, eating some super healthy boring person breakfast while I eat my sugary cereal, and when he's not working late and I'm not with June or Lainey, he'll sit with me on the deck chatting.

We're...friends.

"Claire," his voice bellows, and I roll my lips into my teeth, stifling a laugh. God, I've been giddy for this confrontation almost *all day.* "Claire, come down here right now."

I should wait, make him hold out because he's already mad, but I'm eager to see what he thinks of the fruits of my labor.

"Yes, Daddy?" I ask from the top of the stairs, looking down the railing at him like a kid who knows she's about to get in major trouble.

His jaw is tight, and his shoulders are raised as he glares toward the kitchen.

That hasn't changed, at least, my incessant urge to tease Miles just because it truly unsettles him. That's my self-assigned job this summer: to rattle Miles Miller a bit out of the cage he's made for himself.

Or, at least, that's what I've been telling myself is why I flirt incessantly with him. It's definitely *not* because I have a full-blown crush on my ex's older brother.

No. That would be wrong. So, so wrong.

Right?

"Get the fuck down here," he says through gritted teeth, a look of exasperation already on his face like he's resigned to this fate.

I behave and make my way down, standing in front of him with my hands on my hips.

He's still in his work boots, adding an inch to him, making him tower over my bare-footed face even more, and I fight the urge to wipe at the small spot of grease on his cheek. The backward baseball hat he wears to keep his messy hair back is the cherry on top.

No, I lied. The *glare* he's giving me is the best part. It shouldn't be so hot, but here we are.

"What the fuck is that?"

"What's what?" I ask, tipping my head to the side like I have *no* idea what he's talking about. His glare deepens as I stand there, fighting the urge to grin. God, he really is too easy, isn't he?

"That. On the counter." He points to the four clear plastic containers with colorful tops. "What the fuck is *that*?"

"Oh," I say as if I'm just now understanding. "*Those*. They're hermit crabs."

He closes his eyes and takes in a deep breath, attempting to center himself or find some modicum of patience.

I don't think he quite gets there.

"And how did they get here?" he asks slowly.

"Oh, I saved her. And her sisters."

"Her?" I shrug, then explain. "I mean, I'm pretty sure they're girls."

He gives me a slight nod like he's trying to come to terms with... life in general before taking a deep breath and asking another question.

"How does one know this?"

"Google says the girls have dots on the back of their legs, but one's been a little shy, so I haven't gotten a good enough look to make an educated guess about if all of them are girls or not."

Miles closes his eyes and takes a deep breath, running his hand over his face. It smears that little dot of grease, and it takes a Herculean effort not to run my thumb over it to clear it off myself. "And when you say all of them..."

"Six," I say before he can finish asking his question.

He nods, eyes still closed like he's trying to find his happy place that is undoubtedly far, far away from here.

"Six hermit crabs," he repeats.

I walk into the kitchen to where they all scramble along in their shells.

"It was all I could grab while they were distracted. I did manage to get Big Gina, though, so that was the real win. She's a real beauty."

"Big Gina?" Exasperation has entered his words, which, in my opinion, probably means I'm wearing him down.

"This one," I say, then point to the one in a white bedazzled shell. I'm still in the process of figuring out just how ethical it is to keep them in painted, much less *bedazzled,* shells, but I'm hoping to find out that it's fine.

"Who distracted them?"

"June." He nods like he should have known. "Don't worry, no one caught us."

He stares at me, pieces clicking, I assume, before he leans onto the counter like he no longer has the energy to stand. "Claire, how did you get these hermit crabs?"

"I rescued them."

He rolls his lips between his teeth and then nods before asking his next question. "Do you and the police have a different definition of rescued?"

I roll my eyes and shake my head left and right before answering. "I think everyone has a different definition of what *rescuing* means, you know?"

"No, I think there's really just one definition of rescuing when you're talking about an animal." I don't respond to that. "Claire, if you don't tell me what happened, I'm marching you back down there and making you return them."

He says it like he's a disappointed dad, and without my mind's permission, I think about how much my dad would like him.

He never cared for Paul, and I always knew deep down from the day I met him that my dad and my older brother Nate would probably see right through him, but I deluded myself into thinking he would change.

But they'd like Miles.

I came to this decision a while ago, because the truth of the matter is I *like* Miles Miller. He's sweet when he wants to be, and he's funny without meaning to (heavy on the *not meaning to*), and we get along in a strange way, his cautiousness balancing out my wild, even if his cautiousness is a bit *too* cautious sometimes.

That's why I made that list for him. Because, for whatever reason, the man is so damn serious, so focused, and if there's one thing I'm good at, it's having fun. *And* making other people have fun.

And, it seems, hermit crab-napping.

"Okay, okay, so June and I were taking our morning hot girl walk because I didn't have work today. Honestly, it was pretty cold, so we had our sweaters on, but then it got warm, so we took it off and—" I start explaining my morning, and he glares at me.

"The hermit crabs, Claire."

I lift a hand.

"I'm getting there! It's relevant to my story!" He rolls his eyes, but I continue. "So we were walking, and there was someone opening the gift shop the surf shop owns—like they were *just* lifting the front door, no one was inside or anything yet, lights off and everything. That's when I noticed the little display for the hermies—what I've named their pop group." He looks at me like I'm insane, but I keep going. "Was outside. *All night*, Miles. They left the poor babies outside! And it was *cold*! So cold, *I* needed a sweatshirt!"

"Okay, let's not be too dramatic. It was, like, sixty-five last night," he says, and I slap his chest.

"They're Caribbean crustaceans, Miles, they weren't built for this kind of weather." He closes his eyes and takes in a deep breath, but I don't think he's much calmer. "Anyway, so we kept walking and looped back around at our normal spot, but I couldn't stop thinking about the poor babies and the conditions they're stuck in. And when the display was *still* outside when we came back around, I had June go in and distract the guy working."

"And you..."

"I grabbed what I could hold and ran. Then I came back here."

Long, long moments pass as he stares at me, his gaze moving from me to my new babies and back.

"And now I have a half dozen hermit crabs in my kitchen?"

"Well, they're going to be in my room in a little bit. I just needed to clean a spot for them upstairs."

He closes his eyes and rubs his face with both hands. "What happened to no pets?"

I shrug, not worried about his stupid, useless rules.

"This house is empty. You need to bring some life into this house."

He blinks at me. "And you decided a hermit crab was the solution?"

"I mean, petting one is on the list," I say.

"*You* made the list, Claire," he groans, clearly overwhelmed, and I pat his shoulders.

"I know. This is all very exciting."

"Claire—" I'm losing him, I can see that, so I shift gears.

"It was inhumane, Miles. I know that no one there was going to be able to handle the responsibility of a hermit crab. Do you know how long they live?"

"Have you considered that they'll just...buy more to replace the ones who were gone?"

I hadn't, if I'm being honest, but that's long besides the point.

"Maybe I should start petitioning to end the sale of hermit crabs," I say, contemplating how I could organize that. I think the only business that sells them right now is the one I stole from, and from what I understand, the locals don't necessarily like the people who own it, so it might be an easy sell.

"You can't just steal from small businesses, Claire," he says with a sigh, and I can hear genuine apology in the words, like he feels bad that he has to be the adult in this situation. "You have to bring them back."

"Look, Surf has, like, four shops on the boardwalk, all of them have hermit crabs. And Deck says they're shitty employers, so—"

He cuts me off, his intrigue piqued. "Surf?" he asks, his frustration slightly dissipating.

I nod. "Yeah. Deck says they suck, and Helen says they're always causing issues, so don't try to make me feel bad for 'hurting a small business.' I don't think half a dozen hermit crabs is going to hurt their bottom line."

"Trust me, I wasn't going to say that," he grumbles, and I wonder just what made him get that look of hatred on his face. What has Surf done to him to make him hate them so much? Or is it just the principle of the giant complex? That sounds like something he would be against inherently.

"So can I keep them?" I ask with a wide smile, trying to strike while he's distracted. I move to one of the containers and pick up Big Bertha, who instantly hides in her shell. "Just look at her! She really wants a good home to live in."

"She looks traumatized," Miles says.

"Probably because she was left outside all night!"

"Definitely couldn't be because you ran from a store while committing grand theft crab?"

"Oh, that's a good one. Maybe grand theft hermies?" I suggest with a smile, and he fights one of his own, shaking his head at me. After a moment, he sighs, taking his hat off, running his hand over his hair, and replacing it once again. "They need a good home," I pout.

"I just don't understand why the good home has to be *my* home."

I smile wide because that's basically a yes.

"You won't even know they're here! I'll even make sure they stay in their little home the whole time."

He tips his head and gives me a semi-alarmed look. "Why would they not stay in their home, Claire?"

"I read they can be escape artists, but I already ordered a large tank and the right lid."

He closes his eyes and groans. "Claire."

Finally, I pull out my secret weapon that worked on my dad and my brother, and every man who ever passed my path for nearly my entire life. I pout.

Big eyes, pouty lips, hands in front of me in a prayer position.

"Please, Miles? Please, please, please?" I make my eyes wider, knowing I'm moving past a cute girl you can't say no to and into a comic book character, but that's fine. "I'll do *anything* for them to stay!"

And then it happens.

A heated flicker in his eyes because, despite what he wants to think, he is *not* immune to my charm or...other things about me.

He snaps out of it quickly and shakes his head. I think I've lost the battle before he steps away and starts walking toward the stairs and toward his room.

"Just keep them away from me," he grumbles.

"I can keep them?"

He pauses on the stairs and looks at me. "If it makes you happy," he says, moving up the stairs.

"So you admit it," I say when he's at the top. I probably shouldn't press my luck, but I just can't help it.

He pauses and looks down at me, a guarded expression on his face when he sees my triumphant smile. "Admit what?"

"That you want to keep me happy!"

He shakes his head in response and walks away.

Yet another success in my book.

FOURTEEN

CLAIRE

After another busy weekend due to an unseasonably hot June weekend, when June calls me on Monday and *begs* me to come to the bar Lainey's dad owns and where our friend works, I say yes instantly.

I could use the break, and I miss my friends. School isn't out yet, so June's still working like crazy, and since I work every weekend for the foreseeable future, our free time hasn't overlapped much. Even though Lainey is *technically* working tonight, we'll still get some time to hang out and chat.

I'm running a bit late, as per usual, which is why I'm overjoyed to see a spot right out front of the Seabreeze, in the small gravel drive.

"The party has arrived!" Deck yells as I walk in, and I laugh out loud, all the heads in the quiet bar turning toward me.

"Sorry I'm late," I say as I approach the small group, since I told June I'd be there thirty minutes earlier. I give my best friend a hug, then give Lainey an awkward one over the bar she's standing behind. "I got distracted doing my makeup after work and then decided I needed to eat a bowl of cereal before I came out."

"What, you don't want me to have to call my brother to rescue us again?" June asks. "He's coming in a bit, so Deck won't even have to call him this time."

I laugh and shake my head, though I do wonder if that means Miles will be showing up later on.

"Unfortunately, no. I have to work in the morning, so just one for me today."

"Boooo," Deck says, hands cupped around his mouth, and I laugh, rolling my eyes.

"Sorry to disappoint."

"Did you find the place okay?" Lainey asks, since the only times I've ever been here were with June, and the old bar, which is only really frequented by locals, is a bit out of the way.

"Yeah, I made a wrong turn, but I got here all right. Plus, I was shocked when I got the best parking spot. June always has to park on the street."

Every time I've been to the Seabreeze since I've been of age, the very small lot has been full, and cars lined the road leading to it, so we always had to park and then walk. I was shocked when I pulled up and saw a spot front and center.

"You got a good spot?" June asks, brows furrowed as her head tilts to the side.

"Yeah, right out front," I say with a smile.

June looks at Lainey's dad, Benny, whose smile is spreading wide. Then, Deck and June look at one another, some kind of silent conversation going on between them. "Should we—" she starts, but Deck shakes his head.

"No, no. It'll be way more fun this way." He laughs. June takes him in, then nods. I watch this all play out before me, slightly confused and still entertained.

"Do I even want to ask?" I say, and June shakes her head with a laugh.

"Nothing important," Benny says, his signature pipe between his teeth bobbing.

Smoking indoors has been illegal in New Jersey for decades now, and even though I don't think I've ever seen the pipe lit, something tells me that Benny doesn't really care about the rules. Besides, there's no way anyone who frequents this dive would tattle on him.

"So I hear you're a real local now, workin' with Helen. Think we can convince you to stay long term?"

I laugh, then shrug. "You know me, Ben. I go where the good times are. Right now, the good times are in Seaside Point."

"Damn straight they are." His name is called from across the bar, and he gives me a wave. "I'll be back, but you save all of the juicy gossip for me, okay?"

I let out a laugh and pat his shoulder. "Of course," I say.

Lainey watches her dad walk away before leaning on the bar, her face assessing.

"So you're officially a local," she says, pouring me a rum and Coke before sliding it my way. "How is all of that going?"

"All of what?"

June glares at me. "Oh, come on. Don't hold out on us! Living with Miles. I don't think I've ever seen the man enjoy himself, so living with you must be a...change for him."

I let out a small laugh and shake my head. I want to argue to defend his honor, and that alone should be a red flag.

"I made him a bucket list," I say with a laugh, "of fun things we have to do this summer because he's so boring."

June lets out a loud laugh. "I'm sure he loved that."

I think about it and smile. "I won him over eventually. He actually woke me up early a few days ago because watching the sunrise was on there, and he wanted to check it off."

June's jaw drops, and I realize that it's been a minute since I've had a gabfest with my friends, since we've all been so busy with work.

"You're kidding," June says, giving a side eye to Lainey.

I shrug. "I made it because he came up with a list of rules for the house, and they were so boring, I needed to offset them."

"Rules?" Lainey asks.

"I'm not allowed to flirt with him. It's against his rules."

June lets out a deep belly laugh. "You?" she asks when she catches her breath, and I nod.

"That's what I said. Flirting with Miles is basically my favorite pastime. He always looks so uncomfortable."

Lainey and June give each other a knowing look before June rolls her eyes at me.

"That's because he's obsessed with you," June says, and I shake my head. "Always has been."

"No, he is not. He's always *tolerated* me. He had to, since Grant is his best friend and June is mine. We've been thrown together a lot."

Both of them give me a side eye like they're not buying it, and if I'm being honest, I don't even know if *I'm* buying it anymore.

"You should go for it," she says. "I bet he would be *amazing*—"

"What are we talking about?" Grant says, walking up to us at the bar. June's eyes go wide, and I give her similar *shut the fuck up* eyes.

"Nothing," Lainey says.

"Sex," June says.

"Periods," I say at the same time. The three of us all start laughing, and Grant gives us a look like he thinks we've finally cracked before shaking his head. In an effort to change the subject before things get weird as fuck, I look around.

"So this place hasn't changed."

The room is open, a bar against the back wall with bottles lined up and photos and memorabilia from the town along the walls. A dozen or so mix-and-match tables are dotted along the room. In one corner, there is a big bulletin board with notices, and next to it is a calendar shouting out specials for each day and events. Tuesdays are bingo nights, while Thursdays are ladies nights.

"The good ol' locals bar," June says with a smile. "Too dingy and off the beaten path for the tourists."

"I like it," I say, looking around again. And it's the truth: ever since we first came after my twenty-first birthday, I've loved it here.

"Don't lie," Deck says with a laugh.

"I'm not! I genuinely like it. It's cool. A little quiet, though." I don't know the last time I was in a bar without some kind of music on, and without it, it feels like something is missing. But upon my perusal, I see a few speakers in the corners of the room. "Do you think the sound works?" Lainey nods.

"Oh, yeah. Tuesday is bingo night, and they have a whole setup for number calling."

"Do you think it could play music?"

Lainey shrugs. "I mean, yeah. I set it up when I'm cleaning up sometimes with an aux cord."

My eyes light up.

"We should dance," I say, a wide smile.

"What?" June says with a laugh.

"Come on! It'll be fun!" The few sips of my drink are already making me feel warm, brave, and a bit chaotic. Or maybe it's just this place, this town, my friends.

I've always felt right at home, the most *me* version of myself, in Seaside Point.

"Hey, Benny?" I call as he walks away from whoever he was talking to.

"What can I do for you, little lady?"

I smile wider.

"Do you think we can play some music?" I ask, and he looks to the speaker in the ceiling, then back to me. "I want to dance!"

A wide grin spreads over his face, his eyes wrinkling at the edges.

"Only if you agree to dance with me."

I put a hand out to shake.

"Deal."

FIFTEEN

MILES

"Fucking *tourists*," I groan as I turn onto Sandshore Road, almost hitting a family that's jaywalking across it.

The father turns to me and starts screaming at me while the mother continues walking, staring at her phone like nothing happened. I point to the very clearly painted crosswalk he is decidedly *not* standing in and flip him off.

He continues to curse at me through the window that's down.

"There's a crosswalk for a reason," I say as they finish crossing the road, then move on toward my destination.

I should have been there almost an hour ago, but at the last minute I had a tourist come into my shop telling me their AC wasn't working. When I told them it wasn't a simple cabin air filter issue, they proceeded to argue with me for an hour before leaving with nothing. It's pretty typical this time of year, but fuck, does it drive me up a wall.

But at least I'll always have the Seabreeze. The bar and grill in the corner of Seaside Point with little to no atmosphere is far enough off the boardwalk that it isn't too interesting for tourists and is mostly just a local hangout.

It's where my parents met, where they got married long ago, and where I go in the summer to avoid the chaos.

When I pull up, I find the normal cars lining up the narrow road, and a sense of peace washes over me.

Except...when I see a bright fucking yellow Beetle parked in my spot.

Of course.

I contemplate double parking her and going in to argue with her, but the last thing I need is the grapevine in this town to go wild about me storming into the Seabreeze arguing with the new girl in town. Instead, I pull back out of the parking lot, cursing and grumbling under my breath before parking on the street.

It's not until I'm closer to the bar that I realize there's *noise* coming from inside, which is strange because it's Thursday, and the only times the Seabreeze gets rowdy in the summer are on bingo nights and the monthly trivia night.

But when I open the door, loud music comes blaring in, confusing me.

Until I see it.

Long blonde hair pulled into a ponytail, a tight white tank top, and long tanned legs in a pair of shorts that should be fucking illegal.

I walk further in, sure my eyes are deceiving me, when Grant catches my eye.

"Miles!" he says, smiling wide and tipping his head to the center of the room. "Just in time!"

But my eyes stay locked on Claire as she's swung around the room by Benny, who is probably much too old to be moving like that. When her eyes catch on me, her steps slow, then stop before she leans in to say something to Benny with wide eyes. His head tips back with a laugh before he pushes her in my direction.

"Hey, there," she says with a wide smile. I try to fight the way it warms me over, momentarily forgetting that I'm supposed to be annoyed with her.

"Your car's in my spot."

She looks from me to the car she can probably see through the window, then tosses her hair over her shoulder before tipping her head to the side. She uses a hand to fan herself, and I notice then the way her cheeks are flushed, the way her chest is rising with labored breaths from her dancing.

Cut it out, I tell my rampaging mind.

"It doesn't have your name on it," she says simply, a smile playing on her lips like she knows it's going to annoy me.

My jaw goes tight, and I wonder what the enamel of my teeth will look like by the end of the summer.

"I don't have to. It's *my* spot."

"How is anyone supposed to just know that?" She puts her hands on her hips, shifting her weight to one leg and cocking out her knee.

"The people who come here are regulars. Regulars know the rules."

"Rule is being incredibly generous," June says, overhearing our conversation.

I glare at my best friend's sister, and she puts her hands up in surrender but doesn't hide her laugh.

"Why do you get to park there? What makes you so much more special than any other customer here?"

I cross my arms on my chest and look down my nose at her.

"I won the fishing contest last year. It gets you a parking spot for a year," I say, though I suddenly feel ridiculous saying it out loud, sounding like a childish excuse.

Her eyes go comically wide.

"Wow, so fancy," she says in a way that clearly shows she isn't impressed at all.

"It's the rules, Claire. You win the contest, you get the spot. And it's my spot. I got it because I won the contest, but I had to park halfway down the road because you're in my *spot*."

Her lips roll into themselves, trying not to laugh, and her eyes go wide as if pretending like she's taking in what I'm saying, but she really just looks like she's humoring a child.

"Wow, sounds like you've got a lot of big feelings about that."

"I don't have *big feelings* about it," I grumble. "I just want my spot."

She pouts at me and pats my cheek. I can see Grant giggling behind her, entertained by my misery.

The asshole should be on my side.

"There are a bunch of spots on the street," she says.

"That *you* could have parked in."

"I got here first," she says, lifting her hands in the air and stepping closer. We're almost nose to nose, her hands now on her hips, looking up at me from her short height, me towering over her, and for a split, fucked second, I think about the fact that it wouldn't take much to kiss her.

I bet that would shut up her incessant need to argue with me.

She's my tenant. I remind myself. *She's only here for the summer. And you have more than enough on your plate to deal with a handful like Claire.*

After our morning together where she told me more about her doomed relationship, I've removed *that she's your brother's ex from my reasons I can't be into her, and before that, I removed that she's too immature and young.* The slowly dwindling list can't be a great sign for my restraint, but I'll worry about that another day.

I shake my head and step back.

"Claire!" Benny shouts over the music. "Is he giving you a hard time?"

"No, Benny boy, he's just chatting with me," she shouts over her shoulder, but her eyes and her wide smile are still directed at me.

Benny boy. Fuck, why do I like her fitting in here so damn much? She slides right into this place, not sticking out like some outsider, making nicknames for Benny and friends everywhere she does, as if she's always belonged here.

"Come on, Miles, let my dance partner be. She was teaching me the Cha-Cha Slide." I look over Claire's shoulder at Benny, his smile wide and teasing, his usual Hawaiian shirt unbuttoned over a white tank top and a pair of cargo shorts, pipe for once out of sight. "Who knows how much longer I have to live?"

I shake my head, then look down at Claire, who is smiling wide at me.

"Yeah. Are you really going to deprive an old man of fun to argue with a girl about a parking spot? How very alpha male of you."

A million thoughts run through my head, and more than one of them revolve around showing Claire *just* how much of a Neanderthal I can be by hefting her over my shoulder and carrying her out of here.

But I don't. Instead, I shake my head, then gesture toward the bar for her to carry on before moving to see Grant.

"Come on, my man. Let's get you a drink," he says like it's a consolation prize as he leads me to a larger table where half a dozen drinks sit in various states of empty instead of the normal high-top table we usually sit at on Tuesdays.

"I think I'm going to need it."

I look around the dive bar. It's more crowded, since it seems someone pushed the tables back to make Claire a makeshift dance floor. Lainey and June twist and turn together while a few other couples do the same.

Despite myself, I have to accept that this is what Claire brings everywhere she goes: joy, chaos, and a lightheartedness that can't be denied.

It drives me fucking crazy.

"Looks like they're having fun," Grant says an hour later, tipping his chin to where patrons are now spinning around the dance floor. Some old 80s song I vaguely recognize is playing, and each time I look up, Claire is dancing with someone new, her head tipping back with laughter. She's come to the table a handful of times to take a drink of water or chat with June or Lainey, but most of the night, she's been at the center of the bar, dancing.

"Hmm," I say noncommittally.

"You should go dance with her," he says as if it's a casual suggestion, but I know my best friend enough to know it's anything but.

I look at him and shake my head.

"Why not?"

"Not the dancing type, and you know that."

He shakes his head like he's disappointed in me. "Looks like fun."

"No," I repeat, grabbing up the beer I've been nursing all night and taking a sip.

"You're fucking scared of her," he says with a laugh after a beat. "Never thought I'd see it."

"Scared of a five-foot-two blonde? No, I'm not."

"You totally are," June says next to him, though I'm not sure when she got here.

My eyes shift to Claire's best friend, and I glare. I open my mouth to argue, but then June's brows furrow, and I look up, following her line of sight.

Sam Fields, an asshole who graduated a year below me is standing next to Claire, his hand on her bare shoulder. Claire gives him a small shake of her head, then tips her head toward our table. Instead of getting the hint, he takes a step further into her space, and Claire's body goes tight. She shakes her head once more, and Sam's hand goes out to grab her wrist.

I don't know what happens next.

Something inside me snaps, and I'm on the other side of the room before I can even recognize I'm moving.

"Claire," I say, reaching out and grabbing her free hand, tugging her toward me. Sam immediately drops his hand and steps back.

Sam is an ass, a player, and a loser, but he's not an idiot.

"Sorry, man. I didn't know she was yours."

I tug Claire into my chest, and without even missing a beat, she slides her hands around my neck. I watch as Sam moves off to someone else, this one more willing.

"Thank you," Claire whispers when my eyes travel back to hers.

"He's a dick. Not a problem usually, but when he drinks, he gets a bit weird."

She nods, and I could step away, lead her back to the table, go get her a drink, take her outside for some air. But...

I don't.

Instead, I wrap an arm around her waist, pull her in close, and start to sway to the slow '70s rock ballad that's now playing.

This is such a fucking bad idea. A horrible, terrible fucking idea, but I can't seem to stop myself all the same.

"A dance?" she asks, a small smile on her lips.

"Don't want to make a scene," I lie because, for all intents and purposes, the scene has already been made. I can see it by the way Grant and June whisper to each other and the way Lainey is back behind the bar, smiling.

"Hmm," Claire says like she doesn't believe me, but she leans into my body, swaying to the song with me.

I take a deep breath, her strawberries and cream scent filling my lungs, forcing myself to commit it to memory.

As if it's not already there.

"Does this check something on my list?" I ask without meaning to.

"Are you having fun?"

I should lie.

I should tell her I'm not. That she's ruining my relaxing night, that I much prefer when this place is quiet and the tables are normal and no one talks to me, but I'm a fucking idiot, so I don't.

"The most fun night I can remember having at the Seabreeze."

"Yeah?" she asks with a hopeful smile, and I nod. "What's different?"

I shift a bit to look down at her, her face hopeful and glowing, and once again, I can't find it in myself to lie.

"You. You're here."

Because I can't help myself, I put a hand to her hip, tugging her in closer so our bodies are melded, her soft breasts pressing into my worn T-shirt, and she beams up at me as we continue to sway.

The music isn't fast, but it isn't slow, either. Instead, it is stuck in that normally awkward in-between beat where you're not sure what to do, but with her, it feels natural. My body just knows how to move with hers.

I lift my hand, pushing the hair that's fallen into her face back as we sway, and she looks up at me with wide eyes that shift from my eyes to my lips, then my eyes again.

It would be easy to kiss her.

Too fucking easy.

Except, then, the song changes. I should be relieved, but instead, an alarming sense of disappointment fills me, but not Claire. She gasps, her eyes going wide at the tune I don't recognize.

"OH MY GOD!" June yells from the other side of the room.

"It's our song," Claire whispers, still in my arms.

"You should probably go dance with her," I say.

"I guess." But she doesn't let go. "Thanks for saving me, Miles."

"What?" I ask, confused.

A smile spreads across her face like a wave. "I knew it," she whispers, then moves to her toes and presses her lips to my cheek.

I don't know when she did it, but the next morning, on the paper pinned to the fridge, she added a new item to the bottom.

Dance at the Seabreeze

And she crossed it out.

And when warmth fills me, I realize once again just how fucked I am.

SIXTEEN

MILES

"I'm fine, really, Helen!" Claire says as the front door opens. It's barely nine, so it can't be a good thing that she's back this early, much less with Helen in tow.

"No, you're not. The doctor said you need to lie down and rest! Where's that Miller boy?" Ignoring the way my pulse beats a bit faster at the idea of Claire being hurt, I move to the entryway from the kitchen, Helen ushering Claire to the sofa in the living room. When she sits and Helen leans back, I can see there is a giant goose egg on her forehead.

"Jesus, Claire, what happened?" I ask, moving around the couch quickly to check her out.

"Nothing, Helen is just being a bit overbearing," Claire says, though when she rolls her eyes, I don't miss the small wince she makes.

"Overbearing my ass!" Helen shouts with a glare directed at Claire, then shifts her gaze to me. "Kids were playing baseball on the beach, not paying attention. Seems the sun got in their eyes, and one of the kids got her in the head. She was out cold for a few minutes."

"Please stop exaggerating," Claire says with a sigh, sinking back into the couch. "I was not out cold for a few minutes. A few *moments* at best."

"A few minutes or a few moments, it's kind of the same, Claire," I say, because neither sounds great.

"It's a huge difference. If I was out cold for a few *minutes*, they wouldn't let me leave the doctor's office. The other is where I am right now. I was dazed, not concussed." She glares at me with a venom I didn't think someone with a head injury could muster. I'm proven correct when she winces, her hand moving to her head, then mumbles, "Shit."

"See." Helen turns to me. "I'll be expecting her to stay home for at least two days." She turns back to Claire then, giving her a motherly, chiding look. "And you'll need the doctor to give you a note saying you're good to return."

Claire's shoulders drop, and she gives Helen a deadpan look. "Is that really necessary?" she whines.

"Yes," Helen and I say together. Helen turns to me, nodding approvingly.

"You'll keep an eye on her today? Doc says someone should make sure she's not losing it. It's not a concussion, but she got knocked pretty good."

"I don't need a babysitter," Claire grumbles.

"Yeah, I've got it, Helen. You covered at the beach?"

She nods and waves a hand at me. "Yeah, no worries. Feel better, Claire." And then she's off, nearly skipping as if she didn't just deliver an injured employee to my door.

"Has she always been this bossy?" Claire asks with a low grumble.

I let out a laugh.

"Yeah, pretty much. At least she has been since I was a kid." I look at her standing there before I sigh. "Come on. Let's get you comfy on the couch, you're going to be here for a while." I could bring her upstairs to her room, but I'd rather have her somewhere I can comfortably check in on her occasionally.

"Oh my god, not you too," she says. "I swear I'm fine. My head just hurts a bit, and I'll have a bit of a knot on my head for a little while."

"Humor me, okay?" I ask. She looks at me with a bit of a glare, but she must see the resolve in my eyes because she rolls her eyes, then winces at the move before settling into the couch with a sigh. "Where's Margo?" I feel stupid calling her water bottle by a human name, but it makes her smile, so it's worth it.

"In my bag," she says, tipping her chin to where Helen dropped a tote bag near the door.

I dig through it, finding her water before shaking it to check its full and handing it over to her.

"Staying hydrated will help. Want TV, or will it hurt your head?"

"TV should be fine. I don't want to die of boredom."

I chuckle at her dramatics before sitting on the other side of the couch, turning the television on, and lowering the volume. Then I grab my phone and shoot Steven, the other mechanic at my shop, to let him know I won't be in today. It's not the best case since money is tight, but I'm not leaving her alone. If I get to sit on this couch with her all day to make sure she's okay, that's a hit I'll willingly take.

I force myself not to look at that impulse too closely.

"Why are you doing this?" she asks some time later. When I look over at her, her eyes are closed, her head is back on the cushions with the blanket I draped over her earlier pulled up to her chest.

"What?"

"Why are you doing this? Taking care of me, sitting with me. You have work today. I know you called out. You didn't have to do that."

"Because you're hurt," I say simply, not wanting to dig into the deeper answer of *because I'm starting to* like *you, and I can't like you, but I also can't change that, so here we are.*

It's the same conclusion I jumped to when I saw Sam trying to dance with her: I just couldn't stand the idea of someone else pulling her in close. The same reason I can't seem to say no to any of her chaotic ideas, the reason I check her fun list every day and try to think of ways to check them off.

"I would have been fine by myself. You didn't have to inconvenience yourself with me," she murmurs under her breath.

I groan and then shift closer to her on the couch. She looks too helpless like this, her confident shine waning like she doesn't have the energy to keep it up, and that weakens my defenses.

"I'm with you because I care about you, Claire. And you know that," I say, reaching over to push a strand of her hair that's fallen into her face. I tell myself it's to look at her bump, and even if it's a lie, I inspect it a bit.

The swelling has gone down thanks to the bag of frozen peas I brought her, and the spot on her forehead, while red, doesn't seem to be darkening, which I think is a good thing. A long beat passes before a soft smile slides along her lips.

"Yeah, I guess I do know that. You're kind of in love with me."

I let out a small laugh, baffled by how she can still be flirting when she probably has a killer headache.

"Well, at least I know you still have your twisted sense of humor." I gently brush my fingers over her bump and watch fascinated as a small shiver runs through her, that smile still on her lips.

"Can you at least admit you like me? If I die, at least I'd die knowing you finally admitted you're into me."

I drop my hand then, crossing my arms on my chest and letting out a deep laugh, and turning back to the television where some movie I haven't been paying attention to is playing.

"You're not going to die, Claire."

"So you're denying me my last wish?"

"I'm not denying you anything," I say, but when she doesn't speak, I turn to her, her eyes closed, her tongue lolling out of her mouth. She opens one eye, then smiles and goes back to her dead face. "Do you even know how to be normal?"

"I can't answer. I'm dead. There's only one thing that would bring me back to life," she stage whispers.

"Jesus Christ. I—" I stare at her, her tongue still out, her eyes closed, and a smile tipping at the edges before I sigh, giving in. Whatever. What does it even matter anymore, pretending?

"Of course I like you, Claire. How could I not? You're...Claire."

"I knew it!" she says, springing to life with a wide smile and turning to face me. "I knew you liked me."

"You need to rest," I say, determined to change the subject. "Lay down. Relax."

She looks at me for a long moment before she smiles in a way that I know means trouble before she shifts her body until she's lying along the couch, and before I know it, her head is in my lap.

I freeze, unsure of how to respond, but don't get the time to overthink it when she turns to her back to look up at me.

"Watching a movie is on our list," she says.

"Then I guess today we'll be checking it off, won't we?" I ask.

She smiles, then turns again to face the TV. Without meaning to, my hand moves, fingers shifting to her hair to push it back and over her shoulder, then repeating the move. As I sift through her hair, she lets out a small, contented sigh, and my heart skips a beat.

"This is nice," she says quietly as she moves a fry through ketchup before eating it.

When I asked her what she wanted for an early dinner after she slept through what would have been lunch in my lap, she told me she wanted french fries and dino nuggets. I'm pretty sure it was another step in her *make Miles have more fun* scheme, but I couldn't find it in myself to argue with her.

So I called up Grant and asked him to make a quick run to the store for us and then baked her dinosaur-shaped chicken nuggets and frozen french fries.

And honestly? Better than I thought.

"What is? Having a concussion?"

She shakes her head with a laugh, tossing a plain fry at me. I grab it off the table and pop it into my mouth.

"No, you dummy. I told you I don't have a concussion. I just mean..." She waves her hand around the kitchen where we're eating, then to the plate. "This. You taking care of me."

"I'm sure you've been taken care of before, Claire."

I've heard many stories over the years about her family, her two older sisters and her brother, and her parents, all of whom are apparently very close. Still, she shrugs.

"By my mom. By my family. People who are forced to tolerate me, who have it ingrained in their mind that they have to care of me. But not...other people. Not a guy."

With that, with the hint of shame in her words, my brow furrows as I look at her fully, reading between the lines.

"You've never had a boyfriend take care of you?" I don't know why I ask it since I know Paul wasn't the *take-care-of-someone* type, and I regret it instantly.

"Don't give me that pitying look, Miles Miller, or I might start crying about how depressing my life is," she says with a laugh, playing it off as is her way. When she sees my face, which is probably a mask of panic and guilt, she lets out another giggle. "I'm just joking. I'm not going to start crying, at least not right now. But what about you? Ever had a lady friend take care of you?"

I mull it over, then shake my head. "Nope. Never had the opportunity."

Her brow comes together, and she stares at me, confused.

"Is that a dig on never getting beamed in the head with a baseball by a little kid?"

I let out a laugh, something I do often when Claire is around, before I clarify.

"I've never really had someone in my life I've been that close with."

Her face transforms again, eyes going wide with shock. "Oh my god, Miles, are you a virgin?"

"Definitely not," I correct quickly, then feel an embarrassed blush burning at my cheeks. I don't know why it is I always seem to fumble my words around Claire. "I mean. No. I'm not a virgin. At all. I, uh. No."

Real smooth, Miller.

"So you've only had fuck buddies?"

I choke on the water I was trying to sip to cool myself down.

"No. God, I just mean I've never had a serious girlfriend, one who would be living with me to have to take care of me." Then I pause, repeating what I said and explaining. "Not that you're my girlfriend. You're my tenant. You're just living with me. Fuck—"

"You're so easy to fluster," she laughs, letting me out of my misery. I glare at her as she eats another nugget before asking, "Why haven't you? Had a serious girlfriend, I mean."

I shrug. "Never really had the time. Between updating this place and building up the shop, I haven't had time for one. Women aren't really into a man who works all the time and, as you like to point out, never likes to have fun."

She gives me a soft smile.

"I don't know, I think I'm doing a pretty good job at rehabbing you. You're getting pretty fun."

I can't help but smile back. "All thanks to you, I suppose."

She quirks a shoulder and puts a hand under her chin, and I let out a laugh at her antics.

"I bet by the time summer is over, you'll be a whole new person."

I smile and nod, though it reminds me that she's only here until the end of the season. The thought of her leaving is unsettling.

"What's next?" I ask. "After the summer, I mean."

She shrugs, and fuck, I wish I had her carefree energy. That not-knowing alone would eat me alive.

"Not sure. I'll probably head back to Evergreen Park, maybe work at my brother's girlfriend's dance studio again."

"You don't sound too happy about that."

She tips her head to the side like she's trying to decide how much to reveal before she explains.

"I love my hometown, and I love my family, but it can be a lot. They all expect me to have everything figured out, to find a job and stick to it, and get on with my life. They mean well, but it can be suffocating, having that in your face every day." I nod with understanding. "Being here has been nice. No one asks me what I'm going to do with my life or what my ten-year plan is. I get to live day by day and figure things out as I go."

Silence fills the space, and we both sit there for a beat, lost in our own thoughts before I blurt out without thinking, "You could always stay here, you know." I don't know *why* I say it, but I do all the same.

"What?"

"You could stay in Seaside Point." She's staring at me, and I focus my attention back to my dinner. "You fit here. Everyone would be happy to have you here more."

I jolt when her hand reaches out, hand covering mine.

"Even you?" she asks softly. I look up then, seeing a vulnerability that is so opposite of how Claire is, it looks strange on her. Without thinking, I twine my fingers with hers and give her a soft smile.

"Especially me," I whisper.

We sit in silence, and for a split moment, I almost lean in and press my lips to hers, throwing all common sense to the wind, but then there's a loud knock at the front door before it opens.

"Hello?" the familiar voice of June comes calling in. "Claire, I hear you got hurt! Where are you?"

Claire squeezes my hand once, then lets go, smiling at me before she stands and goes to find her friend to assure her she's fine.

SEVENTEEN

MILES

"Whole lotta beach, Miles," Claire says, five days after her injury, stepping off her towering lifeguard chair and moving next to me as I set my board in the sand. There was a small bruise on her forehead the next day, but it's already gone.

"Yeah?" I ask, trying to keep my eyes on the bag I'm unpacking.

After June walked in, I needed space. Thankfully, I had a full schedule for the next few days, meaning I was able to avoid her completely. But when I realized I had the second half of my day off today with nothing else to fill my time, I decided to grab my board and hit the waves.

It definitely had *nothing* to do with Claire asking me when the last time I surfed for myself was.

"Yeah. I think it's interesting you chose the stretch right in front of my chair to set up."

My jaw goes tight as I realize what she's saying and, even more, that she's not wrong. I could have picked nearly anywhere on the mile stretch of shoreline that is Seaside Point, but instead, I chose the stretch between 16th and 17th Avenue, knowing damn well that's where Claire would be.

The more I deny my pull to her, the worse it seems my subconscious tugs me.

"I like this spot," I say nonchalantly, looking to the water once more before shifting my gaze back to her.

She tips her head to the side, her long blonde ponytail falling to the side as she smiles, and I know damn well that means she can see right through me, whether or not I want her to.

"So you're not ignoring me now?" Claire asks with a smile.

A light blush burns on my cheeks, but I hope it can be explained away as just the heat. "I never was," I say, even though I definitely was.

Claire keeps telling me I'm into her, teasing and taunting and being an overall brat, but as much as I deny it, she's not wrong. Something about Claire Donovan calls out to me, even if there's no universe where she can be mine.

Not with her leaving after the summer and surely not when I need to keep my fucking head down and concentrate, take on as many odd jobs and surf lessons as I can in order to buy out Paul.

Especially with how Brad has been sniffing around lately.

"You're a bad liar, Miles," she says.

Even I can't argue that fact, but I don't have to when her name is called. She gives the lifeguard a nod over her shoulder and starts walking backward, her gaze still locked on mine.

I shake my head and smile at her as I lift my board and walk toward the water.

"What are you up to?" I call out two hours later as she stands at the edge of the water, watching me as I walk back onto the shore, surfboard in hand.

There weren't too many waves, though every time I caught one, I could see Claire watching me, and I don't think it was because it was her job.

"I'm off for the rest of the day. I was just moving up the beach to make sure no one needed anything before I head out," she says, putting her hands onto her full hips before tipping her chin to the water. "Saw you out there."

"Nice to be able to surf without having to teach some kid or keeping an eye out for them." It was also a reminder of how much I love being out on the water and how freeing it is to be out there with no responsibilities or worries.

"Yeah, I'm sure. I wish I could do it."

I shouldn't say it. Really, I shouldn't, because the less time I spend with Claire, the better, especially if that time is spent while she's in a small bathing suit and soaking wet.

But because I'm a moron, I say it.

"I could teach you."

Her head moves back like that's a shock to her. "Really?"

My desire for her to be happy beats out common sense, and I shrug. "I don't see why not. It's kind of my job, you know."

"Yeah, but you hate spending time with me," she says with a fake cringe.

I roll my eyes, and her smile goes wide. I realize she's fucking with me, and my voice drops a bit. "I don't, Claire, and you damn well know it."

"Well, I'm glad. Now we just need to get you to admit you think I'm hot, and you haven't been able to stop thinking about me since I moved in, and it's driving you crazy that you can't have me." She winks at me and reaches out, brushing off some sand from my shoulder, and I don't know what happens.

Blame the beating sun or exhaustion, or maybe that tumble I took out on the water.

No matter the reason, something in me snaps, and I reach out, gripping her wrist, wrapping my fingers around it, and pulling her in close. Instantly, her hand moves to my shoulder, holding herself steady, while mine moves to her waist, holding her to me.

My voice sounds low even to me when I say, "Never once have I denied you're gorgeous or that I can't stop thinking about you. But let's be clear: you and I both know I could have you if I wanted."

Her breath hitches at my confession, her mouth dropping open just a hair, her lips full, and I wonder what she would do if I leaned down, if I pressed my lips to hers. The look in her eyes shifts in a heartbeat, moving from awestruck to that snarky and teasing one.

She lets out a small laugh, and the sound of it, the way it vibrates through me, makes my fingers tense.

She is too fucking sweet, too fucking good-looking, and far too fucking tempting in this bikini.

What am I saying?

She's tempting in a pair of pajamas or those little cut-off shorts or one of her workout sets or...or...or.

She's just *tempting,* period.

"Could you now?" she whispers, her fingers wrapping around the back of my neck, and right then, I decide to throw common sense out the window and begin to lean my head down slowly.

What option do I have when I have this dream of a woman in my arms, when she's smiling at me like that, when—

Her eyes shift to somewhere behind me, and her face changes almost instantly.

"Fuck, please. *Please* hold this thought," she says, eyes closing as she takes in a calming breath, and I furrow my brows in confusion. It grows when she steps away from me and then jogs in a direction behind us.

When I turn, I find eyes moving in her direction, a magnet to her at all times. She's moving with a purpose toward a group of kids, four older kids, probably fifteen or sixteen, a few of whom I recognize from around town, and a smaller one, maybe twelve years old. They don't realize Claire is moving their way, her shoulders back, her pony-tail swaying behind her. When she's still ten feet away or so, one puts a hand to the smaller kid's shoulder, pushing him.

Fuck.

I recognize the kid now, Jonah Davis. He's smaller than most of the other kids, and I've always had a bit of a soft spot for him, considering I, too, was raised in this small town by a single mom and faced similar teasing because of it.

Quickly, I grab my things and tuck them beneath the lifeguard chair, out of the way, before moving in their direction.

"Hey, Jonah!" Claire says, none of the irritation I can see in her shoulders bleeding in her voice, as she starts jogging now, closing the gap and waving. Instantly, the older boys step away from Jonah, their eyes going wide.

I follow behind a bit slower, closing the gap but taking in what's going on.

"Oh, uh, hey," Jonah says.

"Hey, gorgeous," the older of the kids says, with what I'm sure he thinks is a slick, playboy smile on his face as he gives her a head-to-toe look.

I catch Claire giving him a pitying smile, then shifting her attention back to Jonah.

"I've been looking for you all afternoon," she says. The youngest boy's eyes go humorously wide.

"You know him?" one of the other kids asks, and Claire looks at him like he's crazy.

"Well, duh. He's my favorite coworker. We work really closely together," she says, putting an arm around his shoulders and pulling him in to her.

"Really? But he's so—" The girl pauses, looking at Claire, who raises an eyebrow at her, visible beneath her sunglasses in a challenge.

"Cool," Claire says, giving the girl a look. "He's so cool, right?"

It's effortless, the way Claire works with these kids. She's young and cool enough to be on their level and admired but old enough to be respected. It's a fine line not many can straddle, but Claire kills it. The girl looks absolutely crushed that her idol is so obviously disappointed with her, though I don't think Claire will ever express that disappointment aloud.

"Hey, Claire, did he say yes?" I ask, walking up and putting a hand to her lower back. The warmth of her skin penetrates my palm, and when her head turns, a hint of shock melting into pleasure written there, I feel that warmth spreading through my chest.

I am *so* completely fucked.

"I haven't asked yet," she says with a curious smile.

"Jonah, Claire and I were about to get ice cream—do you want to come?" With my words, her body melts a bit, leaning into my side, and I hold her tighter.

So. Totally. Fucked.

"Ice cream?" he asks nervously. "Oh, uh, yeah. I have some money in my bag—" I shake my head, then tip my chin toward the boardwalk.

"No need, we've got you covered. Later, guys," I say, giving a flip of my hand to the other kids, two of whom I recognize as kids I've given surf lessons to a few times over.

Fucking spoiled assholes.

The boys look from me to Claire, then to Jonah, something clicking before their shoulders fall a bit, but I barely pay attention as I lead Claire and Jonah to the boardwalk. The hand she slipped around my waist tightens in a quick thanks.

"Does this count?" I ask twenty minutes later, tipping my chin toward Claire's half-eaten cone, and her brow furrows.

We're on a bench on the boardwalk, eating the cones that we bought, Jonah finally taking a moment to stop talking. As soon as he got away from the kids, he started talking about anything and everything, clearly comfortable around Claire. I know for a fact her so clearly taking him under her wing the way she has will have a long-lasting impact on him.

Which is just another thing making me warm to her.

"What?" she asks, popping a finger into her mouth and sucking it off.

I was focused on them chatting and laughing together as we ordered and waited for our ice cream, but once it was served, all I could concentrate on was not being a fucking creep, watching Claire lick at her cone or her fingers when it melted quicker than she could eat.

A unique kind of torture.

"Get some ice cream. I think that's your list, right?"

Her smile widens, and she looks from me to Jonah and shrugs.

"I'll allow it."

"His list?" Jonah asks.

Claire turns to him excitedly, always eager to share her experiment with anyone who will listen. "I made Miles a list of fun things to do this summer because he's so boring."

Jonah nods, looking older than his age suddenly. "Oh, totally. He's super boring."

I groan and look to the clear blue sky. "Jesus Christ, does the whole town think I'm boring?" I ask, and Jonah nods, then shrugs.

"Yeah, pretty much."

"I think that was a rhetorical question," Claire says in a stage whisper before they both laugh at my expense. And even though it's simple, just ice cream on the boardwalk in the town I grew up in with Claire and a twelve-year-old kid, it's the most fun afternoon I've had in years.

EIGHTEEN

CLAIRE

I've been on the clock for barely four hours of my ten-hour shift, and I'm already exhausted.

This is the first time I can really understand why Miles can't stand the tourists who descend on this town. It's the first week since most of the public schools in the state were let out, and families have started to show up tenfold.

So far I've had to go into the water after an adult let their inner tube drift out too far, only to do it *again* an hour later. That resulted in my sending Helen a text to consider banning the tubes in the water, a rule we're enacting starting tomorrow.

I also had to take a kid to the first aid stand when he stepped on a crab, then listened to his mother tell me I should do a better job at making sure there is nothing that can hurt her child on the *natural beach.*

Finally, ten minutes ago, I had to leave my post and argue with a family who decided to set up camp dead center in the roped-off area right in front of my chair. The dad spent half the time arguing with me, half of it staring at my boobs before his wife finally told him to go find another spot.

I'm grumbling to myself as I climb back up to my chair when I get a new text from Miles.

> Do you need this?

I smile at the text and the accompanying photo he sends, my sticker-laden water bottle on the counter, the one that's nearly surgically attached to me most of the time. I realized I left it behind this morning and grabbed a plastic one from the lifeguard house but in this heat, it got warm and gross in less than a half hour.

> MY BABY.

> I can't believe I left her at home.

I try not to think too much about calling Miles's place *home* or how much it actually feels that way.

> Want me to bring it to you?

I smile wide, then look around to see if anyone is watching me. It feels like some kind of secret every time Miles texts me, since I don't think I ever see the man scrolling his phone or even using it for anything other than calls.

But he texts me.

> I would do crazy things for you if you did.

I should send a follow-up text to explain and make it less weird, because I can just *picture* him blushing, and even though I refuse to stop altogether (I think I'm physically incapable), I have been making an effort to tone it down lately. But before I can, he replies.

> Where are you posted?

I look at my watch, then at the boardwalk, and decide I can take my break a bit early. I turn to Carly, who is on post with me, and tell her I'll be back in thirty before moving down the beach toward where my things are to grab them, and so I can tell Helen I'm headed on break.

> Lifeguard house? I'm about to take my break.

I ignore the way I want to add, *to hang out with you.* It wouldn't be the first time. Occasionally, Miles would have his lunch on the boardwalk, grabbing a slice of pizza or a sausage sandwich, and I'd meet him there, sometimes June or Grant joining us, and sometimes just us.

> I'll be there in five.

> I'll meet you on the boards.

With a rush of girly excitement, I make my way down the beach to where the covered lifeguard beach house is on the sand, opening the door to grab my bag.

"Wow, what happened in here?" I ask as Helen sits at the desk, her graying dark hair in a messy knot on top of her head, dozens of papers around her.

"The devil," she groans, and I let out a laugh.

"I'm sorry?"

"Budgets. The devil. Same thing." I nod with understanding, even if I don't *actually* understand. Helen sometimes speaks in a code only she understands, but if you give her a minute to process, she always interprets and clarifies. "I don't think the department can fund the soccer league this fall," she says with a sigh.

Instead of reaching for my bag like planned, I take a step closer, arms crossed on my chest. "Do they normally?"

She nods. "The coaches are all volunteers, and we try to make it so the kids don't have entry fees. But we still have to pay for league fees, field rentals, jerseys, snacks...unfortunately, the town cut our funding this year. I think we'll have to charge for the program."

I see the scattered papers before her and tip my chin toward them.

"Do you mind?" I ask. "If I take a look?"

She waves her hands at me, then shifts her rolling chair back to give me room. "Not at all. My old eyes aren't too good at these things anymore."

I scan the columns of money in and out, noting the salaries, beach badge income, and the cost of the lifeguard program, as well as the projected fundraising from the upcoming events, before finally I point to the block party.

"Can we add something here? A contest or some activities that cost something? We can also look into getting some of the local businesses to fundraise, give out flyers, and a certain percentage of sales would go to the department that day."

Helen looks at me like my relatively basic ideas are new and exciting.

"That's...that's a great idea. We used to do more at the events, but with everyone spread too thin..."

I shrug.

"I could take it over." She gives me a wary look, then shakes her head, but I speak before she can. "No charge, I'll do it off the clock. I love planning things. My mom is a PTA president, a class mom, the whole nine. It's almost in my blood at this point. We could do some stations of crafts at the block party and contests with entry fees. We could raise this money easily."

"You think?" she asks, tipping her head like she sees me in a new light.

"In a town like this? Where half of the people are tourists already primed to spend money? Hell yeah. Honestly, you guys should be amping up this time of year, honing in to bleed the tourists dry to pay for the people who make this place what it is."

She smiles at me, leaning back with her arms crossed on her chest.

"You know, you're good for this place," she says, and I smile, suddenly self-conscious.

"I've had a lot of jobs. They all end up building on one another. Some people see it as a bad thing, the job hopping, but I see it as skill building. That way, when I have a friend who needs to know how to perfectly wrap a gift or someone who can choreograph an eight-year-old's dance recital, or someone like you who wants some fundraising advice, I've got you."

She tips her head, reading me in a way I *do not like.*

"Have you considered working in recreation? Or fundraising? That's basically the skill set that's needed: a jack of all trades."

I shake my head with a laugh. "God, no. Much too structured for me."

"I don't know about that," she says, tipping her head toward her disaster of a desk with a laugh.

I shrug, suddenly feeling like I'm under a microscope when I very much do not want to be, something she must read on me.

"Sorry, sorry, not trying to be a nudge. Go on your break." I smile and nod. "But later, maybe we can talk about some things. Like I said, you're good here."

"Yeah, okay," I say noncommittally, then head out the door.

"Hey, Claire, right?" a voice asks as I close the door behind me, and my entire body stills, hand still on the doorknob.

In the window, Helen gives me a curious look. "Do you need help?" she mouths, but I give her a slight shake of my head and a roll of my eyes. It's not uncommon for beachgoers to try and come to this building for something, though they don't typically know my name.

"Hey, yeah, I'm Claire," I say, slightly uncomfortable but trying to play it cool. "Do you need something?"

"I'm Brad. And you're actually just the person I was hoping to see."

I tilt my head to the side, confused, but then I notice he's in another white polo, but this time, it has the logo for Surf on it. It's tucked into a pair of khakis, and he's wearing dress shoes despite the fact that there's sand grinding beneath his feet. In contrast, I'm in an oversized lifeguard sweatshirt and shorts, my flip-flops slipped into my bag.

Somehow, I just know the guy is a tool, and he looks the part, too.

"How can I help you?" I ask with a tight smile, eyes moving to the boardwalk to keep a lookout for Miles.

"I need to hire some lifeguards." My jaw goes tight. "The older ones, above legal age." My brow furrows, and I fight an actual grimace moving across my face.

"Excuse me? This is a township recreation department," I say. I want to add *not an escort service*, but considering I'm technically on the clock, I resist the urge.

He lets out a fake laugh, and it grates against me in a way I hate more than anything.

"Of course, I know that, Claire." I don't like the way he says my name, like he's holding the knowledge of it over my head. "You see, I'm hosting a beach games tournament, and we were told we need to hire township lifeguards and EMS to get the proper permitting. I just thought it would be nice for the participants and guests to have some kind of...eye candy, you know?"

I fight a gag at the way he gives me a once-over.

"Beach games?"

"We're going to start promoting it soon, but yes. It's going to be quite the event, teams competing in different games, a winner, a big party after."

"Wow, that's pretty cool," I say, because even if I hate this guy, I bet beach games *would* be fun.

"You know, I've even meant to talk since our first meet got a little...interrupted," he says, then steps closer to me. I give him a tight smile and step back. "At Surf. You started dancing and then were dragged away."

"Yeah, sorry about that, but—"

And then we're interrupted once again.

NINETEEN

MILES

I see her bright red sweatshirt and her blonde hair before I really see Claire, but as I approach, my jaw goes tight. That's because she's standing on the steps of the lifeguard house talking to Brad Baker.

The bane of my existence.

When she takes a step back, he mimics it, and something snaps in me when I see how uncomfortable she looks.

I move across the sand, my weight shifting in a way that if I didn't run on this sand regularly, it might slow me down, but thankfully, I'm to her quickly.

Just in time to see Brad Baker reach out and brush a lock of Claire's blonde hair aside. She tries to shift away as his fingers touch her face, but there isn't much room on the steps.

"Hey, baby," I say, too loud to be casual, but I'm fighting back a myriad of emotions in my gut that I refuse to look at too closely.

Because if I do, behind the simmering irritation, I might see I have a thing for Claire Donovan.

Both heads snap toward me. Brad gives me a dirty glare, while Claire looks at me with intrigue before a small smile that's hiding a healthy amount of relief.

"You know him?" Brad asks, and Claire looks from me to Brad, clearly trying to weigh whether she's more annoyed with my antics or annoyed by this dickhead.

She looks at my outstretched hand and at me before she reaches out and grabs it.

"Oh yeah. Miles and I go way back."

I tug her down the two stairs and away from Brad, pulling her into my side. Her hand moves to my chest, heat burning there, as her body presses to my side, and she smiles at Brad. His jaw has gone tight, his eyes narrowing in on my hand that's on her waist.

"Brought you your water," I say, lifting her bottle, and she smiles genuinely this time.

God, she's so pretty.

"You're the best."

I take a step away from the building, and she follows, hand in mine.

"Uh, Claire, I really need to talk to you about the lifeguards—" Brad starts, but I interrupt, ignoring him and directing my question to her.

"You're on break, right?" It's meant as a reminder that she is *off the clock* and thus not required to speak to him about work things. She nods. "Come on."

"I was talking to her—" Brad starts, clearly annoyed by my interruption of his hitting on her.

"Helen is inside," Claire says with a polite smile. "She'd be more than happy to talk to you about hiring some lifeguards."

"But I—" Clearly, he's not getting the picture, and suddenly I'm even more happy I came in to interrupt their conversation because he wouldn't have stopped.

"Excuse me, Brad, I gotta talk to my girl," I say, putting a hand around her waist and tugging her away.

"Miles, what are you doing?" she asks low, a hint of a giggle in the words, but I don't respond. "Where are we going?"

"Far away from him," I say through gritted teeth, spotting the shaded spot underneath the boardwalk.

"Oh? Why's that?" she asks, a teasing lilt to her tone.

"That guy's an ass," I say, stepping away from her once we're in the shade, crossing my arms on my chest. She looks at me with feigned irritation before mimicking the move. "And he made you uncomfortable."

"You seem to be making quite the habit of saving me from unwanted advances." I shrug, and she takes a step closer to me, a teasing smile on her lips. "You know, I don't think you pulled me away because you don't like the guy, Miles."

"Then why else would I?" I ask, staring down at her.

"You did it because you were jealous someone else was giving me attention."

I roll my eyes, hearing the footsteps and laughter overhead.

"Trust me, I am *not* jealous of Brad Baker," I say, but it even *feels* like a lie on my tongue. When she says it, I realize it's the exact feeling that was coursing through me. I *was* jealous of the attention she was giving him, whether she wanted to give it or not. I was jealous of how close he was to her, of the way he was about to touch her.

"Oh, you so are," she says as she leans back against the beam of the boardwalk. The light filters in through the boards, moving over her face and highlighting her smile. "Just like at the Seabreeze when Sam was trying to dance with me."

I roll my eyes. "That was not a jealous thing. It was because he wasn't taking no for an answer. Why would I be jealous of either of those assholes?"

She shrugs. "Because you're obsessed with me."

I shake my head and let out a small laugh, taking off my hat and settling it back on my head. It's a nervous habit of mine, and, god, does Claire make me nervous.

"You're out of your mind," I say.

"You're so into me, Miles. It's okay, I can't blame you."

"No, I'm not."

"Yeah?" she asks, a teasing lilt in the words.

"Yeah." I say with all of the false bravado I can conjure. She straightens up, then takes a step closer to me. "Then prove it."

"Prove it?" I ask, lifting an eyebrow.

"Prove you're not into me." She takes a step closer to me until there's barely a foot between us. "Kiss me," she says, this time the words coming out in a breathy whisper.

My heart flips like I'm a kid with his first crush, but to be honest, that's how Claire makes me feel: completely out of my depth, lost and nervous, and like she can see past everything I normally hide.

"No."

"Because you're chicken," she says, crossing her arms on her chest, the sleeves nearly covering her hands. The huge lifeguard sweatshirt she wears makes me wonder if she *asked* for a size that would swallow her up or if the department ran out of sizes that actually fit her.

"I'm not chicken. I'm not going to kiss you just because you're bullying me."

She smiles at that, continuing to look up at me.

"Oh, this isn't bullying you. If you want me to bully you, I can." I let out a laugh without meaning to, and she shrugs. "Some people like that kind of thing."

"You're insane," I whisper, and without meaning to, my fingers shift, touching a strand of her long ponytail that rests on her shoulder. It's so fucking soft, if a bit knotted from the wind off the ocean. For a delusional moment, I think about how much I'd like to sit here for an hour, gently detangling her tresses with my fingers. "And you're a deadly fucking flirt."

"I'm so happy you noticed," she says with a wide, gleeful smile like she genuinely *is* glad.

"Hard not to when you flirt with everyone you see."

She pauses and then looks at me, a slightly puzzled look on her pretty face as I cross my arms on my chest. "What?"

"Oh, come on, Claire, don't deny it. You're a helpless flirt."

She tips her head to the side, and a smile spreads over her lips as she takes a step closer to me. "Who do I flirt with, Miles?" she asks, and I stand there, rolling my eyes as I try and think of who to name and quickly realize...

No one.

"Well..."

Claire might be *flirty* with lots of people, but that's because it's her personality, but she doesn't outright flirt with everyone. I would know: it would drive me insane, having to watch it.

But she sure as shit flirts with me.

"Are you trying to say you only flirt with me?" I ask hesitantly.

She rolls her lips into her mouth and gives me a shy smile.

"If I say yes, what are you going to do about it?" she asks, and the challenge in her words, the smile on her lips, the way she stands there in her sweatshirt, and her full lips...

Without thinking, I reach out, grabbing her around her waist and tugging her against me. Her eyes go wide, and her mouth parts just a bit, making her look even more beautiful, something I didn't even know was possible, yet here we are.

I hesitate, terrified to cross this line, but then I press my lips to hers. At the touch, my hand tightens on her waist on instinct before I deepen the kiss, needing to savor every moment of it.

It's an idiotic move.

Maybe the stupidest thing I've ever done.

I probably could have survived this entire summer with her. With her teasing and her toying and her flirting.

But knowing what she tastes like when I kiss her? The way she gasps when my tongue slides into her mouth and the way her hands shift, folding around my neck like she wants to get closer?

I don't know how I'm ever going to continue to keep my distance knowing all of this.

We kiss like this, my tongue sliding along hers, her fingers digging into the skin at my neck, my hands desperately trying not to dig into the flesh of her hips, and I realize I'm totally screwed.

Kissing Claire is so much better than I thought it would ever be, like a part of me is snapping into place, a sense of calm taking over, battling with the consuming need that flares in my chest.

A tiny mewl leaves her, pulling a groan from my chest and fraying the last thread of control I have.

I want to get her home.

I want to get her naked.

I want to be inside her.

"This is a bad idea," I say, my lips moving down her jaw and to the soft skin of her neck. I can feel her smile as her hands move under my shirt, caressing across my back.

"Is it?"

"Possibly the worst one," I say, nipping her ear before sucking at the skin beneath it. She lets out a breathy laugh.

"Then maybe you should stop," she whispers, the words breathy and going straight to my dick,

"In a minute," I say.

"God, you're so gone for me."

"No, I'm not." I lie, my lips moving back to hers and tasting her again, our tongues twining.

Her nails bite into my back, and it's hot and untamed and strangely familiar somehow, like this was always where we were supposed to end up.

I break the kiss again, moving down the other side of her neck, wanting to grace every inch of exposed flesh I can.

"You are. You just won't admit you want to be with me."

Those words have me hesitating, reality crashing back in as I rest my forehead against hers. "I don't have time for a relationship, Claire."

Something curls in my stomach, canceling out the peace and excitement that was just dwelling in there.

"I'm a relationship kind of girl," she admits, something that, despite it all, I knew.

It's why Paul stayed with her instead of just fucking her and running once he got what he wanted.

I stand there, staring at her with her kiss-swollen lips and the dazed look in her eyes, committing it to memory.

Because I won't ever see it again.

I can't do the same thing my brother did to her, taking what she so willingly gives without thinking about what *she* needs.

"We shouldn't do this," I say, and her body goes tense.

"Excuse me?"

"We shouldn't be doing this, Claire."

"I don't have time for...whatever you want this to be." The words twist in my gut and taste sour on my lips, but I know it's what needs to happen.

She steps back, anger playing over her face.

"Don't make it seem like I'm forcing you into something, Miles. You kissed *me*."

"I know, I know," I say, running a hand over my hair. "Trust me, I know. And god, I fucking want to, Claire. I really do. But I can't."

The sad smile that moves over her face puts salt in the self-inflicted wound. She steps further back and shakes her head, disappointment clear on her face, hurt hidden beneath it.

"You don't have to sacrifice everything all the time, Miles. You know that?"

"If I could have you, I would, Claire."

She gives me a pitying smile.

"Except, you already do. It's totally crazy, but I like you. And you like me too, but you're so caught up in your responsibilities and what you think you *have* to do, that you won't give yourself what you want."

She shakes her head and takes another step away from me, each one feeling like I'm losing something vital before she turns completely away. When she's almost in the sun, she looks over her shoulder, giving me one last look.

"I do wonder, Miles, just how happier you'd be if you just *let yourself.*"

Then she's gone.

And even though her words echo in my mind throughout the night and into the next day and the next, I make the decision that I'm going to keep away from Claire Donovan to the best of my ability.

TWENTY

CLAIRE

It's been a week since our kiss under the boardwalk, and Miles has made one thing glaringly clear: he is making every effort to avoid me. It's like a single moment together flipped some switch, reminding him that we can't not only be something *more*, but we can't even be friends.

We're barely *acquaintances* at this point.

Two days in, I took the list off the fridge and crossed out *eat ice cream*, leaving it on the counter for him to see. I was somewhat mollified when he didn't crumble it and toss it in the trash, instead putting it back on the fridge where it belongs.

But besides that, there has been absolutely no contact.

It's why when, on my day off, I meet June, Lainey, and Deck at the beach, I'm shocked to see him arrive with Grant thirty minutes later, dropping their things into the sand at the little camp we set up.

I push my sunglasses down my nose and watch as Miles takes his ever-present backward hat off, flipping it around so the brim hides his face a bit.

"Wow, did you tell Miles I was going to be here?" I ask as he pretends to be looking for something in the black bag he bought.

"What?" Grant asks with a confused look.

"I just figured if you told him I was going to be in attendance at this little friend gathering, he would have found some new, strange excuse not to come."

The group looks from Miles to me, a blush growing on his cheeks despite the hat.

I take him in from behind my glasses and ignore the tiny pinch in my heart. I genuinely thought we had gotten past whatever was keeping him so closed off from me, but clearly I was so wrong.

Miles is off fighting some fictional battle in his head about God knows what, but I learned once before that you can't make anyone want to be with you: they have to want to do that on their own.

And I refuse to fight for a man to grace me with his attention.

"Are you two fighting?" Deck asks from where he's sitting in the sand beside Lainey.

"No, she's being ridiculous," Miles grumbles, and my eyes go wide, not expecting a response.

"Oh, Miles is just being a dick because he realized he's super into me but he's mad about it, so he's taking it out on everyone around him. Feel free to ignore him."

Grant lets out a snort laugh, but Deck doesn't bother to hide it, laughing out loud.

"Why is he being a dick?" he asks.

"Because he kissed me under the boardwalk. You know, because he's so in love with me." I smile angelically, taking a sip from my water and setting it back down. "But then he panicked about it, so he's ignoring me."

"It did it to prove I didn't like you!" he says, and Grant gives him a deadpan look.

"Bro," he says, and Deck lets out another loud laugh.

"Yeah, he was all, '*No! I can't do this! I'm not good enough for you!*'" I say.

"That's not what happened, Claire," Miles argues, that blush deepening, be it with irritation or embarrassment, I don't know.

"Do you want to share with the class then? Feel free to correct me. Maybe they can decide who is in the right and who is dead wrong," I tell him, giving him a raised eyebrow. "That's what I thought," I say when he doesn't respond. "Anyway, I told him I didn't want to play games because I am an adult, and he's been avoiding me for the last week. This is the first time I've seen him since then, actually."

"I haven't been avoiding you—" he starts, but Grant cuts him off.

"Dude, you literally came to my house after work and showered there yesterday. Is that why you didn't just go home? Because you're afraid of a little blonde chick?" Grant asks with a laugh.

My eyes widen with the confirmation. I smile, but secretly, somewhere, I would very much like to ignore the sadness that leaks into my bones.

It was only an assumption that he was ignoring me, since I know in general, he works a ton, but the confirmation is...not what I was hoping for. I guess I was hoping there was some incredibly logical explanation that might, possibly, come with a romantic confession of love.

A girl can dream.

"I'm going in the water. Anyone want to come?" I ask, in desperate need to get away from the awkward tension. I stand and look behind me only to find Miles's eyes glued to my ass exposed from the high-cut bottoms that show off half of it. Despite myself, I smile, shaking my head when I catch him, and he shifts his gaze quickly.

"I'll come!" Lainey says eagerly, standing.

"Me too!" June agrees, both of them clearly ready to gossip.

"I'll come," Deck says, but Lainey glares at him. "Just kidding. I'll just...stay here with the two Mr. Denials."

My mind moves through the *two* comment, but I don't have the time to figure out who else he's referring to because June and Lainey are putting their arms through my elbows and dragging me toward the water. We don't go in fully, just barely up to our knees, because the water is still chilly.

Once we're officially far enough from listening boy-ears, Lainey gives me a look.

"You guys kissed?" she asks, eyes wide. "You didn't tell me!"

"This is the first time I've seen you in a week," I say with a laugh.

"You could have texted me!"

"And miss your reaction in person? No thanks," I tell her with a smile.

"She told me," June brags with a smug smile, and I turn my glare onto her.

"That's because you're off for the summer and spend each day right next to my stand." She shrugs like she isn't going to bother arguing with that.

"Okay, okay, okay," Lainey says, eager to get back on topic. "But like, how was it?"

I sigh.

"It was...amazing," I whisper.

"I *knew* that man would kiss good," June says.

"Lethally," I agree.

"But what happened? Because if Miles Miller kissed me, I'd never stop." Lainey looks at me. "No offense."

"None taken. Trust me, I didn't want to. It just..." I sigh. "He said he doesn't have time for a relationship and that he knew that would be what I wanted. He works too much, blah blah blah."

"So, he's a big baby chicken?" Lainey asks, and I snort out a laugh.

"Kind of." I nod as I watch a small wave crash against my legs.

"Do you like him?" June asks seriously. "Like, really."

I let out a deep breath, look to the sky, and admit my truth. "Unfortunately." Lainey lets out a small laugh. "I think I always did," I whisper.

"No shit," June agrees with a laugh. "You deluded yourself into being into Paul, but we always knew which Miller you really liked." Guilt that Paul doesn't deserve moves through me, but I don't have time to let it stay there. "Okay, so now that we've got that confession out of the way, what are we going to do about it?"

I turn to her. "What?"

"What are you going to do about it?"

I frown. "Well...nothing."

"Nothing?" Lainey asks, clearly shocked by this.

I shake my head. "I won't chase a man who won't admit he's into me."

June looks at Lainey, and a look passes between them, but I don't pay it any mind.

"That's so fair," Lainey says.

"Totally. Either way, it looks like we're in for an interesting summer," June says with a laugh.

"I'd kill for a date. I feel like it's been an eternity since I've been out with someone. Even just to get drinks and have a night out. I want to dress up and look pretty," Lainey says a few hours later.

We've played in the water and taken a few walks, watched the guys throw a football, and got lunch from the boardwalk, though the entire time, Miles has basically ignored me.

"Everyone in this stupid town is too chicken to ask a girl out," June agrees, and I wonder exactly who she's talking about since June rarely says anything without intention.

I make a mental note to ask her about it later, but in the meantime—

"Just do it yourself," I say with a smile. "Dating is so antiquated, waiting for him to make a move? We all know men can't decide on a single thing. If you want to go on a date, just ask him."

Miles lets out a scoff, and I shift my gaze to him. I fight the all-consuming urge to start to heckle him and scream, *I was talking about you, dipshit!*

But instead, I decide to be an adult.

Kind of.

"What's funny?"

"That you'd give that advice, since you'd never do that."

My eyes go wide, and my mouth drops open in shocked irritation. He's barely talked to me in a week, and this is when he decides to?

You've got to be kidding me.

"Excuse me?"

"You would never do that, Claire. You're a wait-for-the-guy-to-make-the-first-move kind of girl."

My jaw goes tight, despite the fact that he isn't wrong.

I like the guy who makes the first move to make me feel wanted. That's why when Miles makes the first move, and his actions do not match his words, it hurts.

"So you're saying I wouldn't ask a guy out on a date?" I challenge, crossing my arms on my chest.

He shakes his head in response.

I nod and give him a smile because the universe loves to give me bad ideas, and one is walking our way.

"It wouldn't bother you at all if I got up and asked someone else out right now?"

Miles shakes his head, though I can see his jaw twitch just a bit.

"Go right on ahead," he says.

He's so fucking stubborn, but I don't have the time or energy to coach an adult man to use his big boy words to talk about his big, big feelings, so instead, I nod, then scan the beach for a moment before finding the perfect option. Then I stand and walk over to where I spotted Brad.

"Hey," I say, with a sultry smile, when I reach him.

I place a hand against the post that separates the regular beach-goers from the exclusive beach seating, Surf leases from the town. Heads turn, but I keep my eyes on my target, and when he looks my way, I smile wider. His eyes widen when they take me in, then his face goes smug as he says something to the guy he's talking to before walking over to me.

"Well, hello there. What can I do for you?"

I put a hand on my hip, sliding my hair over my shoulder, and looking toward my group of friends. Deck and Grant look horribly entertained by me, while June looks a bit concerned. Lainey is intrigued, like she's taking notes for future reference, and Miles looks...angry.

No, not angry. Absolutely *livid*.

Good.

He wants to play the hot and cold asshole, I can too.

"So, my friends kind of dared me to ask someone out on a date because they think I won't actually do it, and you might be the lucky guy," I say, giving him the honesty Brad deserves.

His eyes look over my shoulder, taking in my friends, and I look too, before wiggling my fingers at Miles. Even from here, I can see his jaw is clenched tight enough to crack a tooth.

"Is that so?"

"Yeah. Does tomorrow night work?"

His arms cross on his chest, and he leans back. That's when I notice the khaki shorts and polo tucked into it. Looking at the other employees, I note that this is *not* some kind of uniform he's forced into, but instead something he chose intentionally.

I take a deep breath, telling myself that I can get over that.

Probably.

"You with Miles?" he asks, something I find strange, but he probably remembers Miles pulling me away from him last week.

"No. I'm not," I say simply.

"Well, then, yeah. Definitely. How does tomorrow at seven work?"

I smile wide. "That would be perfect."

"We'll have our date here, at Surf."

My brow furrows, but then again, I've been on enough shitty dates to not care about adding one to my tally to best Miles.

"That works."

"Perfect. Here, give me your number," he says, and I call out the digits before shaking his hand like this is some kind of business transaction. Finally, I turn back toward my friends with a thumbs-up and a smile.

Despite winning his little dare, the look on Miles's face doesn't make me feel like I won anything.

TWENTY-ONE

CLAIRE

The next morning I'm sitting at the kitchen island eating my breakfast when I'm surprised to see Miles come down, making it the first time I've seen him at home since our kiss.

"I won't be home until late," I say, taking a bite of my cereal when he doesn't say a word to me.

"What?" he asks, confused as he pours coffee into a mug and turns toward me.

I keep my eyes on the bowl as I take another bite. I wait until I chew and swallow, weighing my words before I respond.

"I won't be home until late tonight. I have that date. Remember?" I don't see it since I'm avoiding looking at him, but I can *feel* Miles's body go rigid at my words.

"What?"

"I have that date. The one I made yesterday? We're going to Surf." Finally, I look up at him and see his jaw is clenched.

"The fuck you are."

I fight a small smile as I take another bite of fruity cereal, chew, and swallow.

"Says who?"

"Says me."

That's when I start to get annoyed. "I didn't realize I had to run my social life past you," I say. "Plus, you're the one who told me to go ask him."

"I didn't think you'd actually do it," he says.

I give him a smile as I stand, moving toward the sink to dump out my milk and rinse the bowl. "You should know by now that I always follow through with my threats."

His shoulders straighten, his arms crossing over his broad chest and tightening the Miller Automotive tee perfectly across it as he glares at me.

"Is that what this is? Some kind of threat?"

I tip my head to the side as I put the bowl in the dishwasher and lean on the counter.

"Now, why would I be threatening you?"

He throws his hands up in the air. "Because you're throwing a hissy fit that I'm not falling to my knees for you. Because you're mad that I'm not taking things further. I don't know how your brain works, Claire."

I roll my eyes, officially annoyed by him and his attitude.

"If I wanted you on your knees, I'd just have to say the word, and you know it, Miles," I say, only half joking. I think if I told Miles I was okay with just hooking up, he'd strip down right here and now, but I've never been the kind of girl who liked hookups. With my challenge, he steps closer, and my breathing halts.

"Then say the word."

My heart stutters in my chest, that stupid, idiotic hope flaring up with it.

"Miles," I say, my breath getting caught in my lungs. He steps closer until I'm pinned to the granite of the counter, his body pressed against mine. "What are you doing?"

"I have no fucking idea." But clearly, that's a lie because then his lips crash down onto mine, and my entire body ignites. My hands reach up, twining around his neck and pulling myself up.

His arm wraps around my waist, holding me tighter, as the kiss deepens, as his tongue brushes against my lips, and I open them to let him in. He tastes like dark coffee and a hint of toothpaste, and my heart beats wildly.

It feels right, the same way it did last time, like a wave crashing over me, washing away all of my mixed emotions from the last week. His hand moves up, fisting in my ponytail and using it to move me to exactly where he wants me, a firm hand to guide the kiss along. His erection grinds into me and makes me moan. My nipples scratch along the bathing suit top under my sweatshirt, and I curse the layers of clothes between us.

"Miles—" I groan, shifting my hips against him.

But something about the single words snaps the moment between us. He pulls away from the kiss, eyes closing as he rests his forehead against mine, breathing heavy.

"We shouldn't be doing this, Claire," he says, regret heavy in the words, and my gut drops at the repeat of what happened under the boardwalk.

"Don't say that," I whisper in a plea, the words aching at my throat as I say them. "Please. Don't."

"I'm sorry, I'm so sorry, you have no idea. But I don't have the time or energy to devote to you, not in the way you'd deserve—" I push on his chest until he gives me room to step away, then point an angry finger at him.

"Don't you tell me what I deserve, Miles."

"You know what I mean, I—"

"No. I don't. I don't know what you mean, because since I've gotten here, you've done nothing but make assumptions and tell me things *about myself* as if you know me better." I close my eyes and take a deep breath, shaking my head to stop the tears that are always eager to fall. "If you can't have me because I'm too much work and you don't have the time, that's on you, but you never bothered to ask me what *I'd* need out of a relationship." He opens his mouth to argue, but I shake my head and keep going. "You never bothered to ask, Miles, but if you had, I would have told you all I would need is to be yours."

The last word cracks painfully, but I still keep it together.

A beat passes as we stare at each other across the kitchen before he speaks, a whisper of words. "Don't go on that date."

My body is on fire, my heart pounding, my belly filled with millions of hopeful butterflies.

"Why not?"

I want him to give me a reason to stay. To tell me he doesn't want me to go because he wants me for himself, because he wants to kiss me and taste me and give this a shot. He opens his mouth and closes it a few times, and my hope dissipates slowly.

"Because he's a fucking asshole," he says, and it all drops. The butterflies float away, and the warm feeling turns to ice-cold disappointment.

I let out a breath as reality sinks in, that the kiss that felt like my world changing was just something he did out of passion, not out of emotion, and it meant nothing.

"What, so just because you don't want me, you decided no one else can? I'm just some toy you get to tease and play with until you're bored or too busy or whatever is your issue, but I have to sit waiting in the corner for you?"

"No, that's—"

Anger is flooding my system as I take a step away, grabbing my water bottle and hefting my bag over my shoulder.

"You're like every other man, Miles. Happy to let a woman sit safe in the corner, play games of will he, won't he until you see another man try and play with your toy. Except I'm not a toy, Miles. I'm a woman, and I'm not the kind of woman who waits around for someone to make a move."

I can't be here right now. I can't stare at him and feel the all-consuming desire for him twining with disappointment that we'll never be anything more than a desire he won't give into.

"You know," I say when he doesn't add anything as I move toward the door, with him following me as I do. "I thought you'd finally tell me the truth, but here we are." I take another step backward, giving him a sad smile I can't force myself to hide. "It's just more of the same bullshit."

And then I'm out the door.

Almost twelve hours later, it's painfully clear I shouldn't have gone on this date.

Not because Miles told me not to, because fuck him, but because the man sitting across from me is *intolerable*. I've been sitting here for a total of fifteen minutes, ten of which he has spent talking about himself, his job, and his position in expanding his firm's presence. And has yet to ask me a single thing about myself.

"Are you from here?" I shake my head and then open my mouth to give a full answer, but he interrupts. "Good. This place is dreadful."

"I like—"

"I can't wait to leave this town in the fall," he says, lifting a glass, and my brow furrows. "My father has me overseeing another project in North Jersey starting in September. Where will you be in the fall?"

I'm almost shocked he knows how to ask questions about other people that require more than a yes or no, if I'm being honest.

"My family is in Evergreen Park. I'll probably find a new job up that way." Something I try to ignore twists at the idea of it, at the thought of leaving Seaside Point.

"Ah, Evergreen Park, that's a nice area. You know, I spearheaded a campaign to—" He starts going on again about some project he worked on for Baker Brothers, and I smile tightly, nodding as I do.

I get a reprieve from his bragging about himself and his job and blah blah blah when we get our drinks. Grateful, I take a large sip because I can feel it's going to be a long ass night. I'm contemplating going to the bathroom to send an SOS to June when he asks me the second question of the night.

"So, how do you know Miles Miller?"

My head tips to the side, a bit confused. "Miles?" I say the name, feeling that stab in my chest once more.

"Yeah, he's interrupted us a few times now." I guess he would see it like that. "How do you know him?"

"Oh, uh," I start. "He's best friends with my best friend's brother. I actually dated his brother for a bit." I don't know why I added that last part, and I instantly regret it because I don't want to talk about Miles or Paul tonight. I just wanted a few hours where my mind wasn't completely wrapped up in Miles, and here I am, talking about him.

"But you two aren't together anymore?"

I shake my head. "No, we broke up, but I came down to Seaside Point for the summer to hang out with June, and Miles had a room for rent. It was nice being able to stay with someone who wasn't a total stranger."

Brad nods like he understands. I hope that's the end of that, but I quickly find it is not.

"What does your ex think about that?"

My jaw tightens before I answer. "I wouldn't know, him being my ex and all." A creeping feeling starts to move through me at his interest in Miles and Paul, and alarm bells are ringing loudly.

"Don't they talk?"

"I don't know," I say, clipping the words short. "I honestly don't really talk about my ex much." My bluntness takes him off-kilter.

"Oh, oh, of course. Sorry, I just find small-town drama so interesting, you know?"

I give him a tight smile, once more wishing I hadn't been so fucking stubborn to go on this date. And even worse, why did I have to choose *him*? The most obnoxious, self-absorbed man on the beach.

I know the answer, of course, is because of the reaction it got out of Miles the first time he saw Brad in my vicinity and my undying need to get a reaction. I wish Miles was less of an idiot, less stubborn and uptight, and could just admit there is something between us.

But instead, I'm stuck holding my ground right down the beach from him. I look over my shoulder at the house, where I wish I were cozied up on the deck reading a book or laughing with Miles, interested to see if the lights are on and if he's home, or if he left.

Except I don't see the house, not really, because I'm distracted by something else. Instead, I spot Miles strolling down the beach, no shoes on, eyes locked on me, and looking like he's on a mission.

I want to be annoyed, especially considering he's got that *look* about him, half pissed as fuck, half devious, like he's planning something.

But I can't.

Because from the moment I showed up here, this date has been an absolute misery. I have girlbossed way too close to the sun this time by going out with the most boring finance bro known to mankind, who won't stop rambling on about himself, his investment portfolio, and his *plans* for the town.

Which, strangely enough, I suddenly find offensive because this little town is perfect the way it is.

But also because, for better or worse, I haven't been able to think about anything—or anyone—but Miles since I got here.

What was he doing? Would he be mad when I got home? What did he think when he saw me waving at the video doorbell on my way out, all dressed up and ready to go? He was nowhere to be found while I got ready, and I silenced my phone for this date, but I'm itching to check it now to see if he called or texted me anything.

"What's going on over there?"

I don't answer, too absorbed in watching Miles stalk closer, lost in the way he's looking at me.

"Jesus Christ," Brad grumbles under his breath, but I'm not even on the same planet as him anymore, lost as I watch Miles, his T-shirt clinging to his chest as he moves, sand kicking up with each step.

When Miles realizes my eyes are on him, he smiles wide and mischievous.

"Come on, Claire," he calls before he's even at my side.

"What?" I ask, then he steps over the small fence on the sand, moves until he's at my side, and puts a hand out to me.

"Come on, we're going home."

TWENTY-TWO

ONE HOUR PREVIOUSLY

MILES

"Are you going to tell me what the fuck is going on?" Grant asks.

I look at the clock on my phone and cringe. It's six p.m., so she's probably getting all dolled up to go out with Brad fucking Baker. Taking a sip of my beer, I remind myself that this is what I wanted and force myself to relax my shoulders that were up near my ears.

"What do you mean?" I ask.

"So that's a no," he says, then lifts his beer and takes a sip.

We're at the Seabreeze, where her ghost seems to haunt me. The tables are back in their original place, but Lainey is glaring at me as if she's trying to shoot darts into my eyeballs, and I can almost feel Claire in my arms when we danced here. I never realized how quiet this place was, but like all things, it seems once Claire shows me the sunshine, I eternally miss its warmth.

She's ruining my hometown, and I don't know what to do about it.

"What do you want to know?" I ask

"First off, you kissed her?" I sigh and look at the ceiling. "When?"

After the disaster at the beach yesterday, I've added my best friend to my growing list of people I'm avoiding, not wanting to deal with the questions.

With a deep release of air, I confess. "Last week. She dared me to."

He gives me a look that says *don't be an idiot.*

"She dared you?"

My jaw goes tight at his disbelief and the fact that I have to justify this bullshit.

"She told me I was too chicken. It was to prove I wasn't into her."

He lets out a laugh, and I can't even be mad. It sounds idiotic even to me.

"And then...?"

"And then I stopped and told her we can't do that because she's someone who needs a relationship, and I can't give her that." Grant glares at me. Because I just need to get it all out, I add with one last breath, "And then I avoided her."

"What the fuck, man? Why do you think you can't give her that?" he says in a calm voice he must have adopted from his sister.

"I don't know!" I say, throwing my hands into the air. "It's too fucking messy, and I have too much going on." I let my head hit the bar top and groan. "Because I've got too fucking much going on. Because she's Paul's ex. Because she's going to leave at the end of the summer."

Silence hangs between us before Grant speaks again.

"Come on, man. She was never Paul's."

I lift my head from the bar and look at him. "What?" I ask, my blood going cold.

"It was always you, Miles. She always had a thing for you, but you convinced yourself she was too young and that she needed to enjoy school or whatever the fuck bullshit excuse you use to separate yourself from things so you can't have anything good in your life."

I open my mouth to argue, to tell him I don't do that, but he gives me a look, and I close it.

Do I do that? Create barriers and excuses for why I can't have good things?

Instantly, I see the truth in his statement.

A dozen moments in time flash in my mind with his statement, a dozen examples of not letting myself have something I wanted. Letting Paul have things that he didn't even *attempt* to earn just because I was the older brother, and that's what I was supposed to do. Not letting myself have a social life in order to build my business into something bigger, something I could be proud of, when everyone around me was already proud of me.

How many times have my friends and family told me they were worried about me and my nonstop need to work?

How many times has my mom told me she's terrified I'm going to work myself into an early grave like my dad? My dad, who never let himself have a day off because he was *saving* for retirement or some big family vacation or a bigger house or a better life, when looking back, I would give up all of that just for *time* with him.

Fuck, I *just* told Claire I was too busy to give her what she deserved, didn't I?

But Grant's statement cracks something inside of me inexplicably. If I'm too busy working for a better life to enjoy the great one I have, what's the fucking *point* of it all? What's the point of working myself to the bone if I have no one to share it with? My mind runs through at least a dozen other times over the years where I haven't gone after something I wanted because I convinced myself I couldn't have it, that I hadn't earned that freedom of time off.

Hell, Claire had to make me a *bucket list* because she is so aware of how little I do things for myself.

Six years of telling myself I didn't deserve Claire, only for her to tell me she only wanted *me*.

And then I told her it wasn't enough. The sad look that slid through her eyes in my kitchen this morning flashes through my mind, a knife to the heart.

"It's the same shit you're spewing now, years later," he adds, his eyes filled with accusation. My mind is reeling as he continues to speak, and if I'm being honest, I don't know if I *want* to hear what else he has to say. "That summer, she was done with school, and you told me you were going for it. But your brother was there, and Paul, being the fuckwad Paul is, had to have what you so clearly wanted. We all knew it was happening. Except for Claire, of course."

I remember that night very well, of course.

We were at the Memorial Day party Surf was throwing on the beach, and despite hating the place, Grant had dragged me to it. I was sitting with Grant and Paul, who was telling us about his newest get-rich-quick scheme. I can't even remember why he was home for the weekend, which was a rarity since he graduated from high school, though he was probably there asking for money.

That's when I realized she was back, when I heard the magical laugh that I'd grown to both love and hate. My head turned in the direction it came from, and I saw her, dancing with June, a drink in her hand, head tipped back in laughter.

"Is this going to be the year?" Grant asked. He looked at me with that knowing smirk I always want to hit off him, but I couldn't deny it. I smiled back, ready to finally give myself just *one* fucking thing I wanted.

Because I had always wanted Claire Donovan.

"Yeah," I said simply.

I'd always thought she was the most gorgeous woman, but I refused to even think about starting something with her knowing she'd be going back to school in the fall. She deserved that, to enjoy college without having to worry about some older boyfriend back in his hometown, wallowing away as a mechanic and desperately trying to make ends meet.

"Who is she?" Paul asked, and looking back, I realize I shouldn't have said a goddamn thing, not with knowing the way he is. But back then, I still had the blinders on, the desperate hope that one day, my brother would grow up and snap out of it. Unfortunately, I've learned narcissism isn't something you just *grow out of*.

"That's June's college roommate," Grant said. "She comes down occasionally, hangs with Lainey and June."

Paul always could tell when my interest was piqued.

I turned to ask Grant something, to try and change the subject, but I saw it even then, the look on my brother's face. A new prize for him to win. Because any time he saw I might want something, he had to have it first.

The next morning, I went to my mom's for breakfast, not seeing either of them for the rest of the night, and a shy, smiling Claire walked in on Paul's arm. That was the first time I ever really wanted to punch my brother in the face, but Claire looked happy, and that was all I ever wanted for her, so I let it go. I let *her* go.

"He did it on purpose, you know," Grant says, snapping me back to the present.

"I don't think—" I lie.

"I do. And if you let yourself see it for what it is instead of with rose-colored glasses, you would too. I've watched it a million times over, Miles. Every time you get something, he either wants to take it from you or ruin it for you. It's been that way since you were kids."

"Look—"

"When she stopped coming down without him?"

My body stills, and Grant nods like he knows I know what he's talking about.

Claire spent nearly every weekend down here for the first two months of the season to hang out with June. She even came on weekends when Paul was in the city or out with some record exec trying to get a deal. She'd come and spend time with June and Lainey on the beach, and more often than not, Grant and I would tag along under the guise of trying to keep them in line. But really, the three of them, and occasionally Deck, were just a blast to hang out with.

And then she stopped coming out of nowhere toward the end of July. That's when June started going up to her place on the weekends instead.

"He told her that you thought she was annoying. June confessed it to me a week ago or so."

My body stills. "What?"

Grant takes a sip of his beer before he answers.

"The way I see it, he didn't like the idea of you two spending time together. Everyone knew that despite your constant bickering, you two were close. You would have fun talking, picking on each other, walking on the beach, whatever bullshit you two did. I don't think he liked it and knew exactly what to say to get her feeling self-conscious. *A master manipulator who knew her soft spots,* is what June called it."

Nausea fills me as I realize that even though she was nervous about my thinking she was annoying, she asked me for a place to stay. And then I continued to confirm that was how I felt once she was back in town, making it seem like she was irritating me at every turn.

And yet, she still made an effort. She still made that fucking list to try and convince me to give myself some time for myself, to have fun this summer. Still told me she wanted something with me, only for me to tell her I couldn't give her the time she needed from me.

You never bothered to ask, Miles, but if you had, I would have told you all I would need is to be yours.

That's what she said. Telling me straight up that she didn't need any of the millions of things my brain had convinced myself she needed in order to be mine.

She just needed *me.*

"I fucked up," I whisper.

"No shit."

"*God,* I fucked up. This whole fucking time, she'd been giving me a chance."

"Uh-huh," Grant says like he's waiting for me to continue to come to terms with my idiocy so I can move to the next step in some master plan I don't have.

But don't I? She handed it right to me.

She doesn't need some grand gesture—she just needs me to want her.

Which I do. I always did.

I stand, my stool scraping along the worn wooden planks loudly so all eyes in the bar turn to me, but I don't care. I swipe my keys and phone off the bar top and slide them into my pocket.

"Where are you going?" Grant asks, a sinking smile on his lips.

"To get my girl."

"Thank God," Benny yells as I move toward the door.

"I'll settle my tab tomorrow," I say with a wave.

"You get that girl, and we're even."

I smile at the old man, that fuck-ass pipe in his mouth, and nod.

"Got it."

And then I go to get my girl.

TWENTY-THREE

CLAIRE

"Excuse me, we're on a date, Miles," Brad says, his voice tight, but I'm not looking at him at all.

My eyes are locked on the man before me, his hand outstretched, waiting for me to grab it. Miles finally breaks his gaze from mine, shifting it to the man sitting at the table with me, and looks at him as if that's the first time he's seen him before he shakes his head.

"Not anymore. Sorry, my girl's just trying to prove a point, aren't you, baby?" he asks.

I want to be annoyed. I really, really do because is he *serious* right now? But then he steps forward, his outstretched hand moving to the back of my neck and burying his fingers in the hair there, gripping and shifting so I have to look at him, and his touch makes my brain short-circuit the way it always does.

"I don't know, I'm kind of enjoying myself," I lie, staring into his eyes with a small smile on my lips. I sense more than see Brad's chest puff out.

"See? Get out of here before I have to call someone."

"Claire, I fucked up," Miles says low, only for me to hear, looking at me, and any pretense of trying to prove a point in front of Brad falls away, and I see him.

It's not jealousy and possessiveness in his eyes.

Well, okay, yes it is, but it's not the first thing I see. The first thing I see on his face is a gut-clenching level of regret. Beneath that is a level of pleading I don't think I've ever seen from another person, much less this man who is so self-assured and so self-sufficient, it looks out of place on him.

His hand reaches down for mine, and I give it to him without a second thought, letting him pull me up to stand next to him.

"Claire, this is crazy, we—" Brad starts, but his words turn into mumbles like the Charlie Brown teacher, as Miles pulls me in tight to him, my chest pressing against his.

I want to be annoyed—hell, I *should* be annoyed—but when his head dips, pressing a barely-there kiss to the now-exposed skin between my shoulder and my neck, his mustache grazing along sensitive flesh, I can't find it in me.

A shiver runs down my spine as he whispers his next words.

"You're right: I've been too scared. I fucked up, and I want to fix it." He pulls back, looking in my eyes. "Come home with me."

"Miles, I can't go." His face falls, and I'm pretty sure Brad speaks to continue to argue in my defense, but I can barely hear it as I smile up at Miles. "I'm in heels. There's no way I can walk through that sand," I say as if that's the only reason I can't just leave a date.

He pulls back just enough to look at me, his gaze burning over my skin as it skims down my body, down my legs, landing on the four-inch sandals I slipped on.

He smiles wide.

"I can fix that" is the last thing I hear before he bends down and drapes my body over his shoulder.

Then he steps over the barrier in the sand back onto public property.

Brad stands, clearly irritated by the turn of events, but I just wiggle my fingers at him.

"Sorry, Brad! It was nice seeing you!" I shout over Miles's shoulder as he walks back toward the house.

"The fuck it was," Miles grumbles.

"Oh, hush you," I say, slapping his back. "I'm still mad at you."

"That's fine, I like you mad," he says before shifting me as he walks through the sand, never faltering in his mission to get us home, until he's holding me bridal style. Once my arms are securely around his neck, he bends down and nips at my bare shoulder.

The brush of his teeth on my skin goes directly to my clit, I swear to god.

Still, I force myself to collect my thoughts as we make it to the boardwalk because I can't afford to let my mind get jumbled. Not when he owes me a true apology and an explanation. I can't fall into this without some kind of surety that this isn't just envy taking the reins.

June suggested a fling, but that's not something I do. Not even just because I don't do flings, but because I couldn't bear to have Miles as *just a fling*.

Once we're off the sand, he sets me down, his hand moving to mine, but when we're at the front door, I step back, putting my hands to my hips and glaring at him.

"What was that, Miles?"

He looks at me with a hint of confusion. "That was me saving you from the world's most boring date."

Something in my heart deflates. Was this just another example of Miles letting his jealousy get the best of him?

"I didn't ask you to do that. I'm a big girl, Miles."

His jaw goes tight, and he takes in what seems to be a steadying breath before speaking. "I know, but I still wanted to get you out of there. You shouldn't have gone out with him. He's not good enough for you."

"Oh, what, and you are?" I cross my arms over my chest and glare at him.

He shakes his head, surprising me.

"Not even close, but unlike him, I'll keep working until I get there."

My heart skips a beat at his confession, but I shut that flickering hope down.

"Miles—" I start, startled by his honesty, but the word dies on my lips when he steps closer, backing me against the door of the house. My breath catches in my chest with the serious look on his face, with the way his head dips to look at me.

"I should have told you that the reason I didn't want you to go on this date wasn't because I fucking hate that man, which, to be totally up-front, I do. I hate him and what he's doing to this town, but I hate more that he got to touch you. That he took you out before I got the chance. I spent the last six years wanting you, and I should have told you that the reason I didn't want you to go is because I'm crazy about you, because I want you for myself, but I'm chicken shit, so I didn't. But now I don't want to be anymore, Claire. I'm just hoping it's not too late."

A lump grows in my throat as that hope blooms out of control with the sincerity in his words and the ones written all over his face.

"You want me?"

"You know I want you." He says it like it's obvious, yet it's anything but to me, so I shake my head, feeling my hair move against my skin.

Every inch of me is a crackling mess of on-edge nerves, my mind capturing every single moment for future inspection and dissecting it, as if I *know* this is a pivotal moment, for better or worse.

"No, I don't. I know you're attracted to me because, duh, just look at me," I say, going for silly and aloof because that's who I'm supposed to be, right? "I know you're stuck with me because I live here, and I flirt with you, and it annoys you—" I would continue, but I can't.

I can't because Miles has pulled me into his body, his strong, sun-kissed arm wrapping around my waist and pulling me in so tight, the breath leaves my lungs. His other hand goes to the back of my head to pull my face to his before he's kissing me.

Hard, deep, tongues and teeth clashing, and it's like he is trying to prove something to me by showing me before he gets to tell me. Or maybe like he couldn't help it, like the need to have me won.

But for a moment, I don't even care.

For a moment, I bask in the moment of being held and wanted, my hands moving to his neck to hold him against me, the same need and desperation coursing through me as he kisses me.

Finally, he pauses it, pressing his forehead to mine, our panting breaths mingling in the small space between us.

"Then let me correct that horrible fucking misstep of mine," he whispers, his lips brushing against mine with each word. "I wanted you when you were nineteen and too fucking young for me. And I wanted you when you were twenty and started flirting with me because it got a rise out of me. I wanted you when you were twenty one, and I told myself I'd go for it once you graduated so you could enjoy your carefree years without some boyfriend waiting for you in a dead-end town."

My breath catches in my chest.

"But then Paul beat me to it, and I wasn't going to step in because I thought you were happy, and that's all I wanted for you. But make no mistake about it, you were always supposed to be mine. My biggest fucking regret is not running across the beach two years ago and going for what I've always wanted—you."

My mind flashes to that Memorial Day party, when June and I looked across the beach to see Grant, Miles, and Paul. June laughed that maybe this would be the year Miles pulled his head out of his ass, but I told her there was no way he would ever be into me.

That was the night Paul came over and used all the right lines until I was putty in his hands, a feeling that carried over for too long.

I also remember the look of pain and regret I thought I saw flashing in Miles's eyes the next morning.

"Oh my god," I whisper, eyes wide.

"I never hated you flirting with me, never thought it was annoying: I was mad that I wouldn't let myself act on it. I didn't want you changing your life for some idiot mechanic in a small town waiting at home at night for you to call. I want you so fucking bad, I can't think straight. I go to work and I wonder what you're doing. When I come home and you're not there, the house feels empty. Seeing you at my kitchen table eating your shit cereal that's going to rot your teeth out makes my fucking morning. When I think about you leaving in the fall, I get downright depressed. You think I think you're childish and flighty, but in truth, I envy how you never care what anyone thinks, so long as it makes you happy. I wish I could be like that. I wish I could be like you, Claire, but the truth is, I'd much rather *have* you."

"Oh," I whisper, heart pounding and overwhelmed with what he's saying.

"So here's what I have to know: are you able to forgive me? Can you get over my being so fucking blinded by what *I* thought *you* needed that I almost let you walk away from me? Or did I come to my senses in time to not lose you?"

I stand there, pinned between the door and his body, the warm summer air ghosting along my skin as his big towering body pins me in place, his brown eyes staring me down, and for the first time, I see there's nothing there: no walls, no denial, no worries and concerns. Just pure fucking longing and need and something else under there that's been simmering for years that I don't think either of us would be ready to name.

Some sane part of my mind warns me he might change his mind in the morning. That this might just be the consequence of him seeing me with another man. It wouldn't be the first time we took one step forward and three steps back, after all.

But like I always do, I trust my gut and decide to jump.

"It's not too late."

TWENTY-FOUR

CLAIRE

I barely even get that final word out when his lips are on mine, and instantly, I know this is different. There's no hesitation, no hint of *should we be doing this*. Just his lips on mine, my hands pulling him tighter so I can get him as close as feasibly possible.

One hand moves to my hip, tugging me in closer, and the other fumbles behind me on the doorknob, attempting to turn it as he continues to kiss me. I let out a giggle as the door opens, stumbling back, but he catches me, a similar smile on his own lips.

We move through the door, and as soon as we're inside, he slams it closed with my back, pressing me there and grinding into me. My lips move to his neck as he locks the door behind us before the hand not holding my ass moves to my chin, redirecting me to his lips, where he kisses me again.

It's heaven, and it's heated, and it's everything I knew this moment would be if we ever managed to finally get here. His lips start to move down my neck, the scrape of his mustache sending more heat ricocheting through me as he nips and sucks down the column of my neck. My fingers twine in his hair as he trails kisses down to my clavicle, his tongue running along the bone there.

"Miles," I whisper, and I feel his smile against my skin more than I see it. "I need you." He lets out a pleasure-filled breath, the heat of it coasting along my skin as his fingers play at the hem of my tank. "Please." I don't even know what I'm asking for, but I'll take whatever he will give me.

He tugs the pretty tank top I wore on my date up, revealing my breasts in a bra, and he audibly groans, like the sight alone has done him in. It sends a rush of wet between my legs as his thick finger grazes along the seam of my bra, my breath hitching.

"Yes," I whisper, afraid that if I speak anything else aloud, I'll ruin the moment.

"So fucking pretty," he groans, leaning forward from where he's now on one knee to press a kiss to one swell.

"Do you want me to—" I'll do anything right now if he takes this further. Absolutely *anything*.

"No, no. I've been dreaming about unwrapping you for years, Claire. Let me have this." I can't help but let out a small laugh at that, but it's swallowed by a moan when he tugs one bra cup down and wraps his lips around my nipple.

He tongues the needy bud, and my chest arches into him, one of his hands going to the bare skin of my back to hold me there. His teeth graze along them before he pulls back, then sends a cool shot of air from parted lips to coast over the nipple.

"Oh, god," I groan, my hand on the back of his neck moving to get him closer. A deep chuckle leaves his lips when he doesn't budge.

"Oh, this is going to be fun," he says low, almost as if he's talking to himself.

"Miles," I say, but his name gets caught in my throat when he moves to the next breast, pulling the cup down and sucking the nipple into his mouth in the same moment. "Ahh!" I pull his head further into me, and he bites down on my nipple, more wetness soaking my already ruined panties.

As he sucks, his hand moves up my calf to my inner thigh beneath my skirt. I attempt to subtly shift my legs wider, needing more, needing everything. He chuckles against my breast, and I groan at the vibration, my hips rocking forward to try and get some kind of relief.

His hand begins brushing along the sensitive skin of my upper thighs before his mouth shifts to the other nipple again. I let out a groan, and he looks up at me.

The man is smiling, clearly finding satisfaction in my frustration.

"What do you want, baby?"

"I want you to touch me." I've never been coy about sex: why should I be? But whatever vein of bashfulness is out the window now: I'm certainly not going to be shy with the man I've been dreaming about for years.

"Like this?" he asks, thumb grazing slightly higher on my thigh, but still not where I want it. I shake my head, frustrated. He smiles. "Like this?" His voice is huskier now, as his thumb moves slightly inward, barely brushing a line across my underwear. I shake my head again, my breathing growing even more shallow.

His thumb grazes along the fabric over my swollen clit, and even though it's a gentle graze—barely even a caress—I gasp before eagerly nodding.

"Yes," I breathe.

"God, I can feel how wet you are for me already."

"Please," I beg.

His thumb presses a bit firmer this time, pressing along my soaked slit and then up to my clit. I groan, my hips bucking at the touch. His mouth descends on my nipple again, and I shriek as pleasure pulses through me.

But it's not enough.

It's so much, and it's so good, but it's *not enough*. He could do this all day, the most perfect torture, and it wouldn't be enough: I wouldn't fall. And somehow, I know he'd find joy in keeping me on this teetering edge all night.

"Miles, I need more," I whisper.

His eyes look up and his mouth unlatches, and that smile appears again before he says, "Okay."

And then he's moving.

He's pushing my skirt up my hips, and without even thinking, I grab eagerly at the hem to hold it in place as his fingers tuck under my underwear at my hips. He tugs them down, and a deep, satisfying groan leaves his lips when he sees me bared to him, a gleam in his eyes as his thumb traces the same path as before, but on heated skin.

"What are you doing?" I ask with a laugh, but his face is so serious, it fades from my lips quickly.

"I told you I would get on my knees for you."

"Oh."

His thumb brushes over my clit, and I moan, my head hitting the wall with a light thud. He runs it back and forth, then in circles over my swollen clit before my hips chase more. I should have known this is how things would be, unending teasing and torture, because that's us after all, isn't it?

He slides his thumb into me, and all thoughts leave my mind. My pussy tightens around it as I let out a shocked gasp. Looking down at him, he's smiling wide, taking in every response I give and finding pleasure in it. Then his head descends, his lips moving to my clit.

"Wait, wait, wait," I say, and instantly, he stops, looking up at me. I quietly groan at how he looks on his knees before me, my fingers gripping my skirt.

"What's wrong? Do you want to stop?" His face is a mask of panic, worried he's overstepping.

I shake my head, a smile spreading over my lips. "Shirt off. The visual will be so much better."

He stares at me for a long moment before he lets out a loud, deep laugh, and god, I hope it's always like this with us: this ease, this chemistry. It's a relief to see it still exists even like this.

He obliges, taking his shirt off in one smooth tug and tossing it to the ground. I groan when I see his toned and muscled shoulders I've daydreamed about far too many times.

"Better now?" he asks like I'm inconveniencing him, a hand moving to my calf to lift my leg to his shoulder so I'm spread before him.

"You can proceed," I nod.

He laughs, and I smile, but it's cut short by my moans when he does, in fact, proceed. He licks me from entrance to clit, wrapping his lips around my clit before he sucks.

"Oh, god."

When he pulls back, his eyelids are drooped, his face enamored like he's actually in some form of heaven.

"I've been such a fucking idiot, Claire," he says against me, before he drags his flattened tongue up over my pussy, sending shockwaves through me. "Let me make it up to you." A hand moves to my calf, gripping and lifting until my heel is resting on his shoulder, opening myself wide before his mouth moves back to me.

My hips start to gyrate in a rhythm of their own, as I try and get more from him, as a finger slides into me and he laps at my clit. I can feel the ball of tension, of all-consuming pleasure, swirling in my belly, folding in on itself and multiplying as he starts to suck on my clit, as he adds another finger inside me, curling them to press on the spot no one but myself has ever touched.

My eyes drift shut, the feeling too overwhelming, but just as I do, he pulls away, his fingers still fucking me.

"No, no," he says, and when I open my eyes to look down at him, he's looking at me intensely. "Eyes on me. I want to see you fall apart. Want you to watch me finally fucking worship this cunt."

I tighten around the fingers buried in me at his words, and he feels it, his own eyes drifting shut as that brings *him* pleasure, too. Before I can say another thing, his mouth descends on me once more. Sucking on my clit, seemingly on a mission now, his eyes are locked on mine as I stare down my body at him. My orgasm builds back quickly, and I know I can't put it off a moment longer, not even to bask in the beauty of him like this for another moment.

"Fuck, fuck, fuck," I grit out. When his teeth graze along my clit,

I detonate, yelling as I do, and even though I want to let it wash away all of my senses, I keep my eyes locked on Miles as he finger fucks me and licks up every drop of my orgasm.

I'm still quaking as his fingers slip out of me, and I'm grateful when that hand moves to my waist to hold me steady, his wet fingers resting on my heated skin.

Slowly, he stands, eyes still on mine, adjusting his hard cock in his shorts. "Good?" I wipe my thumb along his mustache, the hair there wet with me. I moan at that, a thought I've had way too many times to be appropriate this summer, a fantasy I'm now living.

I shake my head at him.

"No?" he asks, confused.

"No, I need you to fuck me. Then I'll be good."

He smiles wider.

"God, you're fucking perfect for me," he says.

I barely have time to bask in the statement before his hands grip my ass and he lifts me. My skirt is still bunched at my waist, so I wrap my legs around him, my wet core pressed against his bare stomach, and we both groan at the way it feels. I just came, but somehow, the need to come again is almost worse.

It's consuming everything, and this need to have him inside of me, fucking me, filling me with his cum...I need it.

My hands go around his neck, and he smiles, pressing his lips to mine again. Instantly, with the taste of me on his lips, my back arches into him, my arms pulling him tighter to me, my lips sucking at his. It's feral and needy, and my hips rock against him with need.

"Your room or mine?" he pants when we manage to break the kiss, and I smile wide.

"Yours." Miles wastes no time at all, climbing the stairs as I pepper kisses on every inch of his skin I can reach, my hands grazing up and down his back to memorize the muscles there, to feel his warm skin, and commit it to memory. Before I know it, we're stepping through the entryway of his room, and he's tossing me onto the bed. I undress quickly, tugging off my tank top and bra at the same time, then sliding off my skirt before lying back and watching him.

"Are you on the pill?" he asks, but I can't really hear his words. Not as he's sliding down his shorts and underwear in one smooth movement, leaving him naked before me and...

Oh. My. God.

I've seen Miles in low-slung shorts and even glimpses in his tight boxer briefs before, but I've never seen him like this.

He's a fucking god. All sun-kissed skin and toned abs, shoulders so broad it almost feels comical, strong arms—

"Claire," he says, grabbing my attention.

I move my eyes from his long, thick cock and to his face, which is smiling with pride. "Huh?"

His smile spreads into a grin.

"Are you on the pill?" I have to work hard to understand the question before I nod. "I was tested six months ago," he continues, "and everything came back normal. I haven't been with anyone since."

As if without meaning to, his hand moves to his cock, squeezing and stroking once, and my jaw drops. I want to watch that: him jacking off while watching me. My pussy clenches at the mental image I've made, filling in gaps and creating an entire scene ending in him coming on me, and I lick my lips.

"Claire," he repeats, but there's humor in the words. I move my gaze back to him with more difficulty this time. "Can I fuck you without a condom?"

That.

That's what I want. That's *definitely* what I want.

"I had my annual not too long ago. All clear." I smile again and lose all pretense of looking at his face, going back to focus on his cock.

His hand is slowly pumping now, and my hand starts to creep between my legs, with a mind of its own. He lets out a deep, pained groan as he starts to move, his cock bobbing with each step he takes toward me until he's standing at the foot of the bed. His hand pumps himself one last time; the tip is red and weeping with need before he puts a knee on the bed. I'm on one elbow, one hand gently playing between my legs as I watch him approach with heated anticipation.

"Lay back, baby," he says softly as he climbs onto the bed, his body sliding over mine, and I do as he asks, dropping from my elbows, and then he's face-to-face with me.

I expect the same frantic energy, the same intense need and desire. I expect him to push me back, to slam into me, to do... something.

But it all changes. The way he moves, that look in his eyes, the way his fingers graze along the skin of my arm. Gone is the frantic energy, the need, moving as if this would disappear in a moment, and in its place is...reverence.

Such sweet, all-consuming reverence and longing, it makes my heart skip a beat, makes my body shift softly toward him, my hand moving up to cup his jaw and look into his eyes.

Suddenly, it's me and Miles and nothing else. Gone are our history and location and bills and future. It's just us, right here, right now. He notches the head of his thick cock into my entrance, and my eyes sink shut, my breathing turning labored with anticipation.

"No," he says, low and gravelly. "No." My eyes open, and his hand moves off the bed next to me and rests on my face as he holds himself up with just one strong arm. "You're going to look at me the first time I sink into you."

"Miles," I moan, my hips shifting to get him deeper, to push him to fill me.

"The first time I give into this, when I finally admit to what you've known for some time, you're going to watch it take over me. Watch me become yours, for good."

"Miles," I whisper again, this time without the irritated pleasure, instead filled with the understanding that Miles is *mine*. I fight the urge to cry, but that's suddenly gone as he slides into me, as his thick shaft stretches me in the most perfect way, as inch by inch, he fills me.

Once he's fully seated in me, he stops, his eyes still on mine and open and filled with everything I wanted to see a week ago. Everything I saw this morning, but he wouldn't admit to. Desire and acceptance and friendship and a million other things I don't have the time or presence of mind to identify.

"This changes everything," I whisper because I won't let him play with me that way. "This changes everything, Miles."

"Good," he says, then he pulls back, dragging along swollen and sensitive flesh before slamming back in. I moan loudly, a leg wrapping around his hips as he slides out again and thrusts back in. "I want it to."

"Oh, god," I breathe as his cock slides against sensitive nerves, sending a bolt of ecstasy straight to my core, that pleasure swirling as it does. It's too much. It's too good. It's too consuming, I think it might break me. I hold on to his back, and he pounds into me, my nails biting as I try to hold onto reality.

"I know," he says through gritted teeth. "Me too."

Because he feels it too. That perfect rightness, the total and complete change, the knowledge that nothing will ever be this good, this right. This is me and Miles, and the rest will fall into place, so long as we have this.

Us.

"I'm going to come," I murmur, a panic flitting over me at the thought. My breaths come in pants as my hips move up with each slam inward, and he adds a grind now, friction to my clit as he does.

"Good, take me with you, baby."

I don't know if it's the permission or the acceptance or the mere thought that my orgasm will trigger one of his own, but with his words, my back bows, my cunt tightens around him, and my head falls back as I scream his name.

I come, and I come, and somewhere in my distant consciousness, I feel his body tighten, feel him go somehow deeper still, and feel him spill into me, groaning my name into my neck as he comes inside me.

And with it, I know I am ruined for any other man.

TWENTY-FIVE

CLAIRE

Miles stays on top of me for long minutes, both of our breathing evening out before he gently rolls off. His feet quietly hit the floor, and he pads to the bathroom when I hear the sink going.

I lay on his bed, trying to gather the courage to get up as well, trying to not overthink things too much, but he returns before I can. Without a word, he moves to me and then something warm moves between my legs.

A washcloth.

Miles is cleaning me with a warm washcloth after he just fucked me to oblivion. I keep my eyes to the ceiling, trying to rectify this with the version of Miles I know before he's done, disappearing into the bathroom once more.

Slowly, I sit up, pulling the covers that are haphazardly thrown off the bed up to cover myself as the ceiling fan above us runs slowly, sending a cool breeze along my body, and finally, I take in his room. He's lived here for years from what he's told me, but it's so sparsely decorated, you'd think he just moved in recently. The rest of the house is the same, which is confusing to me since, at the very least, you'd think it would be filled with knickknacks from his grandmother. While there are a handful strewn about, it's not a house that was lived in for any stretch of time with love and laughter.

Without my permission, my mind starts to move along the walls, putting in photos, furniture, or decorations I think would fit Miles's personality. I saw a giant old poster of the original map of Seaside Point while thrifting with June recently that, in the right frame, would look stellar over his bed.

Eventually, he reenters the room, a pair of shorts riding low on his hips, no visible underwear to be found. He has my water bottle in hand and a glass of water for himself. My heart skips a beat at the sight. He smiles at me, and the look of it warms me to my core as I sit up.

"I brought you Margo." I smile at his use of the silly name I gave my water bottle, putting my hands out to grab it because all of that did, in fact, make me thirsty.

Before he gives it to me, though, he gently presses his lips to mine, sweetly, melting me on the spot.

"Thank you," I whisper as he sets his water on the bedside table and then climbs into bed next to me, tugging and shifting me until his back is to the headboard, my back against his chest, nestled between his legs. Finally, he reaches down, grabbing something from his pocket: a plastic baggie he must have filled with different cereals, handing it to me. He even reaches in, grabbing a few and popping them into his mouth.

"Food *and* my emotional support water bottle?" I ask with a silly giggle, looking over my shoulder at him. "You give good boyfriend, Miles Miller." He chokes on the cereal, and I smile. "Oh, hit a nerve, did I?" He coughs once, reaching for his water, and suddenly, my nerves kick up. "We don't have to—I didn't mean—I'm not saying—" I start a few different sentences but can't seem to find the right words to finish a single one because the truth is, I want Miles to be my boyfriend, and the thought that I may have just jumped into this without any kind of thought makes me feel sick.

In the heat of the moment, I told Miles this changes everything, and I meant it: I won't go back to flirting and teasing that goes nowhere. I'm happy to keep the harmless arguing because I think that could end pretty entertainingly for both of us, but I'm not going back to *just friends*.

But as seems to be Miles's way, he puts that fear to rest instantly, setting his water to the side and using a hand on my chin to keep me looking at him over my shoulder. "You said everything changes, and you were right, Claire. I've spent far too long pretending you aren't everything to me, and I'm not going back to that, especially not now that I've had you."

Relief washes through me and with it, emotions. My mind runs over a dozen other examples of how this is turning into something more.

I should be nervous about that, since I was only supposed to be here until September, but I've never lived by anyone else's schedule, much less my own. Maybe this is me finding my place, finding my people.

I fucking *love* Seaside Point and the people here. I could easily find myself settling into everyday life here.

With Miles.

It's been a long night and a long summer and, honestly, a long year, and all of it rushes over me at the same time, emotions bubbling to the surface.

"Hey," he says as I sniffle. "Are you crying?" He shifts me in his lap so my head rests on his chest, both of his arms wrapping around me.

"I'm a crier. Get over it." A blush burns over my cheeks, the tears spilling up as I turn away from him with embarrassment.

"No, no, no," he says, a hand moving to my chin that I've buried into his chest and forcing me to look at him. "I like it." His thumb brushes over my cheek, swiping away one of the wet tracks.

"You like that I'm a crybaby?"

He smiles at that, the wide, carefree one I like most of all.

"I like everything about you, Claire. But mostly, I like that you don't hide things, don't hold them in. You get a feeling, and you feel it. Not many people do that."

"Like you?"

"Like me," he agrees softly.

A beat passes, and I lift my hand, resting it on his cheek and looking over his face.

"What are you keeping in, Miles?" I whisper, my thumb brushing over his mustache. I liked it before, but now that I felt it scraping between my legs while he ate me out, I like it even more. I fight the shiver that wants to roll through me because this is *not* the time.

"I kept how much you affected me in for a while," he says, and I let out a laugh.

"Sorry to tell you, bud, but you didn't really do that too well. I knew I affected you, just not that you were totally obsessed with me." I'm smiling as his eyes go softer.

"The first time I saw you," he whispers, and my body stills. "The first time I saw you, I knew I wanted you." I let out a slow breath in an effort to still my heart, but it doesn't work. "You came with June to some party, and Grant dragged me along because he wanted to make sure she didn't drink, since she was underage."

"We totally did," I confess. "We pregamed before we went, and we got so sick the next day." I choose not to tell him Deck got us the liquor or that he was our "supplier" every summer until we turned twenty-one.

He smiles and nods. "We know, trust me. But I remember sitting on the beach, and there was this big bonfire. You guys were on the other side, and I heard this ringing laugh—your laugh—and I knew I wanted to find you."

"It was so loud that night," I whisper, remembering the music and people talking. It was some kind of rec department event on the beach.

He shrugs, a smile on his lips as a rough thumb moves over the apple of my cheek.

"I've always been zeroed in on you, I guess. I spotted you, saw you with June, and tipped my chin to ask Grant who his sister was talking to. He told me it was the infamous Claire, the girl she got into trouble with at school." I smile wider, loving that my reputation preceded me, even then. "You were so fucking pretty and so happy and so...*young*. I told myself if you were still around once you were done with school and had some time to figure out what you wanted out of life, I'd shoot my shot. But then..." He doesn't have to finish his thought, but he does it anyway. "Paul went after you."

Dread fills my stomach at the thought that I could have been with Miles all this time, that I could have had him, but...

"I'm glad he did."

"Excuse me?" I ask with a laugh.

"This way..." He uses a hand to push my hair back. "This is the way it was supposed to be. I needed time; you needed time. We needed...the past two months."

"Of you hating me?"

"Of me coming to terms with how crazy I am for you," he says, confidently.

"Are you crazy for me, Mr. Miller?"

His thumb moves along my jaw before leaning in.

"Wildly," he whispers against my lips.

"Who knew you were such a romantic?"

"You know what? I think you did, Claire. I think you knew all along, and you were just waiting for me to catch up. If you didn't, I don't think you would have been so patient with me." I smile up at him, realizing he might just be right. "So what now?"

"What now?" I ask, my heart thumping as I bite my lip because I just had the best sex of my life and I would love to do it again and again, but...

"Well...you called me your boyfriend."

A blush creeps up on my cheeks at the reminder.

"I was talking figuratively," I lie. "Because you were doing boyfriend things. But you never asked me to *be* your girlfriend."

He looks down at me with a smile. "I'm thirty-one, Claire. I don't think you do that when you're thirty-one."

I raise my eyebrow at him accusingly. "So, what? I'm supposed to just go around assuming I know where we stand just because you're old? That doesn't sound very fair."

He moves his fingers on my side, tickling me and making me giggle. I shift away from him, but he holds me tight.

"Are you saying I have to ask you out?"

"I mean..." Before I can continue, he rolls me over on the bed, hovering over me, hands on either side of my head and a wide grin on his lips.

Fuck, he's handsome.

Too fucking handsome, especially since he *knows* I find him to be so.

"Claire Sophia Donovan," he whispers, and I wonder when he learned my middle name. "Will you be my girlfriend?"

I move a hand up his chest, the coarse hair there tickling at my fingers before I slide them over his shoulders and twine my fingers around his neck.

"Because you're crazy about me?"

"Because I'm crazy about you, and the idea of everyone not knowing exactly what we are, including you, makes me a bit feral. Because I want you to introduce me to people as your boyfriend, because I want to walk into the Seabreeze by your side and have everyone in this town know you're mine and to keep their fucking hands off of you."

"I think I like when you get all possessive," I admit in a whisper.

He smiles, somehow wider. "Good, because it's how I always feel about you." His lips move, kissing my neck, his mustache scraping along the delicate skin. "You haven't answered me, Claire."

"What was the question?"

"Will you be my girlfriend?"

My heart skips a beat, and even though I've been secretly dying for this for years, I shrug. "I don't know, you haven't really given me a compelling argument for why I should say yes."

"A compelling argument, huh?" he asks, his lips moving to my collarbone.

"Yeah," I say, breathy now. His lips shift again, moving to my nipple and sucking deep. My back arches off the bed as he does.

"Then let me plead my case." His lips move down my belly, and he does, in fact, plead his case.

At the end, before we fall asleep after round two, I say yes to being Miles Miller's girlfriend.

TWENTY-SIX

MILES

The next morning, I wake up before Claire to find her wrapped around me, her head on my chest, and an overwhelming sense of relief. After years of wanting this exact moment and not letting myself have it, it's even better than I expected.

Slipping out of bed, I use the bathroom and shuffle down the stairs, checking the weather and water temperature before I decide this is the perfect morning for what I have in mind. Next, I check if her coffee is in the fridge since I know there's no way I'm getting her out of the house early if we don't have coffee. We do, thankfully, so I quickly make her a to-go one and refill Margo, grabbing a few things and tossing them into a bag before I move back upstairs.

She's in the same position but curled around my pillow like she realized I wasn't there and needed a replacement. Too fucking sweet. I'm almost tempted to scrap this whole idea when she lets out a sigh and snuggles in deeper, but instead, I grab the bottom of the blanket and tug until it's on the floor.

Once again, I almost abandon my plan, seeing her naked body curled into my bed, a leg hitched up on the pillow, and I can see her pussy again.

Nope, not now, Miller, I tell myself. *She wants boyfriend things; we're giving her boyfriend things.*

Except right now, she's glaring at me in the most adorable way.

"What are you doing?" she asks as I tug on her arm. She looks toward the window where the curtains are cracked and gets even more skeptical. "It's still dark?"

"Surprise," I say, whispering. I feel stupid acting as if I need to be quiet so I don't wake someone, but it's just the two of us here. And, of course, half a dozen hermit crabs.

"I know this thing with us just got official and all, but you should know I don't do extra early mornings." She glares at me with more venom than one person should be able to muster first thing in the morning, and even though I should hide it, I let out a laugh.

"You don't say."

Her glare intensifies. "Especially when I don't get the details of why I'm so rudely dragged out of bed."

"We're going to knock something off your list," I say.

"What?" She blinks a few times, looking adorable.

"We're doing something on your list. You're not working today; I'm not working today. As much as I'd love to spend the day in bed with you, let's go. I know a place."

"A place? What kind of place?"

"Do you have to question me on absolutely everything I ask of you?" I reach out, placing a hand on her waist and pulling her into me. I can't help but smile down at her as she melds her body into mine. I couldn't tell you the last time I felt this way: light and airy and just...content in the world, like this piece I didn't realize I was looking for finally snapped into place.

"It makes life a whole lot more interesting if I do," she whispers, and then I dip to press my lips to hers. Her hand slides up my back, tangling in the hair at the back of my neck. I break it before either of us gets any ideas since we're on a bit of a deadline.

"You're sure right on that," I whisper against her lips, then tug her out of bed to get on our way.

We drive to a stretch of the beach that's on the very edge of the town, then climb up onto the jetty before walking down to the very edge of it. The ocean is calm this morning, the low tide just barely lapping at the dark rocks, working in my favor. The sky is starting to lighten up, and I set out a towel on the ground for Claire to sit on, then hand her a coffee and a cereal bar.

"I was going to do the whole nine, but I figured after this we could go to Seaside Coffee."

"But... your mom..."

"Hate to tell you, babe, but if my mom finds out I finally got the nerve to give this a shot, we're really fucking in for it."

"What?" she asks, an eyebrow raised at me.

"My mom was the first one to call me out for not telling her you were living with me. That day with the cereal boxes?" She nods. "I went to the coffee shop, and she gave me a talking to. She's the one who helped me see what an ass I was being."

Claire gives me that bright smile I love so much. "You *were* being an ass."

"Yeah, I was being stubborn," I whisper, pushing back her blonde locks that are being blown around by the breeze. "But I finally came around to common sense." She smiles wider then and nods.

"Thank God for that. Took you long enough."

"Yeah," I whisper. "Thank God." I turn for a second, scanning the ocean, almost forgetting why we're here, and that's when I see it. I turn her in the direction I'm looking.

"Right there," I say, pointing out into the distance. The sun is starting to lighten now, reflecting off the ocean.

"Right where?" she asks, the forms dipping back beneath the ocean.

"Just wait. You'll see it." She looks at me skeptically before I turn her face back toward the ocean. For a moment, I think we may have missed the chance, but then—

"Oh my god," she whispers, eyes wide. Fins break the water, four or five of them, and even though they're pretty far out, it's clear enough to see what it is: dolphins.

I always wanted to see dolphins, she told me the second day she was in my house. I remember that morning thinking that in July, when the water is warm, I should take her to the jetty and show her, but also thinking it would be too intimate.

All I want with Claire is intimacy now.

"This time of year, I almost always see them if I come out this early. Don't know what it is about this time, but they come over and say hi."

"Oh my god," she whispers again as the dolphins go under again before reappearing a bit closer. "Look at them!" She claps quietly, excited, and I smile in return.

"I think there's a baby," I say.

"Oh my god," she whispers, her voice strained, and when I look at her, I see my soft girl's eyes watering.

"Are you going to cry?"

"No," she bites out.

"You're a liar."

"Shut up and let me watch the dolphins," she says.

I brush my thumb along her cheek where a single tear falls, then let her watch the dolphins.

I don't watch the dolphins.

I watch her. I watch every possible emotion under the sun cross her face: excitement, joy, and awe. I take it in, a wash of warm, calm falling over me.

It's then that I realize I'm falling for Claire Donovan, and I'll do whatever I have to do to keep her at my side.

When the dolphins disappear, I grab her hand, and we make our way down the shoreline, her eyes on the sand looking for shells. It's something we've done a million times before, usually with June chatting away or as I throw a ball with Grant, but this time, we're walking down the shore hand in hand, and a sense of peace comes over me.

She feels it too, I know, because she says, "I always loved it here, Seaside Point."

"Mmm," I say, squeezing her hand but letting her guide the conversation.

"Sometimes I look back, wondering why I put up with Paul for so long." I force myself not to tense up, knowing that he is a part of her history neither of us can erase, and I have to be okay with that. "It's because I love this place."

Another beat passes as she watches the sand, but I know she's not shell hunting. She's lost in her memories.

"When I look back on it, the only moments in our relationship when I was *really* happy were spent down here, and sometimes, I wonder if maybe I just loved being here more, you know? Like, I loved Seaside Point so much, and being with him meant having another excuse to spend time here." She shakes her head and lets out a small, self-deprecating laugh. "That makes me sound like a bad person, I know, only wanting to be with someone because of where they live."

"It doesn't," I say quickly.

"No?" she asks, hopeful as she looks up at me.

I pause our steps and move closer to her, my hand moving to her chin.

"No. Not at all," I whisper. "There is no one in this world who knows better how amazing this place is than me. And I have to think that you wanting to be here, me wanting to stay here, June living here and being your roommate was always some thread keeping us together."

I brush a thumb over her cheekbone, and she leans into my palm.

"Fate kept giving us a million chances, and we were both too stubborn or too blind to see them." Then her face moves to a bit of a glare, and I laugh. "Okay, *I* was too stubborn and blind to see them. But now it's startlingly clear, and I'm not letting you go."

A long moment passes as we stand like that, her hand lifting to hold my own cheek, her thumb brushing over my mustache the way she always does, the way I love, before she speaks.

"Promise?" I almost don't hear the whisper over the waves, but when I do, I wrap my arm around her waist and pull her in close.

"Promise," I whisper against her lips, then kiss her, sealing the deal.

"There," I say a bit later, tipping my chin toward the sand as Claire searches at her feet for the perfect shell.

Her gaze follows mine before she sees it there, wet and with a few pieces of sand on it, but perfectly together. A scalloped seashell. She bends to inspect it and then grabs it, stepping into the water to rinse it off before turning back with a wide smile on her lips.

"It's perfect," she says, walking back to me. "Look at it! The colors are so pretty." She looks up at me with a happy grin, and I remember all of the times this exact moment has happened over the years: the times we'd wander off, me accompanying her while she scours the shoreline for shells, yammering away while I listen silently, then handing them off to me for safekeeping as she found them.

But now she's mine.

I pull her in close then, pressing my lips to hers in a firm kiss before breaking it.

"I've always wanted to do that."

"What?" she asks, looking confused.

"You always look so happy, finding a shell. You'd smile at me, and every time, I'd have to fight the urge to just..." I press my lips to hers again, and she smiles against mine. It feels like accomplishing some grand life goal, being able to kiss her whenever I want, anytime she directs that bright smile at me.

"You were always my lucky charm," she whispers, and I smile wide, knowing this to be true.

"I'll do it for as long as you allow me." Her stomach growls, and I let out a loud laugh. "But maybe we head back to the car and get you some breakfast. I think you're going to need the energy later." I tug her in closer, then nip at her ear, and she giggles, free and sweet, and again, my heart seems to expand in my chest.

"Energy, huh?" she asks with an amused raised brow.

"Oh, yeah."

A blush burns on her cheeks, but without a word, she takes my hand and turns around back toward the car. We're walking past a life-guard stand when, as is her way, Claire shocks me. You'd think I'd be pretty prepared for it by now, but I don't think I'll ever be prepared for Claire's version of wild intrusive thoughts.

"We should fuck on the beach," she says with a sigh.

"What?" I ask with a laugh, and she turns to look at me.

"We should fuck on the beach. That would be hot."

"There would be sand everywhere, Claire. Trust me."

She gasps, a hand going to her chest. "Miles Miller, are you telling me you've done this before?"

I roll my eyes, but I feel a blush burning. "No, but I grew up here. Everyone has tried it. I tried once and decided pretty soon that it was a terrible idea."

Her arms are crossed on her chest and somehow, despite being nearly a foot shorter than me, she looks down her nose at me.

"You tried to fuck someone on the beach but won't fuck *me* on the beach?"

I let out a laugh and pull her into me, although she tries to step away. I press my lips to hers, and her body eases, her arms moving around my neck as she deepens it.

When I pull away, I press my forehead to hers,. "I won't because it wouldn't be good for you."

"We could bring a towel," she whispers.

"That won't stop the sand."

She bites her lip, and I see it then, her stubbornness easing in. "What if we were up high?"

"Claire—"

"There's no sand on the lifeguard chair."

I let out a loud laugh and shake my head. "I feel like you could lose your job for that."

"It would be nighttime, *obviously*. And honestly, you've met Helen. She'd probably go on some kind of rampage about sexual freedom and tell me new positions to try."

I grimace, knowing she's probably right. "Even more reason not to do it."

"God, you're so boring," she says, and I smile.

"One of us has to be," I say, spotting my truck in the distance.

"I like that," she whispers, her stubbornness seemingly to have been forgotten.

"What?"

"You being the serious one who uses logic, me being the chaos gremlin I am." I smile, using a hand to push her hair back.

"Yeah?"

"Yeah. We're a good match."

TWENTY-SEVEN

CLAIRE

"So," Miles starts, seemingly nervous even though he's literally been inside me more times than I can count in the past week. It's like we're both making up for years of lost time, and if I'm being honest, that debt is still not paid. My body craves his every waking moment. "One car?"

I stare at him for a silent moment before I burst into laughter. He stares at me, unentertained, while I continue laughing before I finally settle down.

Today is the annual summer celebration, but my first time attending. According to Miles, the crew has done this for as long as he can remember, with everyone meeting up at the bay beach behind the Seabreeze and enjoying a delayed celebration, since almost every local in Seaside Point works on the actual fourth.

It's also our first outing as a couple.

"Yeah, Miles. One car should do the trick," I say with a smile, pressing a kiss to his lips before we make our way to his truck.

"Finally," Deck says, the first to spot us when we walk to the cove hand in hand, a sigh of relief leaving his lips. I look up at Miles, whose brows are furrowed in confusion, then start laughing again, loud.

"What did I miss?" he asks me low, and I smile, shifting to my tiptoes and pressing a kiss to his cheek.

That makes Deck hoot louder, and Lainey and June join in too. Grant just shakes his head with a smile. I look over to where Miles's mom is sitting at a picnic table with Helen, both of whom give me a thumbs up. Benny sits in a lawn chair, so tan by now I worry his skin might crack, a faded trucker hat on and that ever-present pipe between his teeth.

"It happened," Lainey says, cheering.

Although they know since I've texted both of them a million details, I've been so busy with work, so I haven't actually seen them since Miles and I got together. When I look at Miles, he somehow looks even more nervous and anxious. It takes everything in me not to laugh at him again. The poor man is so confused.

"You guys finally got together!" Lainey adds, and it clicks for him, a deep blush burning over his cheeks.

"Does *everyone* know we..." he starts.

"Yup," Deck says, coming over to us and slapping a hand on Miles's shoulder. "Everyone knows you banged your brother's ex."

Miles pushes him away, though it's half-hearted, and Deck stumbles away.

"Ew, Deck, do you have to be so...gross?" June asks with a cringe.

"Is that not what happened? You were just cheering for it," he says, confused.

"We're cheering because they're *together*, not because they fucked," Lainey says.

"His mother is here," June adds, though Mrs. Miller doesn't seem put off at all. If anything, she seems more excited than Deck does.

"Whatever. I'm just glad we don't have to see Miles moping around, pretending he's not crazy for Claire anymore," Grant says.

"Same," Deck says, sitting down at a table.

"Oh, for sure," Lainey says.

"You can say that again," June adds.

"So, everyone knew I was into her?" Miles asks, embarrassed, running a hand over his head.

"Yeah, honey," I say gently, patting his shoulder.

"God, I fucking hate small towns," he grumbles, then lets go of my hand and moves toward the cooler sitting in the shade. "You want anything?"

I shake my head, but June and Lainey are at my side before I speak.

"We have a *lot* to talk about," June says, grabbing my hand and tugging me toward the other side of the small beach for a much-needed gossip session. I hesitate, but when I look over my shoulder, Miles is cracking open a beer and cheers-ing with Grant. He winks at me, then waves me off, so I allow myself to be dragged away to spill everything to my friends.

"Hey, Blondie, you ever fished before?" Deck asks two hours later.

It's long past my filling Lainey and June in, which included many muffled squeals and laughs, and past when Miles's mom, who insisted I start calling her Sarah, forced me to eat the biggest plate filled with picnic food known to man.

Now I'm sitting on a fold-out beach chair next to Benny, previously watching Miles and Grant toss a football back and forth, though now we're all accumulating on the dock, arguing over who knows what.

I smile wide and shake my head. "No, my dad and brother do, but normally, I'd much rather catch a tan than deal with gross worms and stinky bait."

He puts a hand out, and I grab it, letting him tug me up as he puts an arm around my shoulders, moving me toward the fishing gear on the dock.

"Come on, you've gotta do it. It's tradition. We all compete to see who can catch the biggest fish. This place is our secret hideaway. Fishing's always great here because the tourists don't know about it." He tips his chin to my boyfriend, who watches with a simmering hint of jealousy I love. "Miles is our reigning champ, beats all of us every year. I think he cheats, if you ask me."

Miles throws a piece of bait at Deck's head, which luckily misses me as I duck out from under his arm.

"I don't fucking cheat, you just suck. I just got skills, my man. Sorry you don't," Miles says as Deck guides me onto the dock and toward a collection of fishing poles.

"Skills, huh?" I ask, picking up the fishing pole and looking at it. "How much skill could you need to use this thing?" I move it like I've seen my brother and dad do a million times before Miles grabs the end of it, glaring at me.

"Well, for one, you've gotta make sure no one is nearby when you're casting, so you don't hook anyone." I roll my eyes, then look around, noticing that, besides Miles, no one is nearby. I wonder if they all ran the second I grabbed a pole. "And second, it goes this way." He shifts the pole, twisting it so the reel is on the other side and the line isn't twisted.

Okay, that's a fair point.

I smile wide at him. "I think you're just scared I'm going to kick your ass."

He rolls his eyes, and I look at Deck.

"What happens if you win?"

His smile goes wide. "You get Miles's spot."

"Oh yeah, I forgot he won that," I say with a smile. "So only people here today have the chance to park there? Don't people get pissy that they won't get a shot?"

Deck shrugs. "I don't know, maybe?"

"It doesn't matter. That's how we do things here," Benny says from his chair, watching the interaction with entertainment.

"Huh," I say, thinking about Evergreen Park and how, even

though it's a relatively small town, compared to Seaside Point, it feels like a city. A system like this would *never* fly there.

"The town is small, but it's even smaller come fall. Locals know the local rules. That's why Miles got all pissy at you when you parked in his spot," Grant explains, sliding bait onto his hook with ease.

I fight the grimace at the look of it and instead smile and shake my head. "No, he got pissy because he's obsessed with me, and before, that made him mad."

"And now?" Grant asks.

My grin widens.

"Now he's come to terms with it. He doesn't really have a choice, you know? I'm pretty stubborn, and if I decide I want something, I'm persistent," I inform him matter-of-factly.

"Yeah, that was what won me over," Miles says, "Your persistence. Definitely not your ass."

My eyes go wide and my mouth drops with shock, and I push him jokingly. "You know what? I can't be mad. I do have a great ass."

Deck's eyes move to try and look at said ass, but Miles pushes him in the shoulder, and he just barely saves himself from falling into the water.

"Don't even fucking think about it," Miles says.

June lifts a hand and waves it at her face. "Oh my god, I never thought I'd be into possessiveness, but my *god,* that was hot," she says, and I smile at her, agreeing.

Grant, in contrast, grimaces. "That's my best friend, June," he says. "He's known you since you were a baby."

June shrugs. "Doesn't make it less hot."

"Totally," Lainey says in an equally dazed voice.

"It really doesn't matter about the spot, though, because I'm obviously going to win again," Miles says, a hand going to my waist and tucking me in close before I push him away.

"So cocky, aren't you?"

I prop a hand against my hips, the other holding my pole awkwardly.

"Always."

"Well, I think I'm going to kick your ass. Then the only way you'll get to park there is if you ask me *really, really* nicely."

Miles rolls his eyes and shakes his head.

"Someone bait me up," I say, looking at Grant and Deck.

"No, no, no. Gotta do it yourself if you're gonna compete," Miles says, and I cringe at the bucket of moving worms, knowing there's no universe where I can do that.

Parking spot be damned.

"That's not in the rules, Miller, you don't get to make 'em," Benny says with a fatherly chide. "Grant, son, bait up Claire's line."

"I can do it," Miles grumbles.

"I don't trust you not to fuck it up so you win," I say, sticking my tongue out at him and handing the pole to Grant.

"You're not going to win, Claire, no matter who baits you up."

"We'll see," I say with a wink.

"Ahh!" I shout a half hour later when there's a tug on my line.

It's been an increasingly boring half hour, and honestly, if Miles hadn't already caught a fish and deemed it "the winner," I probably would have given up. But since then, Helen, Sarah, Lainey, and June have all deemed this effort to be a girls versus boys type thing. I can't back down now.

My pole is bending, and my heart races as I try to figure out what's next.

"Okay, now take it slow," Deck says. He's also team Claire, telling me he would love nothing more than to see Miles losing. He verbally guides me through reeling in the fish, each circle getting harder and harder before it comes out of the water, flapping like wild.

I jump excitedly. "I got a fish!"

"I think it's bigger than Miles's," Lainey says.

"No way, let me see," Deck says, helping me bring it onto the deck.

"Ahh," I shout as it flops, almost touching me. "Oh my god, stop, it's going to touch me!"

"Jesus, she catches the biggest fish, and she doesn't even want to touch it," Miles says with a laugh, stepping in to help.

"I'm just a girl, Miles," I shout, averting my eyes back to my prize. "Oh, no, do you think it's mad at me?"

He lifts it by the fishing line and looks at me confused, the poor thing flopping around.

"I mean, he's not happy," June says with a laugh.

"Put him back then," I shout, hopping from flip-flopped foot to flip-flopped foot.

"We gotta measure him, Blondie," Benny says, grabbing a measuring tape.

"I hate this. He's drowning."

"How is a fish drowning?" Miles asks, walking the fish toward Benny's measuring tape.

"Because he's in the air! He needs water." I look at him with pleading eyes. "Miles, he's air *drowning*. He needs to go back to his home."

My eyes start to water at the idea of this cruelty, and he hands off the fish to Grant before pulling me into his arms.

"It's fine, Claire. Once Benny measures it, we'll put it back."

"Oh my god, the girl did it," Benny says with a laugh. "She beat the record."

"Oh my god," June shouts, jumping and clapping.

"Picture," Lainey shouts, and then they hand me the line. I stand with everyone, holding my fish with what I can only imagine is a look of panic before Benny takes the fish and quickly unhooks it. He finally tosses it into the water again where he swims away happily. I let out a sigh of relief.

"That's my sweet Claire," Miles says, pulling me in tight. "Would key your car, but couldn't bear to watch a hook taken out of a fish."

I look at him and smile.

"Does this mean I won?" I ask, coming back to myself now that I don't feel like a fish serial killer, and Miles smiles wide. Benny laughs and nods. "I won! I get the spot!"

June and Lainey come over to grab my hands, and we jump, laughing and excitedly celebrating.

When I come down from my high, Miles is sitting at the picnic table with Helen, and I make my way over there.

"Happy to concede to you, baby," he says, pulling me onto the bench next to him and pressing a chaste kiss to my lips.

"I keep meaning to talk to you about the block party in three weeks, but you're always bopping from post to post, and I never quite know where to find you," Helen says.

"You give the assignments, Helen," I say with a laugh.

"You go above and beyond, filling in wherever you're needed, and you know it."

I blush a bit at the praise from my boss.

"You have my number," I add and she shakes her head.

"No, no, I like to ask favors to people's faces, get their honest reaction so I can know if they actually mind helping out."

"I never mind helping you out, Helen. What can I do for you?" I ask, leaning forward onto the table, Miles's hand resting on my lower back comfortably.

"The block party is in three weeks, and I just can't handle it all anymore. So much to keep track of and people to contact. Any chance you'd be willing to take on some of the planning? You'd be paid, of course."

I shake my head.

"No, no, I don't need the money! But I'd love to, however I can help. I can get a group of the kids, have them ask around and see if they want some volunteer hours. What about donations? Are we covered there? I can go around to local businesses and see what I can get? I know you mentioned a sandcastle contest, do we have prizes lined up?" I ask, my mind reeling and excited.

Helen lets out a loud, belting laugh. "Goodness, I didn't think you'd be this fired up. But yes, all of that would be great. We can talk details tomorrow, cut your shift short and head to my office an hour early,"

I nod, though I don't plan to do this on the clock.

"I told you. My mom was the PTO president when I was a kid, so I helped with many events. How about I come in early tomorrow, and we can make a plan? Then in the afternoon I can start making my rounds after my shift and see what businesses might be interested."

"Paid," Helen says, glaring at me. "I insist on it being on the clock."

I shake my head but smile. "We can argue about that tomorrow, yeah? Today is family day."

The smile she gives me fills me with warmth, and I realize the truth in that statement.

Because that's what this is.

My little shore family that I never expected to have but am finding I would do anything for.

TWENTY-EIGHT

MILES

The past two weeks have been some of the best of my life, even though tomorrow is my first day off in that whole time. Every night, I spend time with Claire, either just her and me hanging out in bed or on the deck together or with friends, sometimes at the Seabreeze, sometimes at Grant's place. Last week, we spent the night like tourists, going to the boardwalk to do some rides and then playing in the arcade. I won Claire a giant stuffed animal of a cat that she put in the living room right next to the hermit crab tank she set up not long after her theft.

Now I'm standing in the kitchen a week after our afternoon at the Seabreeze, waiting for Claire to be ready for trivia night, when my phone rings in my hand.

I expect to see a call from Grant or maybe Deck, bitching that we're running late since I texted we'd leave almost twenty minutes ago, but Claire is taking longer than expected, as is her norm. I wonder if I should start changing times, telling her we'll leave at five when we have to be there at five thirty, just so we're on time.

I'm smiling to myself and my thoughts about a future with Claire, but I look at the screen, and my stomach drops.

It's Paul.

All happiness leaves me when I see it, knowing he only calls me when he needs something or if he wants to drop some fucking bomb that is going to ruin my day.

With a deep sigh and a look over my shoulder to see if Claire is in the room yet, I answer and lift the phone to my ear.

"Hey," I say as I instantly begin to pace the kitchen. "How's LA?"

"Did you talk to your lawyer?" my brother asks abruptly, no need for a hello.

I sigh, closing my eyes as I tip my head to the ceiling and try not to snap at him.

"Nice to talk to you too, baby brother. I'm good, Mom's great, how are you?"

"Stop being a dick, Miles."

I roll my eyes at the irony of Paul calling me a dick, much less calling him out for not even bothering with niceties.

I'm the one being a dick? You just called me up about money," is what I really want to say, but I don't.

As annoying as my brother is and as ready as I am for this whole fucking mess to be over with, he still owns a chunk of this house and has the power to completely fuck me over if he really wanted to.

I take in a deep breath and force myself to sound pleasant and brotherly.

When I remember that I was eating out his ex's pussy just a few hours ago, that task becomes shockingly more simple, a rush of calming pleasure washing over me.

"Yes, Paul. I talked to my lawyer. I, unfortunately, don't have your full payout on hand right now. We tried to offer to double the payments for the time being until I either have the full amount or you're paid out in full. My lawyer hadn't heard from yours, so for June we sent the single amount, but I'm happy to wire over more if it's what you want."

"I fired my lawyer," he says simply.

"What?" I ask, blinking. I suppose that's why Paul's lawyer never got back to us.

"I fired him. Everything's going through me now."

My jaw tightens, knowing that can't be a great sign, overall.

"Why'd you fire him?" I ask, straightening.

"He's too expensive and was taking too long. You said you'll double the payment?"

I close my eyes and fight back the guilt eating at me. This is the most desperate I've ever heard him. Maybe it's just because I'm finally content in my life, but he sounds miserable.

"Paul, are you okay?" I ask, trying to be as gentle as I can.

"I'm fine. Double it?"

"I mean, yeah, we spoke about doubling it, but it would halve how many remaining payments you'd get."

"When can you get the money to me?" he says instantly.

Now my nerves start to rise because even if my brother is an ass, he's still my younger brother. It was instilled in me from the day he was born that keeping Paul safe was my number one job. Sometimes, I wonder if I took that too seriously, especially after Dad died, not letting him learn and grow on his own.

Maybe if Paul had to be more accountable for his mistakes, we wouldn't be in this position.

Or maybe we just would have gotten here quicker.

"Paul, seriously, are you okay?"

"I'm just in a tight spot right now. My record company is fucking with me, and that bitch Claire left, and she was supposed to cover rent, so—"

"Cover rent?" I ask, fighting the urge to tell him not to talk about Claire like that. In a perfect world, Paul won't find out about my relationship with Claire until after I have the amount to pay him out. It's not that I want her to be some kind of secret, just that I don't need him finding out and throwing a temper tantrum.

"I mean help with rent. Whatever. Shit's expensive out in LA."

Unease builds in my gut with a healthy dose of familial guilt I always feel regarding my younger brother.

"Look," I say with a sigh. "Why don't you come home? We can—"

"Fuck off, Miles. Drop the caring brother act; I know it's all bull-shit. Just get me the money."

My jaw goes tight, and I go to speak, to tell him I won't send a thing until he signs an agreement at the behest of my lawyer, but then I realize the line has gone silent.

I close my eyes and take in a deep breath, shooting off a quick text to my lawyer. He's probably going to insist Paul sign something, stating that he's okay with the number of payments halving, which I know Paul isn't going to want to sign, but he'll want to make sure I'm financially and lawfully covered.

"Everything okay?" Claire asks, walking over to me as she slips an earring in. She's in a little tank top with a flowy skirt that stops at her knees and a pair of sandals, and as always, she's fucking gorgeous.

"What?" I ask, taking a step closer, always distracted by her.

Why did I used to think that was a bad thing? Right now, getting distracted from the mess of Paul is exactly what I need.

"You okay? You look stressed."

I smile and shake my head. "No, just normal shit. You ready to go?"

She stops into my space, her hand lifting to cup my cheek, her thumb brushing over my mustache in the way I love before she smiles.

"Yeah, baby," she whispers, then moves to her tiptoes to press a kiss to my lips and step back. "Let's go."

TWENTY-NINE

MILES

"One car?" Claire asks as we walk out of the house. "We can park in my spot."

I glare at her as she gives me a wide smile, then tug her into me, pressing my lips to hers.

"You gonna let me live that down?" I ask against them.

She shakes her head. "Maybe next year."

"Next year, huh?"

"I have to try and keep my reign," she whispers. But all I can hear as I help her into the passenger seat is that she's planning on being here next summer.

"I can't believe they're already putting up signs for fall," she says a bit later, tipping her chin to an apple festival sign as we drive past it.

"Yeah, but the Apple Fest is fun, though. Have you ever been?" She shakes her head, though I already know the answer. I've been taking note of when Claire is in town for as long as I've known her. "We'll go together. The bakery makes apple cider donuts and sells them fresh; it's my favorite thing every year."

She smiles at me, and I reach over to squeeze her knee. Her fingers trace over the veins in my hand before she speaks again.

"You know, technically, my contract is up in five weeks."

"I know," I say, because I do. I'm intricately aware of just how long Claire has a job in Seaside Point.

"What do you think..." she starts to say, then hesitates, then restarts her sentence. "You know, we are new..." Then her words fade off again.

I look at her quickly before moving my eyes back to the road, turning off the main road toward the bay. "We'll figure it out, Claire," I say, squeezing her knee again, then shifting my hand to grab hers, twining our fingers together.

"Really?" she asks, disbelief and hope in the words. When I slow to a stop at a red light, I turn to her, confused.

"What do you mean, really?" My pulse quickens, because what if we're on separate pages and I didn't realize?

"We'll figure it out?"

My brow furrows as I realize there's hope on her face, and I shake my head gently. "What did you think I'd say?"

She shrugs. "I...I don't know. I thought..." I sit patiently, waiting for her to find the words so I can understand where she's at. "I wasn't sure how things would go at the end of the summer. We haven't talked about it, so—"

With that, I put the car into park at the red light and shift in my seat to face her fully.

"Miles—"

I quiet her by pressing my lips to hers before leaning my forehead against her.

"I'll never be done with you, Claire. Don't you get it? I've waited six years to have this. I'm not going to just have it for one summer. I'm in this for the long haul."

Her breathing hitches as her eyes widen, and I smile.

"I'll come see you; you'll come down here if we have to. Whatever you want, I'll make it happen."

She smiles then, wide and happy, and I know I said the right thing. I hate that I keep messing this up, but I'm on a mission to

change that, to make her as confident as I am in our relationship.

"Okay," she whispers, and I smile again, leaning to kiss her once
more before a car honks behind us. Claire lets out a laugh, and we
both look to see the light has gone green. The car behind us lays on its
horn now, and I roll my eyes, sticking an arm out the window to flip a
bird to the person behind me, as I put the car back into drive and
continue on to the Seabreeze.

"Fucking tourists," Claire says with an exaggerated eye roll.

I let out a loud laugh, the sound free, and then we drive off to see
our friends.

"Boys versus girls," June shouts, pushing her brother away from the
table she secured. "You can't sit with us!"

We've been here for approximately five minutes, and already, I'm
regretting it.

"Are you kidding me, June?" Grant asks.

"Girls versus boys. May the best team win."

"What about me?" Deck asks, putting a hand to his chest. "I'm an
honorary girl."

"Not tonight, you're not. Go to your side of the bar," June says,
arguing.

She and Deck go back and forth as they tend to do, and while
they're distracted, I start to stealthily move Claire to the opposite side
of the room from June because the girl kind of scares me on days like
these. I always forget just how insanely competitive June is.

"No, no, no," June says, her attention snapping to Claire and me,
my arm around her waist. "No. You two separate."

"Excuse me?" I ask, raising an eyebrow at my best friend's little
sister.

"No, no, Miles, that won't work on me. I've heard stories about you now." She puts a hand on her hip and then grabs Claire's elbow. "Your grumpiness is no longer effective."

"Uh, what kind of stories?" I ask, looking from June to Claire, whose face has gone suspiciously red.

"All kinds. I know things I never wanted to know about you, but because you make my best friend so happy, which means she'll probably be closer to me more often now, I accept it. But the line stops at trivia night."

"June, come on," Claire tries, but June turns her ire on Claire.

"No. You can spend a single night not attached at the hip." She then shifts to me with begging eyes. "Give my best friend back for one night."

"Oh, stop it, we're not attached at the hip, June," Claire says with a laugh, but still, she steps away from me, and I give her a glare.

"Where are you going?" I ask, reaching for her once more, but she steps away.

"It's boys versus girls, bud," she says with a smile. "You're the enemy."

"The enemy?"

"Oh yeah," she says with a teasing smile, taking another step back toward the table where Lainey is already sitting with Helen, who, it seems, they conned into being on their team. A boon for us because Helen is terrible at any trivia that happened before the year 1990. "May the best team win."

Something about the way she says it and the look in her eyes sets me on fire, and I lean forward, grabbing her wrist and tugging her into me. She stumbles before falling into my chest.

"And what happens if I win?" I mumble low enough so only she can hear.

"If you win? You're not going to, so that's no problem." Her grin is wide and cocky, but I continue to look at her. She rolls her eyes. "Fine. I'll give you the parking spot." I nod, accepting her offer. "But if I do?"

I raise an eyebrow, and her cheeks go a bit pink. She bites her lip, and I have to fight my dick getting hard in this.

"You know what you'll get," I whisper, pulling her closer, my lips moving to her ear. "Lifeguard chair."

Her cheeks grow even pinker. "Really? But you said it would be too dangerous," she says, suddenly seeming excited.

I have no desire to fuck my little daredevil in the lifeguard stand, but there's also no chance she's going to win trivia today. It happens once a month, and the whole town comes out, hence the packed room. Her team consists of a few women I recognize, my mother and Helen, neither of whom are even the slightest bit decent at trivia.

We have Grant, who is alarmingly good at all history trivia, and Deck, who, for some reason no one quite understands, can recite all celebrity trivia starting in 1980 and on, though if you ask him about the '50s, '60s, or '70s, he's a lost cause. When I look over the rest of our team, I see a pretty even spread, so I know there's a solid chance we're going to win.

"You're not going to win, so I'm not worried," I say with a smile, then step back from her.

"Oh, Miles, baby, I don't think you know what you just did," she whispers before she turns to her team, who bring her in, all of them whispering and giggling.

"We're Team Trebek's Rejects," Deck says with a laugh when Benny, our moderator, asks for the team name. Benny rolls his eyes but writes the name at the top of the giant chalkboard. Usually, it's a few smaller teams playing, but it seems we're really leaning into this boys versus girls thing.

"And you ladies?"

"Team WAP," Lainey says. My mother bursts out laughing, and I look at Claire, who seems far too pleased with herself. I can almost guarantee it was her idea because she gives me a sassy wink, and I shake my head.

"WAP?" Benny asks, clearly confused.

"It's a song," Claire says with an angelic smile.

Benny, clearly sensing her mischief, just shakes his head.

"Okay, tonight we only have two teams, but the rules are the same. I ask a question, and the first to raise their paddle gets to answer. If you answer wrong, you lose a point, and the other team can steal. If you answer right, you get one point. I got some fresh questions, so be ready to be stumped!" Benny says, and we all look at one another, both intrigued because Benny rarely adds new questions to the roster.

"Edie Falco and James Gandolfini star in what series about the life of a New Jersey mob boss?" Benny asks, and Deck, our resident guido's hand, shoots out, slamming the table.

"*The Sopranos!*"

"Don't look so happy with yourself, Deck," June says, rolling her eyes. "Literally everyone knows that."

"Crazy, because you didn't even raise your paddle."

"Neither did you, so wouldn't that disqualify you?" June asks, her paddle in the air.

We all glare at Deck, whose smile starts to fall.

Benny lets out a loud laugh. "Girl's got you there, Jagger. Yes, Team WAP?"

There is something so fucking wrong with Benny saying WAP, but here we are.

"That would be *The Sopranos*," June says, batting her eyes at Benny.

An hour later, the crowd is getting rowdy. The score is just about tied at thirty-five to thirty-four, with our team one point down. It's so close and so heated that Benny even took his pipe out, setting it to the side for the night.

"All right, this one is for the win, five points to whoever gets it," he says. "So I've gotta make it a good one."

Looking over to the girls, I see them giggling and whispering, but as always, my eyes are on Claire, who gives me a small smile and a wink before pulling out her phone.

The room quiets as Benny shuffles through his papers, looking for his next question.

My phone buzzes in my hand, and considering almost everyone who texts me is in this room, my brow furrows as I reach for the device. Upon lifting it, my brow furrows deeper, seeing Claire's name on my screen. I look up and see her head tipped back with laughter at something June said.

My heart fills like a sap because she's so fucking beautiful, and I love having her like that, happy and overjoyed.

"You know what I mean?" Deck asks, and I lift my head to look at him and nod.

"Definitely," I lie, because I have no idea what he's saying, but he smiles and nods before sliding me the paddle, but I can't focus on that because I just tapped open my texts and read the message Claire sent.

I can't wait to ride you on the beach.

All the blood leaves my body and goes straight to my dick.

There is noise around me, cheering and booing, but I can't do anything but look at Claire.

Then my phone buzzes once more. I slide it under the table because who the fuck knows what she's going to send next, and I'm glad I did because this time, it's a photo.

Claire, in the primary bathroom mirror, her hair is full and loose, clearly taken today because the makeup is the same, completely naked. Her arm covers her breasts, but I can see the edge of a rosy nipple, and she has her hips popped backward, legs crossed to hide her pussy, but still, I know it's there. I know what she's hiding.

And I want it.

My chair moves back with a loud screech. With it, everyone in the room turns to me, but I only have eyes for Claire. Hers are wide like her smile, and she leans to June, whispering something, but her gaze never falters from mine as I move across the room to her.

I grab the back of her chair, tugging it, and thus Claire, back when I reach her.

"Miles, what are you doing?" my mother asks, and I force myself to forget that my girlfriend is *sexting* me while sitting next to my mother.

Without answering, I bend down, grab Claire, and lift her over my shoulder. I know she waves at the girls as I make my way to the door, feeling her move and the chorus of laughs behind us, but I can't focus on anything but getting my girl out of here and alone.

"Girls win!" I vaguely hear Benny shout with a deep belly laugh.

THIRTY

MILES

"Miles, what are you doing?" She giggles as we walk out of the Seabreeze, Claire over my shoulder.

Never in my life have I ever been more grateful for that stupid fucking fishing competition. Because of it, the truck is right outside for me to put Claire into before jogging around the front and getting in. Gravel ricochets along the underside of the truck as I back out and then make my way to my destination.

"Miles," she says with a louder laugh. "What is happening? What are you doing?"

"You wanna be a bad girl? I'm going to make it happen," I say low, reaching over as I drive faster than I should and gripping her thigh, pulling one to the side. "Be good and widen your legs for me."

She looks at me, and when I glance at her, her lips are parted, and she is panting.

"What?"

My fingers dig into her thigh. "Open your legs for me, Claire. Give me some room." I'm grateful when she doesn't argue, instead parting her legs as I slide further up her skirt and then down the front of her underwear, finding them already soaked against the back of my hand.

"So wet already," I groan, my fingers sliding through her sweet, wet pussy with ease.

"Miles," she whispers, but doesn't stop me. Instead, she sits back further, legs parting wider, and she slightly shifts to give me better access as I drive on a mission. I groan at her acceptance and her eagerness for me to slip a single finger inside. I don't finger her, just hold it at her entrance, her hips rocking gently, shifting the heel of my palm against her clit.

By the time I get us to the other side of town, where there's less foot traffic on the beach this time of night, my hand is soaked.

Once parked, I take my hand out of her, then I slip the wet finger in my mouth to clean it off as I leave the car and jog to her side. I open her door and grab her hand to pull her out. Then I press her back against the car and pin her there with my body.

"What are you doing?" she whispers into the night.

"You won. You get a prize now."

A low moan leaves her lips, and her breathing gets heavier as I press my lips to hers. The kiss is wet and needy, filled with lust and the subtle hint of naughtiness at the thought of what I'm about to do. Our tongues twine, and I taste the wine she was drinking mixed with her pussy, and I push my hard cock into her belly.

Her hand twines into my hair, and I realize she would let me fuck her here against the car if I asked. That has me pulling myself together, stepping back, and taking her hand. I lead her to the beach, giving her barely enough time to kick off her sandals as we continue to move toward our destination.

I'm so grateful she wore a flowy skirt tonight. As we approach the lifeguard chair, I'm also relieved that this wasn't a night when they put them away.

"Miles." She stumbles in the sand before I catch her, her body against mine. I steal another kiss. "What are we doing here?" she asks when I break the kiss.

"Fucking on a lifeguard chair," I whisper into her neck, sucking the skin beneath her ear. "On your list. Now it's on *our* list." I pull back and then move up the steps, brushing off the bench, then sitting.

"Miles—" she says, cheeks flushed in the moonlight, the waves crashing in the distance. Her lips part as she stands beneath me.

My dick jumps at the sight of her.

"Come on, Claire." I take myself out of my loose shorts, stroking my cock once, twice, and letting out a low groan. "Now."

Her eyes go wide when she registers what I'm doing, and then she's moving up the stairs quickly. Soon, she's standing in the small space between us, my hand still slowly working my cock. I slide my free hand under her skirt, stopping at the seam of her panties between her pussy and thigh and moaning when I realize she'd soaked through them.

"So fucking wet for me, aren't you? Does this turn you on, Claire? The idea of me fucking you outside, where anyone could see?"

"Yes," she whispers instantly, and I bite back a moan. This woman was made for me, you can't convince me otherwise.

"Or maybe it's the idea that I can't even bear to waste the time to go home; I need to be inside you so bad."

A mewl leaves her lips as I slide a finger underneath her underwear and glide it along her wet slit.

"Please," she whispers.

"Please, what?"

"Please fuck me." Her eyes drift shut as I slide a finger inside, her hips shifting to get more as soon as I do.

My greedy girl.

"Gotta make sure you're ready first."

She moans quietly as I slide out, then in, then slide my thumb over her clit. Her panties dig into my hand and probably cut into her hip, but somehow, that adds to this even more. I slide in and then out, slowly finger fucking her, bending them to graze along her G-spot, and making her hips buck.

"Fuck," she groans. "I need you." Those words always do something to me, especially when my own hand is still wrapped around my cock.

"Think you can stay quiet?"

"What?" she asks, her eyes going wide, but when I swipe my thumb across her clit again, she lets out another little mewl.

"Can you stay quiet, Claire? We can't have you out here screaming my name when I'm deep inside of you." Her pussy tightens around my fingers, and I swallow a moan of my own.

"Miles—"

"Can." I brush over her clit. "You." Another swipe. "Stay." Another. "Quiet?" This time, I pinch the bundle of nerves, and she lets out a shaky breath before nodding. "Or else I'm going to have to get creative."

Her hands move to my shoulders to hold herself steady as I start to move my fingers faster. I know I won't last long, and truly, we *can't* take too long out here, so I need her right on the edge when I slide into her.

"Miles," she moans.

"You have to stay quiet, Claire, or we're going home where you can be as loud as you want."

She shakes her head, which has dropped to my neck, her arms on the wooden back of the chair behind us holding her up.

"Or I could have you on your knees, fucking your mouth and leaving you needy until we get back home. That would keep you quiet." I think that would be a threat, leaving her unfinished, but the slight hesitation of her hips as if that's the best course of action has me groaning. "Fuck, you like that, don't you?"

She lifts her head, and her slight nod takes me higher, closer to the edge I know Claire is already dancing on.

"Maybe next time." I start to fuck her faster with my fingers.

"Miles, please," she groans, not even trying to temper her noises.

"Yeah, we're getting creative." I slide a hand out of her and up to her hip under her skirt, looping a thumb under her underwear and tugging.

"Miles—"

"Step out," I whisper, and she does as I ask. When I have her panties in my hand, I ball them up and put a hand on each hip to help her straddle me, one of her knees resting on the wood on either side of me. I use one hand to line my cock up with her cunt but keep it wrapped there so she can't lower herself onto me.

"Open," I whisper.

She pulls her head back and looks at me, eyes dazed with lust. "What?"

"Open your mouth, Claire."

Her eyes go wide as she understands and does as I ask before I shove her panties inside. Her eyes go even wider, and a soft, muffled moan leaves her lips. My cock throbs at the sound of it.

"My girl is so dirty, isn't she?" I rub the head of my cock through her wetness, and her eyes close just a bit. "You like having your wet panties stuffed in your mouth, don't you?" She nods, and I reward her honesty, notching the head of my cock inside of her and giving her an inch of me. She's tight and dripping onto my hand. I groan into her neck as she tenses over me.

"Mmm," she mumbles through the panties, and I smile. In retribution, she tenses on me again, slamming on the head of my cock. The feeling is exquisite, but I want more, so I slide my hand down a few inches so she can take more of me.

"I like you like this, Claire," I whisper into her ear. "At my mercy." Her hips move, and I slide a hand up her back, tangling into her hair and tugging. "You only get what I let you have,"

She lets out a pleased, muffled moan.

"Your prize, but I decide how you get it." I let her get another inch of me, biting back a moan of my own. She looks at me, pleading in her eyes, and I smile. "Is this torture, Claire?" I ask, and she nods. "Good. That's what you do to me every moment of every fucking day. Any moment I'm not buried in you, when you're teasing me, sending me dirty pictures while sitting in a bar? You're torturing me."

Her head rolls to the side, her hair tumbling as she lets out a soft sigh. And then my hand is gone, shifting to her hip and pushing her down so I fill her fast and hard. Her head snaps back, and I groan as I hold her down onto me, feeling her pulse around my cock. Once I've caught my breath, I speak.

"Ride it, Claire." She lets out a heated breath against my neck. The fingers of my hand dig into her hip as she rises and falls, the other on her neck holding her face into the crook of mine. Her little moans are constant now, sending me higher with each muffled sound.

"God, you grip me so good," I growl into her neck, my own sounds becoming too loud for comfort, despite the loud sound of the ocean waves and the lack of people and houses on this side of the shoreline. Her hips start moving faster, losing their precise rhythm, the noises coming from her going more frantic before she starts rocking on me, no longer riding and scraping her clit against my pelvis with each move, and I know she's close.

Thank God, because I don't know how much longer I can hold on.

"I need you to come, Claire. Do it, and I'll take you home and fuck you all night long; you can be as loud as you want there."

After another moment, she tightens around me and comes all over my cock. I use a hand in her hair to push her face into my neck, the panties in her mouth only able to muffle so much as I do the same into hers, my hips bucking up as I spill inside her.

"Fuck, Claire," I groan, my hips jerking with each clench of her pussy, each grind of her hips as she rides out her orgasm, forgetting everything except for squeezing every last drop of her own pleasure out.

I love that about her, the way she takes what she needs from me.

It makes me want her again already, though I know that's not in the cards, at least not until I get her into our bed. Slowly, her hips stop rocking, her body stops quaking, and her head drops to my shoulder.

I move my hands to her mouth, tugging out the panties and

smiling before I shift her and use the panties to clean her up. It's not my normal aftercare, but it will do for now.

Then I press my lips to hers, her eyes still hazy as she smiles. "Can we check that one off?"

And when she laughs, it's not quiet; instead, it fills up the night air.

And I somehow fall just a little bit harder for her.

THIRTY-ONE

MILES

Two weeks before Labor Day weekend, Claire and I slide into my truck and head down to Evergreen Park for her niece's birthday. Apparently, on Saturday there's a party at some play place, but on Friday we're having a family dinner at Claire's parents' house.

When we pulled up, I sat in the car for a minute too long, staring at the decently sized but still cozy home that Claire grew up in, trying to get the nerve to step inside.

"Can't sit out here forever," she whispers.

"I mean—" I start, and when she glares at me, I smile in return.

"Come on, before my sisters—"

Except it seems that she spoke them into existence because two blondes who look similar to Claire come out of the house and head straight for the passenger side door. A brunette comes out behind them, followed by a young girl who I know, from photos Claire has shown me, like the proud aunt she is, is her niece, Sophie.

As soon as the car door is open, the little one jumps onto Claire's lap with a happy squeal. "Aunt Claire!" she yells, and Claire lets out the sweetest, most joyful version of her tinkling laugh as she holds the little girl tight, melting everything inside of me.

"Sophie, baby!" she says, then shifts with the girl still tangled in her to slide out of the car and onto the sidewalk.

Realizing I can't stay in here forever without looking like a weirdo, I follow suit, sliding out of the car, slamming the door shut, and walking around to where Claire is hugging her two sisters, Sutton and Sloane, while Sophie is still clinging to her. She finally sets her down to properly hug her brother's girlfriend and her former boss at the dance studio, Jules.

I stand back like an idiot, uncomfortable and startlingly realizing I've never done this: meeting the family of someone I'm in love with, much less when they're a close-knit family like Claire has told me about.

"Your man is looking uncomfortable as fuck, Claire," another voice says as it approaches, and instantly I know this is her older brother, Nate.

Claire turns to me with wide eyes and cringes.

"Oh, shoot, sorry. You guys, this is Miles. My." She bites her lips like she's nervous suddenly. "My boyfriend. Please, be nice to him. I like this one a lot, and I don't want you to scare him off."

"Us? Scare off your boyfriend?" Nate says with a very unconvincing gasp. "We would never."

"Yes, we would," the sister, who I'm pretty sure is Sloane, says. "Though we should have tried harder to scare off Paul." Sutton elbows the oldest Donovan girl with wide eyes before she corrects herself. "Oh, shit. Sorry. I forgot he's your brother."

I shake my head and smile. "No worries, I know intricately about my brother's faults."

Claire closes her eyes and sighs.

"You guys, I gave you *one job,* and you're already failing. Don't talk about his fucking brother or how I dated him first," Claire nearly whines, and I can't help but smile at it. It's so interesting to see her in little sister mode. I'm used to this from June, but I've never seen Claire in the role.

"Oh, come on, it would have been the elephant in the room,

Claire Bear," a deeper voice says, and when all of the heads on the sidewalk outside the Donovan residence turn toward the sound, I see who is clearly Claire's father moving our way.

"Hi, Daddy," she says, the group stepping back to let her father go to his daughter, where he hugs her tight. When she pulls back, I see Claire's eyes shining.

"My Claire, always wearing her emotions on her sleeve," he says, then squeezes her shoulder.

"She's a girl—" Sutton starts.

"Yeah, yeah, you're a girl," he says, and it's clear this is a common conversation in this household. Part of me warms to know Claire has pulled me into it, into that part of her life, but I can't think about that too long because Claire turns to me with a wide smile.

"Dad, this is Miles. Miles, this is my dad."

Her dad takes me in for a long moment, and I do the same, seeing a plaid button-down tee tucked into cargo shorts, graying blonde hair, and a kind face. He looks almost identical to her brother Nate but obviously older. For the first time in a long, long time, I get a pang of jealousy, wondering if my dad would look like me but older if he were still here.

I've seen photos and can come to the conclusion that the answer would be yes, but every once in a while, when I least expect it, that pain comes and bites me.

I push the unwanted thought away and give the man a wide smile.

"Hi, Mr. Donovan. I'm Miles. So great to finally meet you." I say then put a hand out, and it hangs there for a long moment. Sweat starts to form on the back of my neck in the summer sun. I think I'm clearly failing whatever test this is before he lets out a loud laugh and takes my hand, shaking it hard.

"Great to meet you, Miles. Been hearing about you for years now." Then the big man puts an arm around my shoulder awkwardly because I'm a few inches taller than him.

"Are you all just going to stand out here with the door open, letting out the cold air all afternoon?" a new voice asks, and when everyone looks up to the house, an older version of Claire stands on the front step with her arms on her chest. God, I've seen that exact face a million times, and something about it makes me smile.

"Mom!" Claire says, then bounds up the walkway to her mother, who wraps her up in a hug. Everyone makes their way inside, but Mr. Donovan guides me, arm still on my shoulder.

"Not gonna do the whole *threaten you with a shotgun* thing, because I think Claire would come and kill me in my sleep if she found out." I let out a laugh and nod. "And because from what I hear of the two Miller boys, you're the good one. Just going to say that I'm glad you finally got your head outta your ass, and if you hurt her, I won't come after you, but her sisters will, and they're much scarier than I am."

"If they're anything like Claire, I would, in fact, be terrified of them."

He stops walking and drops his arms, turning to me with a smile.

"You'll fit right in here," he says, then leads the way into the Donovan household, and somehow, I know I passed a test.

"So what's next in your grand plan, Claire Bear?" Mr. Donovan asks, and I feel more than see Claire's body go still. When I look at her, her face is tipped down toward her slice of birthday cake, a bright pink extravaganza with extra sprinkles that I learned Sophie made with her grandmother and Jules.

"I, uh..." she says. "I'm not totally sure yet. My contract ends in September, and right now I'm having a great time helping to plan a block party fundraiser for the recreation department."

"Oh, that's so fun!" Mrs. Donovan says with a smile.

"Yeah, it is," Claire says, agreeing, but her fork continues to push around the thick layer of frosting. "I'm just kind of playing it by ear, seeing what jumps out to me next.

Silence takes over the table until Sloane breaks it.

"Must be nice," she says, and my eyes shift to hers. "Just bouncing around, doing whatever you want."

"Sloane," her mother says in a chiding tone.

"Oh, come on. That's what she does. She's never going to decide what to do when she grows up because she refuses to grow up. That's a luxury we don't all have. I'm just saying, it must be nice."

I can feel Claire sinking in on herself as she sits next to me, and without meaning to, I speak up.

"I think it's great," I say, and the room goes quiet. Next to me, Claire lifts her hands, picking at her nails. "Having the ability and the forethought to want to find something she's going to like and want to do for the rest of her life? I think that's great."

"Well, yes, but eventually you have to settle down, figure it out," Sloane says.

"Why?" I ask, and Claire reaches under the table, grabbing my knee. I don't know if it's just to have that contact with me or if she's quietly telling me I don't have to defend her but I don't plan to stop regardless.

"Miles," Claire whispers, but her mother speaks first, surprising me as she does.

"Well, at some point, you have to stop looking for the perfect job and just take one. Life keeps moving, and it won't stop just because you don't know what you want to do for the rest of your life."

"But she's not struggling," I say, sitting back. This is a misunderstanding I myself had, and guilt eats at me now to realize that I wasn't the only one from whom she was getting this judgment. No wonder it hurt her so much: she thinks that everyone sees her this way because, in a way, they do.

"But she doesn't have a *plan*, either."

"Is that so bad?" Jules adds, and since she's the only other outsider here, it feels like she's on my side. "Look at Ava. She didn't know what she wanted to do and eventually found the perfect thing for herself."

"Ava is a force of nature all on her own," Nate says of Jules's best friend who won the Miss Americana contest a while back.

"So is Claire," Sutton says with a shrug. "I don't know why we're all so weird about wanting her to have some boring-ass big girl job from the get-go. She'll figure it out eventually."

"And she's *right here*," Claire says. "Can we stop talking about me like I'm not in the room?"

"Mom, I love you, you know I do. Nate, I so appreciate you always looking out for me, but I'm not a kid. I'm an adult. I don't spend money superfluously, and I have no debt since I got a full ride." This is news to me, but somehow not surprising. "And I have a degree and a *killer* résumé, if I do say so myself. I know I do things a bit differently than you guys would, but that's because I'm not you. And I would appreciate it if you stopped treating me like I'm some little girl who doesn't think about what's next."

"Not for nothin', Claire, but just a few months ago you came home crying because your boyfriend broke up with you," Mr. Donovan adds, and her fingers tighten on my knee.

"Yeah, Dad, because I was upset, and my family is a safe place for me to be that way. I was upset that things didn't work out the way I had hoped, and I thought that was valid. At the time, it sounded like a fun adventure, and while it might have felt out of left field when I left for LA, it was something I thought out and planned. That's why I had a job lined up there, why I saved up, and why, when it wasn't what I thought it would be, I left and came home to my family who I knew would comfort me." Her jaw gets tight before continuing. "I hate thinking that next time I make a mistake, I won't feel comfortable doing that because I'm worried you're going to hold it against me."

"Claire—" Mrs. Donovan says gently, and Claire opens her mouth to say something, but Mr. Donovan speaks first, his face thoughtful.

"You're right, you should feel comfortable to make mistakes. That's what your mom and I always wanted for you four anyway, the freedom to do what you wanted, make mistakes, and have a safe place to land." He reaches across the table to hold her hand, and her eyes start to water. "I'm sorry that we started to use that against you."

"I didn't," Sutton says matter-of-factly, and I decide right then that I really like Claire's older sister.

"Sutton—" Mrs. Donovan says.

"Me neither," Sophie says, and it's the perfect amount of comic relief needed to break the tension.

Mr. Donovan squeezes Claire's hand one last time, then lets go.

"Okay, who's ready for Pictionary!" Mrs. Donovan says, clapping her hands.

Instantly, everyone starts to move, clearing off the table with what seems to be already assigned chores, working like a well-oiled machine. I guess for a family of six, that kind of thing is required to avoid chaos. As I awkwardly stand to follow whatever Claire's task is, Mr. Donovan puts a hand on my shoulder and tips his head to the living room.

I step in with him and instantly start to apologize. Kind of.

"Sorry if you think I overstepped, Mr. Donovan, but I also don't really care. Your daughter means a great deal to me, and I don't like anyone making her upset," I say.

He looks at me stoically, and I contemplate standing down, but then a wide smile spreads on his lips. "No, you were right. We're too hard on Claire, and she has never given us reason to be. She's just the baby of the family, and we all care a whole lot about her."

"That makes sense. I care about her, too," I say, meaning it in a dozen different ways and when he looks at me and nods, I think he can see that.

"Call me Tom," he says.

"Your brother," he says, and my gut tightens. "No offense—"

"My brother's an ass. Trust me, I know."

He smiles then. "Family is important, but sometimes, you gotta know when to cut them off."

"Trust me, we're on the same page with that. That's something I've been working my way up to."

He nods like this is an appropriate response.

"I always thought all my girls would settle down in Evergreen Park, close to their mom, so she wouldn't have that empty nest she always feared. But I always knew Claire would jump ship somewhere else. Happy she picked somewhere we'll be happy to visit, though. Real pretty down there." I open my mouth, unsure of how to respond to that, but I don't have to when he keeps speaking. "All I care about is that Claire is happy. She's always been a bit head in the clouds, and I've always loved that about her. My wife and her siblings give her a bit of a hard time about it, but I always knew she'd figure things out eventually."

I smile then. Finally, something we can agree on.

"I agree."

"That includes where she wants to be and who she wants to be with," he adds, and again, my back straightens. "Only thing I ask if you take her out of this town is you make sure she comes home often and has a room for her sisters when they want to come down. They're close, and they need their time together."

A long beat passes before I nod with understanding.

"You have my word," I say, putting a hand out to him. He inspects me, then takes my hand to shake, but surprises me when he pulls me in for a hug, patting me on the back.

"You're a good kid, Miles. You're good for my girl."

And then he walks off, and again, I think I have gotten Claire's dad's seal of approval.

THIRTY-TWO

CLAIRE

"Ahh!" I yell, running across the bar in my hometown, when I see Ava Bordeaux—no, Ava *Wilde*—walk in, a big man standing right behind her. "Ava!"

"Claire!" she yells, abandoning her husband to run my way with her arms in the air.

"It's so good to see you! Jules didn't tell me you were coming!"

She shrugs. "You know how much I love a dramatic entrance."

After dinner and cake at my parent's house, my mom insisted she have a sleepover with Sophie, and we all went out for a fun time. My sisters were in immediately, though it took a bit of convincing from Jules to convince Nate to come with. There was a bit of whispering and a *Jesus, Jules*, that I refuse to think about too deeply before he agreed, and now we're here.

It's a dive bar at best, much like the Seabreeze, but one I've been to more times than I can count with my sisters and with Jules, Ava, and Harper. I've even brought June here on winter break in college, who instantly told me the vibe was like a younger Seabreeze.

"Harper coming?"

Ava rolls her eyes and shakes her head. "No, she has some work thing."

I nod and shrug, not very surprised since it usually takes a lot for Ava and Jules to convince their third friend to go out for the night since her boyfriend, Jeremy, is never willing to tag along.

"I hear you brought a *man*," she whispers, and I let out a laugh, tipping my head to the side to show where Miles is chatting with Nate. I'm so grateful my brother hasn't gone into weird older brother territory and seems to be playing nice with Miles.

"Oh, he's *fine*," Ava breathes, eyes wide.

"Excuse me?" her husband, security to the stars, Jaime Wilde, says.

She rolls her eyes and slaps his chest. "I said he's *fine*."

Her husband's jaw goes tight, and again, Ava rolls her eyes. She does that lot where her husband is concerned. I've never met two people who clash more but fit so perfectly together the way Jaime and Ava do.

"Calm down, Jaime; we all know no one could handle Ava except for you," Reed, bassist for Atlas Oaks, says, flopping into a seat next to Jaime. Now it's Ava's turn to glare at the big goofball that is Reed, though it bounces right off him.

I shake my head at people who have become my close group of friends here thanks to Jules. When I see everyone is here, I stand in front of the table we're all sitting at and put my hands on my hips.

"Okay, quickly, because I'm only doing this one more time," I say. "Miles, this is Ava, her husband Jaime, Reed, and Wes. Everyone, this is Miles, my new boyfriend. He's a nice guy. Yes, he's Paul's older brother. Yes, he hates him as much as all of you do." Miles closes his eyes and sighs at the ceiling, but I keep going. "I don't want to catch any of you interrogating him, arguing with him, trying to trap him in some kind of weird fight for male dominance." Sloane lets out a small laugh, and when I look at Miles, his eyes are cautiously wide. "I don't think it'll happen, but I'm setting the ground rules now."

"Uh, okay?" he says.

"Everyone agrees? I like him a lot, and I don't want you guys to fuck this up." I purposely lock my eyes on my brother. "That includes you."

"I'd be more nervous about Sloane," he says under his breath.

I turn to my sister, who is smiling.

"Me? Never."

Another fucking lie because my sister does, in fact, like to run the men I date through the wringer. Miles stands and pulls me into his side. "Claire," he says. "I think it's going to be okay. I can handle a little interrogation if need be."

"That's what I like to hear," Sloane says, rubbing her hands together, and I roll my eyes.

"I would apologize, but I'm not changing anything," I say, with a smile.

"I wouldn't want you to."

"You're a brave man, Miles, dealing with that one," Sutton says, and I turn to my sister, my mouth dropped open and my eyes wide.

"Traitor!"

"How am I a traitor?"

"Because you're supposed to be on *my* side! You're *my* sister!"

She rolls her eyes like it doesn't matter, then turns to Miles. "How long until I have to wear some ugly-ass bridesmaid dress?"

My mouth drops further, and I reach forward to hit my sister or push her or something, but Miles wraps an arm around my waist, keeping me back.

"Not too long, if I have my way."

I turn to him with a glare, but there's a hint of happy shock rushing through me.

I want to be mad.

Really, I do. It would be easy.

But instead, my insides are melting. Instead, Miles is smiling wide like he knows he caught me, and he looks so happy and carefree; I can't find it in me to be mad.

How could I possibly be mad right now? Miles Miller just told my sister he wants to marry me.

I turn my glare to my traitor of a sister.

"It wouldn't be ugly," I say.

"It will probably be something that Sophie will find very pretty," my sister says in a way I know is meant to be underhanded, but I take it as a compliment.

"Sophie has *great* taste," I say.

"She's six," Sutton deadpans.

"And?" Sloane rolls her eyes.

"I see the sass runs in the family," Miles says under his breath, and I smack his arm, but when he puts it around me and tucks me into his side, I can't do much more than melt into him.

Two hours later, Nate and Jules are already out of here, probably off to enjoy a kid-free night, and Sloane asked them to take her home on the way because she had an early morning. I sit blissfully tipsy with Ava and Sutton, and Miles sits next to me but talks with the guys about random things, and a sense of utter joy washes through me at him sliding so easily into my Evergreen Park life.

"How is everything going? How's the house?" I ask Ava. The last time I saw her, she was just doing the finishing decor touches on the house she and Jaime bought and renovated.

"Amazing! We're all settled in."

"And Peach?" I ask of her beloved cat.

She rolls her eyes and lets out a sigh. "Great, except Jaime wouldn't let me bring her tonight."

I roll my lips between my teeth as Jaime overhears, turning his head to his wife.

"Ava, we can't bring a cat to the bar."

"Says who?" she asks, tipping her head at him like she doesn't believe him.

"Says everyone," he grumbles.

"We have hermit crabs," I say, turning to Miles. "Our little shell babies, right babe?"

He glares at me, but I know he loves them as much as I do. I always catch him putting a bit extra food in when he thinks I'm not looking.

"Hermit crabs? Oh my god, how cute!" Ava says, clapping.

Sutton looks at me, always knowing there is more to whatever random story I have.

"They're rescues," I say with a serene smile, and Ava gasps, holding a hand to her chest as if I adopted a whole-ass child instead of a few crabs.

Jaime, on the other hand, is rightfully skeptical. "How does one rescue a hermit crab?"

"When she says rescue, she means *she stole them* when the shop owner wasn't looking," Miles adds, and I elbow him in the side.

Jaime gives an unsure look, and Ava's eyes go wide.

"Typical Claire," Sutton sighs, and I glare at my sister.

"They were being mistreated," I explain, throwing my hands into the air. "They were left outside all night long!"

"That's animal cruelty," Ava says, not a hint of sarcasm in her words.

"I think, technically, having hermit crabs as a whole is inhumane since they aren't even from this area," Jaime adds. His wife turns to him with a fierce glare.

"Well, what is she supposed to do, Jaime, just let them be free?" He shrugs. "She's doing what she can with the tools she has available to her."

"That's what I said!" I say, smiling at Ava. "I can't undo their trauma, but I'm doing my best to give them a better life."

"I so get you," Ava says, taking a sip of her drink.

"How did she con you into keeping them?" Jaime asks with an all-too-knowing look, tipping his head towards Ava. "This one found a stray cat in an alleyway with fucking worms."

Miles cringes.

"She had tummy troubles, Jaime; she's just a girl," Ava says, then turns to Miles. "She's all better now, the perfect little princess."

"And then she made me cart the thing across the country with us."

Miles lets out an entertained laugh. I should have known Jaime and Miles would get along because Ava and I are so similar in personality. Any man who could endure us with a smile is bound to be friends.

"Why didn't you just make her take them back?" Sutton asks, confused.

"I can't stand the guy she stole them from, so it seemed like a good compromise."

Jaime nods sagely, as if that makes perfect sense to him. Honestly, I should have realized earlier that Jaime and Miles would hit it off.

"Plus, it was on his bucket list."

"A bucket list?"

Miles sighs and takes a look at the ceiling.

"You made the poor man one of your bucket lists?" Sutton asks with exasperation. She knows all too well my love of bucket lists since I made her live out many a bucket list while we were growing up. Being barely sixteen months apart in age, Sutton and I were the closest of our siblings, which is probably why we also butt heads the most. But it meant that most of the trouble we got into, we got into together.

Okay, so I got us into trouble, and Sutton had to endure it. Potatoes, potatoes.

"Of course I did. He wasn't having any fun until I came into his life."

Miles glares at me but doesn't argue, probably knowing he doesn't have a leg to stand on there.

"Inevitably," Ava says.

"How was stealing hermit crabs on your summer fun list?" Sutton asks, a speculative brow raised.

"*Petting* a hermit crab was on my list," I say like it's obvious.

Jaime blinks at me confused, before opening his mouth to ask something.

"Don't ask," Miles suggests.

"What else was on your list?"

"I'm so glad you asked. See dolphins, which we did. Get ice cream, eat s'mores, go for a walk on the beach, play volleyball. We ended up merging his with *my* summer list since we're now attached at the hip, so I got to check off hook up with a local, and we went to the be—" Miles's wide hand covers my mouth, cutting off what I was going to say.

"Beach?" Reed guesses by some miracle, and I nod feverishly. I lift my hands to try and mimic what Miles and I did, but that clearly is the tipping point for him.

"It's been great, you guys. I gotta get this one out of here before she gets into any huge trouble or confesses everything we've ever done that her sister really shouldn't know about." He stands, hand still on my mouth, as Jaime also stands.

"Yeah, I gotta get Ava home for the same reason."

"I would never get into trouble." Jaime glares at her, and she rolls her eyes. "I'm only going because I'm tired," she mumbles, and he smiles, pulling her into his side. That's when Miles lets go of my mouth and lifts me, carrying me over his shoulder, heading towards the exit.

He seems to really like doing that.

"Later. Let's do this again next time we're back in Evergreen," he says, and I realize my bag is looped over his other shoulder. "Or down at Seaside Point—I've got rooms for you guys to stay." Then he turns, and I wave at my sister and my friends.

That is, right before I shout, "Fuck on a lifeguard chair!" as we walk off.

"Jesus Christ, Claire," Miles groans, but he doesn't put me down as we leave the bar, and I could swear I feel the rumble of his laugh as we walk.

THIRTY-THREE

CLAIRE

The buzz from the few drinks I had at the bar only adds to the pleasure coursing through me as Miles fingers me.

His fingers pump into me as he hovers over me, and I've never been happier to be in a hotel room than right now as I moan out loud. Even though my parents repeatedly told us it was silly to stay in a hotel room for one night when my childhood bedroom was free, we did anyway for this exact reason.

Before I hit the edge I'm building toward, Miles pulls his fingers out, and I watch with misery, lust, and a little bit of awe as he puts them into his mouth, sucking them clean with a groan.

"Yeah, I've gotta eat that clean," he mumbles to himself before he moves to his back next to me. He then rolls me over, shifting and positioning me to my knees, until I'm straddling his face. Instinctually, my hands move to the headboard behind us, gripping it for stability, then looking down my body at Miles before I groan.

The image could be hung in museums. His face framed by my thighs, his eyes heated with lust, lips tipped in the hottest smirk known to man...it's a masterpiece. And then his hands go to my hips, thumbs against my hip bones, the others splayed over my ass.

"Ride my face, baby," he says, then tugs me down onto his mouth.

"Fuck!" I shout as soon as his lips touch my sensitive clit.

His lips wrap around it, his tongue flicking and teasing me. The pleasure rockets through me as I ride his face as requested, his eyes locked on mine. His tongue moves, slipping into my pussy, fucking me, and I let out a deep moan.

"You're so hot," I say, leaning back just a bit so I can feel his tongue slide into me, his smile widening as his mustache scrapes along my swollen clit. "Oh, god!" I twine my fingers into his hair to hold him right where I need him as my hips move, taking what I need.

His fingers dig into the skin of my hips, helping my hips move as I buck against his face, and that alone does it. I'm falling, coming on his tongue as I moan his name. My body is still ricocheting with my orgasm when he slides his tongue out and moves from under me.

My hands still on the headboard as I try to come back to this universe.

He shifts around me on the bed, and when he's behind me, there's a quick pull on my hips to tug me back, my upper half falling to the bed. Then he positions me until my hips are up high, my knees and elbows in the bed, back arched deeply. The tip of his thick cock slides up and down my entrance before he slowly, so fucking torturously, slowly, starts to slide into me.

A pained groan leaves him, and I look over my shoulder at him. His hair falls to the side, and I see his eyes are focused on where he's sinking into me, his jaw slack, tongue in his cheek.

I lied.

This is what I want a picture of. I want it plastered on every surface, burned into my brain, into a permanent spank bank material for me to use forever.

"You should see how you look, Claire," he says low, his eyes never leaving my pussy, never leaving his cock sliding into me. "Taking me so perfectly. Spread around me. So fucking wet from my mouth making you come."

The previous pleasure of that orgasm was long gone, a distant memory, but the need to come around him and total lust for this man are already taking over my body once more. It seems to be a constant state of being since we got together, if I'm being honest.

I thought it would fade, that the need that lives in my bones would start to ease, but it's anything, it's worsened. Everyday, I wake up wanting Miles more, remembering the new positions he twists me into, the new highs he brought me to.

It's no different now, when he bottoms out in me, and we let out a mutual groan in pained pleasure. I'm so full, especially bent like this. I try to shift to my hands, but his hand on my back pushes me so I can't.

"Stay down, baby. Let me see your ass work."

I moan at his words, at the way the thumb of his other hand digs into my flesh, a bite of pain left in its wake. I do as he says, staying with my chest to the bed, arching my back further and shifting my hips so I'm fucking him, meeting him thrust for thrust, my fingers between my legs, sliding against my clit, then up to feel where he is sliding into me.

"Fuck, you're so hot," he says, then pulling out and slamming back in. "Let me see this ass move."

I oblige, more than happy to take over. I shift my hips back and forth, rocking on him, falling myself and retreating, slamming back again. His hands are ghosts on my hips, there just to have a hold on me as I do all of the work, a frame for his own dirty fantasy. It builds in me as I fuck his cock, as I hear his groans of pleasure and adoration from behind me. A hand slides down my spine, then back up, tracing to my ass and the tight hole there. His thumb grazes over it, and my pussy tightens, my hips faltering.

I've never done that. Never even felt the vaguest desire to. But right now? With his thumb gently pressing there, with his breathing getting heavier?

I want *everything*. Whatever he'll give me.

"You want my cock here one day, baby?" he asks, the question almost entertained.

I nod frantically into the bed, my hips trying to move up, to get whatever I can. I'm so lost in a cloud of another orgasm I know will swallow me whole.

"Yes, yes," I breathe out, my hips still fucking him though the movements are stilted, no longer able to keep up any semblance of a rhythm.

He slaps my ass with his free hand, and I scream his name out as his thumb presses just a bit harder against my asshole.

"God, I wanna take that," he says as if to himself.

"Yes, please, fuck." I want everything—anything—in this moment.

A dark chuckle leaves his lips, though it sounds strained with the same need coursing through me.

"No, no. Not today. We have to get you nice and ready first. Work up to it."

I lose the pressure, and I groan at the loss, but then I hear him spit, it lands on my ass before his thumb is back, rubbing the wetness in and pressing on my asshole. I moan at the pressure of him against me in this new way and the way he groans in response. My hips move back, both onto his cock and the thumb against me, the tip sliding in.

"Fuck, you're so hot," he says as his thumb continues sliding into my ass. It's tight and feels foreign, but he moves slowly, my body accepting every inch he gives me. When his finger is all the way inside, his palm against my lower back, I moan deep and uncontrolled, my hips bucking. I'm full, and the stimulation on both of my holes is too much.

"Fuck, Miles, fuck," I whimper, my hips moving frantically. The sound turns into a shriek as both his cock and thumb shift out, then back in, fucking me.

"The hottest thing I've ever seen," he moans, sliding his hips back until just the tip of his cock is still inside. Then, he slams back in, filling me, and pressing his thumb in deeper. He repeats that same move again and again, each time his thumb moving inside me with the rhythm of him fucking me, my hips bucking back to get more, to get deeper, to come around him.

"Fuck, Claire, you gotta get there soon," he groans through gritted teeth like he too is teetering on the edge and needs me to fall first. "Claire."

That last small plea of my name is what does it. I tip my hips back to get him in as deep as I can, my chest collapsing further into the bed as he slams in, and I come, hard.

His thumb presses in deeper, and it somehow intensifies my orgasm, stars shooting behind my eyes. Sound fades away as the world shifts to nothing but colors and feelings, pleasure washing over me. His loud moan fills the room before I feel him throbbing in me, spilling his cum into me, hips bucking to get just a bit deeper.

When I fall asleep after we clean up, I do it completely exhausted and utterly happy.

"I wish I had something like that," Miles whispers in the quiet of the dark. He rolled off me eventually after we both caught our breath, cleaning himself before coming back with another wet washcloth to clean me up as he loves to do. Then he dragged me into the shower with him, where he cleaned me up before he dried me off and helped get my tired body into bed.

That's where I am now, curled around him.

I turn to look at him, confused. "What?"

"What you have here. A tight-knit family. Siblings who care about one another. Family dinners. Everyone is hanging out together." Silence fills the room as I wait for him to continue, knowing he has more to say on the topic. "My mom and my grandmother did great, did what they could, but they had to make ends meet. They were always working, always busy."

It reminds me of the man himself and makes me wonder just how much of his inability to slow down and enjoy life is something that has been ingrained into him.

"And, of course, there's Paul. You have your sisters and Nate, and I know some of it is because you're the youngest, but there's...camaraderie with you four. Even when you fight, you get over it; you support each other. Respect each other."

After dinner and Pictionary, and after dad talked to me, both Nate and Sloane came and found me, apologizing even though I told them it wasn't necessary, that I understood. It's what we do, and I never thought to take it for granted, but seeing it from his viewpoint, I see how one could envy that.

But I also realize then that Miles doesn't see it.

"You do, Miles. It just looks different," I tell him gently.

"No, I don't," he says with a scoff. Then I untangle myself from him, shifting to look at him better, seeing that he actually means it.

"You're out of your mind if you don't realize what a family you have."

"Mom's great, but she was an only child, so was my dad. I just have my mom, really."

"Honey, you have an amazing family. Grant and June and Deck and Lainey. Helen and Benny and—"

"They're all friends. And they aren't blood."

I shake my head.

"Family is what you make it, Miles. You've made yourself one hell of a family," I say, and he stares at me, taking me in for long, long moments before he smiles, understanding spreading over his face, a peace I've never seen settling over him.

"Yeah, I guess you're right." Then he leans forward, pressing a kiss to my lips and burying a hand in my hair. "And I can't wait to continue doing that."

I don't ask what he means because the moment feels precious and sacred, but I can see it in his eyes all the same.

I want to continue making a family...with you.

THIRTY-FOUR

CLAIRE

"Thanks for helping," I say as I take Miles's T-shirt from him, putting it with his other things, far enough from the dunk tank that, hopefully, they won't get completely drenched when he goes under.

Grant, June, Deck, and Lainey are standing to the side, and Grant already has a wad of cash and a wide smile, so Miles is *definitely* going under.

I asked him for the favor very carefully after he was well exhausted after making me come with his mouth *and* coming in mine. I crawled up his body, snuggled into his side, and quietly told him that we needed to fill in a few more spots for the dunk tank.

"I've never been able to say no to you, Claire. Ever," he says, smiling wide and not missing my perusal of all of his tanned skin.

"That's bullshit," I laugh, pushing on his shoulder, but he stands straight, unflinching, before he wraps an arm around my waist.

"I'm serious." I roll my eyes, and he uses his free hand to hold my chin and direct my gaze to him. "Tell me when I've told you no, Claire. When I followed you into the cold-as-fuck ocean? When you showed up at my door looking for somewhere to stay? When you brought home half a dozen hermit crabs? When you wanted me to fuck you on a lifeguard chair?" I look around with wide eyes, but he pulls me in even closer, pressing his lips right below my ear. "I'll do whatever you ask of me, Claire. Every time."

It hits me then that I actually can't think of a time when Miles has told me no, and the knowledge of that short-circuits my brain.

"Come on! Stop sucking face, and let's get to dunking!" Grant yells, and the small crowd surrounding him cheers.

Miles heaves a sigh into my neck before groaning and walking away from me.

"Let's get this thing over with," he grumbles before stepping into the dunk tank.

"Three balls, five dollars," I say to Grant ten minutes later.

He's already dunked Miles five times and clearly is out to do more. Now, Mrs. Miller—Sarah—is tossing balls at Miles's target while he teases her. Everyone—locals and tourists alike—have been wandering the boardwalk all afternoon, playing games, eating food, and enjoying the gorgeous day.

It's been the most perfect afternoon, and without even having a tally, I already know we raised a ton for the department.

"Do you have tap to pay?"

I give him a look.

"Grant, this is a community event. No, I don't have a credit card machine." He rolls his eyes, and I smile sweetly. "But there's an ATM over there," I say, tipping my chin to the other side of the boardwalk. I expect an argument, but he moves toward it with excitement, and at the sight of it, I let out a laugh.

Sarah uses her last ball, missing again, but I watch as Miles reaches out of the cage he's in and hits the target she missed by a long shot before falling into the water. Everyone cheers and laughs, and Miles shakes his wet hair when he comes up out of the water, wiping it out of his eyes before looking straight at me. I smile, and he returns it before he resets the stool and climbs back on, June now heckling him with balls in her hand.

For not the first time, I feel it—that happy feeling in my chest from just being here, with these people, supplying this community. It's starting to feel like I was pulled here for a reason, not to give myself space to find myself, but because this is where I *belong*.

"How many for a hundred?" a voice asks, pulling me from my daze. I turn to find Brad in front of me, that cocky smile on his lips, but it's no longer laced with kindness to try and win me over. He's in that ugly-ass white polo and khaki shorts, and I give him a tight smile.

"Three for five dollars," I say.

"Come on, a deal for a friend?" he asks.

I shake my head. "It's a community fundraiser, Brad. No discounts." He truly is *such* an asshole.

He takes me in, then looks to Miles. "Of course, just joking." He hands me the hundred that's so crisp, it must be straight from the bank unless he irons his cash, which I wouldn't put past him. "Just three, keep the change."

I lift an eyebrow. "You sure?"

"That's all I'll need," he says, and I roll my eyes, taking the cash and handing him three softballs.

"Stand at the line, then throw," I say.

He nods and gives me a cocky grin before moving toward the chalk line we made earlier this morning. Everyone stands around him, Miles and our friends glaring at the asshole as he stretches like this is going to be some huge, impressive feat instead of a kid's carnival game before he makes his first throw.

I've never never been more happy to see someone miss a target. I let out a snort that I cover with a cough when he misses, and Miles looks at me with a wide smile. I shake my head at him, then look back to Brad.

"Wind is pretty strong today," he says, and I look to the flag behind him to see it's drooping, showing there's barely a breeze. I nod and give him a tight smile before he winds up.

"Or maybe you just can't aim," Miles says, and I snap my head to him, eyes wide. He doesn't even look at me; just keeps smiling at Brad like he already knows he's going to miss before he releases the ball.

This time he's closer, though he still misses.

"You suck, mister," some kid I kind of recognize as a younger sibling of one of my lifeguards says, and his mother quickly shushes him before Brad glares.

"Come on, man, can't hit a target?" Miles says, taunting Brad. I have to fight a laugh.

"Fuck off."

"This is a family event, Mr. Baker; we'll have to ask you to refrain from foul language," Helen says. I don't know when she got here, but she's also smiling at Brad like she's entertained by him missing his shot.

This whole town is nuts, and I love it. Brad's jaw goes tight. Before he turns back to Miles, winding up and throwing.

The ball misses the target again, and to my pleasure and horror, the kids gathered behind Brad started cheering.

His face goes beet red as he turns and walks off, leaving Miles laughing hysterically before he drops into the water, Grant already taking Brad's spot with his next round of balls.

"This was good," Helen says as he dunks Miles on the first try, the kids cheering again. She stands next to me and places a hand on my shoulder. "Fun for the town and the tourists. You've got an eye for this kind of thing."

I shrug and smile at her. "PTA kid. I've been to more fundraisers than anyone ever should."

"I'm just saying. Something to keep in mind. Anyway, you're on break," she says. "Take that boy with you before Grant spends his life savings."

I smile as Grant throws his last ball at the target, hitting it again, and Miles falls into the water. I nod because the baseball coach is already standing to the side, waiting for the shift he signed up for, a bunch of his players lined up to dunk him. I have a feeling he'll get even more wet than Miles did.

Grabbing a towel, I walk over to the tank. "Time's up, bud," I say, and he gives me a smile.

"Already?"

"I'm on break."

His eyes go soft before he climbs out of the dunk tank. "Does that mean we can go hide under the boardwalk for a bit? Make out?"

I let out a loud laugh, loving this side of Miles that I rarely have seen in the past but am glimpsing more of each day. Playful and fun, less worried, less stressed. Though I like all of the versions of Miles, I like this one best.

"Hold your horses, bud. First, you gotta dry off."

He wiggles his eyebrows at me as he takes the towel, draping it over his shoulders. "So you're not saying no..."

I roll my eyes, and he shakes his head like a dog, his hair sending droplets of water toward me.

"Oh my god, stop it!" I say, but he doesn't; instead, he reaches for me, and despite my backing up with a laugh, he gets to me quickly and grabs me, pulling me into the towel with him and getting me all wet.

Fifteen minutes, and, yes, a mini makeout session under the boardwalk later, I'm making rounds to check on all of the events we have going on. Miles is holding my hand as we walk down the board-walk toward the beach entrance. The rec employee checking badges at the entrance nods us in, even though neither of us has beach bags on us, and I give her a smile of thanks.

Looking over my shoulder at the people milling about, my heart is so full, knowing that we absolutely blew whatever goals Helen had for fundraising out of the water.

Once on the sand, we move down the shoreline to check out the sandcastle competition, taking in all of the creations the kids have made. Some of them are just pushed-together sand piles, and others were clearly aided by parents. There are drip castles and bucket castles, and even someone's dad buried in a sandy mermaid tail, but my brow furrows when I move to the end of the walk and see a group of giggling girls around the last contestant.

"Who's that?" Miles asks, and I shrug but move closer all the same. That's when Miles grabs my wrist, tugging me back so I can't go any further.

"Miles, what—" But the words die on my tongue when one of the young girls shifts, and we see it: Jonah, smiling wide, building an impressive sandcastle, a gaggle of young girls around him, giggling and twirling their hair and— "Oh my god."

"Seems our boy got the much-needed self-confidence boost he needed."

Jonah says something, and all the girls let out a laugh.

"Where did he get that?"

"I may have pulled him aside the other day and given him some girl advice."

I shift to look at him, my jaw dropping. "You're joking." Miles shrugs, and I shake my head, smiling at him. "You know, under that grumpy exterior, you really are a nice guy."

He looks at me for long moments before he smiles again and pushes hair behind my ear. "Don't tell anyone."

"Your secret is safe with me," I whisper.

"We did it, Claire!" Helen says, coming over as we watch about a dozen tables lined up, kids on either side eating their bowls of ice cream, giggling and smiling all along.

"We made the money for the soccer team?" I ask with a wide smile.

"And then some! The wrestling team is already half-funded. And the day is still young."

I pull her into my arms and squeeze her. "I told you! You just need to capitalize on the busy season. I bet you can fund almost everything in the summer season alone. Add another event like this next summer, so you have two, maybe three events throughout the season? Perfect."

I already suggested a monthly or even, if they can manage it, weekly live music on the beach night, and Helen agreed it could be a great idea and brought it up with the town to figure out permit requirements for a temporary stage.

"She's a smart one, Miles."

He puts an arm around my shoulders, pulling me in and pressing a kiss to my hair.

"Don't I know it," he says.

"We're getting together a volleyball team," June says, coming out of nowhere, her fingers wrapping around my wrist and tugging me toward the sand. "We need you."

"I'm still—" I start, but Helen shakes her head.

"Go on! Go have some fun!" Helen shouts at me with a wave of her hand. "You're supposed to be off the clock by now."

"I was planning on helping—"

She shakes her head again. "You're off the clock, Claire. Enjoy your night." And then she walks off, ending any discussion.

"Come on! It's me, you, and Lainey versus Miles, Grant, and Deck." As much as I like girl power, that sounds like a recipe for disaster.

I sigh and turn to Miles. "You in?" I ask. "It's on the list."

He smiles wide, then shrugs. "Where you go, I go."

June glares at him as only a best friend can do to the man you're inevitably head over heels for.

We're on the third round, and, to everyone's surprise, each team has won one round. We both are only two points away from the predetermined ten-point requirement, but it's getting increasingly hard to concentrate.

One, I was up at the asscrack of dawn to work, and it's nearly five. Two, my super hot boyfriend stands across from me, looking, well, super hot. My eyes lock on Miles's, and he smiles wide at me, winking, and my mind spirals on all the filthy things a simple wink could mean.

A moment later, the ball hits the sand right next to me.

"What the fuck, Claire!" Lainey yells from behind me.

"Hey! He was distracting me," I say, giving Miles a glare.

"Gotta keep your head in the game," he says with a smile.

My glare deepens. "Who the fuck are you, Troy Bolton?"

His brow furrows. "I don't know who that is," he says as June tosses the ball over to her brother.

I blink at my boyfriend. "You don't know who *Troy Bolton* is? Oh, god, that's a crime. We need to—"

"Claire!" June yells, her competitive side winning once again. "Flirt with your boyfriend later. We've got some boys to beat."

I look to said boyfriend, who is smiling wide at me, and I realize two can play this game.

While Grant serves, I reach back and take the ponytail holder out from my hair, grateful the wind is blowing toward us so it's not in my face before I stretch my hands behind my back, my boobs pushing out in Miles's direction. June spikes the ball over the net, knocking Miles in the head before it falls to the ground.

I turn to June, giving her a high-five before turning back to face Miles.

"It's so on," he says with a grin as Lainey serves the ball.

"Is it? I didn't realize."

Grant sets the ball, and Deck hits it over right to Lainey.

"You're getting it when we get home."

"Promise?" I ask, then watch heat flare in his eyes as the ball goes to him. He hits it over with ease, right to me, but when I try to hit it, I come in wrong, sending it wild to where no one could save it.

"No!" June shouts on a disappointed laugh.

"Sorry," I say with a cringe, walking over to hug my friends.

We watch as the guys huddle together, all excitedly shouting in celebration.

"They're kind of cute, you know?" I say, watching Deck, Grant, and Miles all jump like they're fifteen instead of over twice that. I can't help but smile as I watch them, both because it's hilarious but also because it's so good to see Miles *happy*.

"I think you're just in love," June says, but Miles is bounding over for a good game kiss before I can even respond.

THIRTY-FIVE

CLAIRE

We're walking along the sand an hour later, looking for shells when Miles is fiddling in his pocket, and I look at him confused. His face turns red as he bends quickly, grabbing something he dropped out of the sand.

"What was that?" I ask.

"What was what?" he says, but he's blushing, so I know it wasn't in my head.

"What did you drop?"

"My wallet," he replies much too quickly.

I stare at him, and if I didn't know better, I'd let it go. Fortunately for me, I do know better.

The blush on his cheeks, the panic on his face...he's hiding something.

And I want to know what it is.

"Miles Miller, what are you hiding?" I say with a smile, stepping closer to him.

"Nothing, let's keep walking—"

I shift my body, my hand going into his pocket before he can stop me to find what he dropped.

"Claire, I—"

I still when my fingers brush it. Three, actually. Gently, I wrap my fingers around the familiar forms and pull them out. He sighs like some grand secret is about to be revealed, and when I open my hand, I see why.

In my hand are three small shells.

Perfect, gorgeous shells.

"Miles..." He doesn't respond as I stare at them and then up at him. "Why do you have these in your pocket?"

A hand goes behind his neck, holding himself there, and the blush creeps down his neck now. "Because I drop them sometimes."

"You..." Slowly, it comes to me.

The beach walks.

My shell collection.

You're my lucky shell finder, I told him. *I always find the best ones when we're together.*

"Do you drop these for me?"

He lets out a sigh, then runs a hand over his hair.

"That first time you found one when Grant and I took a walk with you two, you were so excited." I remember the shell, a dark blue-grey scallop shell the size of my palm that was perfectly intact. I look up at him, asking without saying it, and he shakes his head. "That one wasn't me. But you were so excited by it, how perfect it was. You said you wanted to find a sand dollar one day, and I knew the chances of finding a perfect one on the beach were slim. So I..." He pauses then sighs. "So I bought a small one at a gift shop."

"No way," I whisper, my jaw dropping and my eyes widening as the pieces fall together.

"You came down a few weeks later to see June, and we all went to the beach together. I slipped it in my pocket. It was dumb, but..."

I jump in with the rest of the story and what I know of it.

"I was looking for shells that night. You said I shouldn't walk on the beach alone."

"I stand by that," he says, and I roll my eyes but otherwise move right past his protective streak to the point of the story.

"You dropped it?"

He nods.

"And you were so happy. You being happy made me happy, even then, so I made it a habit of mine. Popped a couple of them in my pocket every time I thought I might see you on the beach."

"How long were you going to let this go on?" I ask in awe.

"As long as I could," he says with a laugh. "Think it kind of loses the magic if you know about it."

I stand there, looking at him, my eyes wide, my entire understanding of Miles and my relationship once again turned on its side.

"Oh my god, you're so in love with me," I whisper with a smile. "And you have been. For like, ever."

I mean it jokingly for the most part, but his face takes on a serious note as he steps closer, grabbing the shells from my hand and pocketing them once more before pulling me in close, his hand going to my chin.

"I really am." He rests his forehead on mine. "I'm so fucking in love with you, Claire; it's made me crazy for six years."

"Miles," I whisper, my throat tightening with *stupid* emotions, and he smiles as a tear slides down. His eyes soften as he swipes it away with his thumb.

"My sweet, soft girl," he whispers.

"You know I love you too, right?"

"Yeah, Claire. I do," he whispers against my lips. "But it's still good to hear you say it."

"I love you," I say, wanting to give him anything and everything he wants. "I love you, I love you, I love you. I have since I was nineteen, you know."

He smiles softly. "And I've loved you since you were nineteen and already driving me up a wall."

I let out a small laugh and a sniffle, a hand on either side of his face as I pull him down to kiss me. "Yeah, I guess you were kind of a creep, weren't you?"

He pinches my side, and I let out a laugh, trying to pull away, but he tugs me into him once more.

"I love you, and I always have. I hate the tourists, but the season brought you every summer, so I used to count down the months, waiting for you to come," he says, a whisper I can barely hear over the ocean. "But I don't want to wait for the summer anymore." My heart pounds, and he tucks hair away from my face. "So what do you think —any chance I can convince you to stay in this little tourist trap of a town with me?"

I stare at him for long moments as his words sink in. As my mind finally understands what I couldn't see for some time.

"This town isn't a tourist trap, Miles," I say with a shake of my head. He gives me a disbelieving look. "This town isn't a tourist trap, you are."

He looks at me confused, but I smile wider at him.

"You're a tourist trap, Miles Miller."

"What?"

I step closer to him, and he puts an arm around my waist, pulling me in close.

"You lure in unsuspecting tourists and make them want to stay forever."

"Is it working? Are you stuck here?"

"I'll stay for as long as you'll have me."

We make love that night. It's not the first time, and I hope to God it's not the last, but it's that: making love.

After, Miles sets up the fire pit and shows me the makings of s'mores he bought without my knowing. I sit on his lap in comfortable silence, eating my marshmallow and enjoying a perfect summer night.

Below us, people are still milling about, chatting and laughing on the boards, and families are out on the beach eating dinner or having dessert.

Sitting here, looking out, I'm hit with the overwhelming sense of home. It's a feeling I've never felt anywhere else, one I felt glimmers of over the last few summers, the most beautiful glimpses, but I only felt it wash over me the day I stepped into this house.

June told me Grant is confused as to why Miles won't just agree to sell the house, make a boatload on the sale, and buy something smaller, more low-key, and off the boardwalk, but I get it. There's something about this house that is so special that I want to keep it forever.

So finally, here on the deck, exhausted from one of the most fun and fulfilling days I can remember, after Miles and I finally confessed our feelings after dancing around it for months—years, if we're being honest—I decide to jump in.

"Hey, Miles?"

"Yeah, baby," he murmurs, hands brushing through my hair as a gentle breeze rolls over us. It's a cooler night, and the sound of people laughing mixed with the waves crashing against the shore and the crackling fire settles my soul. I realize, in this moment, I want nothing more in this world than to keep this.

Not just Miles, but this house. This place where he was raised, this place his grandfather built, this place where I fell in love with him.

I bite my lip, knowing he's not going to like what I have to say next, but knowing I have to all the same.

"I'm going to say something, and you're not going to like it, but before you go off the handle and react, I need you to listen to me. Listen to what I'm really saying instead of how you're feeling." I feel like a therapist talking to him like this, but here we are.

"Okay..." he says. "Should I be nervous?"

"No. But you know I love you, right?"

"Uh, yeah?"

"And you love me?" It might be a bit soon from the grand declaration of love to pull this card, but if I'm being honest, it's been sitting with me for weeks, and I haven't found the right opening to give him my offer and this is as good as I'm going to get.

"Yeah? Claire, where are you going with this?"

"And you know I love this place. Seaside Point, our friends, the Seabreeze...this house." His body goes tense with my last word, and I keep speaking, not wanting to pause and get lost in my thoughts. "I told you to listen before you react, Miles."

"Claire..."

I move, shifting so I'm facing him, my knees now on either side of him. I'm in one of his too-big shirts and a pair of boy-short panties, so the playing field might not be super even, but I'm willing to work my womanly wiles to get my way.

"If something happens—if you need to buy the house sooner than you planned and don't have all of the money, I want you to let me help out."

He closes his eyes and sighs, any hint of distraction from my being in his lap gone.

"Claire—" I cut him off with a soft kiss before holding his face in my hands and forcing him to look at me.

"I don't want to lose this. For you, yeah, I guess, but selfishly, for me too. I love it here. I love that I fell in love with you here, and I broke you out of your shell here—" He opens one eye and glares at me, and I give him a wide smile. "I love that your mom was raised here and that you were raised here. I want to convince Nate to let us watch Sophie for a week on summer break, and I secretly want her to fall in love with Jonah one day. I love lying on your chest and listening to the waves in bed, and I'm going to love watching the snow fall on the shore in the winter."

"Claire—"

"I don't want to lose this. I have the money. I've been saving for years. Call it...call it an investment in my future," I whisper.

He looks at me, brow furrowed, before his face clears, going soft.

His hands move up, ghosting along my back before he tugs me back down to his chest.

"An investment in your future?" he asks into my hair, and somehow, I know he needs this, this barrier where I can't read his face.

I let him have it while explaining.

"Our future. I want to raise our kids here, Miles." I smile at the mere thought of kids with Miles' eyes and my hair. "I just...I have the money. It's just sitting there, and I can't stomach the idea of losing this place just because you were too stubborn to accept help."

I can feel him readying to argue, but I shake my head, on a roll now.

"You don't get it. I spent my entire life waiting for something to feel right, for someone, and somewhere to feel right. I found it here. Let me help you protect it."

"Claire—"

Finally, I sit up and put a finger to his mouth.

"Please, don't say no, Miles. Please. If you want to make some kind of plan to pay me back, whatever, I'll spend it on dumb shit anyway. Just...think about it. Give it a good thought, not just your impulse of no."

"Claire," he starts, and I open my mouth to argue, but he shakes his head. "No. Now it's my turn. Now you're going to listen to *me*."

"Okay," I whisper, eyes wide and definitely not turned on by bossy Miles.

He smiles, knowing I absolutely am.

"Okay," he says, and it takes a moment for me to realize he's agreeing, not just repeating me. "Okay. If we are at a point where time is running out and I don't have the money, I'll let you kick in. But that's you kicking into our life, okay? That means you're stuck here, stuck with me."

I smile then, wide and full, my heart soaring.

"I wouldn't want to be anywhere else."

THIRTY-SIX

MILES

As always seems to happen, once my life settles into something good and easy, it comes crashing down. Two weeks after the block party, Claire is out with Lainey and June having a girls' game night, and I'm relaxing, waiting around for her to make her way home to me when there's a knock at our front door.

Thinking it must be Claire forgetting her keys again, I walk over to the door, a smile on my face as I open it, only to find my brother, who looks a lot more disheveled than the last time I saw him but with a cocky smile on his lips.

My face falls instantly.

"Not happy to see me, big bro?" he asks, snark in his words.

"No, I, uh—" I start because the real answer is *no, I'm not happy to see him,* but I also know giving him that answer will be a bad idea.

The fact of the matter is that Paul only comes to me when he needs something, and him standing on my doorstep is never a good sign. He left Seaside Point when he was eighteen for college, visiting occasionally, and the longest he spent here since graduating was the summer he met Claire, which I now realize he brought her everywhere he knew I'd be just to rub salt in the gaping wound he'd made.

Still, whatever drama he's brought to my doorstep is not something I want the entire boardwalk to bear witness to, so I step aside and open the door wider. "Come on in."

He gives me a look that seems much too happy and makes my stomach churn.

When he walks into the house we lived in for years after our dad died, before Mom got a place of our own, he looks around, taking in the small changes Claire has made since moving in.

She moved her shell collection down to an end table she bought at a thrift store last week and started hanging pictures and art, some of it from piles of things she found from my grandmother in a guest room that either Paul didn't want or didn't sell. In the corner near the door are a pair of running sneakers and my work boots neatly lined up with at least four of Claire's flip-flops in a messy, colorful pile next to them.

His eyes zero in on that before he looks at me again, the intrigue gone from his face, venom replacing it.

For the first time, I let myself wonder what the fuck happened to him. What made him hate me so deeply? I used to wonder what I did wrong, but I've come to realize I did everything I could to repair this relationship, but a one-sided effort only goes so far.

"So, you're dating my sloppy seconds?" he asks bluntly.

My first instinct is to punch him.

My second is *also* to punch him.

My third is to tell him to leave.

I don't get to do any of those before he continues running his mouth, my jaw tightening and my hands curling into fists at my sides as I force myself not to use them.

"I should have known, you know. You always wanted her, always were looking for some reason to get close to her, take what was mine."

I take in a deep breath because *violence is not the answer.*

"Paul, come on—"

"You can have her." He says it like he's doing me a favor, though neither of us needs his stamp of approval. But then a smile spreads on his lips, and I know this won't be good. "You can have her. I was only with her to fuck with you, after all. Mission accomplished."

My jaw goes tight at the thought of him using Claire that way, at the confirmation of what I knew in the back of my mind. But it's one thing to think it; it's another for your flesh and blood to admit it to your face they wanted to make you miserable.

"You think I didn't see the way you looked at her? The way *she* looked at you?" He shrugs. "You two can go run off into the fucking sunset for all I care. Too bad you won't have this place to raise your demon spawn in."

My brow furrows, and nausea churns in my gut, knowing how much Paul loves his dramatics and knowing somewhere deep down where this is going.

"What are you saying?"

He turns to me again, his smile wide, his look fucking *evil*.

I can't believe this fucker came from my mother, the kindest person I know, or my father, who was the most hardworking from what everyone who knew him has told me. I can't believe my grand-mother saw the good in him until the very end.

I *can* believe that he was able to play the game long enough to win Claire because she so desperately wants to see the good in people.

"I sold my stake." My gut drops to the floor. "Yeah, a little bird called, told me you were fucking my ex and gave me an offer I couldn't refuse." Even though he doesn't say it, I can guess who he sold it to, and I'm not going to like it.

"How the fuck—"

"He's got good lawyers, read through our agreement, and there's nothing that says I can't sell my stake, just that I can't sell the house without your approval." His smile is villainous as he crosses his arms on his chest. "And now you get to argue with him about whether or not you sell."

My head goes light with the betrayal as his words sink in, as I come to terms with what he's telling me.

"I can't believe you did this, Paul," I say, low. "Mom is never going to forgive you for this, you know that, right? Grandma would be rolling in her fucking grave."

"Yeah, well, what have they ever done for me?" I stare at him in utter shock, not even bothering to give him the long list of things both of them have done, knowing it will fall on deaf ears. "Exactly," he says as if that silence was because I couldn't think of anything instead of it being because I was coming to terms with the fact that I'll never have a good relationship with my brother, that this is the end of any kind of relationship.

I shake my head. "So what, you cashed out and you're heading off into the sunset? Knowing you, you're going to fucking blow it in a month or two."

"What do you care?" he asks, his jaw going tight. He never likes it when someone holds up a mirror to him and reminds him of his short-comings.

"I guess I don't." I take in a deep breath before I ask my next question. "Who'd you sell to?" I ask finally, though I know the answer.

Of course I know the answer.

With the way I've been poking him all summer, the way Claire embarrassed him at the block party? I should have seen this coming when he asked about my brother. I should have—

"Baker," he confirms, and I close my eyes, taking in another deep breath as reality crashes over me. Time is up. There's no way he's going to give me time, no way he's going to make this easy on me.

"He said to tell you if you want to talk, he'll be over at Surf tonight. Celebrating."

Even though I shouldn't, even though I should drop it where it is and move on, I don't. For the first time in my life, I snap at my brother.

"You're a piece of work, you know that? You did all of this—sold me out, sold the family out, sold the fucking *town out*—for what? Seventy-five grand? One hundred grand? That's all that was left, four years of payouts. And you know, I probably would have kept sending you money because it's what Grandma would have wanted, at least until you got on your feet and figured out what you wanted to do with life. But you fucked me over instead. You took the easy cash and ran, the way you always have."

His face shifts.

"You always had *everything*, Miles," he says with venom, and something in me snaps, the last thread of hope that my brother would turn around dissolving before my eyes.

"What the fuck are you talking about?" I shout. "Are you really so deluded that you believe that? I got a job when I was twelve because Mom needed help. I was the one who gave you a fucking allowance until you left the house because you didn't want to work. You went to college; you got to leave the town you hated so much and go off and pretend to be a rockstar, which, news flash, Paul: you fucking suck."

I have no reason to preserve this relationship anymore. My brother is dead to me, so what's the point?

"And you're so pissed about Claire coming back to town and connecting with me, but you didn't even care about her. You never did. It was always just to get at me because you *knew* she meant something to me. You fucking knew, and just like everything else, you wanted to take that from me."

I expect him to argue, to tell me that's not true, to give me some reason for it, but instead, he smiles.

The asshole fucking smiles.

"And what if I did?"

"Then it makes you a bigger fucking asshole than I thought."

"Just remember, Miles, next time she's under you, moaning your name, she moaned mine first." And then he's out the door.

When he leaves the house, in a fit of rage, I slam my fist into the wall, then sink to the ground in misery.

THIRTY-SEVEN

CLAIRE

Lainey drops me off after girls' night, screaming that I'd better *get it good,* which means when I open the front door, I'm still laughing.

My brow furrows when I realize it's not locked, something that Miles is diligent about. My nerves ratchet high when I walk into the house, though. In the kitchen, I can see Miles, head in his hands, elbows on the granite of the counter.

"Miles?" I ask, my voice coming out in a worried whisper, but he doesn't move, doesn't shift to acknowledge my entering the house at all. "Miles, honey?"

I step closer, dropping my bag at the front and barely closing the door as I rush toward him. But then I stop in my tracks, startled when I see the hole in the wall that's the size of a softball. I look around, worried someone is hurt, until I see one of Miles's hands wrapped in a bag of frozen peas.

"What happened here?" I say out loud, finally stepping into the kitchen and tipping my head to the hole.

"I punched a wall," he says matter-of-factly as if that's not an alarming thing.

I roll my lips between my teeth and nod.

"I see that, but can I ask why are we cosplaying as a frat boy right now?"

He doesn't answer, instead giving me a fake smile.

"You had a long day. Why don't you go take a shower and get in your pajamas? I'll be up in a little bit."

Fuck that.

"Mmm, no, I think not. What's going on here? What happened?"

He sighs, then shakes his head. "Nothing, baby. Go take your shower and get comfy. I've got a few more things to do. When I'm done down here, I'll come up and talk to you."

That's when I notice there are a dozen papers spread around him. From a quick glance, I see they're bills, mortgage documents, and agreements of some kind.

"Miles, there's a hole in the wall. The chances of me going upstairs and pretending it's not there are slim to none."

He looks at me, then sighs, closing his eyes, and I see it there: how tired he is. Not the physical kind, but the bone-deep emotional exhaustion. He's drained because something big happened.

"Let me see your hand," I say softly, stepping closer to him. I move the peas aside and see that, despite a small cut on a knuckle, nothing looks too swollen or damaged.

There's a bit of a bruise on a different knuckle, but I've seen worse when he hits a finger at work. I lean down, press my lips right above the cut, and he lets out a small chuckle before I sit next to him.

It takes everything in me not to look at the papers because even though I'm nosy, I know he'll tell me what I need to know when he wants me to know it.

"You gonna tell me what's going on?"

He leans back with a sigh, closing his eyes.

"I—" he starts, and then he leans forward again and looks me in the eyes. "Do you promise not to freak out, no matter what I say?"

My head tips to the side, and my heart skips a nervous beat. "Uh, no?" I tell him honestly.

"Claire—"

"If you're about to tell me you kissed another girl..."

His smile goes wide despite his grim mood, and he shakes his head, an arm moving around my waist and tugging me out of my chair and into his lap. Having him hold me like this, some of my fears drift away.

"You think I could even *look* at another woman when I have you waiting for me when I get home every night?"

I smile a bit at that, my hand moving to the back of his head and tangling in his hair before I lift the other to cup his cheek, brushing my thumb along his mustache.

"You better not," I whisper. He smiles again, and I feel it against my hand, but it doesn't reach his eyes. "Tell me what's going on."

"Are you going to stay calm if I do?"

My stomach turns again, but I smile all the same, trying to lighten the mood.

"Me? Anything but calm, cool, and collected?"

He rolls his eyes and then tightens his hold on me like he's afraid I'm going to run when he speaks. "Paul came by," he says, and my entire body goes tight.

"What? When?"

"About an hour ago."

"Why?"

He closes his eyes, takes in a deep breath, and I know—I *know* I'm not going to like what he has to say.

"Brad told him we're dating and convinced him to sell his stake in the house." My mouth drops. "I have to talk to my lawyers tomorrow, see what they say, but...I know Brad isn't going to be as flexible as Paul was. He came by to rub it in my face." My heart drops to my feet. "I think I have a plan, but—"

"You have to go be fucking kidding me," I whisper.

"It's fine, Claire. We'll figure it out."

I shake my head, though he's right. We *will* figure it out. First by finding out where the fuck the asshole is.

"Where is he now?" I ask.

"What?"

"Where is he now? Where is he staying?"

Miles shrugs, looking at me skeptically. "I don't know. I think he's at Surf right now; that's what he said at least, I—"

Before he can say anything more, I'm moving, pushing back from Miles and standing. I move to the door, slipping on my flip-flops again before I move.

"Claire," Miles calls, but I'm not listening. I'm out the door, not worrying if it closes behind me because even though he's going to try and stop me, I know Miles is going to follow me and will close it himself.

I start walking faster and look over my shoulder when I'm a few feet from the house to see if he's following me yet. He's probably getting shoes on, but once he's good, he's going to catch up quick. I start going as fast as my flip-flops allow me without eating shit and get to the entrance of Surf quickly.

"Where is he?" I say, looking at Deck, who is luckily on shift as a bouncer today.

"What—"

"Brad. Where is he?" Deck looks from me to Miles, who is moving through the throng of people to get to me, to probably stop me from whatever rampage I'm about to go on.

Deck smiles then, like even though he doesn't know *why,* he knows I'm about to go wild and can't wait to witness the aftermath.

He tips his head toward a door in the corner of the dimly lit bar. "Office."

I don't wait for him to say anything else, instead moving quickly toward the room he pointed to again on a mission.

"Claire!" Miles yells from behind me, but I don't slow down, instead making it to the door quickly and opening it, stepping inside where my ex and Brad are sitting, smiling, across from one another at a desk, a bottle of champagne between them.

The door doesn't slam behind me the way I hope it would

because that would be a dramatic entrance, but it's because Miles is on my heels and follows me in, closing the door with a quiet click and closing out the loud noise of the nightclub.

"Claire—" Paul says, an onslaught of emotions rushing over his face before it is pulled behind his mask. He's seen me full-blown angry twice now: once when I told him I was leaving if he didn't get his shit together and right now.

But this is a different kind of anger, one filled with injustice and betrayal and hurt.

I'm not mad or disappointed; I'm furious.

"Are you fucking kidding me, Paul?" I yell.

My ex's eyes widen, and his jaw sets firmly, but he doesn't speak.

"Claire, good to see you," Brad says, and I roll my eyes.

"Shut up, Brad. It's shitty to see you, as always. More so when you're being an even bigger asshole than normal." I turn back to my ex. "You sold your stake in your family home because, what? You found out I was dating Miles?"

"You were always into him," he says, sounding like a child who lost his favorite toy.

"Oh, get over yourself. If you knew I was into him, then why did you go after me that night? You were so fucking diligent about being together that whole summer, so caring, always hanging out with June and Lainey. Then when we started dating, you never wanted to come here again." I move closer to him, poking him in the chest. "Why go after me?"

He looks at me, then behind me, confusing me, but when I follow his gaze, I realize it being on Miles is the answer to my question.

Then, I see the truth I'd been slowly coming to over the past month or two. The painful understanding that I was just a pawn and another thing to use against Miles because Paul is a spoiled brat who needs the attention. That all this time, I'd been used as just another way to hurt his brother, and I was too stupid to even see it.

I don't know if I'll ever get over the fact that I was used as a way to get at Miles, if I'm being honest.

I, of course, knew this after Miles and I talked, but seeing the confirmation of it written so clearly over Paul's face, his utter lack of empathy for other people breaks something in me. Miles sees it, always so attuned to me, and he moves, putting a comforting hand on my back.

But he doesn't stop me.

"No fucking way," I whisper. "You have got to be kidding me."

"Oh, I'm sure he's told you all about us feuding our whole life. He always got whatever he wanted. For once I wanted to have what he wanted instead."

"You're fucking out of your mind. I'm a person, Paul! Not some toy!"

"And you were obsessed with him! Even when we were together!"

I shake my head because it's not worth arguing.

"You had me, Paul. You *had* me. I followed you across the country, left my family, was willing to pay for everything, but all you wanted to do was party and be some big star. But you didn't want to work, and you surely didn't want *us* to work. So when I said hey, I need you to pull your weight and, I don't know, remember I exist as more than some cash cow, you said no. So I left."

"Right to my brother," he says, pouting.

"No. Not right to your brother, you dumb fuck. Home. To my family. Then I came here for the summer to be with my best friend. I needed a place to stay, and I was lucky enough that Miles was willing to rent a room to me. Yes, eventually, we realized there was something between us, but that was long after you and I were done. But you're such a spoiled brat you think everything is about you."

I turn to Brad, the fucking ringleader of it all.

"And you."

"Look, I get it. Family troubles, but—" he starts, but I cut him off.

"You're so caught up in trying to win that you can't even be happy with what you got." I fling a hand out at the bar. "You have this whole place. A successful business. An entire empire you'll inherit, and there are dozens of people willing to sell to you, but you stood on wanting his. Why?"

"Why?" he asks, like he's confused as to why I would be confused.

"Yes, why were you so vehement about getting that location."

All his good ol' boy facade drops, and for the second time tonight, it throws me back.

"Because no one turns me down the way you did."

My jaw drops with that. "Excuse me?"

"You were a tease, all summer coming over to me and flirting."

"Oh, so you're fucking insane," I say, eyes wide.

His jaw goes tight. "You were flirting with me when I needed lifeguards, and you came to my bar that first night, flirted with me, and then left with *him*. Then I get you on a date, and he carts you off again. I cannot stand for that kind of disrespect."

I shake my head in disbelief. "So you're doing this because of *me*?" I ask, understanding sinking in.

"Claire—" Miles starts, but I shake my head.

"No, you're doing this because I'm dating him, too? You needed to best him by throwing your money around? You two are unbelievable," I say it with a laugh. "You couldn't beat Miles at anything, you loser. That's why you're doing this. Because you're so butt hurt that you suck at everything."

Brad puffs out his chest as if that will prove something.

"I disagree."

"With what? That you're a loser?" I ask, and Miles snorts out a laugh behind me.

"No, that he is better than me at everything. Clearly, I got the property, and now we get to battle about who is better at acquiring and keeping real estate."

"So you agree that you're a loser?" I ask. "That's good to—"

Miles pinches my side, and when I look at him, he's smiling wide.

"You really think you're better than me?" Miles asks, a smile pulling at his lips. He might also be insane because why does he look so...happy?

"Well, of course," Brad says.

"Prove it."

"What?"

"Prove it, Brad. You said money is nothing to you, right?"

Brad's chest puffs out somehow further, and I roll my eyes so hard it makes my head hurt.

"Yeah. That's why you're screwed. I can spend years in court fighting for you to sell to me now that I own a chunk of that property."

Years that Miles could never afford.

"So prove it. You're a big man; beat me."

"I'm not fighting you, Miles," Brad says unsurprisingly.

"Because you'd lose," I say under my breath, and again, Miles's fingers tighten on my side.

"Claire," he says low.

"What? He would."

Miles stifles another laugh before speaking again. "Not a fight. A competition."

"A competition?"

"Your beach olympics? You make a team. I'll make a team."

"And what? We compete for your house?"

"Miles," I say, my voice a whisper as I understand where he's going with this.

"I've got this," he says just as low, looking down at me.

"You win at the beach games, and we settle the ownership the next week, no questions asked. I win; the place is mine, free and clear."

He looks at Miles, assessing, like he's trying to figure out his angle. I too try to figure it out and can't quite put my finger on it. What is he *doing*?

"Or are you scared?" he goads him.

Brad scoffs. "That a bunch of idiot locals will win? Not likely."

"Perfect. Then it's a deal." Miles puts a hand out, and Brad stares at it like he might catch cooties before finally reaching out and shaking it.

"It's a deal."

"I'll send over a contract tomorrow morning," Miles says.

Brad lifts an eyebrow like he's surprised. "You're really going to do this?"

Miles shrugs. "It's that or lose my family house, right? You're not going to play nice, so I might as well go down swinging."

My heart sinks like a stone.

"I hope you're happy," I say, looking at my ex and really, I mean it. I hope he's happy with his choices. He might not have been the one for me, and he might be making the most insane choices, but he's still someone I once cared about.

"I don't," Miles says, then grabs my hand and drags me out of the office as I fight a laugh.

"You're insane, you know that?" I say under my breath when we step out into the cool summer night air. Miles pulls me in right to his side, and I melt just a bit as I look up at him.

"Learned it from the best," he says with a smile, and I roll my eyes. I'm so confused that he's not freaking out, because if we're being honest, I'm freaking out a bit.

"Miles—"

"Don't worry, Claire. We've got this," he says when we reach the house. I look up at him, and he pulls me in close, pressing his lips to mine. "It's just a house. You taught me that. With the amount I have into it and how much it's worth, I'd make more than enough to buy another one in town if I had to sell."

"But it won't be—" I start, and he shakes his head, moving to unlock the door.

"It doesn't matter, none of this shit matters. Not when I have you."

I pause and turn to him. He smiles at me wide, my heart a melted mess at my feet.

"If we win, great, if not?" He pulls me in close. "If not, I got you out of it all."

I smile, but I shake my head.

"Oh, we're going to win," I say.

He gives me a soft smile. "Claire, I don't want you to get your hopes up."

"I'm not. I'm just confident in my abilities."

He looks at me, then sighs and rolls his eyes, pulling me inside. Once inside, I roll my shoulders back and grab my phone.

"Okay. Then we need to get a plan in place."

THIRTY-EIGHT

CLAIRE

> Emergency meeting at the Seabreeze,
> tomorrow at 7. Bring everyone.

The message goes out the morning after we confront Brad and Paul, and I spend the day at work dodging questions about this emergency I texted everyone about.

That night the bar is more packed than I've ever seen it, and I smile as I sit on the edge of the counter, Miles at my side, looking out over this group of people who I've grown to love. Not only that, but the group I've grown to feel like I'm a part of.

"All right, all right," I say loudly, and everyone at the bar quiets down. "I called you all here because Miles needs our help." I turn to my boyfriend, unsure of how much he wants to share, but he sighs, running a hand over his head before he explains..

"Most of you know that when my grandmother passed, she left the house my grandfather built to me and my brother. I've been slowly buying his share from him, but it seems he's gotten..." He runs a hand over his hair again. "Antsy...and sold his share to Baker Brothers."

There's a rumbling from before us, the company clearly not beloved in Seaside Point.

"No fucking way," a voice says from out in the crowd, but Miles keeps talking.

"It wasn't a huge surprise, he has been tight on cash since he moved to California." June coughs out a laugh that sounds like *loser,* and I roll my lips into my mouth so I don't make a scene. "I've been trying to save up the money to buy him out this summer since I kind of had a feeling this was coming, but I'm not there yet."

"That's why he rented out the room," Benny says with understanding, and Miles nods.

"I was wondering why he did that. I thought he just wanted an excuse to live with Claire," Sam says, and I fight a laugh, shaking my head.

"Nah, I had to practically beg him to let me in the door." I move an arm around Miles's shoulders and pull him into me as he presses a kiss to my cheek. It's a shock; what a good mood he's been in, as if a weight has been lifted from his shoulders instead of dropped onto it.

"Fuck, Miles, why haven't you said anything?" Benny asks, his brow furrowed. His pipe is set aside, which tells me he's taking this seriously.

"I knew," Grant says, waving his hand in the air, but we ignore him.

"Don't worry, Benny, he didn't even tell me," Miles's mom says.

Miles went there this morning to talk to her about what happened with Paul. When I got home from work, he told me she was upset but didn't seem surprised.

"Because...I don't know. It's not a fun thing to share, that I'm struggling, and much less to talk about my weird relationship with Paul."

I make eye contact with Mrs. Miller, and she gives me a small, pained smile.

"That's what friends are for, man. We could have—" Deck starts.

"No," he says with a shake of his hand, rejecting any help as always, the stubborn man. Last night I reminded him of his agreement to let me pitch in if needed, but he told me we were focusing on winning the games first.

"We could do a fundraiser," Helen suggests cheerily, and a dozen or so heads nod across the bar.

"No," he says, almost firmer. "Any fundraising goes only to the rec department or something for the town. I'm not taking money from anyone."

Helen looks offended, and I roll my eyes with a sigh.

"Trust me, I offered," I say. "We have a plan, though. One that doesn't fuck with his fragile male ego."

Miles glares at me, and I give him a preening smile.

"He's a little stubborn," Mrs. Miller says.

"No shit," Grant agrees, and I smile, giving them an agreeing wink.

"Excuse me, this was *my idea*," Miles says, and I roll my eyes.

"Okay, so maybe it was Miles's idea, but I refined it so it's way better now. Here's my plan," I say, putting my shoulders back and smiling. "Surf has those beach games next week, and—

"Oh, hell yeah," Grant says with a wide smile, cutting me off. I shoot him a glare.

"Can you let the girl finish?" Lainey asks, irritated. An embarrassed *blush* burns over Grant's cheeks, something I tuck into my pocket before refocusing.

"Surf has the beach games next week, and Miles told Brad if his team won, Miles gets the house, no issue. If he loses, then he has to cooperate with the sale. So—"

"I'm in," Deck says without even hearing the rest of the story.

"Me too!" Lainey says, raising a hand in the air.

"We need six people, and one person is supposed to be under eighteen."

"Jonah?" Helen asks, and I nod. That was who Miles and I already thought would be a good fit after the block party.

"Do you think he'd be interested?"

She gives me a *duh* look. "After all the work you two have been putting in to fix his street cred? I think he'd do almost anything for you both." I smile, happy to hear it. "But, Claire, sweetie—" she starts, and I shake my head, knowing what she's going to say. As head life-guard, I'm expected to work the event and manage the lifeguards on shift for the games, something that Brad asked about specifically when he contracted the rec department.

"I know. I'm working that day. But that works in our favor too."

Helen raises her eyebrow, but June gasps, already knowing where this is going.

"The Sigma Pi Memorial Day Party," she shouts, and I smile wide.

"Exactly."

"Uh, what was the Sigma whatever party?" Deck asks.

"It was this giant contest between my sorority and one of the frats. Claire wasn't in a sorority, so she wasn't in the competition. She stood on the sidelines and, well, did what she does best," June explains.

Miles looks at me and raises his eyebrows. I lift a shoulder and smile.

"Make a scene," I say, fluttering my eyelashes.

"Why do I feel like I'm not going to like this?" he says low.

"Be a good boy, and let me work my magic," I say with a wink, making Helen laugh aloud. "We're working on finalizing our team, but we're still going to need all of your help, both with general cheering and booing, respectively, and for Project Make a Scene."

"I'm in," says Helen.

"Me too," says June.

"In," Sam says, looking shy, probably because he's afraid Miles is going to come in and be all protective hot guy again. The room becomes an echo of *I'm in*s, and I turn to Miles with a wide smile, my eyes watering because of the show of support for him.

"Such a girl," he whispers, pulling me in close and brushing away the tear on my cheek. I press on his chest, but he pulls me in closer. "Thank you, Claire," he whispers for my ears only.

I look up at him, his smile shining down at me when he should be upset or worried or angry. I know then that he meant it, that he's shifted his priorities, that this summer made him see there's more to life than working until you bleed for the far-off possibility of things being good.

And that alone means we already won.

THIRTY-NINE

CLAIRE

"I wish I could help," I say with a sigh as Miles gets dressed in the bedroom attached to the bathroom where I'm doing my makeup.

I lean forward into the mirror, ensuring my sunscreen is completely rubbed in before adding blush, lipstick, and mascara. Usually, I wouldn't bother with the extras for work, but this isn't just a typical day. Today, I'm one of the three lifeguards and first aid members hired by Surf to monitor the beach games event.

"You'll still be there the whole time," he says, and I smile into the mirror.

"Yeah, but it's not the same. I want to kick someone's ass." I know our plan dictates that I *can't* be on the team, but I wish I could be, all the same.

"I don't know how I'm supposed to focus on the tournament when you're dressed like that," Miles grumbles, walking into the bathroom.

I turn in the mirror, checking the fit of my red bathing suit. I'll admit it's a bit revealing, but it still meets the requirements I've been given. I turn fully to him, then lift my hands up, hooking them over his shoulders and pulling him close.

"That's the point, baby," I whisper against his lips. "You can concentrate, knowing when you get home tonight, I'm all yours. The rest of them? They know they can't have it, so it's just a sweet fantasy of theirs they'll never have."

He shakes his head. "You're diabolical, you know that?" he asks with a smile, his hand dipping below the back of my swim bottoms to cup my ass. "But you'll still be a distraction."

"Just know if you win, I'll let you do whatever you want to me tonight."

His eyes widen along with his grin. "Anything?"

"Anything," I confirm. He drops his head to my shoulder, and I let out a laugh at his dramatics.

"Jesus, Claire," he groans into my neck.

"You want to take my ass, baby, it's yours." His breathing goes a bit ragged, and he tugs my hips to his, where I can feel how much he likes that idea. "Not now, though," I whisper, then step back.

"Fuck, now we can't leave for a few minutes," he grumbles, readjusting his hardening cock in his shorts, and I smile.

"Keep that in mind, just in case you lose motivation."

"I don't think that's going to be an issue," he says. "I'm suddenly very fucking motivated."

"Good." I put the cap on my lipstick and throw a lip gloss into my bag before turning back to him. "Ready to go when you are."

When we approach where the beach games are set up, I see some familiar faces that have me stopping in my tracks.

"Is that..." I turn and look up to Miles, who is smiling wide. "What did you do?" I ask, turning to him, my *stupid* eyes watering, and he's grinning now.

"I called up Nate, wanted to see if they'd want to spend the day on the shore."

"I love you so much, I could kiss you," I say.

"Go, Aunt Claire!" Sophie shouts before I can, and I move quickly down the boards and onto the sand, where I grab my niece and spin her around. When I set her down, she starts jumping up and down like a maniac.

"Hey, what are you guys doing here?" I ask with a watery smile. I hug my brother first, then Jules, who is right next to him, before moving on to my sisters. Mom waves from where she's arguing with Dad about how he's putting in the umbrella, and I smile at the sight.

I wonder if that's how Miles and I will be in thirty years, me bossing him around, him doing whatever he deems will keep me happy because he can't care to have me any other way. When I look at him, seeing him setting my beach bag next to my lifeguard chair and shaking Margo to make sure she's full, I know the answer is yes.

God, it shouldn't be legal to be *this* happy. Really, it shouldn't.

"Miles called us, told us you're helping out, and he had a team going," Sutton says, putting an arm around my shoulder.

"I hear he's going to kick that asshole's ass," my dad says, looking around for who I assume is Paul. We found out yesterday when the teams were posted that Paul would be on Team Surf, something that made me more angry than it did Miles.

"He's throwing his hissy fit," Miles had said when I told him I wanted to go find his brother and break his leg so he couldn't compete. "Let him."

Like father, like daughter, if I'm being honest.

"That's the goal," Miles says, moving over to my dad to shake his hand.

My dad pulls him into a backslapping hug, and I fight more emotions that are on the verge. It's like once I fell in love and felt safe in that, all of my emotions were even more prominent, and the thin wall I was hiding behind is completely demolished now that I feel fulfilled in all aspects of my life.

"Hello, Claire," Brad says, walking over with a Team Surf shirt on. It's ill-fitting, and his team stands behind him, looking unhappy to be here, except for Paul, who looks unnecessarily smug. "Shouldn't you be working?"

I give him a smile, then look at my watch, followed by the competition area.

"I didn't know I had to be on before anything started."

His jaw goes tight.

"You work for me, so I don't appreciate you fraternizing with the—"

Helen steps over to us with a dark look on her face, though I have no idea where she came from.

"Actually, Claire works for the Seaside Point Recreation Department, not you, Mr. Baker," she says firmly, then turns to me. "And you're not even on the clock yet, Claire. Enjoy your morning."

"I just think—" he starts, and again, she cuts him off.

"Maybe you should worry about your own employees before worrying about mine," Helen says, tipping her chin toward his team, two of whom are fighting in an escalating volume.

He groans, then moves toward the two beefheads who look like they're about to throw blows. Brad moves quickly toward them, breaking it up but almost getting hit in the process, and I fight a laugh as I watch it.

Miles pulls me to his side, pressing his lips to my hair. "We've got this in the bag, babe."

Each event for the beach games is a bit different, but at the end of each one, each team is assigned points based on their ranking in that game: first place gets ten points, second place gets eight, and so on, until last place gets zero points.

Six teams are registered in total, all vying for the title of *beach games champion*. This seemed alarming to me, and I asked Miles what happens if *neither* of them wins the games. But according to him, they only have to beat *each other*.

Since I'm head lifeguard, I have to work the event, which we decided was best because I can run my chaos in the background and make sure the other team plays by the rules, even if we plan to bend them a bit.

The first event is a tug of war game, and after the Locals beat two other teams, they're up against Surf. I expect Paul to be at the front of their line, facing off against Miles, but I should have known Brad would want to face down Miles.

"Are you ready to lose?" Brad asks Miles with a wide smile. Paul stands behind him, while Miles has Grant at his back. The rest of the team is in line behind him, ready to pull.

"I'm ready to play," Miles says, not giving in to the taunt.

Brad opens his mouth to speak, but the referee starts his countdown.

"Get ready...set...tug!" the referee shouts, and the teams begin pulling. There's a line in between the two teams that if either steps over, they lose, and I watch it like a hawk. With the first tug, Miles takes a small step closer to the line, and my heart sinks. But the smile on his face when Brad lets out a laugh tells me Miles might have some mischievous plans of his own.

"Let's go, Miles!" my dad yells from behind me, sitting in the sand with my family. "Make that asshole eat sand!"

Miles's smile goes wider, but he doesn't say anything or even shift his focus.

"It's going to be a shame, Claire's family watching you lose everything today," Paul says through gritted teeth, clearly trying to egg on Miles despite struggling to pull.

But Miles stays silent, tugging at the rope, and I watch him take a step back as Brad and his team tug a bit closer to the line. My heart starts to pound, my hands sweaty as I jump in place to try and get rid of the nervous energy.

"Because you are going to lose everything, you know," Brad adds. It's clear he's goading Miles, but his cocky attitude is faltering as he's pulled another inch closer to the line in the center. "I can't wait to tear down that piece of junk," Brad says through gritted teeth.

Miles's smile widens then, and he shouts, "Now!" booming and loud, and I realize then the team wasn't putting all of their strength into it. Lainey, Jonah, and June go red as the muscles on Grant, Deck, and Miles all strain, tugging hard and quick.

It happens then and it happens quick: the team is pulled over the line, but not only that, Brad falls face-first into the sand, just like my dad predicted, his hands still on the rope and unable to catch himself.

I give Miles a wide smile and a thumbs-up as the team cheers, and I slowly reach Brad. We decided early on that if something like this happened, I would have to do my job and make sure the other team was okay before I celebrate, so Brad wouldn't have a reason to argue since I'm technically working today.

"You okay, Brad?" I ask as he slowly sits up. There's a small cut beneath his nose, but he doesn't seem injured, just a bruised ego. He brushes sand off his face, eyes glaringly locked on the jumping Locals who won the first game. Paul offers him a hand, but he slaps it out of the way before standing and brushing off the helping hand.

"I'm fucking fine," he grumbles. "Let's get the next game going." And as he walks back over to where his things are, I watch the scoreboard—yes, it seems Brad rented a whole *scoreboard*—turn, giving The Locals ten points and Team Surf eight.

We're off to a good start.

The afternoon goes on, and even though I'm on the clock and it should be a stressful time, it's some of the most fun I've had all summer. I love watching Miles and my friends all compete, beating the assholes at their own game. Half the town is here cheering on The Locals, and even the people who came to cheer on Surf seem to be switching alliances with each round as Brad somehow makes himself more and more unlikable.

His team got first place in the water balloon toss, getting himself ten points to our four (it seems none of our guys have soft hands and popped every single balloon that came their way, something that even though it was disappointing, I laughed so hard at, I couldn't breathe) and got six points to our eight during musical beach towels, though they lost whatever small portion of the cheering section they had when Brad pushed a kid to the ground to win and made her cry.

Next up is Beach Twister, for which we chose former gymnast June to be our contestant. She lasts long, until it's just her and some beefy guy on Brad's team left. I'm not quite sure how the man made it this far, but I don't think he'll be in much longer, not when I spot Benny stepping over with a bucket set a foot from the edge of the oversized Twister mat. I roll my lips between my teeth as I watch him conspicuously dump the bucket in the direction of the game.

Six hermit crabs come tumbling out, including Big Gina, still in her bedazzled shell, though I've given her a bunch of new ones to choose from. Clearly excited to be out and about, they start scrambling along the sand, making their way to the colorful mat.

I catch Jonah's eye and wink at him as he gives me a thumbs up, and then I hear June call out too loudly to be natural, "Is that a hermit crab?"

"What? Where?" the guy twisted next to her yells.

"Left hand red," I say with a bored tone after flicking the spinner.

"Where is it?" the guy shouts again, frantically looking for the hermit crabs June pointed out that aren't even near him. People keep pointing and whispering, and the guy clearly begins to panic.

"The timer is going—Team Surf has to make a move or forfeit the game," I say, ignoring the ruckus.

"Move," Brad yells, his face going red. "Fuck those little roaches."

The guy does, except right as he lifts his hand, he must see the hermit crab a few feet away and shrieks, falling to the ground and then scrambling up, pointing and yelling at Little Tommy, my smallest guy.

Yes, it turns out I got one boy in my grand escape plan.

"What the fuck is that?"

"The Locals win!" I yell, ignoring him, then watch as Jonah neatly grabs five of the crabs. June picks up the last one and kisses his shell before putting him back in Jonah's bucket.

They are so going to deserve a treat tonight.

···○ 🐚 🐚 🐚 ○···

"Next is the watermelon-eating contest!" the event presenter shouts some time later, after half of our team has started on the sandcastle competition on the other side of the beach. "I'll need one team member from each team to participate!"

Miles steps forward, moving toward the table lined with six plates and large slices of watermelon.

I laugh at the irony when I see Paul also move as the chosen team member for this competition. When I look over to where Brad's team is standing, his arms are crossed over his chest, a smug smile as if he thinks this is going to upset me or get in Miles's head. I roll my eyes and then look to the table where Paul is glaring at me as well.

I grab Miles's wrist and pull him in, noting his brother staring at us as I wrap my arms around his neck and pull his face down to mine, moving to my toes to kiss him.

"A good luck kiss," I say with a smile when we break it. He looks over at the table, seeing Paul staring at us, before he looks back at me with a smile and a small shake of his head. Then, I follow him to the table to monitor as part of my job. Miles sits on the end, closest to where I'm standing, and once again, I'm surprised when I see Paul is right next to Miles's seat.

"Surprised you could make time in your busy, rockstar schedule to help Brad out with this. I know your career is just skyrocketing," Miles says to his brother.

I let out a snort of a laugh, and I fail at disguising it behind a cough.

"Well, I have a recent influx of cash, so I have some more flexibility," he says as if that's going to bother Miles. It bothers *me* more than it bothers Miles, though.

"Just make sure you don't spend it all in one place, okay buddy? Put some in your piggy bank for a rainy day, since you lost everyone who would ever be willing to help you out when you crash and burn next time," Miles says low and easy, situating himself before his large piece of watermelon.

Paul's face goes as red as a watermelon.

"I'm about to make it big, so I'm not going to need any of you." He shifts before his own plate, but I can see the irritation written on his face. "When I'm famous, don't bother trying to get back on my good side."

With that, Miles lets out a bark of laughter, and I stifle one of my own before the judge starts telling them the rules: no using any hands, the first person to have mostly white on their watermelon wins, and that will be at the discretion of the judge.

"Go!" the judge shouts, and six heads dip, vigorously eating the fruit.

I watch Miles and instantly wonder to myself, *should this be hot?* Because as I watch him *devour* the fruit, I feel a little warm. Then I look at the contestant next to him and fight a laugh as I watch Paul chase the slick watermelon around, slipping and sliding. In contrast, Miles takes bite after bite, quickly eating the watermelon.

"Looks like you're having a hard time over there, Paul," I say, crossing my arms on my chest. "You always did have a hard time finding the right spots." I almost regret my jab when Miles coughs, slowing him down, but it's a momentary lapse before he continues on.

But Paul stops altogether, looking at me with a glare. I just shrug.

A moment later, Miles stands up and raises a hand, a judge coming over to check his rind before declaring him the winner. The crowd cheers, and Paul comes in dead last, not surprisingly.

"Once again, it's clear which Miller brother is the best," I say, giggling into the sticky kiss Miles gives me. When it breaks, I wipe the mess from his mustache and smile at him.

FORTY

CLAIRE

The sandcastle challenge lasts over an hour while other smaller events continue. The team puts Jonah in charge, and he takes his job seriously. I'm shocked to hear him boss Lainey, Grant, and Miles around during the hour the teams have to build. I have to turn away to hide my laughter more than once, but honestly, the kid is good.

I watch as they make an intricate castle, complete with a moat and seashells, driftwood, and sea glass that Lainey found on the shore, and mentally, I think I want one of them for my shell collection. It's impressive, though I have to admit the other teams have made pretty ones as well.

At the end of the competition, real judges walk by each creation, and I have to wonder just how much money Surf invested in this and if it could ever pay off. I guess a write-off is a write-off, but damn.

They walk up to our sandcastle and take it in. I'm not close enough to hear everything, but I catch glimpses of them talking to Jonah and watch with pride as he beams. No one else on our team talks or gives their own two cents, instead letting Jonah tell every aspect.

When they move to the Surf team, I see their kid team member making a small sandcastle in the corner with some buckets, where June told me she sat nearly the entire time after the other two team members told her to stop messing with their *real* castle.

God, I fucking hate them so much. I can't wait for them to get what's coming for them. I'm *hoping* it will be a big fat L.

When it's time to announce the winners, I watch the judges hand out numbered scores. They announce Miles's team fourth, with a pretty solid score of eighty-nine out of one hundred that has Miles giving Jonah a high five while Grant pulls him in for a one-armed hug. They move through the crowd and give out another score, and by the time they make it to the Surf Club, my heart is pounding because there is only one castle left, and no one has beat eighty-nine.

"Come on," I whisper, eyes on the judges.

"And the score for Team Surf's recreation of a mermaid..." the judge says, then smiles wide before saying, "Eighty-five!"

"Oh my god!" I shout, then stand and run over to them. "Jonah! You did it!" Our team moves around the boy whose cheeks have gone bright red, despite his wide smile.

"Jonah! Jonah! Jonah!" June and I start to cheer, and soon everyone around us is joining in. Miles and Grant grab him, lifting him onto their shoulders as we all cheer his name, laughing and warm with joy at his win.

I look over to where there's a shout and see Brad pushing his teammates over into the sand and then destroying the sandcastle like a kid who lost a T-ball game, and I fight the urge to laugh before refocusing on cheering for Jonah.

The final event is beach volleyball, with four nets set up and teams rotating through them. Two people from each team enter the game, and Miles and Grant are the two for Team Locals. They quickly won each round, beating each of the teams they had gone up against before. Finally, it's them versus Brad and Paul.

With both teams tied at fifty-two, whoever wins this game wins the entire thing, and my nerves are on edge. But as Miles comes to his things to grab a drink of water before the last round, he doesn't seem nervous *at all*. In fact, this might be among the most relaxed and content times I've seen him all summer.

"Why aren't you worried?" I whisper as he sets his water down and pulls me in close. "You guys are tied." Miles shrugs like it's no big deal, then presses his lips to mine, kissing me quick and hard.

"Because we already won, Claire," he says.

"Miles—"

"I'm serious. Look around us, babe. Look at this town, at everyone cheering, everyone who came out to support us. We won. What do they have?"

"Possibly your house?" I ask, and he smiles wider, then shakes his head.

"No, they don't." He's so delusionally self-assured, I wonder if maybe he has heat stroke.

"Maybe you should talk to Brad really quick, see if—"

"No. It's all fine, Claire. No matter what happens, we've got this. I promise."

I open my mouth to argue, but he kisses me again and steps back, a hand in mine.

"Do you trust me?"

I hesitate, but only for the slightest second. Not because the answer isn't an all-consuming *yes,* but because of the look in his eyes.

He genuinely isn't worried, and I'm not sure if it's because he has some kind of trick up his sleeve or a plan for what happens if they lose, but I'm relieved to see it all the same. So I answer, "Always."

He tugs me in once more and kisses me again. "Then let's win this thing."

We move together, hand in hand, to the team, where I look at my friends, this little family we've created, and put my hands on my hips.

"Okay, you guys, we've gotta win this thing. I'm going to do my thing, but we need you guys"—I turn away from Miles and Grant, who will be playing—"to wreak whatever chaos you can. Be loud, be obnoxious, be annoying."

"June's specialty," Grant says under his breath, and his sister reaches out and punches her brother.

"Use your specialty of being a stupid meathead who is good at sports and not much else, and I'll use mine." Grant smiles and pulls his sister into him, using his knuckles at the top of her head to give her a noogie before she dips out.

"Enough goofing off, you two! This is serious! Life or death!"

"I don't think it's that serious, babe," Miles says with a smile, and I turn my glare to him.

"It is to me! I don't want to be living on the street with my hermies next week, Miles Miller."

He smiles at me, then opens his mouth to argue before the judge shouts.

"Teams, get on the court!"

My heart races, and I turn back to my boyfriend and press my lips to his, hard. "Good luck. You've got this. Kick their asses."

"Love you," Miles murmurs, and I fight the melting of my belly.

"Love you too. Now go win for me." He gives me a salute before Grant grabs his arm and drags him off to the last game.

Grant is about to serve, and Miles looks at me with a wink and a smile. I blow him a kiss and then look to the other side, seeing Paul glaring at his brother. Grant serves, and Brad goes for it, setting the ball for Paul, who, still watching me with a glare, misses it completely.

I jump and clap, my boobs very obviously bouncing as I do, and from the corner of my eye, I know Paul is staring. He always had a thing for my tits, and knowing his weaknesses is really going to come in handy today.

Miles gets the ball to serve now, and I look down at my bikini top, grabbing and shifting my boobs as if I'm trying to rearrange them. That's when Miles serves and slams the ball into his brother's face.

"Fuck!" Paul says, holding his now bleeding nose as Miles stares him down from across the net apologetically. "He did that on purpose."

"That was a completely legal serve," the referee says.

"You've got to be kidding me," Brad says. "It hit him in the face."

"He was supposed to hit it with his hands, not his face," the referee says.

I fight back a snort of laughter.

"I want a second opinion," Brad demands, and the second ref comes over from the other side of the net. Since this was the final match, he was also watching from the sidelines.

"I saw it, and I agree with the call. Your teammate was staring off into space." Brad looks like he's about to argue, but someone from the crowd shouts, "It was legal, get over it!" The crowd rumbles their agreement, making it hard to argue further.

His jaw goes tight before he sighs, clearly realizing he's not going to win this one.

"Can I swap out my teammate for the rest of the game?"

I realize then that he probably picked Paul to piss off Miles, and I guess it worked, in a way, just not the way he hoped it would. The ref agrees to let Brad swap, and the game moves on with Paul glaring from the sidelines, holding an ice pack to his nose.

"Game point!" someone shouts ten minutes later as The Locals and Team Surf are tied. The new team member Brad swapped in is much better than Paul, unfortunately, though the bar was kind of on the floor. The game has been tight, but now I need to do my part.

"Team Surf serves!" the referee shouts.

That's when I drop my sunglasses.

"Oh, goodness," I shout, much too loud for a sunglasses drop, but then I turn my back to the court, winking at Miles, who is shaking his head with a small smile, and I bend. The sound of a ball hitting sand hits my ears, and the crowd groans. When I stand and turn, I catch Brad smacking his teammate upside the head, the ball in the sand at his feet.

"Interference!" Brad shouts, grasping at straws. "He was distracted by her!" His hand points to me. I hold my breath, waiting to see what the ref will say since, if he lets this stand, we win.

"Please, please, please," I whisper to myself, watching the judges walk over to Brad to argue with him. I feel eyes on me, though, and I shift my gaze to Miles, who isn't watching the judges or the scoreboard or Brad or anyone else.

He's watching me.

I love you, he mouths, and I smile, shaking my head.

I love you more, I say in reply, and he smiles wider and then shakes *his* head.

Impossible.

As seems to be the way when Miles is looking at me like that, my heart starts to beat wildly, but it tightens when I hear the judges, my head snapping in that direction.

"The ruling stands. The Locals win!" the referee says, and I watch as Brad throws the ball at one of his employees, hitting him in the stomach and knocking him to the sand, but I can't even take a moment to focus on his obvious temper tantrum because I'm moving.

"Oh my god!" I shout, running for Miles. "Oh my god, oh my god, oh my god!" I don't hesitate, don't take note of any people in my way. I just move my feet in the sand until I'm jumping into his arms, peppering his face with kisses as I scream. "Miles! You did it!"

He swings me around, his smile so wide and bright I think it might cause some kind of solar disaster, before he sets me down.

"No, we did it," he whispers, and my eyes start to water as our team comes over to cheer and celebrate our grand win.

This is what I've been missing: community. Friendship. Joy that is based on nothing but making everyone you love happy.

But then Helen and Benny come over, joining in on our cheering, and I can't focus on anything but how much I love this little shore town.

FORTY-ONE

CLAIRE

The Seabreeze is slammed that night, and all of the tables are pushed to the edges of the room, leaving a giant spot in the center of the room for dancing. Lainey is in charge of music, though she's not actually on the clock, as per her father's decree.

She is to *celebrate with her friends*, though she has found herself behind the bar, albeit a bit tipsy, more times than not tonight to help out her dad since the place is packed and poor Benny can't keep up.

We don't need celebration crowns this time because everyone knows we're champions.

I wince as I throw back another shot then smile at Miles, who is watching me from across the room. He winks at me but doesn't move from where he's chatting with Deck.

When I turn to head back to the makeshift dance floor, Helen stops me in my tracks, a soft hand on my arm. "Hey, my girl. I see you're about to go back on the floor, but I just wanted to tell you you're off tomorrow," she says with a smile.

I shake my head, not too far gone to remember that I do, in fact, have work tomorrow.

"No, no. I'm on the schedule."

"Not anymore, you're not. Plus, you should sleep in after tonight."

I cringe, also not drunk enough yet to forget about things like embarrassment. She smiles wider at my grimace.

"I feel like my boss shouldn't see me like this," I say with a laugh, but Helen shakes her head.

"What, happy?" She waves a hand at me like it doesn't matter.

"I was thinking more like tipsy and headed toward being hammered," I say with a laugh. "I should probably pace myself, since I've gotta be up early."

"No, no. I told you. You're off tomorrow. That's your prize. Enjoy it!" She gives me a smile. "I insist."

I take her in and furrow my brows. "Are you sure?" I ask.

"Yes, yes. You had to work the event, now you're good." I nod, and I make a note to tell Miles that I'm off tomorrow before I completely forget. "But on Monday, I want to talk to you, okay?"

My eyes go wide as my stomach flips with worry. "No one likes to hear that, Helen," I inform her.

She lets out an entertained laugh before she pats my arm comfortingly.

"Nothing bad, all good stuff." I give her a disbelieving look, and she puts an arm around my shoulders now, pulling me in for a hug before stepping back again. "I promise."

I continue to glare, and she rolls her eyes.

"Please. Go enjoy your night. Get hammered for me; God knows I can't do that anymore."

"Am I fired?" I ask bluntly, and she tips her head back with a loud laugh that draws attention.

"Not even close," she says, then presses her lips to my hair. "Go. Have fun." And then she disappears into the crowd.

I take a step toward her, but then Benny is at my side, his arm going into the crook of mine and tugging me toward the center of the room.

"No standing still for champions—it's time to dance, Blondie," he says, and I follow him with a laugh, forgetting all of my momentary worries.

"Having fun?" Miles asks later when I make my way to him. He's leaning against a wall, arms crossed on his chest, where he's been chatting with Grant and watching me the entire night like a hawk.

I'm past buzzed and far into drunk, but in that fun, happy way. The way that feels like I could fight an elephant and win, the kind that feels like I could take over the world if I wanted to, but I'm too silly and happy to.

I love this dynamic, the one where I cause chaos, and he lets me, watching from the sidelines, ready to step in if I need him, but not a moment sooner.

I smile wide at him. "The most fun." I run my thumb over his mustache. "You?"

"I always have fun when I'm around you, Claire," he murmurs. His hand reaches up, fingers wrapping around my wrist before pressing a kiss to my palm that sends shivers down my spine. "Though I think we would have much more fun at home. Alone." He presses another kiss to my palm and pulls me closer until my chest is against his. "Preferably naked," he says into my hair.

My eyes widen, and my pulse races instantly.

"We should—" I start, but then a familiar song starts, and I step back. "I'm so sorry, I have to go find June." Miles reads my face, and his brows furrow, not understanding. "Thursdays at Pulse!" I yell, ignoring him and looking around the room for June. I see her then, arms in the air and running my way, just as drunk as I am.

Both Grant and Miles seemed to have decided early on to cut themselves off, which bodes well for my night. When she meets me in the middle of the room, we grab hands, then look around for a table, before Lainey calls my name, then pats the sturdy wood of the bar. June and I laugh but move over, somehow managing to climb up without incident.

And then we're dancing, screaming the lyrics at the top of our lungs to the point that I know my throat is going to be achy in the morning, but I can't find it in me to care, not even a little.

Bar-goers around us hoot and holler, laughing and singing along, and that same feeling I've been feeling all summer long washes over me again.

Home.

Community.

Love.

Family.

My place. I finally found it.

"Claire!" Miles says, and when I look down, I see him standing below me, a smile widening on his lips.

It's so reminiscent of a few months ago, but this time, I'm not surprised to see him, and he doesn't look angry at all. And this time, I don't see my life flash before my eyes because I slip. Instead, I smile, turn, and fall on my own.

He catches me, of course.

I've learned he always will.

"Hey, Miles. Long time no see," I say with a smile, and he turns us, shaking his head at me.

"I think it's time for us to head out," he says as my arms loop around his neck.

"You're right. I think you have a prize to claim," I whisper against his ear. His eyes go wide before he starts moving toward the door.

"Miles," I say with a laugh. "We have to say goodbye to everyone!"

"Bye, everyone!" he shouts as he leaves, and a chorus of laughter and "Bye guys" echoes around us as we make our way to my spot outside of the Seabreeze.

FORTY-TWO

CLAIRE

When we walk in the door, I'm already undoing my jean shorts, pushing them down, and letting them fall to my feet with my panties. I take a few steps toward the stairs and cross my arms over my chest and tug off my shirt and bra in one go.

Miles is smiling at me, locking the door as he tosses his shirt onto the couch. I head for the stairs fully naked as he kicks off his shoes and then takes off his shorts. His cock bobs up, already hard, and my steps falter.

"Eager, are we?" he asks, and I nod, my eyes on his cock as my legs turn to jelly.

"Very," I whisper, licking my lips and turning toward him. He continues moving toward me, slow as can be, and my heart pounds with each step he takes. "You've earned your prize."

I expect heat, but his face goes soft as he steps closer to me, a hand on my bare waist pulling me to him. "We really don't have to do that, Claire," he says, a hand moving to brush hair back.

I reach up on my tiptoes, pressing my lips to his and groaning at the feel of him hard against me. The entire drive I thought about this, about tonight, and I'm already wet because of it.

When the kiss breaks, I whisper, "I really, really want to, Miles." And then because he deserves an extra prize, I sink to my knees and look up at him, my hand wrapping around his cock and tugging once, twice, three times.

"Claire," he says.

I smile wider, letting my tongue slide along the leaking slit at the end of his cock.

"Your prize, but I decide how you get it." His eyes go hazy at that, at the memory of when he said those same words to me, when he teased me to no end. I smile, put my tongue out, and tap the head of his cock on it once, then twice.

"Claire," he says through gritted teeth.

"I'm a kind torturer," I say with a smile before wrapping my lips around the tip and sucking hard.

With that, he lets out a deep groan that throbs right between my legs. He wraps my hair around his fist and tugs, and my eyes meet his. I'm sure he can see the lust reflected there as he pushes the back of my head so a few inches of him go into my mouth before he pulls back, then repeats the move. Teasing himself, but also me.

"Get it nice and wet for me, baby," he says, picking up the speed and fucking my face quicker, his hand in my hair guiding me along his hard length. "Because tonight I'm sliding into that ass of yours."

My eyes drift shut as I moan at the thought, taking him deep until my nose touches his stomach. My legs shift, my thighs clenching as I try to get some kind of friction, some kind of relief from the need coursing through me. I think I could come like this, his cock down my throat, his hand in my hair, his growly moans filling the air around me.

He uses me for his pleasure, and I never—*never*—thought I'd be into that, into a man taking over like this, but here we are. I can feel my own wetness coating my legs, I'm so wet just from this alone.

"Fingers between your legs, Claire," he says in a growl. "Play with yourself while you suck me off."

My eyes go wide, and a near-pained smile spreads on his lips, but

I waste no time at all, moving one hand from his hips to between my legs.

I'm *soaked*.

I moan around him as I swipe over my swollen, aching clit before I slide two fingers inside myself and start to ride them, fucking myself as I suck him off. The sounds in this room are absolutely feral: the wet of my mouth around his cock, his heavy breaths, the sound of my drenched fingers inside of myself.

It's my own personal version of heaven.

Even more so when he starts to move my head at the same pace I fuck myself, making me moan around him.

"God, you look so pretty like this, mouth full of my cock, pussy full of your fingers. I bet you could make yourself come like this, couldn't you? Barely a minute in, and you could come for me."

I nod as well as I can, already tipping on the edge and knowing it would be the first of many tonight. He smiles then, looking almost devious when he's looking down at me before he nods.

"Okay, baby. Make yourself come."

With his words, I start to move in earnest, not having to be told twice. The sounds become even more explicit, my mouth getting sloppy as I moan around him, whimpering as I take myself there, his thrusts getting more uneven, small groans of his own leaving his lips and sending me tighter, my legs starting to quiver.

"Fuck, Claire, I could come just watching this, watching you fuck your fingers because you're so turned on from sucking me off." I loosen my jaw then, my eyes wide as he slides down my throat with ease. "Come for me, baby," he says through gritted teeth, like holding himself back is actually paining him. "Make a mess. Drip onto that fucking floor for me."

Some dirty thought runs over his face, and his cock grows harder in my mouth, throbbing, and that's what sends me over the edge, what has me moaning deep and shaking as he slides deep down my throat one last time as I come, my body falling apart with my orgasm.

His thrusts slow as my fingers do, as I come back to this universe, and when I do, he's smiling at me, using that hand in my hair to pull me back and then up before pressing a hard kiss to my lips. His cock presses between us, pinned against my belly.

The kiss is long and filled with need, tongues twining, and instantly, I need him again. Then he breaks the kiss, stepping back and slapping my ass.

"Upstairs. Get on the bed, belly down, hips up," he says, and a shiver runs through me as I eagerly obey, moving up the stairs and to our room, scrambling onto the bed with a squeal and a giggle.

He follows me in slowly, and I can't see, but instead, I feel him entering the room. Then I hear him, feet passing across the wood floor, then stopping not far from me next to the bed. When I look over, he's standing a foot away. His hand slowly jacks his cock, and I let out a needy noise.

There is something so hot about watching Miles jack himself off, and my knees shift in the bed, my clit swollen from coming once already, but my pussy aching with the need to be filled. He steps closer, his hand going to the back of my neck, gently moving the hair to the side and over my shoulder. It's ironic how gently he's touching me when he just used a grip in my hair to fuck my face just minutes before.

"You want me to take your pretty ass, baby?" he asks, his hand running down my back, stopping on the swell of my ass, then moving back up to the center of my back.

I nod, a mewl leaving my lips at the mere thought of what we're going to do. His hand moves down again, coasting gently before his fingers ghost over my ass and to my soaking pussy. He groans when he feels it, and I echo the sound, my hips moving up to get more of whatever he'll give me.

I groan as he moves featherlight touches over my clit.

"You didn't answer, Claire. I need you to use your words." His fingers gather my arousal, one sliding in and then out and up to my ass again, waiting at the entrance without moving.

"Yes. Please. I need it. I want you in my ass tonight."

He groans at my consent, at my plea, then his wet finger breaches the puckered hole, the tip sliding in, and I let out a breathy sigh. It's foreign, but this isn't the first time he's touched me there. As he continues to push a single thick finger into me, I groan, my hips moving back to get more and pulling a chuckle from him.

"God, you're perfect," he says as he removes his finger then slides it back in, slowly fucking me, stretching me, filling me. But it's not enough.

My hand travels down the bed toward my pussy to rub myself and take the edge away, but his words stop me. "No, no. Not yet. No touching yourself."

"Miles—"

"Not until I say so." And then his fingers are gone and he's stepping away, padding across the room. I go to shift, but his head snaps to me. "No, stay." I arch my back again, and he smiles, the look of it near devilish. "That's a good girl."

I let out an unintentional mewl, the praise sending heat through me, but he just keeps smiling, opening a drawer and pulling out a bottle.

When he moves back, he's putting some in his hand and pumping it over his cock, eliciting a moan from me. He shakes his head and lets out a laugh.

The man *laughs*.

"No, you're not getting this yet. We've gotta stretch you out first, baby," he says, climbing onto the bed and moving back to my ass in the air. This time when I feel the pressure, he's pushing two fingers into me.

"Ah—" I moan, my hip moving back to get him in deeper, the feeling exquisite. The stretch is tinged in discomfort, though not pain, and it adds to the pleasure, my clit throbbing. After a moment, once my body relaxes, he starts to move, slowly fucking me with his fingers.

"God, look at you," he groans, and when I look back, I see his other hand tugging on his cock, making me tighten around him. "Fuck, I can't wait to feel that."

There's another squirt of the lube when his fingers leave me, and then the stretch is back, this time three fingers.

"Oh, fuck, Miles," I say, my hips shifting. It's tighter this time, the discomfort more pronounced but not painful.

"Shhh, baby. Relax, okay?" he whispers, and I do until his finger slides all the way. He repeats the process again, waiting until I'm ready, until my body relaxes before he starts to fuck me with his fingers again until I'm mewling and bucking and begging.

Then his fingers are out, and he wipes them on a towel I didn't realize he grabbed, before he's lubing his cock up one last time and doing more to my ass before getting into place behind me.

I want a mirror next time. Right next to us so I can watch every flex of his hips, watch him disappear into me, watch the look that comes over his face as he slides in.

The thought is gone when the head of his cock lines up with my ass, pressing gently.

He's so thick. So thick and so warm, and my breathing goes ragged.

"We're going to go slow, okay?" he asks, and my hips shift backward, not wanting to deal with slow. He laughs at that. "Claire, I'm going to like this a fuck of a lot, that much I already know. I really fucking want you to like it, but if I just slam into you, you will not like it."

I let out a loud laugh that turns into a moan when he presses the head of his cock inside me.

"Oh, god," I moan, eyes dripping shut because it's too much. Too good. Too thick. Too hot.

"Relax your body, baby," Miles whispers, his hand sliding up and down my back, his words strained. "Let me in."

I do as he asks, and he slides in a bit further, his hand moving up and down my back. He goes an inch, then lets my body relax, letting him in deeper, before going further. It's almost sweet, the calm, easy way he's working into me, the way I know he wants to slide in, but he's finding the control not to.

Finally, he pushes up against the tight ring of muscle, and I force my body to go limp as he pushes. There's a slight burst of discomfort tinged with pain before he's in all the way, his hips against my ass, and then I'm full. So full.

Pleasure cascades over me as he waits there, letting my body get used to the size of him.

"Good?" he asks through gritted teeth, holding onto a thin grasp of control.

I nod into the bed, eyes drifting shut at the feeling. His hand pulls back, slapping my ass, and the movement jerks him a bit deeper. I let out a low moan, every moment of this too much, too much pleasure and feeling.

"I need your words, Claire. Are you good? Are you ready for me to fuck your ass?"

"Please." I whisper the plea, barely able to get words out.

"Fuuuuuck,' he groans as he slowly slides out.

My hips shift back instantly, missing him already, and my pussy makes a mess between my thighs. "Miles," I cry out, the feeling overwhelming the pleasure too fucking much.

"I know," he says, as he slides back in slowly, filling me. The low, deep groan he lets out tells me just how good this is for him, heightening my pleasure with that knowledge.

"Miles, Miles, Miles," I say, a chant now as my hips tip back, as I try to get what I need, though I don't know *exactly* what that is. "More. I need more." The words are a plea, one he understands more than I do, because then he pulls out and thrusts in this time, deep and hard, and I *scream.*

"Yes!" His responding groan is everything, the grunts he makes every time he pulls out send me spiraling higher. His thumbs dig into my hips now as he pulls back and slams back in, my head snapping back as I moan.

"Rub your clit, Claire," he demands through gritted teeth, and I know that voice: he's riding the edge and waiting for me to fall first. "Rub it and come with me deep in your ass."

"Oh my god, oh my god, oh my god," I chant as he fucks me. I move my hand between my legs, my pussy soaking wet as I slide over my clit, my hand instantly covered in my arousal as I do.

It's too much.

It's so good, and it's too fucking much, the pleasure overwhelming me instantly. My back arches, my head falls forward into the bed, a guttural moan leaving my lips as wave after wave of pleasure crashes over me. I think I'm screaming, my body shaking with the most intense orgasm of my life. One of Miles's hands moves to my shoulder, and he thrusts deep inside and stays there, pulsing in my ass as he comes.

"Oh, we're definitely doing that again," I grumble into the bed, my body absolutely liquid, and Miles lets out a long, deep laugh.

After Miles makes me eat and drink about a gallon of water, I'm lying on his chest in his bed—our bed—when I say it. "I'm happy this place is safe," I say. "But for future reference, can we not bid the entire house on a silly game again?"

He smiles at me and shakes his head.

"I was never going to lose this house, Claire," he says, pushing my hair back gently. I blink at him, my brow furrowing.

"What?"

He shakes his head at me. "He was never going to get this place. I'd already figured it out when you came home and didn't have time to tell you my plan before you left in a tizzy."

"A *tizzy?*" I say, aghast. I try to sit up, but his arm firmly holds me in place against him.

"Baby, you ran out of this place like you were going to shoot someone."

I roll my eyes at him. "I don't even own a gun," I say as if that makes any sense in this conversation.

"Thank God for that," he mumbles, but I move right past that, needing to get to the heart of the matter.

"Can we go back to *you weren't going to lose the house?* I came home to you crying over papers and punching walls."

He gives me an irritated look. "I was *not* crying, Claire."

Now it's my turn to look at him with disbelief. "Close enough to it."

"Claire," he warns, and even though I usually like what happens when I don't heed his warning, my body can't handle another orgasm.

"Fine, you weren't crying, but that unpainted patch of dry way..."

"I was mad. That was when he had just left and it was better than punching him, because that would have gotten me arrested. But when you came home, I'd just gotten off the phone with my mom after I'd called my lawyer before that."

"Okay..."

"The contract already in place set the price of the house and how much of it Paul even owned. Brad couldn't ask for more than that. I already had most of the money saved up through the summer, and I called Mom to see if she could lend me the rest of the money."

"Miles..." I whisper.

"I was upset because I hate asking for help, and even more, I hated having to tell my mom everything after I left her in the dark as much as I could about the shit with the house and what a hard time Paul was giving me. But it was a bit late to keep protecting him. So she was upset when I called and filled her in, and knowing I was responsible for it killed me, which was when you came home."

"Oh," I whisper, starting to understand. "So when I stormed into Surf..." It wasn't even necessary, my mind fills in, but Miles just shrugs.

"I knew you needed that, to yell at Paul and finally get it off your chest, and honestly, it was fun to watch." He smiles at my shocked face, then brushes his knuckles along my cheekbone. "Do you really think I couldn't catch you when you were running in flip-flops?"

My nose crinkles because I never could figure that out. Miles runs every damn morning like a sociopath, and I, well...I don't. It didn't make sense that he hadn't caught me before I stormed into the office, but I wasn't really looking too closely at it at the time.

"But at Surf, you challenged him. You told him you'd give him the house."

He shakes his head, a wide, devious smile on his lips.

"No, I said we would settle the ownership without having to go to court. Even the contract my lawyer drew up that Brad signed the next day said the same thing: that we would *settle the ownership on the house as soon as the contest was over*. It basically just clarified that neither of us would contest the contract that was already in place with me and Paul."

"And he didn't realize that when you had him sign it?"

He shrugs then. "Men like that...they're all about whose balls are bigger. He thought he was going to win and thought that no matter what, he'd get the house. He thinks I'm just some dumb mechanic scraping pennies together, partially because I'm sure that's the story Paul sold him. He didn't think I'd be intelligent enough to sneak in something like that."

"You're sneaky," I whisper with a smile.

"No, he's an idiot and a shitty businessman." He's not wrong. "But now I got Paul's part of the house free and clear."

"And his girl," I say, jokingly.

Miles shakes his head then. "You were never his girl," he says, rolling us until I'm on my back, him hovering over me. His lips trail kisses down my neck, stoking a fire I thought was long out.

"Yeah, I was always yours," I whisper, my hips lifting.

And then he spends the rest of the night showing me just how much I've always been his.

FORTY-THREE

CLAIRE

When I walk into work on Monday, nerves eat at me. Even though I texted Helen on Sunday morning, hungover and happier than I'd been in years, to ask what she wanted to talk about, she told me to enjoy my weekend and that she'd talk to me on Monday, which gave me a full day to stress.

Miles continued to tell me it was probably nothing, but I couldn't help but think there was a problem. Maybe she wasn't a fan of the way I tipped the scales of the beach games even though she was in on the planning, or maybe because we're nearing the end of the season, she's going to let me go early. But most of those fears melt away when I walk in and see Helen smiling wide at me.

"Claire, my girl, how are you?" She stands from her desk and pulls me into a big hug. When she pulls back, she takes one look at my face and lets out a loud laugh. "You stressed about this all day yesterday, didn't you?"

I give her a small smile and nod. "I don't do well with vague warnings."

She shakes her head, then sits at her desk and gestures for me to sit in the chair she pulled next to hers. Once I do, I look at her.

"Are you going to put me out of my misery yet?" I ask, my stomach still turning.

"I'm cutting back," she says finally, and my stomach drops. I thought I had at least another two weeks at this job, but it seems... "This is my last summer working full time as the Director of Recreation."

My jaw drops. I knew that Helen was past retirement age, but from what I'd heard, she just loves this job so much, she's stuck around.

Except now, she's not.

"And I want you to take over."

The world spins, and my head goes light. I make an attempt to speak, but my mouth simply opens and closes, nothing of real substance coming out.

Helen lets out a loud laugh at my shock. "What?" She reaches over, grabs my hand, and smiles at me warmly.

"Starting after the summer season, I want to promote you to Assistant Director of Recreation. I'll work alongside you for the next year and retire for good next fall once you have a full year under your belt."

So many things run through my mind, from screaming *yes* at the offer I haven't even really been given yet, to crying, to looking around for the camera crew pranking me.

"Aren't there people who would rather have this job?" I say instead.

Helen looks at me, confused. "Do you not want it?"

I shake my head vehemently, confusing her more before speaking.

"No, no, no, I do. I so very much do. But...shouldn't I work up to it? Should I...I don't know. Work for the department for a while? Learn the ropes?"

She nods. "You'd spend the next year working as the assistant director before you get to be *the* director, but that would just be semantics for the most part. You'd be the one in charge. I'm cutting my hours way back. You'd just be working by my side to learn the ropes."

The air leaves my lungs as she stares at me kindly and patiently.

"I feel...I'm completely unqualified for this, Helen."

She tips her head to the side. "You've been managing the lifeguards all summer, scheduling them, filling in when needed, dealing with their drama, even hiring another mid-season when Tanya quit."

I shake my head, not because I didn't do all of that but because... "That was my job, though."

"You helped Jonah out, boosted that boy's confidence more than I could ever tell you. You got two dozen volunteers for the block party." I shrug, still not feeling like any of that matters. "Did I tell you we funded everything through March?"

My head snaps back. "What?"

"All of the programs are funded. Fall and winter recreational sports will require no enrollment fees. We covered it, based only on your fundraising." My heart skips a beat as a mix of joy and pride washes through me.

"It wasn't—"

"My goodness, do you always cut yourself so short?" I don't answer because I think she knows the answer. "You are good for this town. I had a dozen people come up to me at the block party, tell me how great it was. The mayor himself told me I should do whatever I could in my power to keep you on the payroll for as long as I can."

My spine straightens at that. "He probably meant it in general."

Helen rolls her eyes and heaves out an annoyed sigh.

"My god, girl, take a compliment! You are so hell-bent on everyone else having fun and enjoying life and getting what they want, but let yourself have it too." I sit there in stunned silence. "You are qualified, Claire. You might not have decades in this town or in recreation, but you did more for this town than most people. You'll be my assistant for a year, and I'll hold your hand. But you won't need that because I know you've got this. Hell, half this job is arguing with people, which we both know you're more than great at."

I smile at that, and then she hands me a stack of papers, which is when I realize her decision wasn't made on a whim. This is not something she just came up with, because there is a multi-page proposal in my hands with a cover letter and everything.

"I wrote this up the day after the block party. Brought it to the town council, pled my case, and they agreed. You should know, I told them you'd probably have some big fundraising plans for the Apple Fest, but from what I know of you, you do."

I bite my lips to hide a smile.

"I *have* been kicking around a few ideas I thought I might want to share with you—"

"I figured you would." Her face changes again before she leans in, taking my hand. Hers is soft and warm and reassuring. "You're good for this town, Claire."

My eyes water at her compliment. June, Lainey, and Miles can all tell me that until they're blue in the face, but there's something about having what feels like the matriarch of Seaside Point telling me I'm good for this place that finally lets it sink in.

"I think it's good for me, too," I whisper, and I do. This place helped me feel like I finally had some purpose, helped me find some meaning, helped me find Miles.

"So you'll take the job?" Helen asks, always one to get what she wants.

I smile wide at her, and then, because I can't imagine doing anything else for the rest of my life, I nod.

"Under a few conditions. If it takes away from the budget as a whole, I'll volunteer until you retire, then step in." She rolls her eyes. "That's a sticking point, Helen."

"We already worked in an assistant at the end of the last budget cycle, one I never used and instead funneled into a head lifeguard position." She gives me a knowing look, and my heart jumps. "I knew someone who couldn't handle a summer of wrangling teens couldn't handle this full time, so we were treating that as a bit of a trial run."

I nod, then give her my second sticking point.

"And two, I can't deal with Brad Baker at Surf. Too much bad blood, and I don't want to catch an assault charge."

She lets out a loud, boisterous laugh and shakes her head. "I don't think that will be a problem."

"No?" She shakes her head.

"After the scene he made on Saturday? I think Daddy called him back to the office. Caught him loading his things up into his fancy-ass car Sunday morning. Not sure what's going to happen there or who will take over, but he won't be your problem."

I nod because yesterday I spent a good amount of time watching videos, memes, and spoofs of Brad Baker's meltdown, laughing the whole time.

Finally, I look to Helen, then to her mess of a desk, then out the surrounding windows to the ocean as a sense of peace washes over me.

"Okay then. Yeah. I'll take the job." I don't ask about the pay or the hours or the expectations or insurance or anything I *should* care about because the rest will fall into place. I just know it.

She stands then, pulling me up and into her arms, hugging me tight and swaying from side to side as she does.

"Grateful you found your way to our little slice of heaven, my girl," she whispers into my ear, and when I pull back, we're both smiling, both staring at each other with watering eyes. "Now go. Go tell that boy of yours I convinced you to stay here for good."

I tip my head and shake it. "I have a shift—"

"No, you don't," she says. "You're off for the day. Go celebrate. I'll see you tomorrow."

I think about arguing but then decide against it, smiling at her and nodding.

"You sure?"

"If you don't, I'm taking back the job offer."

I smile and roll my eyes but nod all the same because I really do want to go find Miles and tell him the good news.

"Okay. I'll see you tomorrow. And Helen?" I say as she turns back to her desk, taking in the view before her. She turns her head to me, and when I have her attention, I say, "Thank you."

She knows I don't just mean for the job.

"Of course, my girl. Us wandering girls need to stick together, you know?"

I smile at that, wondering if Helen and I are the same, before I head out to find my man.

I've been here a few times over the past few years, mostly when my car was making a weird noise, only for Miles to tell me something like I was so far past an oil change that he was surprised my car didn't explode.

When I pull up, the garage doors are open wide, and he's on a creeper underneath a car that's lifted up on jacks. He doesn't hear me as I approach, but I wave to John, one of the guys who works with him, who smiles and winks at me.

"Hey, hot stuff, think I can get you to look at my undercarriage?" I ask when I stand above him. The tool he's holding falls to the ground with a clang, followed by a thump, and guilt eats at me as I hear him curse, clearly having hit his head before his booted feet move him smoothly out from under the car.

"Claire? What are you doing here?" he asks, looking confused and worried.

"Think you can take a break?"

"Is everything okay?" he asks, stripping off the gloves he's wearing and tossing them to the ground without a second look. He quickly stands up and moves toward me.

"Everything is great," I say, reaching for him, but he steps back like he just realized something.

"I'm greasy, babe."

"I don't care," I whisper, stepping closer and putting my arms around his neck.

He bends as if on instinct and presses a quick kiss to my lips.

"Is everything okay? Why aren't you at work?"

"I got a job offer," I whisper. His body goes tight, and he looks over my face like he isn't sure how to take that news. I smile again. "From Helen."

His body loosens a bit, and a smile starts to pick at the edges of his lips. "Assistant Director of Recreation until she retires next year." That smile spreads into a wide grin, and his arms tighten on my waist. "Helen says to tell you you have to thank her for convincing me to stay here forever." I whisper those last words against his lips.

"You're staying?"

"I was already going to stay. But now I have a job so I—" I can't finish my sentence because Miles is lifting me, spinning me round and round, his smile now a full beaming grin as I let out a giggle.

When he sets me down, he presses his lips to mine, dipping me back like some old movie. "Now you're stuck in this tourist trap forever," he whispers against my lips once he lifts me back up.

"Happily," I whisper back.

EPILOGUE

Claire

A year later

The summer celebration behind the Seabreeze is even better than last year, but that's because this year, all of my favorite people are here.

Two days after the Fourth, my parents rented a house in Seaside Point, and my sisters, Nate, Jules, and Sophie, all came for a week. Thankfully, Helen was more than willing to work a bit extra this week, though Nate and Miles had a blast picking on me when I worked a lifeguard shift yesterday.

But today, in the cove behind the Seabreeze, all of my favorite people are in one place, and my heart is so full it might explode.

"Okay, girlfriend," I say, jumping up and down beside Sophie, who has a fishing pole in hand. The bobber keeps going under the water, a fish on the line. "Now reel her in, nice and gently."

I have fished a grand total of *one* time this time last year when I won the yearly competition, but right now, I might as well be an expert.

"It's really hard," Sophia says through gritted teeth.

"I know, that just means it's a big one," I encourage her excitedly.

"I can't do it," she says, her face going red with effort.

"Sophie, Sophie, Sophie." Sutton starts chanting, and then Jules, Sloane, Lainey, and I join in, Decker coming in and bringing it down an octave as well. From behind me, I assume either Grant elbowed him when he stops chanting and yells, "*Ow!*"

"You're supposed to be on our team, man," Grant says.

I look over my shoulder at Deck, who is glaring at my best friend's older brother.

"Are you really mad I'm cheering for a seven-year-old girl?" he asks.

Grant doesn't respond, but his jaw goes tight, and I let out a laugh before going back to cheering my niece on.

The cheering does the trick, though, because a splash comes from the water, and my attention goes back to my niece, who starts shrieking with excitement.

"I did it! I did it!" She jumps happily, clearly not worried about the fish the way I was last year.

"You have *got* to be kidding me," Miles says with an exasperated sigh.

I'm confused by his statement, and even more so when Benny starts laughing, loud and wheezing, as he looks at the flopping fish. He comes to my side, putting a hand on my shoulder.

"I think she may have beat you, Claire," he says, and then I let out a laugh with understanding.

"Did I win? Did I do it?" Sophie asks, my brother taking the line from her and holding it up while Grant grabs Benny's measuring tape, holding it out to measure the fish.

"No way," he says, then looks up. "It's bigger than Claire's last year."

"Girls rule," June shouts with a laugh. This year, the group of girls shrieking excitedly is bigger and, thus, louder, something that, again, makes my heart swell.

"Sophie! You won!" I say to my niece.

She smiles wide, hands on her hips. "Of course I did. I'm the coolest, smartest girl ever."

I let out a loud laugh and hope to God she never loses her confidence.

"Duh," I say. "Okay, picture! Soph, hold your fish up!" Nate hands her the line, and she holds the poor, flopping fish up, a smile on her lips as all of us girls huddle in together.

Benny takes a photo, Miles taking one on my phone like the good boyfriend he is. "Must be something about those Donovan girls, you know?" Benny says with a wide smile after Nate releases the fish into the water.

"You know it," Sophie says.

"Who gets the prize?" Deck asks because before Sophie caught her fish, he had the biggest so far. "She doesn't even live here."

"Shut up," Sutton says, rolling her eyes. "You sound like such a whiner."

"Excuse me?" he asks, turning to her with a look of awe on his face.

"I said," my sister says slower. "You sound like a whiner who's mad that a little girl beat you at the fishing contest."

My jaw drops a bit, and I look to June, who is beaming, then to Miles, who is shaking his head.

"There's a prize?" Sophie asks with hope in her words, breaking up the tension.

"It's a parking spot at the Seabreeze," I explain. "Not very exciting."

"Don't think Soph has much use for a bar parking spot," Nate says with a laugh.

"Honestly, if anyone could somehow find a use for it, it would be Princess Sophie," Jules, my soon-to-be sister-in-law, says, the rock Nate slipped on her finger last Christmas glinting in the sun.

"I don't want a parking spot," Sophie pouts.

Miles looks from me to Nate to Sophie like he already has a plan.

From the corner of my eye, my dad lets out a loud laugh from the picnic table where he sits with Mom, Helen, and Sarah.

"Wanna make a deal?" Miles asks, getting on her level.

Sophie looks at him skeptically, hands going to her hips. "What kind of deal?"

"I'll buy you a new Ashlyn doll if you give me the spot," he says. He's spent plenty of time with my family over the last year, including getting to know my favorite niece well.

Her little nose scrunches up, concentrating before she responds. "And the Ashlyn horse," she says, crossing her arms on her chest.

I let out a laugh.

"Sophie—" Nate starts, but Miles puts his hand out for her to shake.

"Deal."

"God, can anyone say no to her?" my brother mumbles, and as I watch my niece and my boyfriend shake hands, I shake my head and laugh.

At least we've got our spot for another year.

"You know," I say, sitting next to Benny. "Love you; you're the coolest person here."

He smiles wider, that pipe moving with the movement. "An honor, darlin'."

"But you gotta quit that thing." His brows furrow in confusion, and I tip my chin to his pipe. "We want you to stay around for as long as you can, Ben."

With that, his lips spread, a wide smile almost making the pipe fall before he grabs it and starts to laugh, full out. His head tips back, and even though I'm confused, I can't help but crack a smile. It's the only option when Benny is laughing like this.

"I'm serious," I say once his laughter dies out.

"Not that kind of pipe, Claire," he says, and my eyes go wide, thinking he means he puts something other than tobacco in it.

"But it doesn't smell like weed—" I start, wondering if maybe Benny is just high all the time, which, honestly, would in fact make sense. But then I realize I don't think I've ever smelled the smoke coming from Benny's pipe. That's when he smiles wide, closes his lips around the pipe, and blows.

Bubbles come out of the end.

Fucking *bubbles*.

"Are you kidding me?" I ask with a laugh, pushing his shoulder.

Lainey laughs at my shock and comes over. "I had that talk with him years and years ago. He said he still wanted it *for his image.*"

"God, you're such a weirdo, Benny." He shrugs like he knows, and he's happy about it. We sit for long minutes, my parents chatting with Helen, Benny, and Sarah, before I see Miles near the shoreline of the bay.

He tips his head for me to come, and I stand.

"I'll be back," I say, smiling. My dad looks at me, reaching out for my hand and squeezing it. I look at him, confused.

"I love this place for you, Claire Bear," he whispers.

My eyes water, and I blink them out, then bend to press a kiss to the top of his head. "Love you, Dad."

He smiles again, something strange in his face, before he tips his head toward where we can see Miles waiting for me.

"Go to your boy." Then he lets go of my hand and sinks right back into conversations with Benny.

I make my way to Miles, who stands there with his hands in his pockets before putting one hand out to me. "Come on. Let's go for a walk."

I don't say another word before he's intertwining his fingers with mine, and we're walking along the water. It feels familiar, though the bay shore isn't as pretty as the ocean, and there are far fewer shells, even without Miles tossing them down.

"Good day?" he asks.

I smile up at him. "Great day."

I hear something fall, and I look down.

It's a seashell.

"Miles," I say with a laugh. "You don't have to do this anymore."

He's smiling at me before he tips his chin to the ground.

"Go on. Pick it up," he says softly.

I roll my eyes, but I do all the same, but when I lift it, I feel something on the underside. Tape. Tape and...

I turn it over, and my heart skips a beat. A gold ring with a perfect princess cut diamond taped to the back of a dusty gray-blue scallop shell, just like the first one I found with him. When I look up, he's on one knee, gently taking the shell from my hands and removing the ring.

Instantly, my eyes water. "Miles," I whisper.

"It took me seven years to get here," he says. "So I think for it to be of full impact, you should be standing." I'm squatting in the sand, my hand out from when he took it from me, but I can't convince myself to move. I shake my head. "God, can you even make anything simple?"

I shake my head again, smiling through the tears starting to fall down my face. His hand reaches out to cup my chin, his thumb swiping along my cheek to brush the tear away.

"I wouldn't want it any other way," he whispers. "But what I do want is for you to be mine. Forever. I want to wake up every morning with you in my arms and watch you eat junk cereal that will make your teeth rot out one day. I want to make a new fun list with you every single season because you're still worried I'm not making the most of every single moment, even if I spend all of my free ones with you. I want you to drag me to every rec department event and force me to volunteer. I'll drag my feet, but know deep down I'd do whatever you ask of me. I want to watch you dance with June, and I want to catch you when you fall off chairs or tables or bar tops. I always want to be the one to catch you. I want to raise our kids in the house my grandfather built, and I want them to be best friends with Sophie because she is, in fact, the coolest, smartest girl ever."

I let out a laugh then, the tears falling faster.

"But most of all, I just want to be with you. Forever."

"Yes," I blurt out, my hand moving to his face.

"I haven't asked a question yet," he whispers, and I shake my head.

"I don't care. You know the answer anyway."

"I don't think that's how that works, Claire. I'm supposed to ask you to marry me."

I smile at him.

"Sounds like you have some really big feelings about that," I whisper, and he smiles wide, his hand moving to mine.

"The biggest," he replies before sliding the ring on my finger, and without giving him another moment, I put a hand on either side of his face, and I beat him to the first kiss.

But I do know I'm going to have dozens and dozens more until the day we die.

ACKNOWLEDGMENTS

My favorite time is upon us: the acknowledgements!

I have gone through patches where I struggled with writing these and others i didn't, and I'd just like to say now that i fully feel like I have curated teh most perfect group of people around me, the ones who cheer me on but tell me when I need to keep my head on a bit straighter, the ones who encourage me and cheer for me and laugh with me when I need it, but also cry with me when I need that, too. I'm so grateful for every one of them, and Tourist Trap would not exist without them.

First and foremost, always, Alex. Thank you for always making sure I have whatever I need at any given moment, be it a snack, my own emotional support water bottle, or a pep talk (or a dozen because let's be real, I need them often.) I'm so grateful we met 14 summers ago (oh my god) and that I get to spend every one until eternity with you. Thank you for being my Miles, my Wes, my Damien, my Hunter, my every book boyfriend always. I love you forever.

To Ryan, Owen, and Ella, thank you for being the coolest kids ever and for letting me be your mom. If I ever find out you ever read this book, you're not getting screen time for the rest of your lives. I hope the self-induced trauma of reading smut your mom wrote was worth it. (love you)

To Rae, because I never could do this without you. Thank you for being the one to keep me in line, to pick up the slack when I inevitably spiral, and for understanding when I disappear because

I'm on some crazy self-imposed deadline and need to catch up. Thank you for being one of my best friends, for never judging me (about the important stuff), and for being the kindest, most understanding person I know. I'm forever grateful that you were on that pre-approved list of Instagram managers.

To Ashleigh, my other ginger. THank you for always tagging along to signings, for always giving me the best, unhinged content ideas, and for letting me info dump my book plots to you. I'm honored to call you one of my best friends, to be able to yap forever with you and never feel like you're going to tell me to shut up. I love you forever (can we do Disney again soon? I think my legs have recovered)

To Taj, the best agent a girl could ask for. Thank you for always championing me and making my biggest dreams come true. Thanks for always sprinting with me and kicking my ass until I get shit done. We're going to rule the world soon. 2025 is our year!!!

Thank you to Salma for being the best Dev Editor and making sure my chaos makes sense. I always appreciate and cherish your notes and direction!!

Thank you to Christine for proofing and helping me refine things.

Thank you, Marlee, for lending me another eye and making sure things are ready for the masses!

To Kayla for being the biggest help with keeping my social media running smoothly and getting the word out, and to Catherine for doing the most phenomenal content pull. I'm so grateful to you both!

Thank you to VPR and Valentine for helping to make sure that this book gets into everyone's hands!

Thank you OODLES to my ARC and content team for being absolutely amazing. I love each and every one of you, and I can never fully tell you what your love and support mean to me. I know that the success of this book is in huge part due to all of you, and I can't possibly thank you enough.

Finally, thank you, dear Reader. I once thought being an author was a pipe dream, but you all told me I could make it a reality, and I'll never be able to thank you enough for that. Thank you, thank you, thank you. I love you all forever.

ABOUT THE AUTHOR

Morgan is a born and raised Jersey girl, living there with her two sons and daughter, and mechanic husband. She's addicted to iced espresso, barbeque chips, and Starburst jellybeans. She usually has headphones on, listening to some spicy audiobook or Taylor Swift. There is rarely an in between.

Writing has been her calling for as long as she can remember. There's a framed 'page one' of a book she wrote at seven hanging in her childhood home to prove the point. Her entire life she's crafted stories in her mind, begging to be released but it wasn't until recently she finally gave them the reigns.

I'm so grateful you've agreed to take this journey with me.

Stay up to date via TikTok and Instagram

Stay up to date with future stories, get sneak peeks and bonus chapters by joining the Reader Group on Facebook!

WANT TO GO TO EVERGREEN PARK?

ALSO BY MORGAN ELIZABETH

The Springbrook Hills Series

The Distraction

The Protector

The Substitution

The Connection

The Playlist

Season of Revenge Series:

Tis the Season for Revenge

Cruel Summer

The Fall of Bradley Reed

Ick Factor

Big Nick Energy

The Ocean View Series

The Ex Files

Walking Red Flag

Bittersweet

The Mastermind Duet

Ivory Tower

Diamond Fortress

All My Love

Made in the USA
Middletown, DE
27 June 2025

77562682R00189